# HAIR TRIGGER 20

A STORY WORKSHOP ANTHOLOGY

COLUMBIA COLLEGE CHICAGO
FICTION WRITING DEPARTMENT
CHICAGO 1998

Cover Photograph
Jed Fielding, *Naples #755,* 1994 (silver gelatin print), collection of the artist.
Jed Fielding © 1994

*Hair Trigger 20*
Copyright © 1998 Columbia College
Story Workshop® is a servicemark (U.S. Patent and Trademark Office Registration No. 1,343,415) of John Schultz.

All rights reserved. No part of this publication may be reproduced or transmitted in any form or by any means, electronic or mechanical, including photocopy, recording, or any information or storage system without permission in writing from the publisher.

Columbia College Chicago
600 South Michigan Avenue
Chicago, Illinois 60605-1996

ISBN 0-932026-50-8

# TABLE OF CONTENTS

## Stories

| | | |
|---|---|---|
| 1 | JOE MENO | *Tender As Hellfire* |
| 10 | LISA M. KONOPLISKY | *Yoko And Me* |
| 24 | PAUL A. MASSIGNANI, JR. | *Explosion* |
| 32 | LAURI COUP | *The Boobs*, parody of Nikolai Gogol's *The Nose* |
| 46 | LOTT HILL | *Tough* |
| 55 | MICHAEL LIPUMA | *The Getaway* |
| 61 | PETER J. MERLIN | *Tube Man* |
| 66 | TAE HEE KIM | *Back And Forth* |
| 72 | THOMAS GWOREK | *Jim Beam & Springsteen* |
| 88 | JUAN A. CORTÉS | *The Jester King* |
| 100 | CARMEN C.A. LLOYD | *Miz Eve* |

## Freshman Level

| | | |
|---|---|---|
| 108 | PAULINE YORK | *Why There Are Stars* |
| 112 | KIRSTEN JOHNSON | *Notes From The Bottom Of A Bottle* |
| 120 | DOREEN J. BERRIEN | *Penny Change* |

## Creative Nonfiction/Essays

| | | |
|---|---|---|
| 125 | HOLLY E. CONLEY | *Lilliputian Jesus—Manufactured In Italy* |
| 137 | J.S. PORCHÉ | *How To Drink A Guinness* |
| 143 | AMBER S. KRIEGER | *In Defense Of Mr. Ramsay* |
| 159 | KAREN STEIN | *How To Live Off Your Girlfriend's Income* |
| 163 | MARY J. HERLEHY | *When The Biological Clock Breaks* |

## More Stories

| | | |
|---|---|---|
| 174 | DREW FERGUSON | *The One-Night Stand* |
| 179 | SEAN LEENAERTS | *Scars* |
| 188 | MARK BEYER | *Lucy* |
| 196 | DAVID BAKER | *Dear Noreenie* |
| 202 | BRANDON ZAMORA | *You Can't Make Chicken Salad Out Of Chicken Shit* |
| 211 | JACQUELINE MARIE HILL | *Fool's Spring* |
| 216 | RALPH HARDY | *Fallow* |
| 223 | ROBERT N. GEORGALAS | *A Little Fire In A Wild Place* |
| 234 | CAREY ARNHOLT | *Cheese!* |
| 245 | KENT MODGLIN | *With Our Secrets Intact* |
| 259 | CHRISTOPHER SWEET | *Mason The Dean*, parody of Herman Melville's *Bartleby, The Scrivener* |

## Special Commemorative Section

| | | |
|---|---|---|
| 281 | EDITORS PAST AND PRESENT | *Celebrating Twenty Issues of* Hair Trigger *Magazine* |

# PREFACE

*Hair Trigger 20* collects prose fiction and essays written by undergraduate and graduate students in writing classes at Columbia College Chicago. These classes include Introduction to Fiction Writing, Fiction Writing I, Fiction Writing II, Prose Forms, Advanced Fiction, Creative Nonfiction, and Critical Reading and Writing, all of which are taught using the innovative Story Workshop® approach, as well as a variety of genre, publishing, and other specialty writing courses.

The success of the Story Workshop approach is reflected in the wide range of content, form, and language background you will find in these writings. That success is also reflected in the numerous awards earned by past issues of *Hair Trigger*, including the equivalent of first place in several national contests. A full list of the many awards won by *Hair Trigger* magazine, as well as by many individual stories appearing in it, is presented in this issue's special commemorative section.

*Hair Trigger* magazine is an annual publication of the Columbia College Fiction Writing Department. Its twenty issues and *The Best Of Hair Trigger* editions descend from a bloodline that includes such widely acclaimed anthologies as *The Story Workshop Reader*, *Angels In My Oven*, *It Never Stopped Raining*, *Don't You Know There's A War On?*, and *f¹*.

## Acknowledgments

Thanks to the student editors, who read through hundreds of manuscript submissions and saw to it that each received equal treatment and consideration. In making selections, the editors were forced to choose among writings of nearly equal merit. Respect for the reader, for content, for form, for point of view and language, and for vividness of telling characterize the selections printed herein.

Thanks to Bill Burck, who was chiefly responsible as Faculty Advisor for supervising undergraduate and graduate student editors in the overall selection and production process for *Hair Trigger 20*.

Thanks to Andrew Allegretti, Don Gennaro De Grazia, Ann Hemenway, Gary Johnson, Patty Lewis, Eric May, Polly Mills, Shawn Shiflett, John Schultz and Betty Shiflett for consulting on matters affecting the student editors' complex editorial selection process. Thanks, too, to the many other excellent and dedicated teachers in the Fiction Writing Program.

Thanks to Linda Roberto for cover design.

Thanks to Deborah Roberts and Linda Naslund for copyediting, proofreading, and supervising crucial phases of production.

Thanks to Deborah Lewis, Hillary Allen, and Amber Krieger for their production assistance.

Thanks are also due to John Duff, President of Columbia College; to Bert Gall, Provost/Executive Vice President; to Caroline Dodge Latta, Academic Dean; and to Lya Dym Rosenblum, Vice President/Graduate School Dean, for their continuing encouragement of this program.

Randall Albers
Chair
Fiction Writing Department


***Hair Trigger 20* Student Editors**
Juan Cortés
John Drake
Venice Johnson
Mike Lipuma
Paul Massignani
Kent Modglin
Dara Ayanna Pressley
Cathleen Quartuccio

***Hair Trigger 20* Faculty Advisor**
Bill Burck

# Tender As Hellfire

## Joe Meno

Do you know, if there is a heaven, it is somewhere within the bathwater of my old babysitter, Val. Val...her legs were the cool white reflection of beauty. Her whole naked form could drive any young mop-headed bastard to any random act of trailer-park violence.

My mother and her boyfriend, French, were swingers and needed somewhere to send me and my older brother every other Friday night. Pill was thirteen, old enough not to need a babysitter, but me, being only ten at the time, and both of us prone to theft and arson and other acts of puberty, lightin' stuff on fire and shouting and running all around and my mother screaming all night and French's walking around in his underwear most of the time, we weren't appreciated there in that gravel-laid motor-home cesspool, so my mother and French paid this young truck-stop waitress at the other end of the trailer park to keep us in her spare boudoir every other Friday night and make sure we didn't burn or steal anything we couldn't afford to pay for ourselves.

Val...spring couldn't have whispered me a sweeter name.

Do you wanna know the truth? Maybe the only woman I'll ever really love is Val. My prom date, Bunny, who shimmered in a strapless blue evening gown, the girl who left the goddamn dance with another lousy man, or even the one and only lady I ever shared a connubial bed with, Teresa, who changed the locks on my door and took off with my poor dog, those ladies hold no candle to the fire that still burns in my heart for my old babysitter.

    Every other Friday, my mother would give me and Pill a brown grocery bag of our clothes and toothbrushes and send us down the gravel road to Val's big silver trailer that was round and looked like a kinda silver space capsule. My brother was never happy about going. He still hated Tenderloin, and bein' cooped up inside on a Friday night when he could be out knocking mailboxes over or pissing someone off musta burned him up pretty bad. He'd kinda sulk behind me with his hands in his pockets as I'd cross the court to her trailer. I'd wipe my nose clean with the back of my hand and then knock on her screen door. Val's trailer was always lit up with a string of white Christmas lights around the door; I dunno if she put them up for Christmas or not, but she sure never took them down.

    Her bare white legs would appear at the door. I dunno what it was about her legs—she was tall, really tall, taller that my mother's boyfriend, French— her legs were just so long that I'd kinda whistle to myself every time I'd see them, not like I'd know what to do with them if I had the chance, but there was something inside my chest that would light up like a match whenever she'd answer the door. Her bare white thighs have been permanently burned in my mind. Before I even think about her name, I see her great bare thighs hung open on the end of her red velvet sofa. Her voice was a honey-coated radiator, husky with sweet tones that would drip off her tongue the way her thick waxy makeup would begin to melt late at night. Her hair was blonde and cut at her shoulders; she'd usually be in her work uniform, which was a yellow dress with a white apron, her hair all done up with a white paper tiara. She'd lead us inside and pat my head and lick her finger and stick it in Pill's ear. He liked her, too, he really did, but most of the time we were there he was in a mean mood, anyways. Her trailer always smelled the way I thought a woman should, like cigarettes and sweat and baby powder. Her mouth was a sweat-wrinkled pink hole that hardly ever closed. Her breath was always hot and musty, moving over some wad of pink bubble gum, and would leave bright red lipstick marks on the spotted white glasses she drank gin from. There was nothing I wanted more than to kiss her mouth and have her kiss my forehead. I wanted to fall asleep in her golden arms without anyone but me and her in her bed.

    Maybe after we arrived, Val would pour us some RC Cola in some giveaway glasses she'd got at a fast-food joint, or maybe she'd light a cigarette as she got undressed, but every Friday night we were there, she'd strip down to her smooth white skin behind this dark black Oriental screen, decorated with a slick yellow tiger, and tie her red Oriental robe around her middle, tucking the edges between her breasts. Man, that would make my teeth hum in my head.

Then she'd take a bath. Honest to God, she'd take a bath right while we were there. She'd close this small wooden door and slip into her pink bathtub and take a goddamn bath. Don't think she was a pervert or anything; she always announced for us not to look, but what the hell, we were boys, we were in the heated vernal season of puberty, it was as though we didn't have a choice at all. Pill always got first look, then me; our greasy white faces would smear against the silver keyhole, breathing shallow so she wouldn't hear, unable to breathe as her cool naked shoulders appeared in our eyes.

My god...my sweet God, have mercy on my poor soul.

My face would get all red and hot, and one time I think I nearly passed out when she suddenly stood and stepped out of the tub and I gazed upon her wondrous naked form, her smooth white belly, her wide hips that slipped down to form the most perfect V I thought I'd ever see. I very nearly blacked out right there, but Pill grabbed me by the back of the shirt and held me up by my collar. His face wouldn't get all red or anything; he'd just get kinda quiet and mad. Heck, I knew why, he was three whole years older than me, and he was thinking he should be out necking with stupid farmgirls named Suzy-Q and making it in their barns or whatever. But since I knew the closest I was about to get to any of that was that steamed-up keyhole, I didn't complain.

Her bare white legs would appear from behind the bathroom door, clouded by steam, still a little wet with singularly perfect beads of bathwater. She'd have her hair wrapped up in a pink towel on the top of her head and be wearing that crazy Chinese robe, all black and red and white and flowery. She'd tuck her legs beneath her and take a seat on her red sofa. Maybe she'd turn on the radio or something, maybe she'd put on a nice record and stare out the screened windows into the dull blue night. By then, Pill would be getting all kinds of anxious—he was a boy with sex on the brain—and maybe Val would send him out to pick up dinner. That was fine with me, just me and Val in the trailer alone. She'd unwrap her hair and let it fall all over her shoulders, or maybe blow-dry it a little, then go behind that black screen and pull a tight gray T-shirt on and some overalls. Anything looked good on her, I swear. We'd sit on her red sofa and watch the night come up, the clouded blue sky giving way to pleasant blackness, me leaning in close to smell the shampoo and soap just evaporating off her body, sweet and heavy like perfume. I'd nearly drown on it all. Then she'd ask me something nice like how many girlfriends did I have or how come I was such a heartbreaker, and just when I was ready to burst with unadulterated passion, Pill-Bug would return with some fried chicken or hamburgers or something from down the road, and we'd all eat, laughing and giggling and throwing food and having the best times of our lives. Well, maybe not Pill. Or Val. But being with them both felt all right to me.

Then when it was time, she'd help us into her big white bed in the spare room, the bed that always smelled like the soft, wrinkled part of her neck where there would always be a greasy dab of perfume. Her head would hang over us as her robe would drop open a little, showing the smooth white plane that she would only share with truck drivers and cowboys who drove pickups. Her mouth would swell as she'd smile and wink us a good-night, and then I'd reach up and kiss her on the soft side of her red, red mouth. That moment, right there, is still what I think about when I think about love. The soft side of someone's mouth. That's it, right there.

My brother, Pill, he would lie on his belly, burying his face in her wide white pillows. I would lie on my back, and then we would hold our breath and listen, because there would always be some lust-filled cowboy coming over to fuck her, because even as young as I was, I knew that's all they wanted with her anyway. Pill would flip and flop around, frustrated, I guess. He'd grit his teeth all night and shake his head, and then we'd hear a pickup or big block-engine Chevy die outside, then the boots, scraping over the gravel, the bare-knuckled knock on the door. The screen door would slide open, they would both be whispering and giggling, maybe there'd be the sharp and clean kiss of glasses striking together. Then it would stop. Then it would be so quiet that I could hear my brother's nasally congested chest rising and falling with each shallow breath. Maybe there'd be the sonorous squeak of furniture, of wood against tile, of metal against metal spring. I'd slip out of bed and stare out the tiny gold keyhole, out into the dimly lit darkness of the living room. Then from only a few bare feet away, my whole world would burn apart.

My Val's long white legs might be straddled around this cowboy's middle; maybe she'd be on her back or bent over the same velvet sofa, but they would be fucking—not gently, not like a sweet whisper or kiss—they would be fucking hard and tearing at each other's clothes and scratching and pulling and rubbing their desperate white bodies together in a way that made me hate her and him and everything about them both. Maybe I'd try to go back to sleep; maybe I'd curl my head under some of her blankets and listen to them fucking all night. These men, these truckers and cowmen had some sorta endurance I couldn't even imagine. All their dumb, hard ignorance must've made them insensitive to any of her. The cold black glimmer in all of her men's eyes was always the same. These men didn't ever make faces or moan or growl, they all gripped her like they hated her with their cold blank eyes and black hair-covered chests. They were full of anger and frustration and wanted to bury it somewhere inside Val's breasts with the flat part of their thumbs, pressing hard to make her hurt, too. Maybe they were just like Pill and me, but older, full of the same hate and rage, and needed to let it go somehow, through someone's soft body.

These men I hated more than anything in my life.

These men would appear every Friday night as soon as we had been tucked in; every Friday night, another cowboy or trucker would have a time with my sweet Val. Only one time did she get herself in a bind.

This one night a big blonde-haired, sweet-faced cowboy in tight jeans came knocking on Val's thin screen door. He was the one with the sandy-colored cowboy hat and silver-toed boots, with his blue Western shirt half-buttoned down to his navel to show off the thin trail of hair that led down to his wanton nether region. He was drunk as hell and stunk like a pig, and my poor Val refused to let him in, not on account of him being drunk, but she was expecting some other visitor that night in tight drawers, stinking of whisky or his wife.

"Just let me in for a second, Val, honey. Just for a second." The cowboy's voice was sweet and cool, his eyes were nearly all red and crossed with sincerity.

"Not tonight, baby," Val smiled, pulling her robe tight around her waist. "Go on home."

"Just a second," he groaned. "Please, honey, just for a single kiss." He clawed at the thin screen like trapped vermin, kneeling in front of the door.

"Don't make a fool outta yourself. Go on home, baby. You're drunk and ornery. I'm not in the mood for any of that."

Val crossed her arms in front of her chest and backed away from the door. The cowboy pulled his sand-colored hat down over his eyes. He yanked himself to his feet, leaning against the door, and tore a big bone-handled knife from the side of his boot.

"Looks like I'm coming in anyway."

He dug the big silver blade into the screen, yanking the knife down and across in a big L-shape. Val let out a scream, and I shot up in bed, rustling my brother awake. Val backed away from the front door slowly.

"I just wanted a single kiss," the cowboy grunted, tripping through the big tear in the door. "That was it, you goddamn tease."

Grinning like a sick dog, he held the knife out before him, a big silver knife with a smooth ivory bone handle. His face was cold and white and creased by his tightened smile. He stepped through the trailer, following Val as she backed away, gliding the knife back and forth in front of him, catching a silver gleam along the edge of the blade as it passed right in front of Val's shiny red robe.

"Now you ain't so proud, are ya?" he snorted.

Val backed all the way into the kitchen, fumbling behind her through thin silver drawers for some weapon, a knife, a screwdriver, anything. The cowboy kept smiling and ginning, moving closer.

Pill and I were at the goddamn spare boudoir door and tore it open. We stood right there a few feet from it all, unable to muster a word or motion.

"Go back to bed, boys," Val whispered, still pleasant, still calm. "Henry and I are playing a little game."

My brother, Pill, didn't move. He stood in the doorway, staring at the cowboy's sweaty face. He stood right in front of me, still and tense, staring right through the shiny bone-handled knife to the cowboy's dull black eyes.

"Don't move a muscle, boys," the cowboy grunted, turning towards us a little. "You both stand right there."

My hands ached with sweat. My whole head felt light and then heavy and then light again like a goddamn fever. My sweet Val had a short screwdriver in her hands, but she was shaking. Her hips shivered against the kitchen counter; her big blue eyes glimmered with big silver tears.

The cowboy took one step closer and knocked the screwdriver right from Val's shaky hands.

"Don't you ever tease a man," the cowboy grunted. He grabbed Val's arm and put the knife right against her thin white wrist. He pressed himself against her, holding the blade against her poor white skin. "Don't ever play me for a fool." He reached his hand down between the folds of her robe, right between her breasts where her heart must've been beating like a scared rabbit. My mouth was dry and hard with terror. I felt my own knees shaking. Pill looked ready to cry. His hands were clenched so tight at his side that his fingernails were drawing blood in his own palms.

"Don't either of you boys move," he grunted. "You're gonna learn how to deal with a no-good woman."

He stood in front of her, veiling her in his shadow.

There was no sound in the whole trailer. No one was breathing. No one *could* breathe. Then a bit of gravel. A single spit of gravel shot up from the ground and ricocheted against the side of someone else's trailer. Then another. The rumble of gravel rolled up right outside along with two thick yellow double beams that crossed the inside of Val's trailer, lighting up the cowboy's face. The big heavy grunt of a pickup died outside. Then the pickup-truck door opened and two boots slid across the dirt and up the steps, and then I heard the single sweetest word I'll ever remember.

"Val?"

Still all silent inside.

"Val?!"

Then the trucker stepped through the gape in the screen, a big square-faced man in blue coveralls. His name was scribbled on a patch on one side, *Buddy*. His hair was black and disheveled a bit; he had a jug of wine in one hand and a single daisy in the other. His jaw was set tight in his mouth as he stepped inside and saw my sweet Val pressed up hard against her own kitchen counter, the cowboy hulking there right over her, holding her bare skin under the edge of a bone-handled blade.

"You best put that knife down, chief," Buddy whispered, setting the wine and flower down on the sofa, "'fore you end up cutting yourself."

The cowboy turned and glared. There were no other words needed right there. Two dogs don't need words right before they set into it, and neither did these men. The cowboy turned and lunged at poor Buddy, taking a wide drunken swipe at him, ripping the front of his coveralls. Buddy lammed the cowboy hard in the throat with a solid punch, knocking his sand-colored hat off. Then Buddy dove right at him, shoving the cowboy over the couch. The two men landed on top of each other, growling and cursing, Buddy on top, trying to wrestle the knife away from the cowboy, who spat and drooled and hissed like a snake. Buddy landed a few more blows, smacking the cowboy's nose, but then something awful happened that will always stick in my head because of how lousy it all was.

The knife blade ran through Buddy's right-hand palm, right through; then the cowboy dropped the knife dully to the floor. Buddy howled, gripping his wrist. He backed away, bowing over in pain. Light ran from the trailers outside right onto the wound; the hole in his hand was silver-dollar size. His face was bright red.

The cowboy picked up his knife and ran out, dove into his truck, and disappeared. He went right back into the dark night that had made him drunk and evil to begin with. His hat was still on the floor. Ol' Buddy kinda tumbled into the bathroom, gritting his teeth in pain. He held his hand under the sink, running the water bright pink over his wound. Val came up behind him and began kissing his neck and saying, "I'm sorry, so sorry, baby," and nuzzled her head against his big shoulders. He wrapped a big pink towel around his hand, shutting off the faucet.

Val hurried me and my brother back into the spare bedroom. Her face was as white as her sheets, and her blue eyes were swimming with tears. She hadn't said a word to us. She was still shaking. She stepped back into the bathroom.

Then, as usual, they began making it. Right in that bathroom. Val fell to her knees and unzipped the man's coveralls and then closed the bathroom door. Then the unmistakable sound of that man and Val, like every Friday night, cinching themselves together, bare and cold, their bodies pressed against the wood door, creating a kind of friction that hurt my tongue. That's when I wished both those men had been stabbed and died right there. That's when I didn't care that this man was hurt saving my Val. This man with the hole in his hand was no different from any of the other men that would come over after Val had put us to bed. He still had that same dumb empty look in his eyes. He still had that same dumb look while he lay his cool naked body next to hers. Most of her men, I guess, were well behaved. But I guess any goddamn fool can act polite if they know what they'll get in return for some lousy sweet talk or flowers or wine.

That's what I hated most about all those men. They weren't any brighter than me. But there was nothing I could have done about any of it. I was a dumb, greasy-faced, trailer-park kid. All these men had snakeskin boots and red pickups with gun racks and decorative mud flaps. What could I possibly offer her besides true, unmistakable love? How could I make her feel the way they made her feel, held down against the dull red velvet, naked and used and bare? My same brother was already asleep in her bed, snoring with the same frustration, not just with tall white legs or truckers or cowboys or trailers but the whole town and not just the ignorant little town of Tenderloin, but of all space and time that sinks down on your head when you feel like a man and still look like a goddamn dumb kid.

All that was too much for me. This man had my Val; they were making it right outside the door or on the sofa or in the kitchen, making a kind of rhythm so mean that I slipped on my own jeans and shoes and climbed out the spare bedroom window, down into the gravel, skidding past the fading light shot from Val's TV or Buddy's bloodshot eyes. I stared at his pickup, same as any other of these men's Valiants, Monte Carlos, big Fords and Chevies that were all made in their awful notion of manliness and desire. I reached down into the dirt and picked up the sharpest rock I could find and lit a match to the fuel line of anger and rage that had welled up in me all night. I let that rock fly hard and straight, busting a rearview mirror. Another stone took out one of the headlights, then another scratched the deeply honed doors before I began kicking in the silver-chromed grill. My whole miserable life lit up in an explosion of hate and anger, until Val's porch light flickered on and I disappeared back into the darkness, back through the window, and back into her soft, white bed, still shaking with rage. Maybe the trucker cussed or shouted and then took off, maybe he stayed and took his anger out on her again, maybe they lay together not touching or uttering a word, both wishing he had left. The next morning the trucker was gone, and I couldn't have been happier. When Pill and I finally rolled out of bed, we got dressed and sat at her small kitchen table. We wolfed down big helpings of yellow French toast and burnt bacon. No one talked. Val stared hard into my eyes and didn't say a damn word. She looked me in my face and then turned away, cold and silent. I didn't mind her being mad. As long as the trucker was gone, she could be as quiet as she liked. I know that sounds real selfish, but she knew there was nothing between her desperate heart and that trucker's heart but being desperate, and me busting up that man's headlights only put a clear picture to all that undeniable frustration. We packed our stuff up and stepped outside. The trailer park was bright and silver and grey with dust. Maybe I turned around and said, "Good-bye," or maybe I was mean and stone-faced and stepped out onto her porch without muttering a thing, but Val stopped me and put her hand on my shoulder and looked down into my eyes and said something like: "You're gonna end up hurtin' someone with all that anger, Dough. You're gonna end up hurtin' yourself and someone you love with a temper like that."

Then more than anything I felt like crying, but I didn't, because Pill woulda never let me live it down, and I nodded and turned away, and me and my brother walked home across the lots of mobile homes, kicking rocks at each other without saying a goddamn word.

# Yoko And Me

### Lisa M. Konoplisky

The important thing to remember is this: I love women. Women's bodies. Breasts, hips, nipples, cunts, bellies. Their hair. Their smell. Their taste. Their lips. Ooooh. Those lips.

And not just any women either. I like women who look like women, not like men. After all, *I'm* a woman and I've got my standards. Buzz cuts, construction boots, hairy legs and pits, beer bellies, and flat butts? You can keep 'em. If I'd wanted that I would have stayed in the old neighborhood and married a marine. No, give me lots of hair, stilettos, and a Botticelli bod that spills out in all the right places, held together by a miniskirt. Now *that's* a woman.

Needless to say, such attitudes do not endear me to my feminist sisters. But fuck that shit. Who do you think has more fun anyway? Them or me? And there's only one word for fun and that word is *women*. I just can't get enough of them despite myself.

Which is what makes what happened with Jennifer all the stranger. I was this close to nailing her. THIS close! But then Yoko showed up. And something gave. Guts. Balls. Whatever.

I did the worst thing you can ever do if your sole purpose in life is seduction. To wit, I let love get in my way. Love. Can you believe it?! Honey-drippin', Cupid's-arrow-flying, *oh-honey-I-want-you-and-only-you-forsaking-all-others-as-long-as-we-both-shall-live*, goddamn-motherfuckin' love. And that's it. I was cooked. Washed up. My reign had ended.

And for that I had Yoko to thank.

But let me back up.

See, it was the second time I'd seen Yoko that day.

The first time I was with Jennifer at Café Figaro. Overpriced coffee. Mediocre food. But oh that view. Figaro sits like a polished little gem, right in the center of the open-air carnival known as the West Village. It's like Rome—all roads lead to it. On summer evenings, when the sun's gone down but the light still lingers, after the trash has been collected, a faintly sweet breeze blows in from Hoboken, and you can sit outside for hours watching people stroll by.

This was such an evening.

The streets were packed. The tourists were out in force. Jennifer was sitting right beside me. Not across from me. Next to me. Like we're at a movie or something. See, I'd been getting vibes off of Jennifer for some time now, and I was thinking that maybe that night we were gonna—you know—do it. Anyway, she leans over, all surreptitious and shit, and whispers, "Check out the chick in the Yoko Ono sunglasses."

My eyes drifted up and left. A dead look-alike. Sunglasses, short, compact frame, black pants and shirt, walking that fine line between New York frumpy and New York cool.

Then it hits me.

It *is* Yoko Ono.

I looked over at Jennifer, and her chin was almost dragging on the table. Her eyes were big and round, like green shooter marbles.

"But...it's...it's really HER," she spat out.

I concurred.

"Shit, yeah."

"Look," Jennifer whispered, a really loud whisper, the kind you can hear clear down the block. "Here she comes!" Yoko was headed our way. Jennifer grabbed my arm hard and dug her nails into the skin.

I yanked it away, "Hey, that hurts!"

Jennifer didn't even hear me. She was bobbin' up and down in her seat like some crazy jack-in-the-box, swatting at me like this was going to help me see Yoko better or something.

Yoko, meanwhile, was walking right past us. I could've reached out and touched her. I was close. Real close. Close enough to see her face, which was soft and kind of lazy. Close enough to see her skin, which was starting to droop a little at the corners of her mouth. Close enough to see her hair, which was bottled-dye black and just grazed the tops of her ears. Close enough to see her lips, which were pressed together just a little, like she was stifling a giggle.

Yoko didn't have an entourage. She didn't need one. When she walked it was like she was parting the Red Sea, gliding seamlessly like an angel, floating like a dandelion seed, riding on a conveyor belt, or being carried along by clouds as thin and watery as gruel.

Yoko turned her head ever so slightly in my direction, an almost imperceptible tilt. She looked straight at me—I could feel her gaze like some superhero comic-book laser beam going right from those Yoko Ono eyes, through the Yoko Ono sunglasses, across the sidewalk, through the thin, sooty, New York air, and straight into the only thing that I was absolutely sure did not exist—my soul.

This must be how the electric chair feels just before your eyeballs pop out and your hair starts to sizzle. I was gonna say she had me by the throat, but it was deeper than that. Whatever part of me it was that Yoko was slipping her dainty little Yoko fingers around, well, it was the right part, all right. At that moment, she could have told me to walk into the East River and I would have obliged. This woman was a witch and I was under her spell. All these crazy, feel-good vibes were filling me up and starting to spill outta my mouth.

"Oh, I like her...," I oozed, not even realizing I was talking out loud.

"What?!" Jennifer's head whipped around. Her nose was about an inch from mine. She looked like an out-of-focus photograph. It took awhile for my eyes to adjust so I could see her tossing a crooked smirk my way.

"Really?" Jennifer's eyebrow arched in interest. "She doesn't seem like your type. Too short. Not enough hair."

"No! Not like that!" I protested.

"Well...like how, then?" Jennifer asked, breaking into a bemused smile.

"Nothing, never mind," I muttered.

But it was true. I *did* like Yoko. And I thought she'd like me. And not like that either. That's what was so weird. Like some prehistoric glacier traveling as slow as Moses, this feeling was working its way up my body, starting at my toes and ending at some place far, far up in the sky. Like the tingling you feel when your fingers begin to thaw on a January day and you aren't wearing mittens, the feeling was comforting and reassuring.

Here was a woman and I didn't want to suck her, fuck her, screw her, do her, or make her. I just wanted to be around her. And, what was even weirder, I *really* wanted her to like me. A total stranger, a woman I'd never thought about twice—a woman who, in my humble opinion, was nowhere near hot or lukewarm, even—and suddenly I was filled with the most tremendous desire, one that had nothing to do with sex.

What was wrong with me?

I couldn't even focus on how unfamiliar, how queer this all felt. I was too busy worrying. Would Yoko like me? Yes, of course she would. I was a good person. Not unkind. And aside from my tendency to use women like disposable styrofoam cups, I was actually quite moral and upstanding. Yes, given the chance—I was certain, yes—she *would* like me. She would see me, the *real* me, find something in me that even I'd never found before. Something hidden and beautiful. She would take me home to the Dakota, feed me whole milk and peanut butter cookies, sitting all the while with her chin in her hand, watching while I ate every last crumb.

*Good cookies,* I'd tell her.

*Thanks,* she'd say, *I baked them myself.*

Jennifer and I watched Yoko until there wasn't any Yoko left to see. She was down the sidewalk and gone, swallowed up by the smash of tourists turning onto MacDougal Street.

I shook my head hard until my earrings jangled like a chain-link fence in a storm.

Whoa, what had just happened to me?

I was disoriented and wanted to stay put and figure out if it was some weird Asian mind-control thing or something. But Jennifer was anxious to beat the tourist traffic back through the tunnel.

We spent the next hour stuck in the tunnel with all the other folks who had the same bright idea. By the time we hit smooth sailing on the turnpike the sun was low in the sky, the color of a peach. Jennifer was playing the tape I'd made for her. Squeeze sang "Tempted." I tried to think about Jennifer, about her body, about the million or so twists and turns that she'd managed to pack onto that five-feet-one-inch frame. I tried to think about the night ahead, plan what I'd say and do. But I had to be honest with myself, I was distracted.

I looked over at Jennifer. She was humming along with the tape. Her shiny black curls sat on top of her head like an ornament, like those red, felt-covered Christmas bells. When she hummed, her eyes did little loop-di-loops, following the path of some roller-coaster ride that only she was on.

I was climbing up a sheer rock face, trying to focus on fucking, but I couldn't get a solid foothold.

In the two years I'd known Jennifer, we'd never talked about how we felt about each other. It was a silent understanding between us that such conversation was off-limits. Actually, not so silent. Once, shortly after we met, Jennifer coyly suggested that she'd like to "try it" with me and proceeded to quiz me on the intricacies of queer sex. I knew she wasn't serious, and I had no patience for shit like that. That night we went to a bar off campus, one where a lot of her sorority sisters hung out. I asked her if she was serious. She said yes. I asked her how she'd feel if people found out she was fucking women. *Fine*, she said coolly. *So*, I asked really loudly, *you wouldn't mind someone calling you a cocksuckin' cunt-eating inverted pedophilic diesel-dyke butch fuckin' femme friend-of-Dorothy limp-wristed leather-chap-wearing fuckin' queer homosexual?* The bar got really quiet and so did Jennifer. I paid for my drink and left Jennifer sitting there. For a week or so I avoided her, but eventually we started hanging out again. But she never brought up the subject again.

Now Jennifer wanted me. Or at least I thought she did. I had the upper hand, the only kind of hand you ever want where sex is concerned. And with all that going for me, what was I thinking about? I didn't want—ooh, how could I even think this and face myself in the mirror—I didn't want to do anything she didn't want to do. All I wanted to do was make her happy. Love. Feeling. Christ, I was turning into some 1940s starlet, willing to suffer anything in the name of love.

Maybe if I held my breath it would all go away. I froze, my body rigid and unbreathing. I was just starting to get lightheaded when I caught Jennifer looking at me, her mouth pulled like a drawstring into a crinkly line.

"What?" I asked.

"Well...like...I was just thinking...about Yoko...you know, how John got shot...you know...like...right in front of her?" Jennifer's chubby little fingers clutched the steering wheel tight.

"I don't know, man. I'd spaz. I mean, that's like nuts or somethin', ya know?"

Jennifer nodded solemnly.

"She must still be in mourning...I mean, like...she's always wearing...you know...black," she said.

"But she *always* wears black."

"Oh...so it's not...like...a mourning thing."

"No, I think it's a monochromatic thing."

"Oh."

"Yeah. She used to wear a lot of white in the sixties. You know, the antiwar, flower-child thing. But now she mostly wears black."

How did I know this? I didn't know this. I was talking like Yoko was my best friend and I didn't even know why.

"Well," Jennifer whined, "don't you, I mean, don't you think she loved John...like...soooo much?"

She threw her hands up and away from her body like she was shooing flies. The Volvo started to swerve into the next lane. It looked like some weird video game until I saw the guy in the truck next to us chewing a cigar and shooting us a look.

"Jennifer, the car!" I yelled.

"Sorry."

She grabbed the wheel. The car rocked a little to each side before she was able to rein it in. We both sat and listened to the music, not saying anything, contemplating the depths of John and Yoko's love. The sun was almost gone now, and pinks and blues spread out ahead of us. I started thinking about the bum rap Yoko had gotten over the years.

"You think she really broke up the Beatles?" I asked Jennifer.

Jennifer's face flattened out and hardened around the edges. Her eyelids came down halfway over her eyes like awnings, making shadows that made her face look somber. "Well, I don't know...maybe, well...those kinds of things...I don't know...you never, I mean....when a band breaks up things can get real heavy," she said reverently. Jennifer took music and everything connected to it very seriously. She'd told me that she dreamed of being a record producer one day. A white, female, upper-middle-class Jewish version of Quincy Jones was how I pictured it.

"Well, still, I don't think one woman could break up an entire band, do you?" I asked.

"Well...," Jennifer's voice trailed off as if to say, *Anything can happen, you just don't understand how these things are!*

"Do you remember when he was shot?" I asked, wanting to get off the topic of the breakup.

"God, yeah! Who doesn't?" she yelled.

"Where were you when you heard?" I asked.

"I don't....I...well...hangin' out...it was soooo terrible...I mean, you know...I was blown away."

When Jennifer got really emotional, her thoughts came in fits and starts, like hiccoughs. Her head jingled a little when she talked, her thick black curls following a beat or two behind.

"Where were you?" she asked.

"At my parents' house," I said. "Everyone was asleep. I turned on the TV—I was watching some old movie, ya' know?—and I was doing sit-ups, I remember that. I thought then that if I did fifty sit-ups a day my stomach would be hard as a rock." I punched my stomach with my fist to emphasize my point and felt it bounce.

"I'm puffin' and gruntin'," I said, "yankin' myself up...twenty...twenty-two...thirty...God, I was trying like hell to get fifty...and this report comes on the TV about how he was shot and all."

Jennifer slowed down to pay the toll. The toll guard was wearing a Walkman and rap music was spilling out of his earphones. He danced in the booth, did a tight little spin, and punctuated the throbbing bass by slapping a tower of change and four one-dollar bills into Jennifer's hand.

I waited until Jennifer merged into traffic before I continued.

"It was so weird, ya know?" I said.

"What, that toll guy?" Jennifer asked.

"No," I said, "John Lennon getting shot. I remember I was confused more than anything. Why would someone shoot John Lennon? It made no sense. Maybe I just didn't get it. I mean, I never was much of a Beatles fan."

"Well," Jennifer asked, "did you cry...or...like...get really upset?" She was concentrating hard on the road, pressing her chest up against the steering wheel.

I knew I should tell her that I'd cried, that I'd gone to a candlelight vigil with thousands of other people, raised my hand in a peace sign and sung "Imagine." I knew I should have said that I hated when rock stars got shot or died under mysterious circumstances, since at least one-third of them seemed to. I knew she'd think that meant I was deep or something. I mean this was it, the chance to really pour it on. First rule of thumb if you really want to get someone into bed is to tell them what they want to hear, right? But no. No. What did I do? I just started talking about how I was feeling—I mean, how I was really feeling.

"No," I told Jennifer, "I didn't cry. But I do remember thinkin' how with the boomers and all it was always presidents or politicians getting shot. First Kennedy, then Martin Luther King, then Bobby Kennedy, Malcolm X, Mahatma Gandhi...I mean...like...did every politician in the sixties get shot or what?"

"Yeah, you got a point," Jennifer said. She did her drawstring lips again, which meant she was thinkin' really hard.

"But then I thought about it and I thought, who did we have? I mean, a

Beatle, ya know?" I said.

"Well, now wait a minute...." I could feel the hairs on the back of Jennifer's neck standing at attention.

"I mean, the Beatles were great, ya know, but...I mean, John seemed like a nice guy...don't get me wrong...," I was scrambling. This would be a bad time to alienate her, I told myself.

"This is true," she agreed solemnly.

"But," I continued, "I figured we didn't have a JFK or a Malcolm or a Gandhi. Lennon was as close as we were gonna get. So I made it a point to remember, for posterity, ya know?"

"Yeah." Jennifer was quiet for a while, then started to hum "Imagine."

Jennifer's parents' house was quiet and dark when we reached it. She punched a complicated series of numbers into the keypad of the house alarm before we could even walk through the front door. Her parents were away in Europe. Her dad was some high-powered attorney in the city and he'd just won a big case. The trip to Europe was the firm's way of saying thanks. Her mom wasn't happy about the trip, Jennifer said. She insisted that they visit only the Teutonic, Bavarian, or otherwise-Germanic sections of the continent. She'd been to Italy before and hated it. The canals smelled, the men were too friendly, and the cooking gave her heartburn. Switzerland, Austria, and Germany, on the other hand, appealed to her true nature which, as Jennifer described it, was on the anal side.

Jennifer took my bag. I asked if I could shower. The bathroom was the size of my apartment. I let the scalding water pour over my body until I was shining bright red. As the water spilled over my face, I thought about Jennifer. I thought about Yoko. Love. Sex. Sex. Love. I thought about how long it had been since I'd gotten laid. LoveSexSexLove. Did it have to be one or the other? Love and Sex. Love or Sex. I'd never bothered to even consider the two together, as part of the same package. SexSexSexLoveSex. First of all, I'd never loved someone and then tried to nail them. Whenever I felt myself falling in love with someone, I was always careful to pick a fight so as not to confuse messy emotions with potentially incredible sex. LoveLoveLoveLove Sex. And if I happened to fall for someone I was already fucking, at least I felt like I already had my position established. Like MacArthur or Patton. I always knew that no matter what, I WOULD return.

But this love thing was fuckin' with me bad. I didn't even know how to do it. How did you get from A to B, anyway? And how did you do it without being eaten alive by that one-eyed monster—monogamy?

It seemed insurmountable. I got out of the shower and wrapped myself in two thick white towels. I gripped hard onto the marble countertop and felt my head spinning. I turned the taps on, filling the sink and dunking my head into the icy water. I had to get a grip. I had to get back on that horse. It was the only way.

I combed out my still-damp hair and put on my softest jeans, the ones that were white—almost translucent—at the knees, and an old flannel shirt. I had to be comfortable. I can't seduce a woman when I'm wearing uncomfortable clothes.

Jennifer led me downstairs to the only room in the house that had escaped the efforts of Mrs. Einhorn's interior designer. It was decorated in early 1960s, swingin'-guy-with-a-turtleneck style. With its exposed brick, mahogany paneling, golfing trophies, defunct bar complete with Budweiser, Lowenbrau, and St. Pauli Girl taps and flashing neon Schlitz sign, it felt wild and untamed. This was obviously where Mr. Einhorn went to retreat from the womenfolk and children.

Jennifer acted nervous and excited, like a teenager who had the keys to the liquor cabinet.

"Do you mind if we sleep down here?" she asked.

"Are you kidding? It's tremendous!"

Jennifer giggled with pleasure. Like we were sharing a naughty secret.

"I always sleep here when my parents are away. My mom never let me when I was a kid. She said it was too damp. Now I do it every chance I get."

"Check out this vinyl!" I yelled.

Her father had shelves full of LPs and an old hi-fi. I immediately located the Broadway musicals. *Brigadoon, Carousel, The Boyfriend, My Fair Lady, The King and I, West Side Story, Bye Bye Birdie, Oklahoma!* And of course, the obligatory *Fiddler on the Roof.*

"What shall we begin with?" I asked formally, like the butler.

"*OKLAHOMA!*" Jennifer screamed.

We sang "Oh, What a Beautiful Mornin'," leapt onto furniture in *faux* ballet moves. Jennifer made a great Curly. When she sang "The Surrey with the Fringe on Top," I was impressed by her bowlegged cowboy strut.

I was winded. Jennifer got me a beer. We threw ourselves into two big beanbag chairs and turned on MTV. I pulled my pipe out. I had filled the bowl before I left home and packed enough in a Baggie for two more.

"You wanna smoke?"

"Sure." I knew Jennifer didn't smoke much, but I needed some chemical sustenance. I lit the pipe and passed it to Jennifer. She sucked so hard the stem whistled. She gagged and hacked, expelling smoke out of her nose and mouth like a cartoon dragon.

"Here, drink this—it'll cool your throat off." I handed her my beer.

"The smell won't stay on the furniture, will it?"

"It'll be gone by tomorrow morning. Don't worry, your parents won't know a thing."

I handed her the pipe again. She didn't cough this time. I took another drag and let the pipe go out. We finished our beers and lit up another bowl. We'd rolled off the beanbag chairs and onto the floor. I laid my head back onto the carpet and stared at the suspended ceiling. If I squinted a little it looked like it was made of popcorn.

"I would have loved to have a basement like this. Did you play down here?"

"Usually I played in my room, when I wasn't at lessons."

"What kinda lessons?" I asked.

"You know, the usual. Ballet, tennis, riding, flute—wait!" Jennifer yelled, "I've got to show you something." She tipped forward and pushed herself up onto one leg like she'd forgotten something urgent. She ran to a wall-length closet on the opposite side of the room and yanked on the plastic knobs to reveal a closet full of toys. I knew them all. Twister, Candyland, Toss-Across, a Wiffle Ball set, one of those inflatable sit-on-it bouncing balls. But what Jennifer extracted from deep within the pile was unrecognizable. It looked like layers and layers of plastic wrap, all wrinkled and stuck together. She flipped it around in her hands until she found an air nozzle into which she began to blow.

"When I was a kid...like..this was...like...it was like my favorite!" she spouted between breaths.

She blew and blew and her face got redder and redder.

What began to take shape looked like an enormous plastic acorn squash. There was an opening which, I assumed, served as an entrance.

"When I was a kid I used to call it the Space Bubble," she said.

Ah, the Space Bubble. I felt like an astronaut entering an unknown world for the first time, silly and wondering, giddy with awe, and this was the strange, claustrophobic, unforgettable world of the Space Bubble.

Her father had brought it home from work one day, a gift from a client he was representing in a wrongful-death suit. The Space Bubbles were designed as inflatable forts for little kids. But one kid took his outside on a particularly hot August day and ended up baking to death in it. As long as Jennifer promised not to take it outside in the summer, it was hers.

"Isn't it cool?!" Jennifer said.

I was impressed. Jealous even. The Space Bubble was exactly the toy I would have coveted as a child. Access to a special secret place all my own. A cocoon of my imagination, of my own making.

She got down on all fours and started to crawl inside.

"Come on." She waved me in.

This was where I really caved in. The sight of a woman on all fours just does something to me. Something chemical, something delicious and completely amoral. I felt my pulse start to race and followed obediently.

"Isn't this AMAZING?" she beamed. "It's SOO amazing!"

"It's incredible." I was starting to sweat. "Kinda hot, though."

I loosened the top button of my shirt and pulled the flannel in and out to kick up a breeze. I pulled my sneakers and socks off and stuck my feet out the opening. I stretched my legs out and rested my head on my arm like a pillow.

"I wish I'd had one of these when I was a kid...your own little world."

"Yeah, that's for sure."

I looked over and saw her staring right at me, barely breathing. Her eyes looked wet, like something inside of her was about to spill out, right through the center of her eyes. I turned and rested on one elbow, and Jennifer started to lean down towards me.

Everything was perfect. Here I was in the basement of forbidden fruits, in the Space Bubble, one intsy-bintsy baby step away from my target. Jennifer was having one of those soft-focus childhood moments that leaves a woman vulnerable and weepy, a perfect opportunity for a gentle, comforting kiss that will eventually give way to a full-scale fuck fest.

They don't come any better than this.

I wasn't about to let this moment get away. I reached up and grabbed Jennifer's shoulders and pulled her down on top of me, wrapping my legs around the backs of her thighs. I pressed my mouth against the hollow of her neck and started to scrape my teeth, then my tongue, and then my teeth again along the skin. I did it real slow. I felt her start to shiver. I reached up and grabbed her earlobe in my teeth, gently sucking the skin into my mouth and working it with my tongue. I could feel Jennifer starting to grind her hips into mine, and I could feel the hot, wet liquid starting to spread between my legs.

I was my old self. Making love to a woman like I was filleting a fish. Working the bones around until the tender white meat just falls away. I felt good. Like Madonna, Ernest Hemingway, and Herman Melville all rolled into one. Jennifer's lips were tugging at mine, hungry and full. Then they stopped. Her legs, her arms, her whole body—they stopped too. Everything stopped. Everything, that is, except me.

I felt my feet were getting hotter and hotter. I looked down the length of my body and saw that they were bathed in a bright white light, so bright I had to close my eyes, and still it lit my eyelids so much all I could see was pink.

Jennifer was just lying there, like someone had flipped a switch and she'd just frozen, a banana slice captured in a big Jell-O mold. Just stuck in time.

I blinked my eyes open and shut and shook my head like a wet dog. I crawled out of the Space Bubble towards the bright light. That's when I saw Yoko. Up went her hands, as if she was offering some sort of benediction. From where I was sitting—mouth gaping and armpits drenched—she looked a mile high. I shielded my eyes with my hand. The glare came from a circle of light around her head. A Yoko halo.

"Wow." I sat back stunned.

"'Wow,'" she barked, "'Wow.' Is that all you can say? You're having a fucking spiritual epiphany and all you can say is 'Wow'? You know how much acid we had to drop when we were your age to even imagine a place like this? Jesus, I don't know why I bother sometimes."

She put her hands on her hips, rolled her eyes in disgust, pivoted on one white silk slipper, walked over to a beanbag chair and plomped herself down.

"I'm sorry," I coughed, "I'm...I mean...I...I don't quite understand what—"

"Understand," she waved her hand at me. "Understand later!"

I felt like Scrooge the night he saw Jacob Marley. I hoped I wasn't in for the three-spirits routine, because as it was I was so fuckin' scared I was just about ready to puke. Things were definitely getting weird.

"Do you mind?" she asked, pulling out a pack of Salem Lights.

I waved her a no.

"Look, I'm not here to lay any heavy trip on you—" She blew a stream of cigarette smoke straight into my face. "I just thought you could use a friend. I saw you on the street today and I said to myself, I said, 'Yoko, that girl's gonna need your help.'"

"I knew it!" I slapped my knee. "I knew it was some weird mind-control thing. Ever since, all I've been able to think about is you. And these feelings, these fuckin' feelings are driving me nuts!"

"Yeah, like what?" she asked.

"Oh, God, you name it! Love, sex, assassinations."

"Assassinations, really?" she asked, her curiosity piqued. "That's a first."

She gestured with her cigarette to the Space Bubble.

"So what's goin' on here?"

I'd almost forgotten about Jennifer. I peeked back inside and there she was, still a banana slice stuck in a big Jell-O mold right where I left her.

"Oh, it's a long story," I explained.

I felt myself getting sheepish. Like I didn't want Yoko to know that I was trying to make Jennifer. Not that I had anything to be ashamed of. I just wasn't in a bragging mood.

"I can't tell you what to do. And I wouldn't even think of it. But I'll tell you this. Long time ago, John had really made it big. The Beatles had just broken up, but his solo career was real good. He let it go to his head. He was chasin' other girls. I looked the other way for a while. 'It's a phase,' I said to myself. Then I said, 'Yoko, you don't need this shit.' I got tired of him treating me like the dirty laundry."

"What happened?" I asked.

"I told him to get out."

"Then what happened?" I asked.

"He left, that's what happened."

"But you got back together, right?"

"We got back together," she said impatiently, "but that's not the point!"

"Sorry."

"The point is this—you really want someone? Well, this isn't the way to do it. And I don't mean sex, either. Nothing wrong with sex. A little more sex and a few less lawyers and we wouldn't be in such a mess. But that's another story. My point is, you're not getting anywhere if all you're doing is trying to fuck with her. And I don't mean fuck her, I mean fuck with her. There's a difference."

I expected milk and cookies, not the riot act.

"So," she asked, pointing to the Space Bubble, "you want her?"

"Yeah, I want her."

"OK. Then don't be a schmuck, OK?"

Yoko stood up and crushed the butt of her cigarette in an ashtray on the bar. "I gotta go," she said.

"Can I see you again?" I asked.

"Don't worry, I'll be around," she said.

Then, just like before on MacDougal Street, she was gone. This time she was swallowed up by the same thing I'd seen just before she appeared—Jennifer, right in front of me, leaning in to me, her lips moving closer and closer to mine.

It was as if someone had flipped a switch starting everything up again.

"Wait!" I yelled.

"What?" Jennifer jumped back and hit her head on the sloping side of the Space Bubble. "What's wrong?"

"Nothing. Nothing, I just—" I was breathing hard, trying to take everything in. Did anyone else see that or was it all my imagination? Jennifer was acting like nothing had happened.

"Just what?" she asked.

"I was just...just thinking."

"Thinking? About what?"

She tried to kiss me again, but I grabbed her arm, squeezing it as hard as I could. I didn't want to let go, I wanted to hold her, to know that she wouldn't simply disappear right in front of my eyes, like Yoko.

"I gotta ask you something," I said to Jennifer. "I need to know if this is really what you want."

She cocked her head and looked at me funny, like she wasn't sure who I was. That's fine, I thought, 'cause I'm not so sure, either.

"Yeah, I mean, I think so." She didn't sound so sure.

"'Cause the thing is, I don't want to do this if it's not what you want. Believe me, when I came here tonight I wanted nothing more than to get you in the sack."

Jennifer's face registered a little horror. "That's a nice way to put it," she said.

"I know, I know. I'm a shit. I would have said or done anything to make it happen. But it's not because I don't care about you, I do. Really. It's because I haven't been honest. With you. Or myself. I was so pissed off at you because I've always wanted you. From the first time I met you. I didn't want you to know 'cause I thought you'd fuck around with me, ya know?"

Jennifer looked confused. I figured I'd blown it.

"It's not that I don't like you," I said. "I do. I like you a lot, Jennifer. But what really matters is that I don't want to lose you."

So there it was. The truth. Just like in the confessional. I planned on going home with nothing more than nine Our Fathers and a sore ego.

I figured I was in for one mighty long dry spell, when Jennifer reached over, grabbed the collar of my shirt, and threw me down onto the Space Bubble floor. "God! I find honesty so incredibly sexy. I want you so much!"

She started at the top of my head and was about one-third of the way down the length of me when I started to feel like the Space Bubble was reaching cruising altitude.

Hey, maybe I was on to something here. Love and sex. Maybe John and Yoko were right. All you need is love. And sex. And love.

# *Explosion*

*Paul A. Massignani, Jr.*

A couple nights ago that nigga Robert and his midget mothafuckin' homey Doop was creepin' the streets in Robert's new car, this slick new one, a Grand Prix. Dark green, real low to the ground, like they do them things now. Blarin' that supersonic rap music doin' about twenty miles an hour top speed, you know, that fuckin' rap shit that sound like a bomb done gone off in they trunk and shit. He stop off at that tall boy Eric's crib over on Sixty-first and Damen, 'cross the street from the park. They was havin' a party, cars parked all jagged up and down the block like you wouldn't believe, all different colors like a line a Chiclets. Aluminum sidin' shakin' and rattlin' off the timbers on that poor old house, windows all dartin' with shadows. Robert and Doop broke on up in there to join in. Seems that Chandra was right in the middle of the front room, grindin' crotches like them young folks like to dance, right there with about six niggas rubbin' all up on her little titties and ass and shit.

    Robert went and found Chandra's brother, that tall boy Eric, and made like he was all straight with him, talkin' 'bout, "Yo Eric, what's up, dog? Yo, this party is live, man, you all that tonight!" Old boy was like, "Aww yeah, dog, I know it's all that, what's up?" So Robert was like, "Let's go out back, I got somethin' fo' you," and they went out to the backyard on the concrete patio and Robert fixed the mothafucker up right. "Yo, Eric check out this bud, dog; it's the bomb." So they smoked it, but Robert didn't tell him the shit was laced like Air Jordans. Eric's ass was ridin' shotgun on the Sherman highway all the rest of the night, dammit. See, that was the plan, see, 'cause Robby scandalous ass knew what he wanted out the situation. He told Eric's stoned ass he gonna take Chandra out for a ride for some more beers, and Eric just smiled with Chinese eyes and put his arms around Robert and Doop and they walked through the crowd from the kitchen back through to the livin' room to where they was all sweatin' and gyratin', hard dicks and hips movin', all them wet pussies, and Eric shouts above the music, "Yo Chandra, come here!" She struts up all sassy out the crowd with her braids up in a ponytail, spandex shorts showin' them pussy lips bulgin' out, sweepin' sweat off her forehead, and smilin' with those big red wet-ass lips.

"What's up, Eric, what you want? Oh hey, Robert, how you livin', sweety?"

Robert was already smooth and tickin' from the Sherm, so to him Chandra was talkin' real soft, and her titties in that shiny spandex donut thang they was caught up in was hella goddamn funny, too.

"Come on, Chandra, haha, yo, ha, ohhh shit." Then Doop see Robert's ass laughin' and he can't help it neither so they both start to crackin' and then Eric joins in. Chandra was like, "Y'all trippin', what you want?" Eric told her to take a ride with them, so she was like, "Yeah," and her eyes lit up and shit, 'cause a ride with Robert was usually a free hit on some of that nose candy and shit.

They left the party all yellin' and shit in the street. Doop grip his midget crotch, and he like, "Whooo, Chandra, girl, you got my dick hard enough to scratch glass and shit." She pout with her hands on her hips, tryin' to play it off, like, "Come on, boy, cut it out, you know you ain't gettin' none a this!" Whoopin' up the whole South Side like that, you dig, they woofin' loud enough to fill every goddamn greasy dark-alley-garbage-can corner west a that twelve-thousand-car-crashin' Dan Ryan expressway over yonder.

They got in the car and start to creepin' 'round the hood, stoppin' at Robby's boy Albert's crib over near Western Avenue. 'Nother rock dealer. Lower than squid shit, you dig? So they peeled off into the night again, and now Robert thinkin' he all slick and bad, he got the seat pushed all the way back, Doop's little laughin' ass in the back seat chillin', and this Chandra girl smilin' at him in the passenger seat, sittin' spreadeagle like she was pushin' out a baby, smilin' real sexy.

Robert kicked the game to another level and held up the little Baggie of nose sugar and she licked them red lips, head swayin' to the music. She asked, "How much you want, sweety?" and Robby tilted his hat down and grinned crooked, real smuglike. He said to her, real calm, "Don't want no money, girl, just have yo'self a party with me and be sweet, aye-ight?" So she snuffed a line off a makeup mirror while they slinked through all them dark squares and grids of South Side blocks, back and forth down them square streets and under train bridges, the night lights crawlin' slow over that shiny new car.

Robert knew what he was up to, though. He rolled the ride into that industrial hood over down Fifty-first behind all them empty buildings by Central Cable and Wire, and parked back there. It was like a T-shaped street with big, square buildings all on every side. The bottom of the T was how you got in.

Every window in every building was dark, ain't nobody in them warehouses after eight or nine. Old girl was like, "Robby, what we doin' here?" He was like, "Chill, baby, we gonna freeze right here for a minute. Yo, Doop, pass me a forty." They all cracked open a cold one and took some hits.

So after a minute or two it went like this: Robert say, "Damn, yo, I'm tired of sittin' on my ass, yo. Let's get out this mothafucker for a minute." Doop spoke up and says, "Pop the trunk, money, let's bump some sounds." So they all got out and Chandra and Robert sat on the open trunk, that rap bomb shit explodin' echoes off a the walls, 'cause they was right down in this service drive between the Central Cable and Whitney Electric buildings.

Chandra gets to rollin' her head back with them braids swayin', and closin' her eyes, head-bobbin' to the beat, and starin' at the stars 'cause it was clear; they was like pinpricks in the sky. Doop and Robert look at each other real sly and smile, staring down at her hot crotch and those mmm-mm, tight little spandex. They got to droolin' over her perky titties, and she was real tight, too, nice flat belly. Robert winked at Doop and mouthed these words, "You down?" Doop pounded his fist to his chest and swigged on his beer, winkin'.

So Robert takes the bold move, reach down while Chandra drinkin' on her beer and rubs the girl's pussy. "Goddamn!" she screamed, and had to cough up some beer that went down the wrong pipe. She was real hot about it, and stared Robert right in the eye, stood up, and was like, "Yo, Robby, don't even try it; you need to ask before you touch, right?"

"Aww girl, I'm sorry, ain't that right, Doop?"

"Yeah, Chandra, we sorry."

"Y'all better take me back to the crib. Eric gonna want me back, come on." Shit, Eric's ass back at the party all Shermed up on the couch. He ain't know where Chandra was, and he ain't care.

Old girl turned around and was gonna open the door to get back in the car when Doop sprang her ass like a gangster frog. Straight up jumped on her back like a monkey, got her in a headlock and shit. Looked like that leprechaun movie, little midget mothafucker. Robert, like the dirty bastard he is, he walked up behind her chokin', clawin' ass and sweep-kicked her right knee out. She let out a hell of a yelp when she hit the ground, but that music from the open trunk and Robert's high-dollar stereo drown her out. Doop pulled her arms behind her back. They was laughin' and really trippin' then and pulled her up hard, her face all twisted up in pain. Robert smiled and cold smacked her hard across the jaw, straight knocked her knees silly, her head all droopin' and eyes rollin'. He told Doop, "Lean her against the car; stand her ass up." She was moanin' in pain. Doop slammed her on the car door hard enough to knock half the breath outta her. He was all excited, starin' intense at the crack of her ass, feelin' her up. "Damn, Robert, she fine, I wanna fuck that ass so hard and bust a mothafuckin' NUT up in that box, yo!"

Robert came 'round from the trunk with some bungee cables. He pushed Doop out the way and wrapped her wrists up. Then he told Doop, "Shut the trunk and come on over here, nigga. Let's do this." Even Doop had to pause when he seen the look in Robby's eyes—he gets into his own zone and you cain't touch him, eyes stone like a pitbull, just get out the way or else. Mothafuckin' possessed by hormone demons. He crunched that poor girl up against the wall of the Whitney Electric warehouse, near a big blue garbage dumpster. Doop came up behind with his forty and watch all wide-eyed, swiggin', while Robert smashed her across the jaw again, and she slumped down the wall a bit, whimpering like a weanin' puppy, and Robert cold yanked her back up like a rag doll and went to work.

He ripped them spandex shorts down real hard—his other hand on her throat—yanking and ripping like a shark on a side of beef, running them down around her ankles and ripping her little white panties off. Her belly shook with fear, poor thing. Doop picked up them panties like a pervert stepson and sniffed the mothafuckers—ooh, he nasty! Robert flipped his hat brim back and breathed heavy hard kisses on Chandra's limp mouth and titties, and unzipped his drawers, lord save us. He pulled out that blackass pole and buried it in her hard, pushing and pushing and pushing. She started to come to, and scream but he covered her mouth with his hand, and she snorted through her nose as he pounded her harder, her ass bouncing against the wall, *fump-fump-fump*.

If that rap music wasn't bouncing, fritterin' off the walls of all the buildings around the empty lots, they woulda heard some floatin' cop sirens a-waftin' with the breeze, comin' all down Fifty-first past the green and yellow neon explosions from Future Video and them Mexican grocery stores and that Submarine Port place, all full of taco-speakin' mothafuckers foggin' up the windows out by the street with they stank; if it weren't for Robby's car stereo they woulda heard that three-squad chase shootin' like blue fireflies straight down Western after some chump nigga in a white van.

But no, Robert turned around, I ain't kiddin', right in the middle of this sick shit and told Doop, "Yo, gimme a hit off that forty, dog; all this hard work makin' me thirsty!" Doop look like he seen a ghost, but he give him the forty. Then that midget weirdo start to strokin' hisself through his pants, watchin' the whole thang. Robert start to screamin', talkin' 'bout, "Awww yeah, yeah!" and finish, then pull out and let her slide to the ground and crumple up on the concrete. What he did next don't no one understand. She was sobbing, jaw all swelled up, and Robby cold took a runnin' start and buried his Nike shoe as far into her stomach as he could. He barked at the bitch, "Yo Chandra, ha ha, what, you hurt, you wanna go back to the crib? Naaaw, bitch. That's right, you wanna show off yo' shit all the damn time, that's right; I got somethin' for yo' ass!" Doop was, like, real quiet, "Robby, dog, let's break, dog, c'mon, she done, let's bust on out—"

"Shut the fuck up, fool!" Robert snapped. "You want second serve, homey? You want some of that box? Get some! Fuck that bitch right now!" He was pointing a hard finger in Doop's face, and his dick was still hangin' in the breeze over his open zipper.

Doop just put his hands up and walked back to the car, sayin', "Naww, dog, that's cool, I'm straight, aye-ight. I mo' be in the car." Robert picked his forty off the ground and killed it. "See ya 'round, Chandra," he mumbled, and then he threw the bottle on her head! Cold. Poor girl's head rang and swelled up some more as they just drove off and left her.

That morning some white mothafucker found Chandra's tattered ass on a bus bench, pretty cocoa face all fucked up with a big bubble bruise on her left jaw and a knot behind her ear, and she was holdin' her ripped up shorts together over her coochie and moaning like a zombie. The cops put her up in the hospital with a junked-up stomach. She still ain't talked much, just laid up. They had Robert and Doop up in there at the police station all of three times last week, but they got some lawyer keepin' they ass out the big house.

Any brother go and do what he done ain't fit enough in the head to be livin'. His old-ass cabbie daddy, and his po' ass momma, bless her soul 'fore she got the cancer and ain't with us no more, they never dropped the boy on his head, don't know why he would turn out with the devil in him. Ever since he started to high school he just get worse.

So the next day Robert be loungin' in his bedroom in the basement, ramblin' on and on to this suburban bitch Keisha Johnson for like an hour. He stretched out on his bed, ain't no concern for the boy that it's already noon and shit, them niggas sell the rocks and they don't even gotta work never! Keisha like, "Boy, don't even tell me no lies. Latesha called me first thing, told me all about it! You better not lie to me, boy. I come over there and pull a .38 and blast your rapist ass to the curb!" Damn, her girl Latesha was at the party and know all about what happened to Chandra 'cause she went up to the hospital with Eric's hungover self and visit the messed-up bitch in the mornin'.

Robert just smile to the phone, sick, man, tryin' to satisfy hisself just picturin' Keisha, like he followin' the phone line up his black concrete basement bedroom wall and out through the ashy white sidin' on that house, over that weed-infested backyard, up to the roof of that fucked-up, powder-blue garage he got out back look like it been picked up and dropped, and out the main line at the pole, shootin' through them hot, stanky alleyways, dartin' and jaggedin' over all them ugly gray mountains a dried-up shingles and hot-ass soft-tar roofs with Coke cans and bottle caps and shit stuck in em' like Pappy's Liquors over on Twenty-Sixth a bit west, you know what I'm sayin', up to those huge tower lines run west towards the water reclamation plant, passin' rows of smokestacks lookin' like they was fenceposts, out over that snakey suburban Highway 55 goes where all the money is, down through Keisha's hood and those in-ground pools between the big ol' backyards over mothafuckin' eight-foot private fences an' shit, three-story cribs, one floor for each mothafuckin' white-ass honky live in there, then down into Keisha's gramamma crib backyard, past the pretty little white veranda out back and through the fresh brown bricks to the garage where Kiesha's little yellow Jap car be sittin', then up in the kitchen where her long, caramel-leg sweetness sittin' crossleg at the kitchen table leanin' over a steamy plate of bacon and sunny eggs. Robby done love that girl and her soft little titties under them white T-shirts and them shoulder-length braids. Oooh, that girl fine.

Robby say to her, "Girl, I ain't did that! Who you be believin' more than me, that girl Latesha, that fat girl that drive a station wagon?"

"She my friend, Robert, don't make fun of her!" Keisha rang Robert's ears with that fussy little scream. Robert say, "Aww, naww, baby, please," beggin' her to listen to him, "naww, baby. Latesha jus' don't like me. I don't know who did that shit to Chandra, hell naw. Wasn't me, though. I'm straight."

Keisha stay quiet for a long time and he got nose-breathin' mad. She bullheaded, but she got money, treat him nice, got a nice crib out where ain't no crazy niggas tryin' to dog his ass and the cops ain't always ready to blast. His mind churn. "Keisha," he say all quiet, "you love me?" She say, "Yeah, boy, come on and answer me!"

"I love you too. You my baby. I ain't never goin' let you go, and you know I ain't goin' play with Chandra like that and lose you. You my world."

She chilled and believed the shit. I guess later they got to fightin' again, but for the time it was cool.

Word around the hood is that tall mothafucker Eric with his greasy little curl came round to the crib to smoke Robert for that shit. Doop and Robert was lampin' out on the front porch of Robby's house. So then here goes this jittery-ass white Cutlass hoopty out by the curb; Chandra's brother Eric jump all tight arm out the driver's side, fist-marchin' on through the fence gate straight up to Robby's face, talkin' 'bout, "Mothafucker, you gon' pay, goddamn, bitch, you about to get smoked!" Face look like somebody sewed them furry-ass eyebrows together at the tip of his wide-ass nose. Robby a strong nigga, though. He ain't scared of no fight, shit. Knocked out a two-hundred-fifty-pound brotha with a bottle 'crosst the jaw three weeks earlier at a nightclub. Robby was straight puttin' fingers right in Eric's face, his head seesawin' back and forth under the streetlight while he jawed at the boy. Then Robert throw his hands up and say, "Yo, ooh, my dick felt *goood* up in them guts, Eric; you got some of that good pussy like yo' sister for me?" Doop's ass just about to hit the deck cacklin' away like a chump then, and two other busters, big boys, got out the tall boy's white Cutlass out on the street.

Well, Robert seen that comin', curl his hand 'round his back, and pulled out a goddamn hand cannon like no one never knew he had, pound on his chest, and told that mad tall mothafucker, "Yo, Eric, this steel about to get live; yo' mothafuckin' homies better bust the fuck out, quick!" Doop was like, "Goddamn, Robert, you raw." Them boys got they ass back in the ride and jetted real quick, Cutlass limpin' down the block. You be three sheets to the breeze 'fore you call the cops on Robert. No sir. Right there on the front lawn by the sidewalk, he told that tall boy with a wave of the pistol, "Get on yo' knees, homey." Soon as the boy knelt down he got the butt of that gun in a chrome slash 'crosst his wide-ass nose. Split it open like a hammer on a tomato. Squish. Poor mothafucker. Musta hurt. His ass was out like Leon Spinks, layin' on the grass bleedin' pretty bad. Doop's ass just lookin' on, laughin' with his hands over his bubble-lip mouth and doin' his arms and hands in a slicin' motion like they swords or some shit, sayin', "Hell naw, that nigga broke, fool! Hell naw!" 'Course that pipin'-ass rock nigga ain't gonna get in on the scrap. Seem funny 'cause them short-ass niggas always be wantin' to prove they so bad. They must call his ass Doop 'cause he a punk retard.

Robert just stood over Eric and faked like he was throwin' fists on him, talkin' 'bout, "How you like that, mark-ass bitch, come up and get some more!" Damn. Him and Doop didn't care none. Sat up on the porch steps and smoked a couple squares, laughin' at how long Eric stayed knocked out, throwin' they burnin' butts at him when they done. Guess Robert got rid of the pistol, 'cause the cops came and took him and Doop away. They went out to the curb laughin' like it was nothin' and let them piglets sweep em' off in cuffs to the department like it warn't no thang at all. Damndest thing you ever did see out of a life criminal.

Gotta feel sorry for that little girl they hurt, though. Cain't even get a good revenge out her brother. That boy had to get CPR and get tooken off to the hospital by a ambulance, he so hurt. He just come to get Robby back for what he did to his sister. Chandra Gray was her name; girl been chillin' a hundred time before with Robert. So's every other ho in the whole South Side, but that's beside the point. Seem like he don't even care none about nobody. He know every mothafucker in the hood afraid of his ass and he like it; you can see in the way he limp down to the corner to huddle with them loud rock-smokin' niggas under the streetlamps.

He got his rep. Any nigga tell you, Robby and Doop do anything; they crazy like that. See some shorties on pedal bikes in a circle on the corner, ten years old, pointin' down the street, doin' they hand like a pistol to another shorty, start talkin' 'bout, "Yo homey, better give up that Shaq rookie right 'fore I do like Robby and put yo' ass in yo' grave." Scare that shorty bad. Everybody start to fearin' Robby. He ain't leavin' the hood never, not creepin' in that green Grand Prix, not walkin', not ridin' the bus. He straight glued his saggy-jeaned ass to a ghetto porch for life. Ain't nobody walk past his crib and see him don't think he ain't ready to die.

# The Boobs

*Lauri Coup*

*Chapter One*

The cool, early morning ocean air was invigorating. Dr. Edward Klottz swung his tennis racket lightly to and fro, fancying that he was a famous player warming up for Wimbledon. His wife, Florence, looked over at him disapprovingly as she methodically stretched her bulbous legs.

"Let's get started, you oaf!" she snorted. "We only have the court reserved for an hour."

Dr. Klottz nodded obligingly from the courtside bench and picked up his brand new can of Wilson tennis balls. The top peeled up with a satisfying *Pop!* and Dr. Klottz reached inside. He pulled out an ordinary-enough ball, delightfully fuzzy and yellowish-green. He bounced it once against the ground, enjoying the pleasing way it snapped up lightly into his palm. He reached in for the second ball, and much to his chagrin, instead of retrieving another downy orb, he found himself grasping something taut yet mushy, with a rather firm eraserlike point at the top of it. He eased it out of the can and reeled back in mawkish surprise.

"Good heavens!" he gasped. "It's a boob!"

Almost immediately his shock was replaced by a strange, somewhat perverted curiosity. He reached once more into the can like a child exploring a Christmas stocking. Sure enough, there was another boob (quite obviously the aforementioned's partner) nestled cozily in the bottom.

"My word," Dr. Klottz said, unaware he was speaking aloud. "This is terribly unusual."

His wife, Florence, who by this time had grown rather impatient, stalked impudently over to the bench, arriving just in time to see him laying out the two boobs (nipples up, of course) side by side on the flat, green surface of the tennis court.

"You goon!" she sputtered. "You infantile, doddering shmuck! I should've known you couldn't leave your work at the office!"

For perhaps the first time in his marriage, Dr. Klottz ignored his wife, and pushed her absentmindedly to one side as he leaned forward to get a closer look at the boobs. They had begun to seem strangely familiar.

"Do you hear me, you stupid gastritic swine? Are you trying to get us kicked out of another country club? You miserable, pot-bellied cretin!"

As if struck by a wayward bolt of lightning, Dr. Klottz suddenly realized whose boobs had miraculously appeared in his can of Wilson tennis balls. He fell back against the bench in horror. The last time he had seen them, they had been perched perkily atop the upper torso of Mitzi Mountebank, star of the hit television series *Babeforce 1*.

"Excuse me, dear," Dr. Klottz said to his wife in a stunned monotone, "but I should probably put these away before anyone sees them. I'll just run right up and put them in my gym locker for safekeeping."

"Are you completely deranged? As if I could settle down to a relaxing game of tennis now! Get rid of them, you puke! I don't want to see your sniveling face again until you've done it!"

And with that, Florence Klottz stormed up to the country club spa to see if she could schedule an appointment with her favorite masseur, Lars.

Dr. Klottz sighed and stared pointedly at the boobs. A stiff breeze had whipped up off the ocean, and it caused the boobs to jiggle slightly as they waited innocently on the tennis court.

"I'll be darned if they didn't jiggle just like that the last time I saw Ms. Mountebank!" Dr. Klottz thought wildly and twisted his hands in the excess fabric of his shorts. He wondered what the medical board would say about this kind of infraction, particularly after last year's botched collagen injections. The thought spurred him to action, and he snatched up the boobs, stuffed them into the pockets of his shorts, and prayed that they would look just like plain old tennis balls to the casual passerby. He strode quickly to his Range Rover and roared out of the parking lot.

It should be mentioned that Dr. Klottz was not a man who performed well in emergency situations. Therefore, instead of driving to another town or to a discreet park, he drove directly back into his own neighborhood. He screeched to a halt a few feet from his front yard and attempted to chuck the boobs inside a nearby mailbox. Unfortunately, his neighbor chose that very moment to walk her dog, and he ended up waving to her instead. He made many such attempts to rid himself of the boobs, but it was a lovely day, and it seemed that his entire neighborhood was outside mowing lawns (or rather, watching their gardeners mow them), sunning, or just standing around doing nothing in particular. In desperation, he drove to the local Burger King and attempted to roll the boobs nonchalantly into a nearby bush while he waited his turn at the drive-thru. However, Mrs. Plunkett, who sometimes came over to play cribbage with Florence, pulled up directly behind him and waved at him merrily through his rearview mirror.

Dr. Klottz drove through the streets of Malibu, munching miserably on his Whopper until, in a moment of brilliance, he remembered the deserted road that led up into the mountains. He realized that once he escaped the highway traffic, he could easily dump the boobs into an unsuspecting ditch. He gleefully tossed the rest of his burger out the window and stomped on the accelerator.

In no time at all, Dr. Klottz found himself standing over a densely foliaged ravine, boobs in one hand, tennis racket in the other. The first boob was served nicely, and soared in a resplendent arc over the leaves of the swaying trees.

"Fifteen–Love," Dr. Klottz whispered, in his most announcerlike voice.

Again he swung the racket behind him, arched his back, and lobbed the second boob even farther than the first. As it disappeared into the valley, Dr. Klottz breathed an almost comical sigh of relief, and began to swing the racket to and fro jubilantly, as if he were embroiled in an intense volley.

"Hey!" a husky voice yelled. "You there!"

Dr. Klottz, caught in mid-swing, turned sheepishly to see a rather brutish woman in a too-tight ranger uniform stomping toward him.

"There's a five-hundred-dollar fine for littering in a National Park, you know!" she cried, shaking a meaty finger at him. "Do you have a pass?"

As the ranger reached for her billy club, Dr. Klottz sputtered convulsively about free tummytucks and discount liposuctioning, but he really made no sense at all, and I'm afraid the rest of that day has blurred into the wavy image of a distant valley road.

*Chapter Two*

Mitzi Mountebank rolled delightedly to one side and stretched her arms luxuriantly above her head, where they encountered her velvet-lined handcuffs still fastened to the bed from the previous night's festivities. She grinned as she pictured the well-endowed Fabio look-alike she had picked up at the party her producer, Marty, had thrown. Mitzi squinted one eye at the other side of the bed, saw nothing but a disheveled nest of sheets, and breathed a sigh of relief. It was one thing to bring home a hottie, but it was nothing but a pain in the ass to fix his coffee in the morning. Mitzi preferred the scummier variety that snuck home as soon as she fell asleep. At least last night's conquest had uncuffed her before he made his escape. She'd had a hell of a time last week after that photographer had left her trussed up. It was a good thing it had been the maid's day to clean.

Mitzi flounced onto her stomach and sighed contentedly before she noticed something was amiss. Her cheek lay flat against the pillow, in a relaxed position that felt altogether wrong. She flipped onto her back and faced the ceiling, so that she could examine herself in the mirror. Her face stared back at her in a comical mask of terror and amazement. Her boobs were gone! Mitzi cupped her hands over her chest, where two, very round, very firm mounds of flesh were supposed to be. There was nothing. A smooth, strangely supple expanse of skin met her trembling fingertips. There was not a curve, not a bump. Nothing but flatness. A strangled mew escaped Mitzi's quivering lips.

"Fuck," she said, in a voice that had been described as whiny on more than one occasion.

But perhaps this would be an appropriate time to get a better idea of just what Mitzi Mountebank was all about.

Mitzi was a stunningly good-looking blonde whose career in television had skyrocketed after she had purchased a rather expensive, but pleasingly pert pair of boobs. She enjoyed her new additions immensely and could be seen flaunting them all over L.A. Men would frequently stop in the streets, mouths hanging open, as she pranced by in her tiny tanktops and minuscule miniskirts. Mitzi used to brag that she had caused more traffic accidents than any other actress in Hollywood. Strangely enough, she was probably right, but I'm afraid that had more to do with her penchant for crossing streets in the middle of rush hour than with motorists being overcome by her bleached-blonde beauty.

So it should be relatively easy to imagine how Mitzi felt when she woke up *sans* boobs. She frantically scrambled out of bed and over to the walk-in closet where she could examine herself more closely in the three-way mirror. She puffed her chest out in the way that had earned her the role on *Babeforce 1*. But it was to no avail. All she saw was the wavy outline of her rib cage, and then the smooth, tanned skin that stretched up in an even plane to her collarbone.

"Shit!" she cried. "What the fuck happened to my boobs?"

Standing there staring at her shapeless reflection only infuriated her further, so she stomped back over to the bed and wrapped the leopard-spotted silk sheets around her to help her concentrate. Suddenly, she was struck with inspiration. It had to be that Fabio guy she brought home last night. He must have taken her boobs! She decided to try and get hold of Marty. Perhaps he would know where she could find the Fabio wanna-be, and then she could get her boobs back. She was supposed to have brunch with her agent, but she called to cancel. The last thing she needed was for him to see her without her boobs. The agency would drop her like a hot rock.

Having a plan made her feel better, so she browsed through her closet looking for something that could possibly camouflage her loss of topography. Unfortunately, she only had outfits that would accentuate her cleavage, not hide the sudden loss of it. In a moment of what she considered brilliance, she remembered the padded bras she had collected before her surgery. With one of the bras and a couple of tube socks, maybe she could get by.

Sufficiently stuffed, Mitzi snuck stealthily out of her house and jumped into her candy red Corvette that was parked half in the driveway, half in the flowerbed.

"Wow, I must have been totally wasted last night," Mitzi giggled to herself, but then she remembered her missing boobs, and the moment was ruined.

She hopped into the Corvette, put down the top, and revved the engine, noticing that her neighbor Bob had come out onto his front porch to glare at her. Bob was a wiener, and Mitzi took great pleasure in annoying him whenever she could. Unfortunately for Bob, that was quite often. Mitzi gunned the engine, then roared out of her driveway, smashing into Bob's garbage cans which stood placidly at the curb. As she sped away she could hear his outraged screams, and she enjoyed it so much that she almost forgot about her mission.

But as she careened onto the freeway, she forced herself to concentrate. Marty was probably having brunch at The Trattoria in Beverly Hills. With a heady look of determination, Mitzi steered the 'vette north. She screeched into The Trattoria's parking lot and winked at the valet as she opened her door and slithered past him.

"Take extra special care of my baby," she cooed, and dropped the pink fuzzy dice keychain into his hand.

She strolled into the impressive marble and gold lobby of The Trattoria and caught a glimpse of her reflection in the full-length mirror. At some point between Santa Monica and Beverly Hills, her tube socks had shifted dramatically, and the right one rested a good five inches higher on her chest than the left. Mitzi gasped, and ducked into the safe haven of the nearby ladies' room which was thankfully empty.

"Maybe I shouldn't have left the top down on the 'vette," Mitzi mused. "The wind must've knocked my falsies out of whack."

Before she could further contemplate the laws of physics, Mitzi caught a glimpse of two strangely shaped strangers passing outside the leaded-glass door of the ladies' room.

"Hey!" Mitzi cried, and scrambled to adjust her tube sock before bursting out into the lobby.

"I'm so sorry, miss," the maitre d' said as she attempted to follow the strangers out onto the trellis-lined patio of The Trattoria. "Do you have a reservation?"

"They're with me...I mean...I'm with them," she stuttered, pointing at the strangers, who were being seated at a lovely table right next to the fountain.

Before the maitre d' could stop her, she brushed past him and out onto the patio where the strangers were just relaxing to enjoy their cappuccinos. Mitzi crept stealthily behind a rather large fern, and her mouth dropped open in astonishment. Seated before her at one of the most coveted tables in The Trattoria were her very own boobs!

"What the fuck?" Mitzi said. She could come up with no feasible explanation as to how her boobs had suddenly happened to turn up at The Trattoria, sipping expensive Italian coffees. They were her boobs, all right, but somehow since last night they had learned to dress very well and had made some great connections. Mitzi had been an important TV actress for months and still couldn't get a table near the fountain in the middle of brunch. She steeled herself, took a deep breath, and pranced up to their table.

"I...I hope I'm not interrupting...," Mitzi began.

"What is it?" said the boob on the left, rather snippily. She was dressed in an impeccable Armani suit, and wore a delicate pair of teardrop diamond earrings, which complemented her silk blouse.

"Do you want an autograph?" the other boob queried, looking up from her menu. The right boob was dressed in a very flirty Anna Sui sundress with combat boots. Mitzi marveled that two boobs with such differing senses of style could have both originated with her.

"Ummm...no, that's not it, exactly," Mitzi stammered. "I think we should just cut through the bullshit and get to the point."

"By all means, do," the left boob said, and laid her chin carefully on her clasped palms with an expression of polite disdain.

"Well, I didn't think I'd have to explain it to you," Mitzi continued, feeling uncomfortably queasy. "I mean, you're obviously not where you're supposed to be."

"Are you from the *Entertainment Times*?" the right boob piped up. "We canceled that interview last week."

"This is stupid!" Mitzi cried in frustration. "I'm a major TV personality, after all, and I can't believe you two could sit here having a nice brunch, while you knew I was at home, worried sick...."

"I do believe she's a bit mental," the left boob said, consulting her partner. "Perhaps we should call over the maitre d'."

"No!" Mitzi cried, and slipped into a vacant chair so that she could address her boobs more confidentially. "Quit teasing me, and just confess! I mean, it's like totally obvious that you two are my boobs!"

The boobs looked at one another and shrugged slightly in annoyed confusion.

"Look, I've seen a lot of desperate actresses in my time, but this takes the cake," the right boob said. "I don't know what you're trying to pull, honey, but you can just forget it. We only work with A-list talent."

"I'd always heard stories like this from other producers," the left boob commented, "although I have to say this is a bit extreme."

Mitzi opened her mouth to set them straight, then out of the corner of her eye spotted her producer, Marty. As usual, he was surrounded by his entourage, which happened to include one virile-looking young man that Mitzi had never seen before. He had slightly wavy black hair and a Latin Antonio Banderas look about him that made her feel slightly weak in the knees. She was halfway over to their table and about to introduce herself, when she remembered that she didn't have her boobs and wasn't completely sure that the tube socks were still on an even plane.

"Dammit!" she hissed inwardly. "I always knew my boobs were something special, but I just didn't think they'd go off and leave me behind."

Frantically, Mitzi turned back to the boobs' table, intending to grab each one by the hair and shake them until they admitted what they really were. But much to her dismay, the boobs had left. They had probably gone to another restaurant where they could have brunch in peace.

Mitzi ran wildly into the street in the hope that she could catch her boobs. She was too late, however, and only managed to catch a glimpse of a black Range Rover carrying two very round passengers as it turned the corner.

Mitzi was at a loss. She was certain there was some protocol for handling such a matter, but she had no idea what that might be. In fact, she wasn't all that sure what "protocol" really meant. She snapped her fingers at the loafing valet, who gave her a sneering look and sauntered to the very back of The Trattoria lot where her 'vette was parked in between a Toyota and a Yugo.

"Well, I just don't see how things could get worse!" Mitzi cried.

She decided to go for a Sunday drive to cheer herself up. But it was Beverly Hills, and everywhere she went she was confronted with pairs of perfectly proportioned boobs, bouncing merrily to and fro on the chests of their happy owners. After one particularly nice pair on a redhead in a sundress, she could stand it no more. She drove north, determined to report the incident to the police. But as she pulled up in front of the station, her heart quailed. She had been arrested in a shakedown of the soft-porn industry in Long Beach last year, before *Babeforce 1* became a major hit. She was sure the cops would take the side of the boobs over a girl with a record.

Beaten, hopeless, and more than a little crabby, Mitzi revved the engine of the 'vette once more and turned toward home. She felt that all that was left for her was a bottle of Jack Daniel's and a Big Mac. But just when all hope seemed dashed, she was struck with inspiration.

"I'll break the story wide open!" she declared, slamming a fist into the dashboard. "My boobs will make *Hollywood's Most Wanted's* top ten list!"

She had met the host of *Hollywood's Most Wanted* last month when they were doing a feature called "Cheerleaders Turned Superstars." Mitzi had been their biggest name. She had ended up seducing Chip Lothario, the host, which had suddenly turned out to be quite convenient, since now she had a press contact. She roared to a stop in front of his comfortable, albeit rented, bungalow in the Hollywood Hills.

She found Chip out back relaxing by the pool and simultaneously rubbing oil on the backs of two abundantly female guests. Chip seemed relatively annoyed that she had chosen that moment to drop by, but never one to turn away any female visitor, he showed her inside and motioned for her to sit down on the red leather couch.

"What can I do for you, Mitzi?" he crooned in his best anchorman voice.

"I have a breaking story!" she began. "And I'm going to give *you* the exclusive!"

Chip conspiratorially brought a couple of mixed drinks over and sat down next to Mitzi. He leaned close to her, and she noticed that he had forgotten to clip his nose hairs that morning. He handed her a drink and then motioned for her to begin.

"It all started this morning," Mitzi began, doing her best to avoid looking at Chip's nose. "I woke up to find something was missing...."

"A burglary!" Chip shouted, squeezing her knee.

"Well...not exactly," Mitzi said slowly.

"Did they steal any valuables?" Chip continued, resting his other hand against Mitzi's shoulder.

"Ummm...sort of."

"Were you hurt?" Chip asked, not unsympathetically.

"Well, kind of."

"You poor dear," Chip crooned. "You must be positively frazzled."

"That's true," Mitzi agreed, and for a moment the feel of Chip's manicured fingertips against her thigh was so distracting that she forgot the problem at hand. However, his hand soon found the problem, and he yanked his fist out of Mitzi's shirt, clutching a red-and-blue striped tube sock.

"Ow-ww-ww!" Chip sputtered furiously.

"I know," Mitzi moaned. "My boobs are gone."

"This is crazy. It's unheard of!" he cried, springing to his feet, and flinging the sock to the ground as if it had bit him.

"So...," Mitzi said, retrieving the tube sock and replacing it in her bra. "Can we do a show on them?"

"A show on your boobs! Are you nuts?" Chip asked, his eyes wild. "We don't do smut stories. Do you know what *30 Minutes* would say about me if they saw me do a missing boob story? The networks would laugh in my face!"

"But what about my boobs?" Mitzi pleaded. "How will I get them back!"

"You're on your own, lady!" Chip said, pushing Mitzi out the door. "And don't tell anyone you were here."

"You suck!" Mitzi screamed as he slammed the door behind her. Dejected, she slunk back to her Corvette, ripped up the ticket she found stuck under the windshield wiper, and drove recklessly home.

Mitzi threw her keys onto the kitchen counter, kicked off her red three-inch heels, and plopped miserably down onto the white leather couch.

"Shit," she said.

She plucked the remote out from under her cushion and punched the button to ignite the fireplace, but the soothing flicker of the gaseous orange flames did nothing to improve her state of mind.

"It's all Fabio's fault," she pouted, sullenly confusing the look-alike she had seduced with the real actor. "I should have told that *Hollywood's Most Wanted* loser that Fabio was the one who stole my boobs. He definitely would have run the story."

She whistled for Poochy, her Pekingese, thinking that maybe a quiet night by the fire with man's best friend might relax her. Poochy trotted lazily in, the pink bows tied to her ears bouncing prettily.

"C'mere, Poochy!" Mitzi demanded, slapping her palm against the cushion. "Mummy needs some love."

Poochy looked arrogantly at her mistress, then deliberately walked over in front of the fireplace, squatted daintily, and peed all over the white chenille rug.

"Poochy!" Mitzi yelped. "You little shithead!"

Luckily for Poochy, the doorbell rang at that very instant, and Mitzi forgot her errant pet.

"What?" she said, yanking the front door open. At best she was hoping for some young stud who had gotten a flat tire and needed to use her phone. Even a reasonably good-looking middle-aged neighbor looking to borrow some butter would have been a welcome distraction. However, it was not a man at all, but a woman, and a rather large one, standing with a blank expression in the middle of Mitzi's front porch.

"What?" Mitzi repeated.

"Is this 315 Montana Drive?" the woman asked slowly. Mitzi noticed with a sneer the tight-fitting polyester ranger suit the woman was wearing.

"Yeah."

"And are you...Mitzi Mountebank?" the ranger said, referring to a small black notebook.

"What do you want?" Mitzi replied with a sigh of boredom.

"I really hate to bother you at home, and so late, but I think I have something that might interest you." For in fact, she was the same ranger who had apprehended a certain plastic surgeon in the canyon earlier that weekend.

"Could you get to the point?" Mitzi said. "I'm having a really shitty day."

"I would imagine," the ranger nodded solemnly. "You see, I think that I may have found your boobs."

"My what?" Mitzi cried, hope swelling in her decidedly unswollen chest.

"Your boobs, ma'am," the ranger repeated patiently. "I believe I have them here."

She thrust a beefy hand into each pocket of her county-issue ranger jacket and produced Mitzi's boobs, which were safely ensconced in two plastic sandwich bags. Mitzi shrieked with delight, snatched her boobs from the ranger, and cuddled them close to her chest, much like a mother nuzzles a young child.

"But...but...," Mitzi stammered, hardly daring to take her eyes from her boobs, lest they suddenly disappear again, "but where did you find them?"

"I caught them over at LAX," the ranger said proudly. "They were just about to board a plane to Rio. I didn't notice them at first, because the airport was so crowded, and they were in disguise. But when I got closer I saw that they were boobs, for sure. A matched pair, no less. The funny part is, a plastic surgeon by the name of Edward Klottz seems to be behind the whole thing. He's somewhat of a shady character, been investigated by the medical board, things like that."

"Edward Klottz...," Mitzi repeated, sure that the name should ring a bell.

"In any case, I'm just glad I can return them to you," the ranger said. "I watch your show all the time. It sure would be a shame if you couldn't do those great swimsuit shots anymore."

"No shit," Mitzi agreed solemnly, and shuddered at the thought of herself, boobless, running down a beach.

Mitzi waved to the ranger as she backed her Park Services truck out of the driveway. She noticed with gleeful satisfaction that the ranger misjudged the sharp curve of the driveway and accidentally crunched Bob's mailbox into the shape of her rear bumper.

"Fuckin'-A!" Mitzi exulted, then remembered her boobs, and hurried them inside before they got too cold. She removed her boobs from the plastic bags, and then placed them carefully side by side on her couch, so that she could get a better look at them.

They looked healthy enough, aside from the fact that they happened to be detached from her body. The left one was a bit scratched up, presumably due to its flight through the dense foliage of the canyon. Mitzi thought it served the boob right, after it had been so snippy with her at The Trattoria. She realized that the next step was to reattach her boobs, which seemed to be a formidable task, but Mitzi was undaunted.

"Now that I've got my boobs back, anything is possible!" she shouted with an upraised fist.

However, the task of resticking the boobs proved to be more difficult than Mitzi had anticipated. Her first thought was that the boobs needed to be heated up. Once they matched her own body temperature, she was sure they would mold back on nicely. She ran a hot bubble bath, and deposited the boobs into the sudsy water. They floated merrily in the froth, bobbing up and down slightly when Mitzi stuck her hand in to test the water. When she felt they had been sufficiently warmed, she stripped off her clothes, plucked the boobs lovingly from the suds, and pressed them gently, but firmly, to her chest.

Unfortunately, as soon as she released her grip, the boobs plopped woodenly back into the water. Mitzi wiped a splash of bubble bath from her eyes and sighed.

"That just wasn't quite the right method," she said doggedly. She carefully dried off her boobs with a pink, fluffy towel and set them gently on the counter. "Maybe they're just not sticky enough."

She rummaged through her makeup drawer until she found the latex adhesive she'd used the year before when she had played a prostitute stricken with a terrible and mysterious case of hives.

"This should do the trick," she thought, and spread the latex over the smooth, flat back of the boobs in generous globs. She lay down on the bathroom floor and pressed them against her chest. But the latex was no match for the weight of the boobs, and instead of perching plumply in their allotted places, time and time again they slid heavily into Mitzi's armpits, and then thudded to the bathroom floor.

During the course of the evening she tried many methods of adhesion, but nothing, not even a liberal dose of Elmer's Glue could make the boobs stick. Tired, disheveled, and rather tacky, Mitzi finally fell asleep on the leather couch, still cuddling her dismembered boobs.

As is often the case in Hollywood, rumors of Mitzi's boob escapade quickly sprang up, and as is also often the case, most of the rumors proved to be unfounded. During the following weeks, *Hollywood's Most Wanted* did a story on two up-and-coming producers who had disappeared on their way to scout a location in Rio. The next day they ran a story on a romantic link between *Babeforce 1* star Mitzi Mountebank and a well-to-do plastic surgeon.

An enterprising young man printed up flyers and sold them outside Graumann's Chinese Theater, promising a detailed map and description of the boobs' Bel Air home. Ray Fetterman peppered his opening monologue of *The Evening Show* with crazy missing-boob jokes. Even Martha Dalters was reportedly wooing the boobs for an exclusive interview on her next special.

Crowds lined the streets at every new movie premiere, hoping to catch sight of the elusive boobs. One astute young reporter named the phenomenon "Boobmania," and the nickname caught on like wildfire, reaping souvenir store owners a veritable fortune in T-shirt sales. Most people treated the boob stories with a good-natured shrug. However, there was a small, self-proclaimed, artistically inclined contingent of the Hollywood scene who were rather put off by the undue publicity the boobs were receiving. One aging starlet commented that she would have gotten rid of her boobs long ago if she'd known it would cause such a ruckus.

But as often happens in the transient mecca of movieland, the boobs were soon shoved out of the limelight by a strange and ultimately unrelated string of celebrity glue-sniffing fatalities.

*Chapter Three*

Had Mitzi been so inclined, she might have reflected on the oddity of chance occurrences in the world around her. Because she was not so inclined, her only reaction to finding her boobs back in their proper places was, "It's about fucking time."

She wasted no time in trying them out. Immediately, she shimmied into her smallest halter top and her shortest shorts and went to the beach. On her way out the front door, she encountered her ill-fated neighbor, Bob, but she was so brimming with the effects of good fortune that she did nothing more than stick out her pointy tongue at him as she bounced by.

She roared to a stop in front of the No Parking sign at the pier and jumped out onto the bike path, almost killing two innocent Rollerbladers as they swept by. Mitzi smiled. It felt remarkably satisfying to have her boobs back, and she exaggerated the bounce in her step in order to feel them bobbing heavily along with her. She ran into several acquaintances and former conquests and noted that none of them seemed to notice anything out of the ordinary. This was the icing on the cake, and Mitzi spent the rest of that glorious afternoon bounding through waves and jogging along the shoreline. She reveled in the admiring male glances that seemed to greet her every movement.

"Yep!" she said delightedly to her reflection in the full-length mirror that evening. "My boobs have come home!"

From that day on, Mitzi could be seen at every semi-exclusive social event she managed to get herself invited to in Hollywood. She starred in several B movies, and was offered a miniseries about a former heroin addict who wins the Miss America crown. She continues her acting career in infomercials and psychic hotline ads to this very day. In fact, if you tend to watch a lot of cable late at night, there is quite a good chance that you may get to see some of her work.

And that, as far as one can tell, is a relatively accurate account of the strange and largely inexplicable events that took place in the greater Los

Angeles area some time ago. Although if you were to think it over, it would become abundantly clear that everything that happened was rather silly. After all, how would a pair of boobs get to be producers overnight? It would be more believable if they had become game-show hosts, or maybe stars of a new detective series. Perhaps, as is often the case, the story simply got blown out of proportion, and the rumormongers of Hollywood saw their chance at some great press. In all likelihood, the missing items probably weren't boobs at all, but maybe a handbag or a nice pair of designer gloves. Even a jet ski or some other recreational water vehicle would have been more plausible than a pair of boobs.

But stranger things have happened in this lifetime, and it would be naive to say that such things will not continue to occur...but who can really keep track of such senseless twaddle? It could give you a headache. Besides, there's a great movie of the week starring Marlo Thomas that's just about to begin....

# *Tough*

## *Lott Hill*

We knew a storm was coming because Dad had called from Richmond to tell us that he wasn't coming home. There was enough snow expected that the roads on the mountain could be closed for more than a day, and Mom had gone to the store and stocked up on everything we might need, filling the station wagon with paper bags full of food. Sam and Jake had spent the whole day after school splitting and hauling wood from the barn to the back porch like ants, back and forth, back and forth, and I had been helping Sara fill jugs of water and scoop the ashes from the woodstove and fireplaces. By bedtime, I was tired enough not to argue and went up to Sara's room, wearing my Slinky on my arm like a bracelet, and waited for Mom to come kiss me good night.

I started sleeping in my sister's room when the nightmares began. I slept with Sara in the old rickety bed that squeaked, left over from our dead Aunt Ola whose girth had pressed an oval into its center, a shallow indentation that cupped one but pressed two bodies together. I slept with her because no one else would have me, both of my brothers stating firmly that they didn't want no babies sleeping in their rooms, and though I wanted to be as tough as them,

I knew the only way to keep the nightmare from coming was by not sleeping alone. When Dad was home, he insisted that I sleep in my own bed like a man. "It's time Adam starts growing up," he'd say. "A bad dream isn't going to hurt him." But Mother, who seemed to be able to detect my every mood, would in her concern let me sleep with Sara whenever Dad was gone.

Mom came into the room still dressed from the day except for her socked feet and smiled, coming over to the bed, "You all right, Adam?"

I was afraid that if I looked at her, she could see right into my head, so I just nodded and kept working the Slinky between my hands. She asked if I was still having those scary dreams and put her hand on top of my head and slid it down to my forehead and my cheek. I stopped the Slinky and looked at it, one wire wrapped around and around in a tight coil. I was ashamed to be eleven years old and still afraid of a bad dream. She pulled my face up by the chin so that I had to look at her, and asked, "Want to tell me about it?" The red sleeve of her dress pulled back, revealing the five gold bracelets that my grandmother had worn. They tinkled together like bells. I shook my head in her hand and she leaned forward, hugging me so tight that I could feel her frown on my cheek. "I love you, honey."

"I love you too, Mom," I said, glancing at her briefly. She got up and walked to the door, pausing and turning back to say, "Sweet dreams, sweetheart," and then she turned off the light and disappeared into the hall.

Sara's room collapsed into the darkness and then the silver light from the winter sky fingered through the five windows along the top and length of the bed like fog pressing into the room, stretching out and away from me. I looked around at how everything looked bigger in that light and how it reflected back from the mirror on the dresser. I slid the Slinky over my hand like my mother's bracelets, feeling the metal cool and pinching at the hairs on my arms. I lay down, the bed cupping my body as if I was sinking into it and into the musky smell of my sister's perfume between the sheets. I let the Slinky slide off my hand and onto the floor in a springy plop, the shadows from the trees outside cast in like moving wallpaper. The front was pushing in, pushing at the windows so that the panes rattled in almost a hum, making the room feel tight and cool. Downstairs, I could hear Jake and Sam in the kitchen arguing about the fastest European cars and which ones they wanted. I couldn't hear the words, but the conversation was familiar enough to distinguish in the muffled voices. The old rocking chair in the corner now looked like an old-fashioned wheelchair, and the piñata that hung from the ceiling above it looked like a huge dark bat. From the hallway, the bathroom door opened and a line of light seeped through, telling me that Sara would come soon.

After a few moments she did, using the light from the hall to see her way to her dresser where she laid down her rings in five metallic clinks. She quietly opened her closet door and pulled off her jeans and wool sweater almost simultaneously like a snake shedding its skin. I secretly watched her, knowing that I could see the silhouette of her nipples as she turned into the closet, her long black hair brushing the middle of her back, her panties creasing at the line between her buttocks in the dim light. She took her nightshirt from the closet and slipped it over her body with up-stretched arms, letting it pause and then fall over her nipples. She pulled her hair from the collar with one hand and pressed the bedroom door closed with the other. I heard the lock click like a whisper and held my breath as her shadow moved toward me and onto the bed, whispering, "Move over."

She just lay there for a while like she was going to sleep, the hollow of the bed holding us together so I could feel the heat of her skin through the nightshirt. Her smell was hot and musky, strong enough that I could taste it in my mouth. I tried to lie very still like I was asleep, but the bottom of the sheets was tucked in and cramping my feet so I had to move them to pull it out. She rolled toward me and said, "Want to play mannequins?"

Mannequin is a game my brothers made up after they saw the ladies pretending to be mannequins at the mall. There were all these ladies who were dressed up in lacy dresses like the kind you get married in, and they were all standing real still. They just stood there and they wouldn't move their arms or even their eyes, even if you waved at them or jumped up and down. We tried to get them to laugh, but they wouldn't move any more than just blinking for a long time, and then, all of a sudden like robots, they would move into another position and then not move again for a long time. So Jake and Sam made this game where one person was the mover and the rest of us were mannequins and we'd have to stand like that. We couldn't move even if they made us stand on one leg or put our fingers in our nose or in our pants. If you kept that position for more than the count of sixty, without the mover moving you, you won, and then you were the mover, and he had to be the mannequin. We used to play it a lot.

I didn't answer Sara, but she pushed the covers down to our feet, letting the chill of the room wash over us, and said, "You be the mover first."

I rolled over and looked at her. She was lying flat with her eyes closed and her mouth slightly open. I moved her right arm so it stuck out in front of her and her right knee up and bent a little so it looked like she was marching. She looked like a Nazi soldier. She couldn't hold it. The branches outside were tapping at the window like they were trying to get our attention. I sat up and put her legs and feet straight out, making her grunt, and her arms straight out too, so that she looked like a doll that was sitting but had been knocked over onto its back. The nightshirt slid up, and I could see her panties underneath. She started to fall over, but I grabbed her ankle to let her get her balance. I let go and started counting. She didn't make it to sixty.

I bent her right leg so the foot was right above the bed and then made the left one match it and moved her hands to her face, covering it so it looked like she was jumping into something she didn't want to jump into. The nightshirt was as far as her belly button, her panties completely exposed, and her belly was still as she held her breath to hold the position. I counted to sixty, trying to go slow, but she held it. When I got to sixty, she exhaled and let her arms and legs drop. She sat up and said, "My turn."

I lay back down, unsure of what would happen next. Sara looked at me, at my face, like she was trying to decide what to do, her eyes squinting and shiny under her dark brows. Leaning on one elbow beside me, she slowly waved her hand in the air over my body from my head down to my legs like a magician showing the audience that no strings held up the floating woman. When her hand returned to my face, her fingers gently closed my eyes and traced down my face to my neck, making me shiver. I could feel her breath on my cheek for a second as she put both of my arms over my head. She put her hand on my stomach and then slowly pulled my T-shirt up to my chest, her tracing fingers making me giggle nervously until she shushed me and said, "You gotta be quiet." The wind outside the windows sounded like the inside of a seashell.

She didn't touch me again for a minute, but I could tell by the sound of her breath she was still looking at my face. Her hand gently ran down my right leg and then my left, lifting them up into the air like I had done to her, but she traced back down the inside of my thighs, pushing my shorts up to my crotch. The cool air tickled and made me afraid that I would get hard, so I tried to think of something else while I tried to keep my legs up. The bed creaked as she sat up. I kept my eyes shut, not wanting to lose, but I couldn't keep my legs in the air. She laughed when I dropped them to the bed, peeking through a squint. Her left hand was between her legs and her right one hovered right above my crotch, close enough for me to feel her warmth, and then she pressed down, her palm soft and warm on the outside of my shorts. I caught my breath and coughed but she kept her hand there; "Shhhh..." sounded like she was consoling me. I got hard immediately. She turned her head toward mine with a slight smile, but I shut my eyes before she could see I was looking. She started to move her hand up and down, gripping my dick and squeezing it. I could feel it in my stomach and my thighs, like the hardness was spreading to every muscle in my body, making me feel tight. I clenched my fists above my head and felt short of breath. Her breath was getting louder, and she started to rock gently beside me. She whispered, "Adam, be very quiet," and then pulled my shorts down and off my feet. My skin was so hot as the cold air washed over my nakedness. I was both terrified and excited, and at the same time, I knew that Sara should not be doing this, but it was something that I couldn't stop and wasn't sure if I wanted to.

Sara pulled my right hand down to her body while still massaging my penis. She pressed my hand firmly to the soft between her legs. I had only touched her there from the outside of her panties, but now it was uncovered and the hair was soft and moist. Her hand stroked and pulled on me, feeling like she was pulling my whole body from between my legs. I tried to keep still as she curled my fingers to the place my brothers talked about on the women in the magazines. It felt like warm fruit, both soft and hard as she gently thrust her hips, squatting onto my hand and pressing it inside her. I spread my fingers a little and she moaned softly, her breath coming faster. The wind was getting stronger, making the windowpanes hum and the branches tap the windows like visitors. The shadows made the room feel like it was moving. The bed squeaked louder, then stopped suddenly, making me look up at Sara as she leaned toward me, the moonlight catching her eyes and making them clear. She hissed, "Be very quiet, Adam," like she was mad. She rolled toward me, swinging her leg over my middle with her head bent forward so her hair brushed across my stomach and chest like a cold wind, and pressed her wet crotch onto my hard one. She sat up slightly and rubbed herself over my penis, the bed groaning under us. I pressed my lips together and tried to breathe through my nose, suppressing the urge to moan. I knew that I was going to be inside of her, and I wanted it like it was something I wasn't supposed to have, something that felt good because it was so bad. Her white nightshirt made her look like a ghost hovering above me. I pressed my hips toward her, holding onto the headboard with both hands. Her hand found my penis again and held it up as she settled down on top of it, taking it inside of her. It was so hot that it almost burned. I shut my eyes tight, feeling tears coming to my burning face. She began to move up and down faster, her face over mine, her breath warm and sweet mixing with a smell I couldn't remember, something metal and dirt-like. My breathing was as heavy as hers, my thrusting up matching her pressing down, and something was starting between my legs that made me push into her harder and not want it to ever stop. The springs were creaking so loud under me that I almost didn't hear the knock at the door, but we both stopped suddenly, looking hard at each other like we were trying to decide if we'd even heard a noise.

The doorknob turned and clicked and then another soft knock, "Sara, honey?" It was Mother.

I was terrified. I knew that Mother should never know what we were doing. Sara put one finger over her lips in a silent "Shhhh..." and moved off me, shoving the covers over me and letting her nightshirt drop down over herself. I pulled the covers up over my head and rolled into a ball, facing the windows, pretending I was asleep.

Sara unlocked and opened the door. "Yeah, Mom?" she asked in sleepy voice, and I knew that her eyes were squinting to the hall light and she was scratching her head like she had just been wakened.

Mom sounded worried. "Why do you have your door locked?" she said as she stepped into the room.

"Adam says it makes him feel safer...," Sara whispered, "from the nightmares."

Mom lowered her voice, "Is he asleep?"

"Yeah, he is," Sara lied.

I lay as still as I could, not wanting Mother to discover my nakedness under the blankets, somehow feeling her gaze on my back from where she stood.

"OK," Mom sighed, "but keep this door unlocked now, all right?"

Sara agreed and climbed back onto the bed, slipping under the covers carefully.

Mother whispered, "Good night," and pulled the door behind her without closing it.

I stretched out my legs but lay flat on my stomach. Sara turned her back toward me and said in a low voice, "Just go to sleep." I lay there for a while, still feeling her stuff on my penis, how my crotch was still wet but cold now. I put both hands between my legs like I was protecting myself and held them cupped there until I fell asleep, trying to think of anything but what we had just done.

The dream came as soon as I fell asleep. It was always the same. I can see Sara in her bed, but dressed with even her shoes on because she knows she'll have to be ready to go at any minute. Dad comes into the room and climbs on top of her, laying his hairy body on top of hers and whispering, "It's time, Sara. It's time."

He looks like he's going to squish her into the bed, and then all of a sudden she's in the barn, kneeling on the ground. The light is all yellow like hay and her arms are hugging the neck of her horse Silver, who's lying on his side.

She's crying and trembling like Silver is; each breath he takes sounds like bubbles being blown in a carton of milk, like plastic marbles being dropped into water. I am standing in the square of light that is cast on the ground from the back door, but I can see Sara and Silver through the barn doors as she presses her nose into his mane, which is now unbraided and sticking out in kinks like an old metal brush.

Mother appears carrying a stack of old towels in front of her like a cake. I am pulled behind her without moving my legs, like I am floating, and behind me I can hear Dad turning the key to the cupboard in his office, the one where he keeps his guns. In the barn, Sara's crying is almost as loud as Silver's breathing echoing off the old wood of the stalls. I know that the doctor had said that his lungs were almost filled with fluid, but now you can really tell. Silver's eyes look like buckeyes pressed into wet boiled eggs, and they bulge from his head, blinking slowly as Sara rubs the hair between his eyes. I can hear the electric fence and taste it in my mouth, like when I got stuck under it and was trapped like a million tiny hands were tickling me until I couldn't breathe. Sara had put her sneakers on her hands and grabbed the line and its power between the rubber soles and pushed me out with her bare foot. I was six then, and Silver was almost twelve, and she'd had him even before I was born.

Mom spreads the towels out on the ground around Silver's head like a quilt, and I can hear Dad coming, cocking the .22, and I can tell by Sara's eyes and Silver's eyes that they know it too. Sara wants to stay with the horse, but Dad pulls her off him and makes her stand away, still crying. The light is blue and shaky, like the air above the road when it's real hot. Daddy says again, "It's time, it's time," and holds the barrel to the soft below Silver's ear. Silver looks at him, and he smiles. Sara yells, "No, Daddy...," and the rifle cracks and smokes from its barrel. Then there is no sound, there is no horse. There is only Mom lying face down on the quilt of towels, which is turning red. Dad is holding Sara, whispering to her, his hands rubbing her and kissing her neck. I am crying. I was always crying when I woke up.

Sara was still asleep, and I could tell that it had snowed by the way the light was coming in the windows. It always got so bright when it snowed, the way it covered the hills and trees thick and shiny white, making the sun reflect a million times like everything was covered in mirrors. I quietly pulled myself out of the warm blankets and was almost surprised to find that I was still naked from the waist down. I slid on my shorts, hopped off the bed, and ran next door to my room to find a pair of sweatpants.

My room was colder but bright with the sun still low in the window, telling me that it was early. Outside, the snow was so thick that barely a color other than white was to be seen, and my breath sent crystals onto the glass. Both the dream and what had happened in Sara's room made me shiver, and I rushed downstairs to the warmth of the kitchen.

Mom was sitting at the kitchen table with her back to the woodstove, humming tunelessly and staring into the steam from her coffee cup. She looked up and smiled as I pulled one of the ladder-back chairs beside her and as close to the hot stove as I could without burning. I was still shivering but the heat was comforting, and she touched my head and said, "Morning, handsome, sleep well?"

I nodded, not wanting her to know that I had the dream while in Sara's room. She took a sip of coffee and ran her fingers through her hair. I looked out the window at how everything looked frosted.

"Looks like nobody's going to school today," Mom told me.

I didn't respond. She looked out the window and then back at me. "Penny for your thoughts."

Startled, I looked at her, suddenly feeling like she could see everything inside me by simply looking, and I became aware of how much I knew that she didn't. I thought that I knew everything that was bad, that I knew everything that was unspeakable. I tried not to think about seeing Dad kissing a woman at the drugstore or about what Sara and I had done. Or about the other things I knew, like how Sam had twenty-two magazines with pictures of naked ladies hidden in the fort on the hill. I knew that Sam and Jake and the Meyers boys would smoke cigarettes there, coughing out clouds of smoke, and pass those magazines around, talking about what they would like to do with those women. I knew that Sara had kissed Kenny Meyers on the lips, down behind the pond, and that they had done more, but I could only see their heads from where I was hiding. I knew from the hole I had made in the back of my closet that I could see into Sara's room, where sometimes, late at night, Dad would sneak in and lie in her bed with her for a long time while everyone else was asleep. I knew that Jake had taken money out of Father's wallet last summer and that he and Sam had gotten a bottle of whisky that they shared with the Meyers boys in the fort. I knew that Mother was unhappy and that she had been for a long time, and that all the things I knew would hurt her even worse.

Mother's hand was on my arm, "You all right, honey?"

I pushed it all away. "Can we go sledding?" I asked.

She smiled with a little relief. "It's pretty cold out there, but I don't see why not. You snow bunnies are pretty tough."

Tough was what I wanted to be. Tough like my brothers and their friends who were always competing to see who could climb the highest, jump the furthest, do the most daring thing, and always yelling down to me that I was a baby, a wimp, a sissy. I knew that if we went sledding, we would compete for King of the Hill, the one who was tough enough to go the closest to the creek at the bottom of the hill before he jumped off the sled.

"I'm gonna be King of the Hill this year," I bragged to Mom, wanting to tell her about our competition even though Sam had warned me that if I ever told her, she wouldn't let us go.

"But of course," Mom said in a funny accent, "but my king needs his breakfast, so what will it be, Your Majesty?"

I relaxed and laughed, "Golden pancakes!"

"Yes sir!" she said, getting up from the table. "And?"

"Silver sausages," I continued, trying to sound like a king.

"Oh! Very good," she bowed low to me. "And?"

"Gilded grits!" I howled, laughing hard and standing up on my chair, loving to see her laugh too. "Gilded grits for the whole kingdom!" The whole kitchen seemed warm and safe, like my mother's arms protected it and me from everything that could hurt us. I spun around and jumped from my chair, grabbing her hands in mine and spinning her with me, singing a made-up song about gilded grits. No place ever felt so alive to me as that kitchen did at that moment, like it was the garden of my mother, like she grew in every corner of it, and like I could always stay that age and that happy if I could keep her there and never leave. That kitchen in that moment was the only place I ever felt completely safe.

# The Getaway

*Michael Lipuma*

So there we was, old Poke cussin' up a storm—fuck this, asshole that—banging shit around in the back, kicking at the side of his own rig. And I'm inside figurin', shit. It's his truck. Better it than me. Know what I mean?

But he stomps around to the passenger side kicking up dust in his combat boots and he's right outside my door and he starts screaming up at me, "I told you to check it. I fuckin' heard myself. Check the motherfuckin' radiator. I said that, didn't I? Check the goddamn radiator. I said that. Check the son of a bitch. I told you to check it. Didn't I, Randy?"

Well, he's right up against the door and—I told you how high he's got that thing jacked up, looks like a toy truck with tractor wheels on it; anyway, all I can see of him is his hands waving around, sticking up out of his red flannel sleeves.

Well, I'm just trying to ignore him, let him blow off steam so's he calms down. You know what a short fuse he's got. Like that time we was in that joint and Maggy goes to the bar to get a beer and as she's squeezing through the crowd, that guy next to her she was smashed up against tryin' to get by? And fucking Poke lays the poor schmuck out—just 'cause the dumb ass says hi to his bitch!

So now he's outside goin' off about the radiator—I mean we're somewhere in bumfuck, middle of nowhere, surrounded by cornfields all brown and shit, getting fried by the sun, ya can't breathe without getting a mouth full of dust. He's out there having a shit fit and I'm thinking to myself that maybe it's got something to do with that little cross-country jaunt he took us on when we lost the cops.

The cops are right on our ass, sirens screaming, yelling over their loudspeakers for us to, like, pull over. Yeah, right. Dumb-ass fuckin' pigs. Like, we're really going to pull over. "Please arrest us, Mister Officer. We didn't mean to rob your little piss-ant bank."

Fifteen hundred bucks! What the fuck shit is that? It's a goddamn bank. Shit-ass little town. We'd a been better off goin' into Mad Town and knockin' off a liquor store.

So the cops is right on us. How they can even see with all the dust we're kicking up, I don't even know. Poke swerves off—I don't know, we were on some county road in Marquette or Adams County—we go in an' out this ditch. I don't know how fast we was goin', but we come flying out of this ditch—no shit, man, all four wheels left the ground. And then we're haulin' ass through the woods, branches snapping. We're practically bouncin' off the trees, me and Poke bouncin' off the walls, windshield, and roof in the cab and I'm thinking, maybe, Poke, you put a hole in your goddamn radiator, or tore off a hose or something, 'cause I checked the mother fucker while he was practically creaming in his jeans talking to the big-haired bimbo in the truck stop.

And then Poke gets totally out of line. Brings my ex into it. I told him to shut up, but he wouldn't listen. He just kept it up.

"Man," he says, "I don't see how your ex ever put up with you. I mean, what the fuck was she thinking? No wonder she threw your dumb ass out. And you got a kid. Whaddya know? You managed to get that right. How did you find the hole? She draw you a picture? But then, come to think of it, she must be one dumb fucking cunt to let you get anywhere near her. Think of that, Randy? As stupid as you is and as dumb as she got to be to marry your sorry ass, that kid you got must be one dumb little son of a bitch."

Well. I don't mind nobody cussin' me out all that much—I certainly done my share of shit to be cussed out for—and I sure as hell don't give two shits what anybody says about my ex, but when it comes to that little girl, well, that's where I draw the line in the sand, if you know what I mean. I mean, I haven't done a whole lot of things that I'm proud of in my life, but if there's one thing I done right, it's bringing this sweet little girl into the world. I mean look at her, that sweet little face? Why, when she gets riled, them little puffy cheeks get red as a fire truck and she stamps her feet and shakes that frizzy black hair of hers, you think her poor little head was gonna come right off. Oh, she can be a terror. And Nadean—that's my ex. Nadean. If that ain't a clue or what? I'll tell you straight. Don't ever get hooked up with nobody named Nadean. You're just askin' for trouble. Anyway, Nadean says she gets that from my side, says there ain't nobody that ornery in her family, like there's something wrong with the kid having her own mind or something. But, I just tell Nadean, "Damn straight! At least we ain't a bunch of fucking boozers." Man, you ought to see that girl drink. Seen her put more than one smart-ass sons-a-bitch under the table. Then she starts hitting on every guy in the place, and when she starts her disappearing act? Well. I ain't gonna stand for that, my momma didn't raise no fool, and I suppose that's why Nadean's my ex and I don't get a chance to see Cally as much as I like to. But I send her a card on her birthdays—Valentine's Day and Christmas, too—without fail. And I swear to God I'd like to do more than I do, but with the way the goddamn Democrats have run this country into the ground and work being slow and all—you know that Rush guy is right. Getting so an honest guy can't make a decent living, giving everything away to all the scum. It's a goddamn shame. I just can't do what I'd like. But that don't mean I love that little girl any less, and if someone's gonna talk shit about her? Well, I draw the line.

So I throws open the passenger door to that jacked-up Blazer. It catches Poke full in the face—I think he broke his fuckin' nose—his eyes is all purple and blue and shit, and it looks like he's got a damn gourd or an eggplant for a nose—knocked him on his ass. And once he gets his eyeballs back from rollin' up into his head, I got my nine on him and I says, "You know, Poke? You know, Poke," I says. And I got my nine out. Not pointing it at him. Just kind of holding on to it where he can see it. Nothing like the old equalizer. Know what I mean?

Anyway, I says to him, "You been riding my ass ever since the damn security guard back at the bank. It's not my fault the fat fuck got in the way. Oh–OK. Maybe I wasted a few shells on the old man, but he pissed me off. He called me a dumb punk."

Called me dumb! I got my nine out and Poke's got that new short little streetsweeper he just got—I mean it's an eight-shot, semi-automatic, twelve gauge—and this asshole old man who's so fat and old he can barely fucking walk decides to give us some shit, and he's calling me dumb? I warned him, but he just wouldn't shut up. I had to let him have it. Right in his fat gut. And then the old bastard starts screaming like somebody cut his balls off and everybody else in the place starts screaming and I'm warnin' 'em that they oughta shut up. I even put a slug in the ceiling. I'm screaming at them, "Shut the fuck up!" But do they shut up? Fuck no! People are really stupid, but some? This teller, let me tell you—nice-looking bitch, tight little red skirt, this sweater, mohair, I think, like my sister used to wear, fucking boobs out to here. Anyway, she starts running around like a chicken with its head cut off. She's screaming, "Ahh! Ahh!" and her arms are flying all over the place and her jugs are bouncing around like they're made outta Jell-O. She was like one of those steel balls caught between two bumpers in a pinball machine, running back and forth between this old guy in a suit, her boss I guess, and some young stud in cowboy boots and one of those faggot string ties. And then she starts running right at me. What could I do? I shot the silly bitch. Then I finished the old man and asked, "Anybody else?" Lemme tell ya. They got real quiet. Know what I mean?

But like I said, some people are real stupid. Mister Cowboy looks at me like I'm some figment or somethin' and he's yammerin' at me, over and over, "You shot her. You shot her."

And I'm like, "Yeah. I know I shot 'er, Sherlock. Shut the fuck up." I mean, could I be any plainer?

But the cowboy won't shut up. "You shot her. You shot my Shelly. You killed her!" and he starts looking around, like he's looking for something to grab, anything, and his lips is curling and his nose is crinkling like a dog's, and he's like, "You mother..."

Well, I put a stop to that right there. I took a step and shoved the barrel of my nine practically up his nose, and Mister Stud Cowboy Thinks He's Gonna Do Somethin' freezes. I mean, this guy is so scared he pissed his pants. No. Really. The asshole pissed hisself.

So I got my gun in his nose, and I get up real close so I'm right up in his face, and I'm, like, not screaming, but talking real slow and even. "You got a problem, cowboy?" I asks 'im. "Am I talking fucking Chinese? You think I'm talkin' 'cause I like to hear noise come out of my mouth? If I want to hear noise I got my little noisemaker here." I give my Beretta a little twist against his nose to make sure he's got a real clear picture. "Now you?" I says to 'im, "You're making me want to hear some noise. You gettin' the picture, asshole? I told you to shut up, so shut the fuck up! Get on the floor. Everybody. Lie on the floor. On your faces. Anybody makes even a peep, I'll have my partner there stick his shotgun up your ass and pull the trigger."

That's when we hear the sirens. I mean goddamn, son of a bitch! Fuckin' nothing ever goes right. So we split with what Poke's grabbed from behind the teller cages. Outside? It was just like the movies. We make it to the truck and we're out of the lot and this squad turns the corner and I climb in the back with my AR and I throw open the back window. This cop is right on our ass and I opened up on 'im. Poke is swerving all over the street so I can't get a decent shot; people are running and diving for cover. I swear, just like the fuckin' movies—you know—mothers grabbing up their children; I'm making Swiss cheese out of the squad, its windshield explodes, the hood flies open, it careens off the road, hits another car, flips over, and explodes. It was awesome, man. I felt like I was Steve McQueen in that movie with Ali McGraw where the cops make them in that parking lot and McQueen blasts out the back window of his own car, except I don't blast out the window and Poke sure as hell ain't no Ali McGraw and the cops back off some, but we still got three squads after us as we roar outta town and that's when Poke decides to go cross country.

So, anyway, there Poke is on the ground and I says to him, "Gimme one good reason why I shouldn't waste your ass."

Do you believe it? The motherfucker says to me, "You ain't got the balls to shoot me." Didn't he just see me waste four...six people? "Shit," he says. "I know you ain't got them kinda balls. You'd have to have a sack draggin' on the ground to have balls big enough to shoot me, big fuckin' Godzilla balls," he says, lying on the ground, spreading his legs like he's bowlegged, holding his hands down there like he's holding onto a couple sixteen-inch softballs. "You got those kinda balls, Randy? Huh? Are those the kind of balls you got? You better have them kinda balls. You better have some pretty big fuckin' balls, you shoot me. 'Cause you know what?" and then he sits up and flings a finger up, pointing at me, and he starts thumping his finger against the air like...like I seen him do against some schmuck's chest when he's tryin' to pick a fight. "You got one fuckin' shot, man," he growls at me. "One fuckin' shot." And at the same time he's talking, his top lip is curled down over his top row of teeth, his jaw is stuck out like he's trying to unhinge it from his head, and his bottom lip is all pushed out showing his bottom teeth all nicotine stained with the big chip in the middle where this big nigger with a fist full of rings hit 'im. It was something to see. They was about the same size, but this boy? One shot. Knocked Poke's ass out cold. Only time I seen that.

"One fuckin' shot, Randy," Poke says, "and you better make it a good one. You better take me out and you better take me out for good, 'cause if you don't, I'll be on you so fast you won't know what the fuck hit you. I'll be all over you in a heartbeat. I'll squeeze your little fuckin' peanut head off and shove it down your goddamn throat. You listening to me, you little fuckin' shit? You hear what I'm saying? You understand me, Randy? I'll give it to ya. You got bigger balls than I thought you had—either that or you're a whole lot dumber than I thought you was, but either way I know you ain't got the balls you need to pull a piece on me. So why don't you put your little gun away before you really piss me the fuck off."

So I'm standing there listening to this tripe, thinking it just goes to show how right I was about how fucking stupid some people can be. I figured it was time to wise his ass up. So I shot him in the knee. He grabs it and starts rolling around on the ground and—you won't believe it—it's just like the cowboy all over. He starts bawling out at me, "You shot me in the knee. You shot me in the knee." I mean, are people really that stupid? I got the gun. I pulled the trigger. Why do they got to tell me what I just done? And then he starts screaming at me that I'm dead, that he's gonna kill me. I mean, don't he get the picture?

"You don't get the picture, do ya?" I asked him. "Maybe this will help." I put one through his shoulder and one in his other knee.

"You fuck," he screams at me. Or he tries to scream. It's more a cross between a gurgle and a scream. I don't know. I musta been off on the shoulder shot. "You fuck. You fuck," he's trying to yell. He's got blood spurting out of his mouth, I shot 'im three times, he's bleeding like a stuck pig, I'm like the only one around who could possibly help his dumb ass, and he's calling me a fuck and babbling about how he's going to kill me. How fucking stupid can you get? I hate stupid people. Ain't got time for 'em.

So anyway, I pop the hood to the truck. A hose come loose. I reconnected it. Filled the radiator with water. There was some in the back of the truck. Meanwhile, I can hear Poke bitching at me some, bawling some, coughing sometimes like he's trying to bring up this monster loogie in his throat, never quite getting it. By the time I'm done, he's pretty quiet. It's like he's lying in this pool of purple mud, breathing real ragged, mouth wide open, blood coming out of his mouth once in a while like one of those boiling mud pots in the hot springs when the bubbles burst, but he's still there. I can see his eyes following me.

I crouched down by him, being careful not to get my boots muddy. His head was kinda twisted but I could see, out of the corner of his eyes, he's watching me. With the barrel of my gun—I didn't want to get my hands messy—I moved his head so he could look right at me. "You shouldn'ta said what ya did about my kid," I told him. "Remember that as long as you can, Poke. Remember that you're dying because ya got a big mouth and you're too fucking stupid to know when to keep it shut."

# Tube Man

*Peter J. Merlin*

What woke him up? Did someone call him from outside on the street? It wasn't the muffled sounds of dishes and water from the downstairs kitchen of the Mexican restaurant. He had become used to them months ago. No, it was a short scraping sound of metal against metal. Where did that come from? He heard the quiet flip of plastic numbers on his digital clock. Then he heard a woman's high-pitched laughter. Was she talking to somebody? He turned his head slowly to the right, as he was on his stomach, to look at the clock. It read 2:26. The streetlight illuminated his apartment through the vertical blinds, giving everything convict lines. He turned onto his back and something rolled off the bed to the floor. He now knew the sound and raised his head off the pillow.

Tubes were everywhere, haphazardly thrown all over the floor, leaning up against his closet and filling the hallway. They were leaning up against his bed, big silver ones that you could put your head into. They had long cylindrical shapes with a seam along the side. He sold a lot of them to air-conditioning companies for their duct work. But what were these tubes doing in his apartment? He sat up in bed, his eyes piercing the darkness, and noticed a slight draft on his head. Window must be open above the bed, he thought.

Had someone actually snuck into his apartment with all of these tubes? It must be Billy with another one of his pranks. Last Sunday, Billy successfully switched golf balls before Jacob teed off on the tenth tee. He thought he hit the ball well and was rewarded with a thick cloud of chalk dust. As he fanned his arms in the white cloud, Billy and the others did the wave and chanted, "Ohh, Jacob, sell us more tubes!" Billy was always trying to be funny as he attempted to sell more tubes than Jacob. No one sold more tubes than Jacob. He sold a lot of tubes to companies all over Chicago. Indiana, Kentucky, Missouri—they all came to him. Arkansas was next. Oklahoma would be easy. He even had a marketing slogan set up with T-shirts that said, *Tube Man.*

He swung his legs out of bed, stood up, and started to walk across the room. His foot rolled over a tube, a four-footer like he had sold to Indiana Air for the Sheraton Hotel in Bloomington. He pitched forward onto his hands and knees, his palms slapping the solid wood floor. He heard a wet flopping noise from the floor in front of him, as if something had fallen a few feet ahead of him. He looked for the origin of the flop and saw a mass of gray matter looking vaguely like thick pasta lying on his just-cleaned apartment floor. There was a slight indentation that perfectly bisected the gray mass, and he knew this thing looked familiar. It was his brain. He remembered the cold draft on his head, and with his left hand he felt the top of his head. It was like the ends of one of the many tubes on the floor, only the walls of his skull were thicker. He felt a ring around the top of his head. It started right above the eyebrows and went all the away around in a nice round circle—or was it an oval? He couldn't be sure. He placed his hand inside, and there was nothing. He thought of feeling around inside his head. Could he touch his eye sockets? Could he feel his eyeballs move around from the inside? With his palm, he felt something soft and warm inside his skull, at the bottom. He swallowed, and he felt the movement. He pulled out his hand and there was a bright red liquid on it.

He reached forward with both hands and, using them like shovels, carefully picked up his brain from the floor and held it over his head. He was on his knees wearing his white *Tube Man* T-shirt and white boxers. *Ohh, Tube Man!* It was deep and throaty. A woman's voice, and she sounded really close. He looked around but saw no one.

Burritos came to his nose, chicken fajitas, and huevos rancheros. He ate at the Mexican restaurant regularly. He often arrived late, around 9:30 straight from work. The office was way west at Cicero and Fullerton, and he spent all day there if he wasn't on the road selling tubes. The restaurant had a hot green jalapeno sauce that he loved to slather on his food. Enrique, who worked the bar near the door, was usually the first to see him. *Buenos noches, Señor Tube Man.* A Tecaté beer and a shot of tequila would find its way to his table promptly.

He let go of his brain and it plopped into his head. The additional weight felt comfortable, like it was just right. Now he had to find the top. He got to his feet carefully, as he didn't want to lose his brain again. He could see the smaller tubes, which lay in piles like sticks on an autumn day. He was reminded of the tire exercise in his high-school football days. He had trouble running through them even then. Very slowly he began to move among the tubes. He raised his knees way up, and feeling through the tubes with his toes, lowered his weight on each foot. After a long time, he made his way to the hallway and bathroom. Despite holding his head erect, he couldn't help but look at all the other tubes about his place. He saw the ribbed, flexible type used with dryers. Their shiny surfaces reflected the streetlight in different directions. His toe bumped into a solid copper tube used by plumbers. He winced with the pain, but stood by the bathroom door quietly, waiting for it to subside.

He felt around the door for the light switch, as the streetlight didn't reach into his windowless bathroom. The light blazed and, through his squinting eyes, he saw the rest of his head sitting on top of the toilet like a quiet animal, resting. His hair was carefully parted, and he marveled at how straight he combed it. He had never seen his head this way. The part of his hair wound across his skull to a little swirl. It looked like baldness at first glance, but it was merely his hairline. That relieved him. He could feel that swirl when he put his hands through his hair and lately was concerned about it. Billy grew his hair very long on one side as he was completely bald on the top. He was always in the bathroom at the office, carefully combing the long hairs over his head. Wind was a big problem for him.

"Tube Man?" He turned his head to listen. Nothing more. He couldn't fathom the voice. Did he know this person? The bathtub was full of air-conditioning tubes. His reflection in the mirror over the sink showed a triangular-shaped face and a narrow chin. Above dark eyes and eyebrows there was a flat line all the way across. Behind that line he could see his brain like a soft mountain range in the distance beyond the trees.

He picked up his top and inverted it, so its inside looked to the ceiling. It had a pale, slightly pinkish look to it, with ridges running along the inside. He was reminded of a turtle shell he saw in the museum once. Opening the medicine cabinet, he looked at the shelves filled with aspirin, Alka-Seltzer, Advil, Anacin, Excedrin, Dimetapp, Tylenol, Bufferin, and Nuprin. He saw the flat tube of Elmer's standing up in the back. Elsie's familiar face was a relief to him, but then he couldn't remember when or why he had placed the glue there. He squinted his eyes shut and was about to rub his forehead in the hope that all of this would disappear and he would wake up in bed. He often rubbed his head and liked pressing his fingers against his skull all through his hair. It felt like a little massage. Realizing that was a bad idea, he opened his eyes and there was his top, still in his hand. He laid it down on the shelf by the toilet and unscrewed the glue. Closing the medicine-cabinet door, he took his top and laid down a thin bead along the edge.

"Oh, Tube Man?" Was there someone in the apartment? He paused, with the glue in one hand. All he could hear were the kitchen noises below him. The voice had gone. Finished, he returned the glue to the cabinet and picked up his top. Arranging it, and careful that he had the right end forward, he held it over his head. He pressed down firmly, his chin dipping down to his chest. The line above his eyebrows oozed some of the clear liquid in little round balls—they had a slightly milky look to them. He counted to ten, released the pressure off his head, then took a Kleenex and wiped along the now-faint line across his forehead. He took a last quick look in the mirror as he left the bathroom.

He waited in the hallway for his eyes to adjust to the darkness. Slowly the silver tube shapes revealed themselves as they lay scattered all over, and he realized how tired he was. His eyes fluttered with sleep.

Reaching his bed, he paused and visualized a way to keep his top pressed to his head while he slept. He lay down, carefully pushing his head into the pillow he had placed against the headboard. He was taking no chances with the glue. Satisfied that the top of his head was now suitably braced, he relaxed, and leaving his knees up and heels pushed into the mattress, closed his eyes.

"Tube Man!" Now the voice was intimate and close. He could feel her breath as she said the words. "Tube Man!" It was as if she wanted something from him. He slowly opened his eyes and saw only darkness. His groin stirred, but he was so tired. Who was she?

A *TUBE MAN* tube store popped into his head. It had *TUBE MAN* in big black letters on a big sign out on the street. He saw men in suits with slim briefcases walking in the door. One of them held a phone and said into it, "Everything is OK; I'm at *TUBE MAN* now." Other men, some with beards, wearing khakis and work shirts and holding clipboards, pushed open the doors. Men exited battered trucks clutching scraps of paper and entered the tube store.

Inside was a forest of tubes: tin, copper, glass, ceramic, and plastic. Heavy cast-iron tubes stood on the floor like sculpture. Men and women wearing black golf shirts stood behind a long counter, selling tubes. He then saw a huge sign on the Edens Expressway and it read *TUBE MAN*. He saw the same sign in Tulsa, Indianapolis, Denver, Phoenix, and Los Angeles. He could see the front page of the *Wall Street Journal*. It showed his face, with his long black hair carelessly falling over one eye, resting on one fist as if he were leaning on a table or desk. The black-and-white image was brief, and he thought he saw some sort of bandage across his forehead. It had a look to it, though, like it was fashionable somehow. *When did they take that picture?* he wondered.

He was sitting up now, his eyes unable to make out anything. Were the tubes still there? His head itched, and he automatically raised a hand to scratch. It came away sticky. He placed one hand on top of his head, then carefully scratched his forehead with the other. That felt better. He swayed with fatigue and reached over for the light. His hand knocked a tube to the floor, and it fell onto others. He leaned back, then with a guttural sound of surprise sat up again. He pulled a tube out of the covers and dropped it over the side. I am in a boat, floating in a sea of tubes. With a sigh, he lay down, bracing his head once more. He thought he smelled perfume, but the voice was quiet. Quiet, he told himself, just focus on the quiet. He no longer heard the voice, and his head didn't itch.

The shadow lines crossed the big block letters of his *Tube Man* T-shirt, and taking an abrupt angle, continued up the wall past the window. A wind blew, rattling the windows of his apartment. Outside, a single tube, reflecting the brightness of the streetlight overhead, bumped into a stubby fire hydrant, then rolled off the curb, into the street.

# *Back And Forth*

*Tae Hee Kim*

I lie in the sun to fire my body, to dry up all the water, to harden and shrink the soft, vulnerable flesh to the bones. As if my body were clay, I will smooth over my pores a glaze made from peach pits and fire myself a second time. The arrangement of my face will cast a moat around me. Condensed, hard, and resilient, no one will get through to the marrow of my bones, to the susceptible organs.

"Soon Gahn-ah, come in. Eat lunch," my mother calls, superimposed over the noise of the kitchen fan, the voices from the TV, and the sweet smells of radish soup.

She doesn't understand that food, fleshy and moist, will counter the immunity I am building up. I can never indulge myself in a serious moment; I'm constantly interrupted. Soon Gahn-ah, take the garbage out. Soon Gahn-ah, what does "miss-in-tuh-puh-reet" mean in Korean again? Soon Gahn-ah, answer the phone, some American asking me too many questions. If he selling something, tell him forget it.

I shift my weight and the plastic bristles of the Astroturf covering the concrete floor of the balcony dig into my backside.

"I'm not hungry," I say, not sure if she heard, and wince because I know she'll yell my name again.

"Soon Gahn-ah, Soon Gahn-ah! Why are you lying outside like crazy girl? What's problem? Come eat. You hear me? Soon Gahn-ah!"

"Yah! Are you deaf?" my father barks at me.

The chipper singsong of a weather girl forecasts another week of the same summer: sunny and in the mid-eighties.

"I'm not hungry yet," I say.

"You have to eat now because you have to go to work soon," retorts my mother.

"Get in here, now! When your parents tell you to do something, you do it!" my father's raised voice commands. It never takes much to provoke my father into raising his voice. It's mostly because he had ten brothers and sisters. That's a lot of competition for attention.

I sit up. I feel adrift and lightheaded. I am in the blur between a secret narrative and the color of my blood in the thin skin of my eyelids. Like leaving a movie theater, I am in transition between believing in projected light and the solidness of the physical world. The sensation of the imprint the fake grass made into me waves up and down my back and arms. Weight slightly forward, my legs press down into the prickly pattern—a tight weave of a child's crayon drawing of green grass. My shorts have bunched up, exposing my thighs. I pinch the insides of them.

"Yah! Soon Gahn-ah, or do I have to call you Sue like your big-nosed American friends? Why don't you have more Korean friends? Don't even think of marrying an American. You know your father, how he would never allow it." Quick random lectures from my mother.

"OK," I say in a voice that's loud in my ears, hoping that neither will call out to me again.

"Everything is 'OK.' But she never listens," my mother says to my father. Then to me, "What you really mean when you say, 'OK?' OK, you will, or OK, leave me alone because I don't want to listen to you anymore?"

"Always, 'OK. Sorry, I forgot.' That's all she knows. She never knows what she has to do. Always looking somewhere else. Focus! You need to focus your mind. You trying to make me drag you inside by your hair?" my father jokingly threatens. "I told you, we should have just left her under that bridge. She cause too much trouble," he says to my mother. The old Korean joke all parents tell their children, that they were found under a bridge.

I ignore them and look beyond the horizontal black metal bars of the balcony. Below me is the parking lot, newly tarred black asphalt divided up by bright yellow lines. Straight across and beyond a wooden fence are dollhouses. Instead of pink plastic, however, the town houses are made of precut, pressed wood. Insert tab A into tab B. I watched the construction crew put them up. From my vantage point on the balcony little men and machines moved about and, in the times my eyes blinked, in the lapses between my observations, houses were built. Leveled ground, then foundations, then erect skeletons, and finally the finished enclosure of space. In a matter of months, the subdivision was done, quick and easy. The crew moved on, hands clapping off dirt before it even had a chance to seep into the veins. The sky touches the roofs, a vibrant pale blue between cottony clouds—the kind drawn by looping half circles together. The new town houses, with their new walkways, trees, manmade lakes, barbecue grills set against the perfect sky, are all too still. There's an eerie tension in the scene.

I get up. Spiders have spun webs in my dry throat. My stomach is tight. I feel too lazy to eat. I open the screen door. It squeaks across its track. I step inside.

"Don't just stand there, help me."

Like particles separating from water and settling to the bottom, my weight is heavy at my feet. I move into awkward motion, shaking from my eyes the brightness of the sun and adjusting to the inside light. My father is in the kitchen with my mother, arguing about whether or not the soup needs more salt. I take the round table from the hallway closet and unfold its four legs that are flat against its top, snapping them into upright place. I put the low table in the middle of the living room and wipe it with a dishcloth. The tabletop mimics the traditional, shell inlay of cranes in glorious, full-winged flight against black lacquer. It's a photograph under a layer of clear Formica. I set the table. Spoons to the left, chopsticks to the right. Rice to the left, soup to the right. In the center, dishes of kimchi—cooked and seasoned with bean sprouts—and fried rectangles of tofu.

We all sit down cross-legged at the table. Mother and I wait for Father to take the first spoonful before we start to eat. Korean table manners. My mother hits my left hand. I've accidentally picked up my spoon with the wrong hand again. Etiquette dictates that one eat with the right. I remember my mother tying my left hand behind my back during meals when I was a child so I'd get used to it. I do just about everything else with the left, but I'm not allowed to eat with it. I take a small spoonful of rice, and my mother reprimands me in Korean and says I have to eat well to live well. She says that I have to gain some weight before my grandparents come to visit because my grandmother will blame my mother for not feeding me well. My mother has been preparing for her demanding mother-in-law's inspection. I wrinkle my nose up in distaste because I suspect my grandmother of selfish intentions. I don't think she just wants me to be plump as a sign of good health as most old Koreans believe, but because she is fat, and what she is is always right.

My father's mouth curls with discontent.

My mother notices. "Everything I make you don't like."

"I didn't say anything."

"Always looking at the table displeased. Only lots of beef and fried food will satisfy your stomach. You only want what is bad for you. That's why you had heart attack. Always eating meat and food dripping of oil, and smoking too much. Oh well, you have to get used to it even though you don't like, because doctor said you have to change."

My father says nothing. My mother's abrasive attitude toward him makes me uncomfortable. I feel protective of my father from such directness because it seems too soon to confront. Although months have passed, the reverberations of that night, the call to 911, the emergency room, the machines, and the tubes are still sharp in my mind.

"Everything tastes really good, tastes as good as honey," I say and take a big spoonful of rice and follow it with soup. Overcompensation. My stomach doesn't accept the sudden rush of food too well.

The garlic, ginger, and dried red peppers of the kimchi taste strong and separate from the salty cabbage. My mother comments that the kimchi isn't ripe yet. In English, the more accurate translation would be that the cabbage hasn't fermented enough. It doesn't sound very appetizing, does it? Nor does it smell fragrant like fresh baked bread. But then again, cheese is old, curdled milk.

I zone out at the TV. The TV is on top of a traditional Korean wooden chest, and behind that is a zigzagging ten-panel screen of calligraphy, a poem of an ancient Chinese language lost to most. The TV with sprouting antennae glows with the Sunday afternoon movie and seems incongruous with its setting. But that's life in America—a collage of different cultures and the past and present.

"Why you stop eating? How you fill your stomach when you eat so little? Why you always upset me this way?" My mother can guilt me into anything.

While watching the news as we eat, my mother asks, "What does 'ex-see-cue-she-un' mean?" I translate the word for her, and remind her that she asked for this translation just the other day. "Oh yeah, you already told me. I forgot. Be kind to your mother. When you wake up one day and you're forgetful old woman like me, then you realize, *I should have been more understanding to my mother.* Then—you too late. My grave doesn't need understanding, just flowers on holidays. I save you regret, OK?"

"*Um-Mah*! Again with the death talk," I raise an irritated voice and stab the air with my spoon in protest.

My mother is so morbid. Actually, the Korean culture is preoccupied with death, rituals for the dead; even the language is liberal with the usage. "I'm so exhausted I could die." The difficult or absurd is described as "sah-rahm jew-geen dah"—killing a person. "You kill me." "I want to die." *Die*, *death*, *suicide*, *kill* roll off Korean tongues easily and all too frequently. Mortality is a cliché.

I put away the dishes, actually pile them into the sink in a rather artful balance of plates, bowls, cups, and utensils. Then I change into a clean, stiff pair of blue jeans and throw on a dark blazer (I'm not sure if it's black or dark blue) over my slightly gray (because it was washed with a black sock), white shirt. My mother hands me a thermos of hot tea and a plastic bag of cut and peeled fruit. I throw them into my bag. As I put my shoes on at the door, my mother is doing the dishes. My eyes line with guilt. Her shoulders seem more rounded, worn down, and the kitchen light, bright against the tiles, exaggerates the shadows in the creases of her skin. I regret that I don't help her more and that she'll be alone as soon as my father leaves. I tell her to leave the dishes, that I'll get to them when I get back, and that she should just relax today. She says if she waited for me, the dishes would never get done, but it's nice to hear me offer. And as always, she tells me to drive carefully. She gets my standard answer, "Yeah, OK." I call out to my father in his bedroom and tell him I'm leaving.

He yells back, asking if I put gas in the car. Driving is like war. My father has a war analogy for everything. Preparation, defense, offense—everything has a strategy, and everything needs to be treated with utmost seriousness, especially since we live on strangers' land. He criticizes me and my generation for not realizing that one has to always plan ahead and be ready for all possible troubles. "You young people don't know how to be prepared because you never experienced war. Why you always wait till car is almost empty to fill it with gas? Somebody take you away if you fill it up earlier?"

As I walk down the short hallway to the elevator, the muscles between my eyebrows and my mouth tighten. Resentment and contempt toward my parents and for my own guilt creep up on me. Often I go back and forth between my obligations to my family and to myself. Tradition binds me to my parents' home and their rules, theoretically until I marry. America is the land of the free, and it's easy to reason leaving by my own will—that my mother chose to be a housewife and I didn't ask to be born—but reason fails to account for guilt and the need for approval, to accomplish as a reflection of parental accomplishment.

In the frustration of going back and forth and waiting for the elevator, I verge on anger. "Even though you live in America, you are Korean" is always the end of a discussion, my father's final words that cut me down, reducing my arguments to immature whining even in my own ears. Tradition and Korean sensibility dictate my role in family and society, dictate my behavior because someone is always watching.

I flick my middle finger at the elevator and head toward the stairs. It's only a flight, but occasionally I prefer to take the elevator. "Too comfortable" is what my mother would say. "Your stomach is too full."

In the parking lot as I get into my car I look up toward the second floor, and as usual my mother is in the doorway of the balcony. Automatically, I wave to her. She lifts a red rubber glove to me. I feel surrounded, that she is too good to me, too suffocating, but then I think I would miss it if she forgot to look out. As always, there's my Um-Mah watching me go off, like a son going to war.

I reverse out of my parking space. I slam on the brakes! A sporty red car with more contrasting curves than an adolescent boy's fantasy girl floors it past. I hear a screen door slide roughly but swiftly against its track.

"Yah! Soon Gahn-ah! Be careful. Don't listen to your music so loud and pay attention!"

"OK, don't worry," I yell out my car window.

# Jim Beam & Springsteen

### Thomas Gworek

The dashboard clock read 2:13 in the morning. Peter's breath rose in front of his face, a milky gray hazing the road in the headlights. The window was rolled open to help keep him awake, his left ear growing numb and his hands and feet cramping with cold. With his left arm dangling over the sill of the car door, Peter felt the outside air rushing by, passing up the sleeve of his coat and down his chest, his arm like the tube to a vacuum, dust swirling up into the bag of his coat like the bright yellow canary feathers sucked up from his Aunt Millie's blue-gray dining room carpet.

He reached forward, warming his left hand in front of the blower that pushed out the heat. "Come on, Billy," he said, clenching his fist open and closed to warm his fingers. "Where'd you go, buddy?" Billy would always drive down I-90 when he was "thinking too much," as he called it, but he usually left a note. This time there was nothing, and Peter had panicked. Billy was not the type of man who broke patterns.

He could hear Billy's voice on the phone earlier that day, when Billy had called to say he'd be late for dinner.

"I need to ask you a question, Peter."

Peter stopped circling letters in the newspaper's daily word search. Billy never called him by his full name; it was always Buddy, or Pete, sometimes Petey, but never Peter. Only his parents called him that.

"If I asked you to go out tonight, would you?"

"Billy, when have we ever not gone out on a Friday together?" Peter knew that wasn't what Billy was getting at. His fingers shook as he began retracing the letters he had already circled, his eyes focusing on the wooden desktop beneath the newsprint. He could hear Billy's sigh, the air letting out slowly between his lips. Peter could almost feel it blowing gently over the back of his ear and down his neck, tickling the fine blond hair on his lobe.

"A date, Peter. A real date." Peter's stomach slid around itself, coiling and then tumbling as Billy's voice grew heavy and tired. "Not roommates anymore, Peter. Something more. No more *It's-my-turn-to-pay-this-week* crap."

"Billy." Peter paused, letting the pen drop from his fingers. "I...don't..."

"Know!" Billy finished the sentence, loud and curt, his voice a short growl that shivered through Peter's back. "I'll be home later. Why don't you just go and eat without me." Billy then hung up.

The yellow and white lines on the dark road streamed past the car in a blur, Peter's eyes trying to read a sign just beyond the reach of his headlights. *Pumpkin Patch 2 Miles—Free Pony Rides.* Billy had talked about getting a bunch of guys together to go grab some pumpkins in the middle of the night when they wouldn't have to pay. "It's called college economics, Pete," he had said, grinning up from his bowl of green beans at lunch that afternoon.

Peter slowed the car and passed the darkened farmhouse, rose up a hill, and then descended, turning off onto the property's utility road. He switched off the headlamps, leaving the orange parking lights on to guide his way. With every knock of gravel spitting against the undercarriage of the car, he grabbed the steering wheel tighter, turning to look and see if any lights came on in the house. Creeping through swaying crops of winter wheat and browned corn, he descended another hill and turned, reaching the edge of the pumpkin patch. In the middle of the field, he saw Billy's truck parked with the orange lamps illuminating the space around it. The full moon shone down, catching hold of the chrome roll bar and fenders.

"Thank God," Peter said, feeling his adrenaline break into a sweat on his brow. He let the car roll to a stop at the edge of the field and quietly got out, tapping the door closed with his palm. His stomach was churning as if he had drunk too much coffee and not eaten enough food. As he walked toward the truck, the soft dirt pressing under his shoes, he heard Billy's voice on the phone again, *A date, Peter. A real date.* And then his response, the one he always gave, *I don't know.*

Springsteen's "Cover Me" was pouring from the cracked-open windows of the truck. There was still no sign of Billy, but as he reached the truck he heard the clamoring of metal and saw Billy's legs hanging off the back of the truck bed, kicking back and forth, up and down, like a child trying to get his swing to go higher. Billy was on his back, staring up into the sky at the moon passing behind clouds that cast a bluish-white light over his face. His eyes were dull, reddened, and when the moon shone from the other side of the cloud, Peter could see the drying tracks of tears. On Billy's right was a half-empty bottle of Jim Beam. Billy reached for it, clumsily fumbling over the ribs in the truck bed before grabbing it. Raising his head, Billy closed his eyes and took one long swig before putting the bottle down, almost shattering it against the wheel well with an echo that rang in the small valley.

"Am I flying yet?" Billy asked.

"Yeah, you're flying," Peter answered, jumping up onto the back of the cab with Billy, his feet giving a hollow thump against the blue steel of the bed. Billy didn't startle. He only looked up, a smile spreading across his face.

Peter stepped over him, putting one foot on either side of his shoulders. His white running shoes, caked with peat and mud, were slippery on the truck bed's chipped blue metal. He squatted until he was hovering over Billy's chest.

"You're flying so damn high, Billy, you have no idea, do ya?"

Billy smiled, the moonlight catching the blue of his eyes. "I was wondering if you'd find me gone again." His voice was half drowned by the music. "How goes it, Petey?" He reached out for the bottle, his right arm roving over the scratched paint. "Have you seen my whiskey bottle?"

Peter withdrew a hand from the warmth of his jacket pocket and pushed the bottle just out of Billy's reach, coughing so Billy wouldn't hear the sound of glass scraping over metal. "Can't say that I see it," he answered, pretending to look about them.

"Did you bring Kevin with you, Pete?" Billy slurred, reaching up and running his hand over Peter's right knee, rubbing it like he would a football, getting the feel of it. Billy's touch was warm, the pressing of his palm strong against the denim, like the time Billy's hand had lingered on Peter's knee while watching the school's production of *Twelfth Night* in the campus auditorium. The woman next to Billy had noticed and caught Peter's eye. Trembling, he had smiled at her.

"What?" Peter asked, forgetting the question.

"Did you bring Kevin with you?" Billy looked at Peter as though he were waiting to gauge his reaction.

"Kevin? Is he what this is all about?" For a brief moment, Peter asked himself if maybe this wasn't about him at all. "No," he said, "I didn't bring Kevin."

"Are you sure?" Billy asked, his speech thick-tongued. "But he's got those eyes. They're so beautiful. You sure he's not with you?" Billy smiled, trying to sit up and look around. He propped himself up on his elbows, straining his neck like a turtle to look over the truck bed's steel walls.

Peter rarely enjoyed seeing Billy drunk, mainly because Billy never chose the right time. But, even in those moments, a child came out in Billy that Peter liked. "Why is there something so adorable about you when you're drunk?" he asked, then reached out and playfully hit Billy's forehead with the open palm of his hand. Billy lost his balance and fell back, his head banging with a thud against the cold metal.

"Owwww." Billy slowly brought his hands to his face, covering his eyes as if hiding for a surprise. "That hurt," he said, his voice slow and childlike behind the sweet whiskey that rose up into Peter's nostrils.

"Sorry," Peter said. He stood and walked over to the edge of the truck bed, leaping over the side and landing in the peat, his weight pushing the soft soil around his shoes. "I think your head's going to hurt a lot more tomorrow."

Peter had had enough of Springsteen's music. Whenever he touched the truck, he could feel the bass line rushing through his skin. He reached for the chrome handle of the door, his bare fingers pulling on the cold metal, but it didn't move—it was locked. Through the pale glow in the truck, Peter could see that the driver's side door was locked as well, and the keys were dangling from the ignition. He groaned, pushing against the door and shivering.

Grabbing the side of the truck like a pommel horse, he vaulted himself back into the bed, then crouched at the back of the cab, pushing the small back window open wider and reaching inside with his right arm. The music sounded even louder as his face pushed against the window, and his breath fogged up the glass so much that he couldn't see anything. He pushed further, pinching his neck until he finally hit the button. The tape clicked off, and the night air filled with the soft, haunting cries of whippoorwills and nightjars circling the nearby marsh. Then he heard Billy fall against the wet mix of peat and mud, followed by the sloshing of whiskey.

"Oh, man, fuckin' hit my head on a goddamned pumpkin."

Billy was sitting with his legs outstretched in a V, rubbing the left side of his head with his palm. Despite the fall, his right hand hadn't relinquished the tight grip on his bottle of Jim Beam. Resting under the bottle was the pumpkin, the same size as Billy's square-jawed head.

"You look like you're about to suck your thumb." Peter hopped down, giving Billy a hand to get up.

"Very funny." Billy took Peter's hand. Peter pulled, but Billy stumbled. Peter grabbed him by the waist, the two steadying themselves. For a moment they stood face to face. Billy then backed off, wiping the dirt off his jeans. "I'm not as drunk as you think, you know." He turned away, looking back at his Ford truck.

"Then why is it that it's thirty-five degrees out, I'm dressed warmer than you are, and I'm the one freezing my ass off?" Peter dug his hands deep into his jacket pockets.

Billy turned back toward Peter, a smile growing on his face. "You're cold 'cause you're one of them thin-skinned queers," he said in his best Kentucky drawl, a laugh growing from deep in his throat. Then his voice fell to a near whisper, and he brought his hand to his mouth as though telling a secret. "And you know, I hear them homosexuals actually kiss when no one's lookin'." He nodded, accentuating his point. "Uh-huh. I hear that's true."

Peter laughed. The two of them played this game often, pretending to be wise men from the small towns they grew up in, trying to guess what men like Billy and Peter did when no one else was around.

"Yeah?" Peter said, as he slipped into his Virginian accent, which wasn't much different from Billy's. "Well, I heard from Mrs. Marian down at the sheriff's place that she was just visiting her sister in New York. She learned that some of these men actually know how to fix cars, do it all day even, then come home and sew buttons on their shirts as if it's just fine for a man to do such a thing."

"Man, I don't want to hear about that. The Lord just says that it ain't right. But even worse, I heard down the street from Dillon that they actually go out to movies together. You know, go on dates and such."

There was an awkward pause. Peter wasn't sure if what Billy had said was planned, or simply a one-liner he hadn't thought through. "Well, I read in *Dear Abby* that those homosexuals even hold hands when they sit at home watching their television shows."

"Really?" Billy stood shaking his head in disgust. "Oh, man, I think I'm gonna be sick."

Peter let out a laugh as Billy made a motion as if he were going to throw up. This was always part of the play—one line, followed by another, and the other person always feigning disgust. But just then Billy fell over, bracing himself with one hand on the side of the truck and the other on the pumpkin. His chest heaved up and then he vomited, whiskey rushing out and splashing from the ground onto Peter's shoes.

"Oh, man!" Peter leaped back, tripping over a pumpkin vine and falling onto the cold, wet ground. "I just bought these shoes."

"I told you I was gonna be sick!" Billy said, holding his side while still cradling the truck. The moonlight caught hold of a line of spit dripping from his lower lip, dangling midway to the ground.

"Yeah, but I thought you were only laughing about...never mind." Peter stood, ignoring the mud caked on his elbows. He reached down to a vine and broke off a pumpkin leaf, trying to wipe the mess off of his feet. He could smell the manure and fertilizer in the mud, and feel the bitter sap from the pumpkin leaf leaking onto his fingers, making them cling together.

Billy started walking down a row of vines toward the marsh, tapping his foot against the larger pumpkins he passed.

"What the hell are you doing out here, anyway?!" Peter shouted after Billy, almost tripping again as he caught up. His patience had waned, yet each time he stood near Billy something inside him took another breath and let out a sigh.

"I'm thinkin'. That's what I'm doing." Billy didn't look at his friend, just took another sip from the bottle and offered it to Peter. Peter took it, keeping it at his side away from Billy.

"Thinking about what? Don't tell me it's just about Kevin."

"It's about Kevin," Billy answered, giving a grin.

Peter rolled his eyes. Was he really thinking about Kevin, or was this another game? "Jesus Christ, Billy. Use your head, will you? Leave the straight ones be!" He flicked an angry finger against Billy's head to accentuate his point, but regretted it as soon as he felt his finger touch Billy's skin.

Billy turned away, his breath rising and fading before his glassy eyes. "Yeah, I know all that, but..."

"No, no buts."

"Kevin's got a great butt," Billy said, a wry smile rising from the left side of his mouth, curling into the smirk that made Peter fall for him when they first met.

"I don't care about Kevin's ass, Billy," Peter said. "I care about you."

"Oh, really?"

"Yes."

They paused, staring at one another. "I just don't want to see you get hurt," Peter said, his eyes falling to his mud-caked shoes. He couldn't look into Billy's eyes any more.

"But Pete, come on, Kevin's a gymnast!"

"What's that got to do with anything?" Peter's eyes traced the strong line of Billy's jaw as it clenched, squaring his face.

"He's a gymnast," Billy said again, his hands rising into the air as if Peter were missing the obvious. "That means he's gotta be gay."

Peter thrust the bottle of Jim Beam back into Billy's chest. Billy took hold of it as Peter walked away. "You are too much, Billy. Too fucking much. So what are you going to do? Kill yourself over a straight boy?"

Billy didn't answer. He just brought the brown bottle to his lips. Peter continued walking back toward the truck, then Billy shouted back, his voice mocking and rough, "If I seem to recall, you started out saying you were straight, too!"

Peter stopped, feeling as though he had been hit from behind and the ground was rushing up toward his face. He didn't turn around. He knew he couldn't do it without a flood of tears and anger overcoming him. Peter saw the night Billy and he had gone fishing in the river under the bridge just a few more miles down the road from here. It was three months after they had become roommates. They had set their poles into the rocks and some time later had begun making out, Billy nervously making the first move by bringing his face in close, neither of them saying a word, Peter not pulling away. Peter was trembling as Billy's soft lips touched his, and he held Billy tight, each of them feeling another man's tongue touch his own for the first time. Peter felt the warmth of Billy's tongue, the bristle on his face strong against his chin, the scents of his cologne and deodorant. Billy then pressed for more, the crickets and frogs around them drowning away any passing cars. "I love you, Pete," Billy had said, running his hands through Peter's blond hair. But Peter was scared, sure that he wanted the touch of a man, but unsure of what he really felt for Billy, or if it was even right. "I don't want to risk losing you as a friend, Billy," he had said. He knew full well, though, how many of his dreams were filled with romantic images of him and Billy, and how many nights he'd sat in bed watching Billy sleep.

For the first time, Peter now wondered how much of Billy's drinking was really his fault. "Goddammit!" he heard Billy shout, followed by a soft thud. Peter turned to see Billy standing with his left foot sunk into a large, rotting pumpkin. He tried not to laugh, but couldn't hold back the smile breaking across his face. "Now I've got this crap all over my boots.... And I spilled all the fuckin' whiskey." Billy tried to get his foot out by simply lifting up, but lost his balance and fell over. On the ground, he pushed against the soft flesh of the pumpkin, removing his foot with a loud sucking sound. Peter could smell the rotten pumpkin as it caught in the light breeze. It was the smell of his candle burning in the pumpkin on Halloween, the insides rotting and the black char of flame mingling with the wax as it sat on his family's front porch.

"Do you want some help getting up?" he asked, feeling further apart from Billy than ever before, his palms sweating.

"No." Billy's voice was flat and labored.

Peter had moved forward, expecting to hear a yes, then stopped, turning and heading back to the truck in disappointment. A lump was building in his chest as a dull throb spread down his arms. He heard Billy's voice under the bridge again, *I love you, Pete*.

He climbed into the back of the truck, trying to figure if it was possible to reach the keys through the small window. He shoved his arm in, pinning his shoulder and pinching his neck, but couldn't get at them.

Billy was now standing next to the truck, resting his arms on the side with his head down as though he were trying to fall asleep. "What are you doin'?" he asked, his eyes closed.

"I'm trying to get the goddamned keys you locked in the car." Peter's voice was slow, talking to Billy as he would to a child he had grown intolerant of.

"The keys?" Billy's face grew puzzled. He dug into his pocket, pulled out another set, and stood jangling them. "You mean these?"

Frustrated and at the edge of tears, Peter walked over and grabbed the keys. "Just shut up and get in the truck."

Billy walked to the passenger door and climbed in, the smell of pumpkin, mud, and whiskey filling the cab. "Where are we goin'?" he asked, clicking the buckle ends together with a cold metal snap.

"Home," Peter answered. "We'll move my car onto the main road and drive yours back to town." He felt sick as the uneasiness in his belly churned, and he tried to sort one thought from the next. He didn't know what else to say but spoke anyway, needing to hear his own voice. "Are you sure you don't want a pumpkin before we leave?"

Billy rested his head against the window, his breath steaming the glass. "Just take me home."

Peter couldn't sleep. He didn't have the energy to try, especially after pushing Billy up the ladder and into his bed. Billy was mumbling about Heraclitus as he drifted off to sleep; about how he thought the world was made of fire, all things, including him and Peter, were broken down to nothing more than fire, tiny flames that consumed and combined, creating the two of them. Peter ignored him, his back turned, and only occasionally looked over his shoulder to make sure Billy wasn't about to roll out of bed and hit his head on the bar. He was standing at his desk pouring the water into his coffeemaker when he heard Billy's first snores.

Peter reached out and turned off his desk lamp, leaving himself in the warm darkness. A glimpse of light was shining through the windows from the streetlamps outside the dorm, the glow lingering over Billy. Peter sat staring at Billy in his bed, watching the way his chest rose in his sleep, rising and falling with each deep breath. Peter found his own chest matching Billy's; when Billy inhaled, so did Peter. He closed his eyes and could see Billy's lips still damp, his tongue resting just behind his teeth.

"This is crazy," Peter mumbled, his voice breaking into the sterile space of the room. He reached back up, clicking his light back on. "I've gotta get out of here." He swiveled his chair so he could reach into the wardrobe for his gym shorts. He stood, slid them over his legs, and then grabbed a plain navy sweatshirt. He'd work out. Going to the gym would get his mind off Billy, off all of it. As he closed the door behind him, the clock read 5:40.

The wind had picked up briskly, cold air rushing up Peter's bare legs. It had rained since they drove back from the farm, and since the sun was just beginning to lighten the sky with blue to the east, he could still see the yellow streetlamps reflect in the puddles as the wind blew ripples over them. He pulled the parka tight around himself and walked across the field toward the gym, a five-minute walk at most.

He saw Billy lying on the back of the pickup bed, his eyes looking up at Peter while he straddled him. He thought of Billy's smile, the way he passed out in the truck and leaned over, his sweaty, mud-covered face resting on Peter's shoulder, rising and falling with the bumps in the road.

Without much thought, Peter turned off the sidewalk that would have taken him to the gym and began to move toward the engineering complex. *You're starting to lose it*, he thought. It had been a year and a half since he found out the toilets on the second floor were a popular cruising place. If one knew the game, there was usually someone hoping to turn a quick trick. Peter wasn't sure what he was looking for, but he continued walking toward the complex. He was shivering by the time he reached the south door. The building was warm, and he stopped to rub his legs. He went up the flight of stairs, made a left, and then took the second right to the washroom in the electrical wing. Only half the hall lights were on as he walked. Except for Peter, the building was still. He had wiped his sneakers off by the entrance as well as he could, but still, every few steps the rubber let out a squeak.

He reached the washroom and pushed open the old oak door expecting it to creak, but it didn't. The door had been oiled since he had been there last, but that was already a year ago. His eyes had to adjust to the crisp fluorescent lights. The walls were still painted powder blue, but it was a new coat, or at least had been touched up. It was no longer chipping, and the water stains from the burst heating pipes were gone. He looked down and saw that the tiles had been changed. They were no longer beige and scuffed with years of boot marks but now a flat, gray linoleum.

The door closed behind him with a gentle knocking of wood. Peter was surprised at how calm he was, the only nervousness felt when he pictured Billy and how he would have looked at him and said, "You're better than that."

He rounded the corner in the washroom and saw no one, facing only himself in the mirror's reflection. It was early yet, and he hadn't set his hopes on finding anyone; it was the possibility of indulgence and chance that brought him here in the first place. He gave a brief whistle to the tune of "The Alphabet Song"—enough to take anyone listening to the letter G, then stopped to listen for a response from the stalls, but there was nothing. He was alone with the fluorescent lights buzzing overhead and the fan rattling unevenly behind the metal grate over the stalls.

He looked at his face in the mirror and tried to rub the weariness from his eyes. Sleep was coming quickly now, and he knew it. Nonetheless, he didn't want to go back to the room, at least not until he was sure Billy would be gone for the day. That was a given when Billy got drunk—no matter how hungover or sick he was the next morning, he would always drag himself to class.

Before leaving, he stepped up to the urinals. They were the old, stainless steel, trough type, like the ones he'd stood at next to his father at football stadiums. As he pulled the front of his gym shorts down and took hold of himself, he heard the door to the washroom open followed by the clicking of dress shoes and the gentle banging of the wooden door closed. Peter's pulse quickened. *You already told yourself no,* he thought, trying to convince himself he was really on his way out the door.

Peter saw the shape of the man step up to the urinals on his right. What he could see through the corner of his eye was a red sweater and that the man was white and a couple of inches shorter than him. Four years earlier, Peter's heart would have been racing, and he would have felt weak and cotton-mouthed, unsure of himself and too busy worrying about getting caught to let go and have fun. But now it was mere formality. Close the business deal and let go.

"Good morning," the man said to Peter. Through the corner of his eye, he could see the man's head rise and fall. His voice came like a low rumble, falling out lazily as the man repeated himself, "Good morning," and undid his zipper. Peter had heard this man's voice before. He remembered it only because he had liked it back then but couldn't put a face to it now.

"Morning," Peter answered, trying to sound disinterested, but when he heard the man's urine hit the metal wall of the trough, his eyes fell and looked down at himself. Then, out of the corner of his eye he looked at the man's penis. It was a nice shape, uncut too, which was always a rare plus. The man must have noticed him looking for he began to grow, his hand gently pulling on himself as his flow of urine began to slow.

Peter looked up from the man's crotch to his face. It was Dr. Sawyer, Billy's first philosophy professor their freshman year. Peter had skipped his own class to sit in the lecture hall with Billy, so he could close his eyes and spend three hours listening to the way Sawyer's voice filled the hall. It was like curling up with a comforter in the night.

That had been four years ago. Now, Sawyer was in his midfifties. What hair remained atop his head was shaved, giving his head a reflection in the lights that looked more like sweat than clear skin. Since Peter had last seen him, Sawyer had changed the style of his glasses to round, silver rims that brought out the gray in his goatee, which was also new. The image seemed an attempt to make him look younger, more appealing, and Peter found himself agreeing with it, warming up to the man's smile. He saw something in the man's brown eyes that would work, something that made him begin stirring as well.

Sawyer turned his gaze from Peter's eyes and looked down. Peter was suddenly aware that he had been stroking himself as well. He had entered the game without thinking about it, without really wanting to. Still, even when he realized it, Peter didn't stop. It was feeling too good now to stop. *You're thinking with the wrong head again*, Billy's voice whispered in his ears.

Sawyer, standing two feet away stroking himself, no longer tried to hide that he was looking up and down Peter's body. "It's a bit cold for shorts, don't you think?"

Peter didn't hear him. He was trying to find a way to walk away and leave, but his body was winning again. It always did. Peter tried looking through Sawyer, trying not to see his erection or the way his foreskin slid back and forth, covering and uncovering. He looked down again, staring at the man's hand as it moved. The back of it was dusted with hair. *It's not smooth like Billy's*, he thought, *and the watch is different*.

Sawyer reached out with his free hand, Peter watching the shadow cross the floor towards him until it met his own two hands, Sawyer's hands now gliding over them. Peter let his arms fall to the side. *Leave*, he said to himself over and over, but didn't move. He said nothing when he felt the soft flesh of Sawyer's palm wrap around him. He let out a groan and withered inside, knowing he was stuck—the body having won out again.

"You like getting sucked?" the man asked; again came the low rumble, the voice he had heard through closed eyes in the lecture hall. Peter's eyes were drawn to the shadows on the floor, to the way the man's shadow-covered belly cast a dark moon on the floor, eclipsing the shadow of the man's own erection. He closed his eyes. This was not the man he wanted to associate with that voice in the lecture hall. Again, the low rumble came, the extra squeeze of the hand, then a step forward so the man's voice was right in Peter's ear now, their chests touching.

"So, you didn't answer. Do you like getting sucked?"

Peter's eyes opened, looking at the man's brown eyes, the steel-rimmed glasses that were becoming more inviting, almost endearing. They were the kind of eyes that were full of temptation, eyes that would have created a sexual attraction between the two had they been the eyes of a friend or a mentor; but they were neither.

Peter looked past those eyes and smiled, nodding his head, taking the next step of the game. "Sure do," he said, and thought, *Let's get this over with*, stepping aside and walking toward the stalls.

Sawyer followed Peter, the two pausing halfway to the stalls as they heard the janitor approaching with his loud, rusty cart. As they stood waiting, Peter sensed a moment to leave and motioned to move. But as if he knew, Sawyer reached out and stroked Peter, again wrapping his soft palm around the warm flesh, his other hand reaching out and cupping Peter's ass. Peter tried forgetting the man, replacing his hands with Billy's hands, the hands that clasped his neck under the bridge. The man leaned in, his voice rolling into Peter's ear, "Come on." Peter tucked himself back into his shorts and followed Sawyer to the stall on the far end, watching as the professor turned and sat on the toilet. As Peter closed the door behind them, he heard the janitor's cart move past the bathroom and on down the hall.

Sawyer's hands clasped around Peter's waist, pulling him close, bringing his mouth to Peter's shorts and pressing his lips into the stretched fabric. Peter wasn't in the mood to draw the moment out or make romance where there wasn't any. He stared up at the ceiling, following the rows of fluorescent lights, and said, "Listen, if you want it, go for it. I don't have much time." The man pulled Peter's shorts down, freeing him again, and then Peter felt the warmth of his hands and the damp heat of his mouth. Peter braced himself against the walls, his arms pushing out as the man began to take more of him in. He closed his eyes and again saw the way Billy looked at him from the back of the pickup truck, tears still damp on his cheeks. He saw Billy's mouth as he slept, his damp lips, and the way he'd sometimes sleep with his tongue hanging out like a puppy. Peter continued sliding into the man's mouth, not knowing it, not really feeling it. Peter was feeling Billy's tongue again, wrapping around his like it did that afternoon under the bridge. Only this time he felt Billy's lips move down his chest, felt him licking his navel while he nervously fumbled with his shorts. He felt Billy's hands on his backside, felt Billy's chin in his lap. Peter wanted to reach down to hold Billy's face now, to tell him how good it felt and how he didn't want it to end.

"Oh, Christ," Peter groaned, "God, I love you, Billy." He took his hands off the walls and reached down to hold Billy's head, run his fingers through his hair, but his hands clasped Sawyer's bald head. "What?" Peter said, looking down at the heavy man below him with sweat dripping down his temples and flesh wrapping over the edges of his wedding band as he started stroking Peter.

Sawyer stopped, his brown eyes looking up through the wire glasses on his overweight face at Peter's puzzled expression. "Who's Billy?" he asked, and began stroking Peter faster.

"I've got to get out of here," Peter said, but the man wrapped his other arm around Peter's ass. "No way," he said, "I almost had you." He pulled Peter deep into his throat.

Peter had to stop before it got to feeling too good again. "I said no," he said, raising his voice and trying to back off. But the man wouldn't let go, his sucking sounds growing louder as the vacuum between them began breaking. Peter reached down and grabbed Sawyer's shoulders, pushing him back hard so that the professor's back hit the wall. Peter pulled his shorts up before the man could grab him again.

"What? What's wrong?" Sawyer sat still, staring up at Peter while one hand continued to stroke himself.

Peter didn't answer, just turned, unlocking the door. But the man grabbed at him, tugging on the leg of his shorts. "Come on, you can't stop now," he pleaded. Peter turned and shoved his arm away. "Sawyer, does your wife know you do this shit?" The man's eyes lit up, realizing that Peter knew who he was. He sat back and let Peter walk out the door.

Peter took his coat off, covering the bulge in his shorts as he walked down the narrow corridor. On his way out, another student came walking in. Peter didn't look at him, only said, "Last stall on the right," then entered the hall, listening to the soft, wooden bang of the door behind him.

By the time he got outside, Peter's tears had already begun rolling down his face, the wind blowing on the salty tracks. He shivered in the cold, his body growing more tired and weary, making him even colder. He wandered through central campus, walking under the towering elms and oaks as their barren branches cut into the light morning sky, the sun shimmering off the light frost and rain puddles. Peter continued walking, ignoring the numbing of his ears, the burning cold in his fingers.

Billy would still be fast asleep, his dreams taking him somewhere; Peter never knew where. Kevin this time? Someone else? He needed to get warm, find somewhere dry to stay for a time before going back to the room. He didn't know what he would say if Billy were still there. He never had the strength to just ignore him, brush past, and say he needed his space. "But what's up? What's going on?" Billy would ask, driving Peter further into himself.

Peter didn't hear the hostess at Denny's ask where he'd like to sit, didn't even see her. He walked down the center aisle, his feet sliding over the brown-and-gold plaid carpet, and made his way to the counter. As he brushed past a waitress, moving to the side to avoid her, his elbow pushed into the belly of a trucker.

"Excuse me," the man said, his voice deep and leering.

"Oh, sorry." Peter withdrew his arm, feeling the flesh fill back where he had intruded.

"You oughta watch where you're going next time, young man," the truck driver said heartily, turning and continuing past him to the register, where the brunette was going to greet him with a big smile and a gap in her front teeth.

"Sorry, I didn't mean it," Peter apologized, but it went unnoticed. Peter looked around. The place was already half full, mainly with truck drivers—some with big bellies, some thin as a rail and wearing glasses. Other than the waitresses, Peter was the only relatively clean-cut person in the place, the only man who didn't look like he needed a shower. He was sure that if the smell of food died off, he would be hit by an overbearing stench of sweat and tobacco. He was odd man out once again. The moment he caught someone's eye he looked away, turning around to sit down at the counter.

"What can I getcha this morning?" the waitress asked. *She's chipper*, he thought. Here was a woman who had been up for two hours already and hadn't let the morning drag her down, a waitress who enjoyed her job. There were few things that amazed Peter, but satisfied waitresses were one of them. "How about we start you off with some coffee? Seems you're a bit slow this mornin'." Peter didn't have time to answer—she grabbed a mug, turned it over and filled it, leaving enough room for cream if he cared to use any. "I'll come back in a few to take your order." Peter felt his eyes roll; the last thing he wanted to contend with was Mrs. Congeniality.

"Thanks," he muttered, his eyes roving over the pictures of omelets and flapjacks. He closed the menu, not much caring for decisions. He'd order what he always got when he and Billy walked into town for breakfast every Sunday morning. "A Denver, easy on the onions, extra peppers, and cheddar, please." Billy always ordered the potato pancakes, oatmeal, a tall orange juice, "Oh, and a side of cottage cheese with fruit, please." That was the first thing he ate at any meal if he could get it. In Montana everyone ate it with black pepper and Tabasco sauce or smothered with Thousand Island dressing. The first time Billy ordered it with fruit, the waitress was astounded. "With fruit?" "Yeah," he said, smiling as he was always doing to strangers. "What's wrong with that?" When she brought it and set it down, she said, "Cottage cheese," and then walked away still talking to herself, "with fruit for the fruits." Billy just laughed. "Oh well," he said, scooping up some in his spoon, "you can't take small minds for a walk on a leash, and you can't shoot 'em."

"So how are the newlyweds doing?" A man sat down next to Peter, his voice directed at the waitress behind the counter and bringing Peter out of his blind stare. He was a big man, the stereotype of what he assumed a trucker would look like: big belly, flannel shirt, red suspenders, worn cap, and a long frazzled beard. When he sat, his bulk shook the stools next to him. His voice, on the other hand, didn't carry the same weight. *It should be deeper*, Peter thought.

"Now, Allen Jamison, you know me and Gary are doing just fine, thanks." The waitress smiled, gave the man a kiss on the cheek and poured him some coffee. "How many times are you going to come in here and ask me that very same question?"

"Until you realize that I'm the man of your dreams, sweety."

Peter had heard almost the same line from Billy a month earlier, the two of them sitting on the couch, watching a rented copy of *Blade Runner*. "You'd think he'd just wake up and realize how much he wants her, don'tcha think?" Billy said of Harrison Ford's character. He was slightly drunk, his words starting to slur.

"Suppose so," Peter answered, taking another swig from the bottle of Jim Beam.

"Kinda like you?"

"What?" Peter turned to look at him, Billy's face flickering in the changing light of the television screen.

"When are you going to wake up and realize it's me you really want."

Peter sat in uncomfortable silence, watching Harrison Ford digitize a photo and look through the reflections in a mirror. He could feel Billy's eyes on him, Billy's hand resting casually on his leg. Luckily, Billy soon passed out, leaving Peter awake, trying to answer Billy's question. Did he really enjoy being free and fooling around with Billy on occasion, or was there more to it?

"You can't deal with it, Peter. You don't have the guts to be who you are!" Billy had yelled a week later, when Peter announced that it all had to stop, they couldn't just keep sleeping together.

With that, Peter had rushed him, throwing him into a wall, knocking down a framed picture of Yellowstone, the glass shattering over the carpet. "Go ahead," Billy taunted. "Hit me. Prove to yourself you're still a man." They glared at one another, breathing hard, chests rising and falling. A shard of glass had landed in Billy's foot. He turned to go wash off the blood, but stopped before opening the door, looking to the open Hide-A-Bed that still had their damp imprints of sweat on the sheets. "You're no less of a man for just having a dick up your ass, Peter.... Or for liking it, for that matter." Peter watched as Billy opened the door and added, "Did I become any less of a man when you fucked me?" When the door closed, Peter slumped onto the bed and cried.

"Here you go, dear." The waitress handed him the omelet, its cheese still steaming. "Now don't eat it too fast, we don't want you to end up lookin' like all these other boys in here."

"No, ma'am," he smiled, sheepishly looking up from his clenched hands, his knuckles white from interlacing so tightly. He could feel the tears welling up, his jaw tightening as he tried to ward them off.

"Hey pal, you OK?" the driver asked him, reaching out and placing a hand on his shoulder.

"Yeah...sure." Peter pulled himself together, "You know, the usual. Wife's gone and left me with two kids, the dog up and ran away, and now I'm a big ol' drunk."

The driver let out a roar, holding his belly and spilling some of his coffee as he set the cup back down.

"Now you don't look old enough to be the married type," the waitress said.

"Well, I'm thinking about it." He felt a smile begin to grow—he liked the way that was beginning to sound. No, he liked the way it sounded—a lot.

"Well, what's the lucky one's name?" she asked, filling her friend's cup.

"Billy," he answered, then quickly added, "Jo, Billy-Jo. It's a pet name her grandad gave her as a kid."

"Well, good luck to ya, son," the truck driver said, patting him on the back. "Good luck."

*Thomas Gworek* 87

# The Jester King

## Juan A. Cortés

When I saw the rainbow-colored suit dancing high up on the rooftop of Los Dos Payasos, the abandoned apartment building across the street, I wondered where my wife Yolli was and if she could see it. It was a twinkle of orange and green leaping high into the air, clapping its belled red feet and landing on ballerina toes at the very edge of the roof corner. Then the suit back-flipped, balancing on one hand, and curled its spine into the letter C. Belled red feet gripped the skull of the suit, and when it wiggled its toes, the purple three-pronged hat that drooped like the roots of a tree jingled into a giggling fit. The suit leapt back upright. From a puffy yellow sleeve, a shiny flute dropped and was snatched by white-gloved hands, and the crowd ten stories below on Whirl-A-Way Avenue applauded wildly, as if the flute had been plucked from midair. Packs of people had already stopped to watch the suit, but when it placed the flute to its laughing lips, they gathered in droves from every adjoining intersection, thickening well into the street. A tune whistled magically down on swoops of wind, twisting around the forgotten Los Dos Payasos building and freezing the ears of all who watched below. Those who tried to walk or to ride their bikes past were staggered by the force of the happy hurricane gales and peered toward the sky. Cars and trucks spun out, clogging adjacent intersections. A red Porsche slammed into a street pole just outside my large picture window, barely missing Señora Reyna, my Wednesday breakfast-buffet regular. I could hear the flute's whistling music through the opening and closing of my restaurant door, as the few customers I had filed outside, as if called to run a drill, to see what was happening. The suit leapt several times, soaring off the side of the apartment building like a daredevil. At first, it dropped a few stories and then snapped itself back as if tied to a rubber string. Next it spread its puffy yellow arms wide, glided high above the crowd, and curved back to the rooftop like a thrown Frisbee.

I wiped down another table, amazed that my customers left half-eaten *chorizo con huevos* to watch the dancing suit on the roof. The picture window that had my name spelled backwards across it was my TV screen to the town, and the crowd that had formed on Whirl-A-Way Avenue was beginning to resemble a mob of protesters. In seconds, fire trucks and police cars had barreled through the crowd below the suit. An ambulance arrived as children began to mimic the suit, doing handstands and playing imaginary flutes. Twelve firemen ran to the foot of Los Dos Payasos with a crash mat. Then the mayor arrived, black suits at his side like castle spires, and was escorted to the front of the dazzled crowd for the best view. Jo-Jo and Jaime, the twin brothers who were my cooks, took off their aprons and joined the mass of people with craned necks.

Within minutes, the entrance to my restaurant was completely blocked. It seemed as if every single person in town had come to watch and now sat spellbound by the singing and dancing of the rainbow-colored suit. Everyone but me.

I scrubbed the same spot on the table closest to the window—waiting to see if I could spot my Yolli in all the madness—until my only view of the city was the backs of slouching old women and the tour dates of heavy metal bands written across black T-shirts. I turned to check the clock above the bar. It read 12:30, and I knew Yolli was ironing or knitting buttons on my *guayaveras* while watching Erik Estrada on *"Dos Mujeres y un Camino."* She wouldn't be out just yet. I couldn't have looked away for more than a moment, but when I turned back a terribly marvelous thing had occurred.

The afternoon sky was suddenly pitch black and the policemen who had been sitting on the tops of their squad cars snapping pictures of the suit were now asleep. The twelve firemen were curled up on their crash mat, asleep. The children who sang and did handstands were asleep. Bikes still between the legs, riders lay on their sides, asleep in the street. The ambulance driver was asleep on her steering wheel. Señora Reyna and the blonde tourist sitting in the Porsche were asleep, their mouths still angry and yelling in midsentence. And at the base of Los Dos Payasos, the good old mayor rested like a baby, butt pointing up at the moon, as the suit, who had just moments before graced the rooftops above them all, slipped off his white cotton gloves and snatched the mayor's wallet from his back pocket.

 I ducked beneath the booth I had been scrubbing. As I peeked over its edge, it gleamed with nighttime stars and I saw the man inside the jester suit stalking the sleeping bodies one by one. He was a walking rainbow in the darkness, but scary as he rummaged through even police officers' pants, pocketing loose change and folded bills. He snatched the pearls from old ladies and gold nose rings from teens. As he skipped closer to my picture window, I could make out more of his face. When he was right in front of the letters that spelled my name backwards, I could see him clearly. He didn't look like anybody I knew, had ever known, or even merely seen through the window of my restaurant. His cheekbones were pointy and his chin was shaped like a W. His eyes were crossed, and his teeth gleamed with an unshakable smile. Muffled through the window, I could hear him singing the cheerful song he had played on the rooftop. The words I couldn't make out, but the melody I could never forget. Its tempo was fast like a polka but simple as a nursery rhyme. I ducked lower and turned away from the sound, fearful the tune might lull me to sleep. The broken streetlight in front of my door shined brightly into my window and dropped the shadow of his torso, sharp face, and three-pronged hat across my floor. One arm on his stomach, the other bent high overhead, I watched his black caricature merengue past me on the tile floor. It bent over a massive shadow I knew was Jo-Jo and Jaime asleep in the entryway, then leafed through their wallets and replaced them in their sleeping pockets.

 I remembered that I kept a bat behind the register at the bar. I wanted to grab it and crush the suit before he could get to me, but what is the strength of an old man? I tightened my soft fists and saw the gray hairs on my arms wither as I tried to summon strength. My round belly snapped the buttons off my *guayavera* and pulled at my dago T. Oh, the profits of owning my own restaurant! I felt straw hairs spreading cold across my balding head, and then a sudden rush of warmth and light passed over my entire body. The front door of my restaurant flung open as if hit by a massive wind. Clutters of people were talking. Señora Reyna found her thoughts and continued yelling at the blonde tourist in the Porsche. Horns honked, engines roared and faded past my door. I looked up from where I sat on the floor, and Jo-Jo was staring down at me, his eyebrows crumpled with confusion.

"Hey, what're you doin' down there, Pete? You missed all the action."

"The action?"

I dusted my pants off and snuck a peek at the bright afternoon sky.

"Yeah, some loon dressed up like a clown or something was dancing on the roof of that old building, Los Dos Payasos. Didn't you notice everybody leaving?"

I broke a sweat walking to the register behind the bar.

"A jester," Jaime interrupted. "He was a jester, not a clown, you idiot. Didn't you see his hat?"

The boys began to retie their aprons around their waists. The drawer sprang open. The little money we had seemed to be there.

"Where is he now?" I called to Jo-Jo. "This jester?"

"You missed that, too! He just disappeared! Man, you work too hard, Pete. Gotta smell the street once in a while, y'know?"

Jo-Jo walked closer to the bar, animating his speech with his hands. Jaime followed after his brother, mocking his every gesture.

"He was playing this flute, right? Doing flips and shit. And then he started spinning real fast and the music he was playing got faster and faster, and the wind was blowing everything until he was like, this blur. Like the Tasmanian Devil! Then he just vanished into thin air. Poof!" Jo-Jo said, snapping his fingers.

Jaime curled his lips and snapped too, like an offbeat retard. "Poof! Poof! Poof! You're such a jerk. There was a hole in the roof about as big as your head. The cops'll find it. They'll search the building and surrounding area. In about three days, one of them'll find some escaped loon with a rusted flute in his hand and get promoted to chief asshole in charge. It'll be a done deal. Solved."

Jaime shoved Jo-Jo in the head as they walked to the kitchen, and continued, "You could get whacked in the skull, sit up admiring chirping birds and never once wonder who swung the bat."

Jo-Jo flicked Jaime's ear and shoved him into the kitchen, responding, "Yeah, and you could see your mother spout water from the top of her head and still deny she's a killer whale."

I closed my eyes as the bickering continued into the kitchen.

Then I had a thought. "Phone's out," I yelled, swinging the kitchen door open with my hand. "Anybody got a quarter? I gotta call Yolli."

Jo-Jo and Jaime checked their pockets but couldn't find a cent, and further, didn't act like they were missing anything. That's when I decided I hadn't been dreaming, and knew that the man in the suit would be back.

The next day was Thursday, the day I usually let the boys handle things. But I strolled through the back door saying my "mornin's" to Jo-Jo and Jaime and my *"buenprovechos"* to Señor Reyna, my early bird who always came fifteen minutes before his wife. I passed the register and hung my coat on the hook behind Señor Alberto and his crossword puzzles and froze. I pulled my hand out from my inside coat pocket, as I did every morning, but my wallet wasn't there. That's when the music that I had heard yesterday struck my ears once more.

I didn't turn around to see if anyone had heard it, because at that moment, I felt it whistled solely for me. It glided through the airtight picture window, zipped across the table where Christina and Nena ate bran muffins and bacon, slithered between Jo-Jo's strut as he swept the floor, spun Jaime around, a tray of O.J. balanced high above his head, paused for two seconds behind my back as I searched through my pockets once more, then it yawned obnoxiously and tapped me on the shoulder with an invisible index finger.

My face ran white as I turned to look back across the restaurant, imagining that everybody—Jo-Jo, Jaime, Señors Reyna and Alberto, Christina and Nena—was staring at me with wide eyes and whistling the merry tune of the flute as they joined hands in a spiritual semicircle. Instead, the gaping crowd was already gathering in front of Los Dos Payasos. First like wandering strays, then like starving rats around a single golden piece of cheese on a pedestal. The musical gales blew through the hair and clothes of pedestrians. Bike messengers stopped again. The mayor was escorted by his black-suited castle spires to the front row again. And *adios mi corazon* if that same red Porsche, *sans* fender, didn't swerve again, narrowly missing Señora Reyna, and crash right into Los Dos Payasos, this time nearly shaking the orange-and-green, purple-and-yellow, blue-and-red suit clear off the building as he balanced on a thumb and forefinger. I turned to warn Jo-Jo and Jaime not to go out into the street with the others, but only saw their aprons suspend in the air and then drop to the floor as the front door slammed closed behind them.

I grabbed the bat from behind the bar and marched past the window, which was darkened again with night and crowded with slouched, snoring bodies.

"Oh, it was the most marvelous thing!" I remembered Yolli saying over the phone. "He must have danced for hours! And the music! *¡Me cubrio en extasis!* I can't believe you missed it!"

I couldn't believe that my wife hadn't been watching Erik Estrada.

I could hear the singing polka and the jingling bells of the flipping suit when I pulled open my front door and saw Jo-Jo lying in the entryway. I laid down the bat and propped Jo-Jo half in the foyer and half on the sidewalk to keep the door open. But as soon as I had him lying perfectly on his side, thumb nestled comfortably in his sucking lips, I turned to pick up the bat and Jaime fell like a domino on top of him. When I rolled him off so he lay next to his brother, their healthy bodies now completely blocked the entry, and I figured I'd brace my footing on their shoulders and hips to get across to the sidewalk. But I stopped once again to pick up the bat, and when I turned back around, I found Señor Alberto lying face down across both of them, his back rounded like a corpse. Now, Señor Alberto is a big man. There was no sense in trying to move him, so I braced one foot on Jaime's shoulder and the other foot on the back of Señor Alberto's head. I got as far as placing my knee on Señor Alberto's shoulder blade when Señor Reyna fell, as if nudged from a part of the sidewalk I couldn't see, and stacked right on top of Señor Alberto's ass, his legs spread open like a snow angel. Both señors and I are big men. So to get over them all, I had to lie on my stomach on top of Señor Reyna and squirm through the top of the doorway.

Even as I got to my feet, I heard the singing fade, and the jester suit was nowhere to be seen. All of the people in the city, however, were laid out one on top of another like sliced cucumbers. It started with Señora Reyna across the street, lying next to the crashed Porsche. She was on top of a drooling policeman, who was on top of one of the firemen on the crash mat. The line of people zigzagged, body on top of body, along Whirl-A-Way, up the fire trucks and down, across the mayor, who again lay with his ass pointing at the moon, over his escorts in black suits, swirling in a line of people around traffic, across to my side of the street, and ending with Christina on top of Nena. From the tilt of her body, Nena seemed to have nudged Señor Reyna, who fell on Señor Alberto, who fell on Jaime, who fell on Jo-Jo when I was picking up my bat inside the foyer. I walked body to body, recognizing faces I hadn't seen in months. It was all one giant snakelike line that must have spelled something phenomenal when viewed from above, but my Yolli was nowhere to be found.

I had searched every face in the line twice to be certain, but it wasn't until I had returned to the row of people in front of my picture window that I saw Yolli lying on top of Señor Reyna, a place I am certain she was not lying before. She looked at peace, hugging my tan *guayavera* to her chin like a blanket as I ran towards her. Her image began to fade like a mirage when I heard the jingle of a spinning fool's hat on top of the apartment complex across the street. The suit laughed as maniacally as a painter in his Cubist period, and by the time I reached Señor Reyna, Yolli was a memory. The sun clicked back on, and I was suddenly one of many in the city with a craned neck staring at a blur of colors spinning into nothingness on the roof of Los Dos Payasos.

"Hey, Pete, whatcha bring that bat out here for?"

People passed me in herds, buzzing about the amazing back-flips and music they'd just witnessed the man in the suit perform, as if seeing it for the first time. Jaime stepped aside, holding his pained ribs as he let Christina and Nena get back inside to their breakfasts. Then he and Jo-Jo glared at me and my bat, hoping everything was OK.

"Oh, y'know, kids...they get rowdy and stuff when things like this happen. I just..." I tried to explain, but couldn't find the words.

Jo-Jo grabbed at the bat I still clutched tightly to my chest and looked down his nose at me as if inspecting the clarity in my eyes.

"You OK, Pete? Maybe you shouldn't have come in today?"

"What you should do," Jaime interrupted, "is charge all these people peepin' in front of your stoop admission for blocking your doorway while the mayor and his circus performs. Somebody's making money off that shit."

Jo-Jo shoved Jaime inside.

"Hey, Pete, nobody's robbed us lately or anything, have they?" he asked, completely removing the bat from my hands. He put his arm around me and walked me to the entrance. "I mean, I'll stay later if..."

"No-no. Everything's fine," I said, opening the door for him.

Jo-Jo rubbed his neck and shook his head, satisfied. "OK. Hey, go get some rest, will ya?" He took the door from me, waved good-bye to Señor Reyna, and followed Señora Reyna inside the restaurant. I saw my plump reflection and, behind me, the dingy entrance to Los Dos Payasos in the glass door as it closed, and the one thing I knew for certain was that I was the only person in the city completely sane.

The next morning I awoke to the sight of two clowns gaping at me, frozen, as if they might crash right into my sleeping body if I didn't get out of their way. The green-suited clown—the terrified one steering the polka-dot bike—had eyes big as uncooked burgers, his legs split like an upside-down V. The orange-suited clown—the one with his legs wrapped around his partner's rib cage—stared down at his partner's horrified mouth from above, mocking the terror-struck gaze with raised eyebrows, a tip of his hat, and a show-biz smile. My heavy eyes traced the letters beneath this picture, along the frayed bottom edge of the faded, twenty-year-old poster. *Los Dos Payasos*, it said, *starring in Those Crazy Clowns*.

I picked myself up from the concrete foyer floor of Los Dos Payasos, which had been my bed the previous night, and dusted myself off. It was a floor that had accumulated a carpet of dust from twenty-five years of nonuse, surrounded by walls that spoke of the town's sentiments toward Los Dos Payasos themselves. *You Abandoned Us*, *Sell-Outs*, *Fakes*, screamed graffiti in colors and variations too numerous to name. My eyes traced the orange-suited clown's outstretched arm again, imagining he held a flute in his hand where the paper had torn away.

"Hey, look up there!" I heard a young boy yell outside, his voice dampened by the dingy glass doors of the entryway. His was a voice I hadn't heard in the previous two days, and I hoped it was an omen of good things to come.

I stood watching the crowd slowly gather before me, as if I was offstage and waiting for my turn to perform. Today, I was going to make a difference, I thought, gripping the handle of the wooden bat I'd held close to my body all night like it was my Yolli. I summoned courage while the music whistled down from the rooftop. It was slow at first, but gathered momentum quickly, happy hurricane winds blowing through the hair and clothes of all those forced to look to the sky. The people gathered in their normal fashion. Pedestrians and bike messengers first. Then Señora Reyna screaming in sync with the screeching tires of the battered Porsche. After that, the ambulance, fire trucks, and cops shooting pictures from the tops of their squad cars.

I scanned the audience of craned necks, watching for drooping eyelids or blank gaping stares that refused to come. Folding chair in hand, the mayor pushed his way towards me to the front row, his black-suited castle spires shoving people aside. He plopped down in the chair, peered up at the rooftop, and watched and watched and watched.

I refused to look away from the crowd or even blink, waiting for the skies to shade themselves, waiting amidst the ghosts tugging on my pants and the voices at my back urging me to look away and follow the script. And not one sky-peering soul closed its eyes, and not one set of shoulders slouched until the music became tangible to me. Only when it turned like a startled cobra and focused solely on me, slipping underneath the dingy glass doors of Los Dos Payasos to tickle me under my nose, scratch the back of my neck, and rub the thick sides of my ribs slowly as a bad Western on late-night TV, did it finally strike me hard with the kind of yawn that makes your eyes tear and stretches the limits of your cheeks. Only then did my eyes squint shut for just an instant.

If the sun hadn't clicked itself off, there would have been a falling shadow on the sidewalk that started as a pinpoint and expanded like a balloon until it was big as Señor Alonzo's backside before the suit landed in front of me on the other side of the glass entryway. I would have had a warning. But in the darkness, it happened quick as a splash of rainbow water in the black air. His rubber body landed with a bounce in front of the dingy entrance, convincing me he could just as easily leap back up the ten stories to the rooftop. His bright orange-and-green back to me, he stepped toward the sleeping crowd, which was all bunched together in the middle of the street today like a pile of French fries. I stepped out onto the sidewalk and snuffed the glass door closed behind me as the suit shoved a handful of folded green bills into his big blue pockets and casually tossed the mayor's wallet back onto his pointing ass.

"The song I sing, the song I sing...," he began.

I stepped closer to the middle of the street, my bat reared back heavily, taking aim at the drooping, belled prongs of his purple hat.

"Is not to bring, is not to bring...," he continued, his voice casually talking the words rather than singing them.

"A sense of glee, a sense of glee..."

The suit turned slowly to face me, emphasizing the words with his fingers like a translator or a great storyteller on stage.

"To you or she."

My eyes watered uncontrollably from the up-close glow of the suit. My arms were pulled back, my batting stance frozen. I must have looked pathetic as he skipped circles around me.

"Are you getting all this? It's important to remember the words exactly," he said as he bounced behind my bat.

"It is to sleep, to put to sleep..."

With every easy step he took, the bells on his hat and feet jingled.

"The town and creep, creep, creep..."

When he made his way back in front of me, I swung the bat as hard as I could.

"Without a peep, peep, peep...," he continued, unfazed.

I swung three more times, madly, his orange-and-green suit, yellow sleeves, red feet, purple hat, and blue pockets focused sharply in front of me each time, but somehow I missed, my thick body twisting around on itself awkwardly.

"Your money I keep," he finished, stopping his apparent dodging with a gallant bow.

I swung one last time, my old body stumbling onto the pile of sleeping people in the middle of Whirl-A-Way Avenue. I pushed myself off of a bike messenger and one of the mayor's black-suited bodyguards.

"You're the son of the Dos Payasos," I stammered.

"Nope," he replied, plucking the sequins off an ugly hat.

My bat clunked off the concrete as I helplessly let it go and walked toward the suit, his glow under the night sky somehow becoming more bearable.

"A brother, a younger brother. You're a younger brother bitter that the town turned its back on the Payasos after they disappeared and abandoned us. You—"

"I'm the Jester King!" he interrupted. He back-flipped, balanced on his pinkies and laughed. A gust of wind picked up as he began again.

"The song I sing, the song I sing..."

"No...you're a thief...a common thief with a trick," I accused.

The suit practiced his flips, landing on a different part of his body every time.

"You really are going to have to let go of your logic if this is gonna work," he said, sitting Indian style, upside down, balanced on the three prongs of his purple hat. "I'm the Jester King! The Dos Payasos are dead," he continued, lying in midair, resting on one elbow.

"True, they had a third brother. He may have been the originator, but..." He settled all of his weight on the tip of his nose. "...that was like five jesters ago. Do you know how much time passes when time stops?"

The suit stuck out his tongue, pressed his body up higher, extended his arms like an airplane and muttered something unintelligible.

Bouncing to his feet, the suit landed at my side. My wallet appeared between his white-gloved fingertips and rested on my shoulder. He turned us around to view the sleeping crowd in the middle of Whirl-A-Way Avenue. I snatched my wallet and knocked away his slithery grip.

"Two days ago you left that at home, and your wife was concerned about you," he said. "That was the only time, though. She really likes those soaps."

"It's wrong," I said, putting the wallet in my back pocket.

"I didn't have a choice," he retorted. "Neither do you." The wrinkles beneath his eyes and his sagging cheeks came into focus for the first time.

"How long have you been here?"

"Your time? One month. Unstopped time..." he paused and looked at the ground, then quickly snapped his arm down, and the flute slipped from his sleeve and into his hand.

"It's best to work from town to town, so they don't go too dry. One month is long, but I knew this was my last stop. Particularly, when you didn't come out the other day. I mean, that's generally how it works. I was a straggler. You were a straggler. There'll be a straggler," he said, fondly caressing the flute.

I scanned the pile of sleeping people for an unfamiliar face or someone I wouldn't mind stealing from. The cops maybe. The bike messengers. But even them I've served. My eyes fixed on Jaime draped on top of Jo-Jo, the two of them forming a comfortable T, and I imagined the elder brother shoving his younger brother off, pushing his face in a half-conscious effort to keep their constant argument alive.

I shook my head side to side.

"And Yolli, my wife? My restaurant...?"

"Maybe it'll be here when you return. Where do you think I'm going?"

The man beneath the jester suit tossed the shiny flute into the air. It twirled and spun like a baton. One month. Thirty days. That meant twenty-seven times I was a victim. Probably caught me on days I walked or was late. No wonder business had been so bad.

I wanted to reach out and catch the falling flute. It glowed seductively like a sparkler in the night sky. But instead it hit me in the chest and dropped into the diving hand of the man in the suit.

"What're you trying to kill me?!" he yelled to me as the sleeping pile of people began to stir. The sky was starting to lighten, and I took two steps back away from him.

"Think of all the money!" he yelled, lying on the pavement, then snapped his fingers and handfuls of green bills swam across the air from his pockets to mine.

"Think of the prestige!" he grinned and vanished.

His distant voice projected from the rooftop of Los Dos Payasos. "Think of the jail time!" And then he laughed.

The mayor slowly opened his eyes. The police and the mayor's black suits awoke next. My pockets were bulging with stolen money and jewelry that was impossible to hide.

I felt the music begin in the pit of my stomach and march slowly up my throat.

"The song I sing, the song I sing..."

My foot began to tap.

"Is not to bring, is not to bring..."

My burly hips swiveled.

"A sense of glee, a sense of glee...

Jo-Jo shoved Jaime off him, with two hands to the face.

"To you or she."

The wind began to pick up, and I heard bells jingling from my hat and feet.

"It is to sleep, to put to sleep..."

The police began snapping pictures of me.

"The town and creep, creep, creep..."

I wiped the sweat from my forehead, the mayor's black suits walking towards me.

"Without a peep, peep, peep..."

And then, suddenly, a flute slipped from inside my puffy yellow sleeve and into my white-gloved hand. The crowd of ants far below me gasped as if I'd plucked it from midair.

"Your money I keep."

A skinny man swimming in my *guayavera* and holding my sagging pants up by the belt line opened the door to the stairwell and scurried down a flight of stairs into Los Dos Payasos. I played the flute until the day went black again and the people below me slept. And then I abandoned them and went on to the next town.

In time, I learned to flip and stand on my hands, and regained some of my youth. But the day has yet to come that I don't miss my Yolli, the restaurant, Jo-Jo, and Jaime. And so I'll just keep spinning into a rainbow blur, the jingle of the three-pronged hat vibrating in my teeth, until the morning I can find someone who refuses to come outside and listen to the music.

# *Miz Eve*

## *Carmen C. A. Lloyd*

Miz Eve was tall, dark, slim, neat as a pin, and clean—whew! At first glance, one might mistake her for her grandmama, Mae. They both had the same dusky dark hue, but Eve's skin seemed to shine with a dim radiance that held a narrow corona of light above its darkness. Mae had been a slave. She had a reputation for being well liked because she kept to her business, kept herself and her things in order, and was smart enough to eventually buy her own freedom, plus the Master had a sweet tooth when it came to dark meat, and Mae was the darkest he had at the plantation. Eve did take after Mae in other ways. First of all, she had a magnetism to the men that was unshakeable. If your man got a whiff of Miz Eve up his nose, wasn't nothing you could do, short of roots, t'hold him. But Miz Eve was different from Mae in this respect: she didn't go with no married man. That got the women respect'n her and not fear'n her; and while not exactly on friendly speaking terms with Eve, they did acknowledge her with a wave or a nod, for many also secretly admired her for being able to hold her own in a man's profession—moonshining. But they did not know the tragic story behind how she had learned that profession.

When Miz Eve had been seventeen, she lay around in the juke houses and wasn't bothered much, since she went in dressed like a boy. She was so tall, five feet ten, and her hair so short, she easily passed. She wore old coveralls two sizes too big in order to hide her breasts and an old cap pulled down to hide her face as she sat in the shadows. An older man approached her one evenin', telling her he had a truck of shine to unload, promised her a whole bottle if a big strong-looking lad like him would lend a hand. Eve looked up into a face that was smooth and unlined except for his forehead, which reminded her of weathered tree bark because of all the crinkles. He was a nice, even-toned, reddish-brown color, like the Alabama clay after a rainfall. He was probably about two inches taller than she was and sturdily built; she figured he was past thirty. She had been smelling a slight odor that came off his clothes that told her he smoked a pipe. The total combination of his being was not unpleasant to her and she did not feel in any danger. She nodded and followed him. They unloaded the truck in record time. Impressed, he offered his hand and asked the boy his name. Eve tried to lower her voice, and told him "Edwin." The man, who was no fool—couldn't afford to be in his game—recognized there was some perpetratin' goin' on. So it was that Lucas Colter recognized the perpetrator's gender. He invited her back to his cabin for a drink. He was intrigued with her situation, plus he wanted a little company this evening, and a female, even one in disguise, would be a welcome guest. Eve panicked, scared to be alone with a man; but she was also scared to arouse suspicions, so she accepted. Lucas sensed her hesitation and promptly produced the whisky as promised and a crisp five-dollar bill. Eve was elated and felt that maybe this could become a full-time job. She piled in the back of the old truck, letting the wind blow in her face.

Now old Lucas Colter wasn't so old; it was just that Miz Eve was quite young. Lucas was thirty-nine and counting. He had been on his own since his wife had died in '23, and except for the occasional whore, he didn't keep female company. Lucas was too busy building his empire. He had been dirt poor when he was a young'un and didn't intend to be that way again. His people, who were originally from Mississippi, had persistence and strong backs, and so were able to eke out an existence. But because they were not skilled at much, their subsistence was meager.

When he was a boy, his mother had passed along to him her talent for brewing a beer that was real potent out of sweet potatoes. What his daddy and brothers didn't drink up, sometimes she sold. And Lucas noted early on that no matter what price his mother asked, up or down the scale, folks had no difficulty coming up with it. So he deduced, at an early age, the laws of supply and demand. He was the youngest son and so his mother always would call him to peel the potatoes; tedious work, she said, but someone had to do it. For a reward, she'd give him some of the money—only a nickel, but to Lucas, it was a fortune. So he quietly peeled the potatoes, which jumped up out of the red Alabama clay like somebody had put a stick of dynamite in each hill. They humped up underneath the dirt and when ready, split the cone-shaped hills open, splaying out of their beds in a five-fingered fan shape. Lucas simply closed his eyes and dreamed of being rich one day, selling sweet potato beer. He sat and peeled pecks of potatoes for his shrewd mother...for it was her enterprise that kept them all from starving. As the memory of his mother faded, dumping him back into the present, all alone now, his mother long gone, dead and buried, he pulled up into a small yard somewhere in White Sands. The black Model-T Ford gave a little shudder and coughed once before dropping into silence, some twelve miles from Decatur. He hopped out, slammed the door, and beat on the hood of the truck as he walked away toward the small house. It was dark and Eve couldn't see, but she had the impression of a well-kept yard. She could smell several kinds of flowers as she approached, and feel that the pathway to the door had been leveled and hard packed. They walked up onto his one-step porch. A misty rain had begun to fall and Eve shivered. Lucas called over his shoulder, "Come on in, son, and I'll have the fire up and going in a minute." Eve hurried in and shut the door. Lucas threw her a blanket and told her to wrap up, so she wouldn't catch "his" death. "I got a bottle of cod-liver oil on the top shelf over here if your blood is thin. Won't do to begin a new job sick."

"I ain't never been sick a day in my life, mister," Eve boasted, "and I don't like cod-liver oil. Anyway I got me a bottle, that'll do jus' fine." She patted the whisky in her coat pocket. (Eve forced every syllable to be monosyllabic, hoping for what she felt was a young boy's voice.)

The man said, "Call me Lucas. And what might your name be?" At this point the fire was going strong, and Lucas stood stock still, a twinge of amusement flitting across his face, as he noticed the girl hesitate and frown.

"They call me..." she broke, started again, "I'm Ev...Everette." That had been her daddy's name. That ought to serve as good as any in this instance.

"Everett, who yer people?" Lucas all but laughed out loud, remembering that the first name she'd given him in the bar had been Edwin. But the test had left no doubt that he had a ringer on his hands.

Eve bristled. "What you want to know for? We come here to drink and discuss business or jaw-jack all night? I got places to go."

Lucas's laugh was strong and sweet (and totally uncalled for, Eve felt).

What was so funny? she wondered, looking down at her clothes to make sure everything still looked proper. Lucas noticed her gaze and followed it. He became aware of the swell of breast underneath the front pocket of the old coveralls, and shook his head as he turned back to the fire. If he wasn't careful she'd guess something was up and be out of there faster'n you could say, "Got the blues." Yep! She was a wild one for sure. He cleared his throat and replied quietly, "Just trying to be neighborly."

Eve looked away sourly. She located the front door again, guessed where the kitchen might be, and in turn, the bedroom. She had to go pee, and she wasn't looking forward to anybody's outhouse—too many snakes out here in the boonies. "You got an inny or an outhouse, Mister Lucas?"

"What I got is a back porch stall, help yourself," he said, motioning to a back door, half covered by a hung sheet that divided the side of the room they were in from his private sleeping quarters.

"Thank you much," Eve said, and almost sprinted toward the opening.

"There's an extra pail of water for flushing," he said, as she dashed past.

Eve went past him and out the back door, onto a little wooden platform porch. The walls were half walls, just high enough to provide privacy, just low enough to allow you to look out and see the stars dancing overhead. Lucas had painted the rough boards on the inside white, and there was a pail of fresh water for flushing as promised. The area was clean as a whistle, and he had devised a sitting area, squared off and boarded, with a smooth opening in the middle for doing your business. No perching your ass in the air holding onto the sides of the stall for support and hoping not to fall in, no couple of loose boards laid across a half-cut metal drum, you praying the edges would not be sharp enough to cut you. This was a first-class operation.

Eve completed her task and returned toward the front of the house. She couldn't figure this old man out. He seemed cultured in some way she was not, nor anyone she knew except a few middle-class colored folks who had real houses. As she passed his bedroom, she expected to see a tick mattress strewn in the corner and maybe a couple of good quilts if he was lucky, laid on some low platform kind of bed. Instead, she saw a big black bed—ebony from the look of it. Her mama had had an ebony bed, but nothing like this one. The headboard arched between two tall armsteads, one on each side going on up the wall; hoisted between the arms was an oval pallette, with a smaller oval in the center. The center turned out to be a piece of mirror, but colored like the windows in a church. The oil lantern on the bedstead had been turned up, warmly glowing, and the jewel-like glass called to Eve to take a closer look before passing on by...so she did.

She walked to the bed and gently touched the gold piece of glass that formed the center of what turned out to be a flower. There she stood in the dead of night in a strange man's bedroom, touching his bed and letting her soul take flight as she discovered something new and beautiful. Tears spilled from her open eyes. She felt joy at the artistry of the glass and wonderment that every color she'd ever seen at sunset was captured in the exquisitely detailed field of flowers and the little sun hovering at the meridian of its own arc, in its own sky.

Lucas walked in at that exact moment with the plate of warm catfish and grits in his hand. He thrust it at Eve, who took it without a word and began to eat, still keeping her eyes pinned to the headboard flower. After she finished, he left to empty the plates. By the time he returned, Eve was fast asleep in his bed.

And that's where she stayed for almost a year, her in the bed, him on the sofa. She revealed her true self to him the next day and they became fast friends. They divided the work equally. She sewed, he cooked. While she tended the garden, he worked on the truck. He taught her the moonshine business, and they had great talks and adventures together. One day the talk turned to marriage. They decided that a small ceremony at the house, in the yard, without any great announcement and hoopla would be enough, a few friends and a little sit-down dinner afterwards. Eve could no longer remember having viewed Lucas as an old man. His skin was rich and satiny. He wore a little mustache that was touched with a hint of sun-bleach. He had steady dark brown eyes and dimples the size of purple plums. His hair was kept cut close and was soft to the touch. He pressed his jeans until they had knife-sharp creases, and his boots always had a shine. Eve liked that he smelled all the time of hickory, because of the stills he tended, and at other times like the essence of his pipe tobacco—Bull Durham—which reminded Eve of the smell of blackberries. His touch was sure and knowing; he taught her about desire. His heart was good and pure; he taught her about love—but he said he would not have sex with her until they were wed, out of respect. Eve prepared her gown, her hope chest, her menu. They invited their small group of friends, and the day was set.

Lucas had seen a special piece of glass when he was in Louisville delivering a load of his homemade hooch. He'd paid the hundred dollars deposit the white man had asked and was told he could pick it up the day before his wedding. He had kissed Eve good-bye that morning, vowing to return by dark. He kept his promise. The two Negroes that brought his body to the door that evening were father and son. They told Eve that they had found him clutching the broken, stained-glass picture to his chest and saying her name over and over. They claimed they'd found him somewhere along the Ohio River where they normally did their fishing. They were from Louisville, but they had felt bound to bring this man home.

　　Lucas had such a fierce determination to live, to see Eve, that they thought "fer sure" he'd make it. But he hadn't. They hauled him in and laid him on the dining table. Eve was standing in the middle of the room, not moving or speaking. The man and his son, whose names Eve did not ask, wanted to leave, antsy about the long, dark ride home. They did not tell her that they had witnessed the execution.

　　Four white men had followed Lucas's truck out of the high-rent district where he delivered his hooch. The restaurant Lucas had made his delivery to was a favorite of several of Louisville's less savory element. These were men who could afford the price of a drink and a good steak, whereas many could not, and so long as they were not boisterous, they were tolerated. But these fellows were what Eve's folks would have called low-ranking, no-account, mean-living people, and as such, should be watched out for—much as one would watch out for a cottonmouth along the side of a river or under an old rotted stump. But Lucas, in his happiness, in his feeling for once like a man in control of himself and his destiny, like a man in love, had forgotten this one time to watch out—for himself and his future. He did not take a shadowy or low profile, but instead walked into the artisan's store and picked up his package, bold as day, and walked out. One of the men in the restaurant had seen his actions through the large, plate-glass windows; Lucas's eyes looking right into that other man's eyes, not down at the floor like a good nigger; Lucas not even standing back to be waited on last, until after the whites cleared the store, but walking straight on up to the counter and announcing his purpose, to pick up his wedding present to his bride. Lucas had gently examined the glass before having it wrapped up. Eve would be thrilled. The picture depicted a great tree with a golden sun setting in the background. Clouds floated and birds dove just beyond the tree's outstretched limbs. Lucas smiled, paid the balance for the stained glass and shook the man's hand.

　　The four men who followed him along the one-lane highway out of Nashville had taunted him with his actions before they shot him in both kneecaps and cut off his penis. "You ain't no man. You just a nigger! And you ain't never gonna bring no more like yourself into this world, hear me, boy?!" one of them shouted. "Your woman gonna need a real man soon, boy.... Maybe we ought to pay her a little visit. You sho' can't help her out now." They left him there to die, lying in the weeds of the riverbank's edge, but not before one of them put his heel through the wedding gift package.

The father and son who had witnessed the murder from their hiding place carried him out and carted him home. They had seen and would never forget every rotten, inhuman gesture of the men. How they had run Lucas's old Ford into a ditch and then jumped in and dragged him out. How Lucas had hit his head on the steering wheel and was semiconscious. How they had pushed him off the highway toward a road the locals used to drive in close to the river. How the smell of pokeweed, red clover, wild blackberries, and wild onion came to them, mixed with the smell of mud, manure, piss, and blood.

Though the man and his son had not told Eve anything at all of what they had witnessed, the condition of the body spoke for itself. The rope burns where the white men had tied him up, hands and ankles together behind his back, were still evident on his body. His body had arched backwards until he looked like the reel of a rocking chair. With his chin and chest clear of the ground, they had aimed kicks at his head and chest until the one who was wearing steel-toed shoes heard a sharp snap along the rib cage. This seemed some kind of insane signal and then they really poured it on. Lucas's chest caved inward, the left side of his jawbone dissolved, and his left eye leapt from its socket. The teeth in his lower jaw exploded outward, as did half in the top part. That's when they turned him over and castrated him.

The hiding man had grabbed his young son's shoulders, pulling his son's face into his own chest to shield him from the sight. The boy had gone limp and his father feared he had fainted. He was not a young man anymore and wondered what he would do if they were discovered—he could not possibly run with the dead weight of his son in his arms.

But as suddenly as the four whites had started, they stopped. They bayed at the moon, pissed on Lucas's mutilated carcass, and sloshed whisky on him. For a minute they thought to burn the body, but seemed not to care to obliterate their act in any way. Finally, they piled back in their truck and sped away.

Slowly, the witnesses—old father and young son—disengaged from each other's arms. Tears stained the old man's shirt and his son's eyes rolled wildly in his head. But the man explained to his son that they had a duty to see this man safely home, so he could die or be buried in peace. He instructed his son to stay back while he checked to see if Lucas was dead or alive, but the boy clutched his father's hand and shook his head no. They loaded him into their truck along with a long package they found, leaving his old truck to act as some discarded monument. One-half mile from home, when Lucas realized that Eve was within reach, he died, feeling totally powerless in the depths of his soul—powerless to protect her, powerless to love her as she deserved, powerless even to father her children. He touched the glass picture to his lips, kissed it, and died alone in the back of the strangers' truck.

Eve left their home that night. The only thing she took with her was the broken stained glass that was to have been her wedding present and the money they had stashed away over the course of a year. She had washed his body, preparing him for burial. She had cut away the soiled and bloodied clothes from his body and burned them. She even burned his shoes, the leather soaked from his blood. She washed his face gently and kissed the closed lids of his eyes—even though one was so bloodied and swollen from his beating that it resembled a baseball painted red and black and glued onto the spot where an eye should exist on a human being; it kind of hung there, obscuring half of his face. Even then, Eve had not uttered a word or a cry. She then went to a tall chiffarobe and got his wedding suit. It was dark blue and had darker blue lines running in wide shadow-stripes vertically; the lining was white silk to match the white tie he was to have worn. The shirt was robin's egg blue and had a pocket handkerchief to match. His shoes were black Johnston & Murphy's, and his hat had been special-ordered from Speakes and Speakes, down on Fourth Avenue S.E. near the L&N Railroad shops.

The man who had brought the body home had sent his son out to sit a while, and he helped Eve struggle Lucas's body into the clothes. He had cried then, but Eve worked quickly and silently. They laid him out on the huge wooden kitchen table, and Eve covered him with one of the white embroidered sheets from her bridal bed. Eve thanked the man and boy for all their help. For a while, they just stood there on the porch looking at each other without saying a word. Finally, the boy hugged Eve around the waist, but she only stood immobile, looking out toward the direction the moon was setting. When the man and the boy left to go home, Eve lit a torch and burned the small house to the ground. Lucas had not needed a monument to his life, and Eve did not want an empty reminder of the life she almost had. In the flames, Lucas's ebony bed burned slowly. The oval glass heart of it cracked from the fire, superheated, finally exploding outward in a shower of tiny colored splinters.

# Why There Are Stars

*Pauline York*

We toasted so hard that we almost broke our longnecks.
"CHEERS!" I ripped a huge belch that reverberated in my rib cage, and J.T. wiped it off his shirt.
"Damn...good tha-a-a-ng it's all liquid."
The bar had closed long ago, but our party continued in a plastic cubicle etched with gang-related artwork and numbers to call for a good time. We were waiting for a cab. The people of the night who used the nearby pay phone for quick fixes and free quarters watched J.T. and me with equal caution.
I was fairly juiced, but not half as blitzed as J.T., who had sat next to me at the Starlite Cafe for the last four hours kicking back malt liquors as if he didn't know what malt liquor did to him. Aside from making him increasingly horny—not that it mattered much to me because I was virtually embalmed with strawberry margaritas, which by experience were due to kick in at any moment so I wouldn't feel nothin' anyway—he just gets to *talkin'* and *talkin'* about stupid shit and he doesn't ever shut up, which is why I go ahead and just fuck him so he'll keep quiet long enough to pass out. But he don't ever make no sense; he gets so silly.

My ass felt like it was fusing to the concrete bench as I tried to get my right and left lines of vision to untangle themselves. J.T. took the liberty to stretch out across the bench, spreading out his sloppy hair in my lap. Under his breath he kept rumbling these throaty little pointless chuckles while staring up at the night sky.

"Lookit, baby...," he cooed. "The stars're shinin'."

I looked up in an effort to see what he saw, but the piss yellow hue from the streetlamp began to singe my woozy corneas. I think he was shittin' me.

"I don't see nothin'...you're stinko...quit makin' stuff up."

"There are stars...whoa," he tried to roll over and nearly tumbled off the bench. "You see 'em now? Look up! Up!"

He thrust his palm under my chin and forced me to look up. I still didn't see nothin', but played along so he'd stop choking me.

I patted him on his gurgling stomach. "Yeah, they're pretty."

"Purr-dee," he repeated, snaking a hand up the back of my blouse. "You know 'bout them stars?"

"What about stars?" I yawned.

As he groped my back, hoping to unhook my bra, he explained his theory. Thankfully, my bra unhooked from the front; it'd take him awhile to figure it out.

"Stars," he began, trying his hardest to sound somewhat PBS-ish, "started billions and zillions of years ago...the devil made 'em."

My ears perked up. "Really?" I asked, almost embarrassed to be a tiny bit intrigued.

"Yep," he replied, taking a moment to swallow back what he burped up. "One day God was walkin'—"

"Wait a sec—I thought you said the devil made stars?"

"I'M GETTIN' TO THAT!" He slapped playfully at me with his free hand. "Boy, you got an industrial latch back there, eh?" he asked of my underwear.

"Yeah, now go on."

"'K. One day God was walkin' 'round in Heaven rubbin' his hands together an' shit, complainin' 'bout how cold it was. God said, 'Goddammit, I'm God! Why is it so cold here? Why can't I make it warmer?' But he couldn't do nothin' about it. After he made the world with all them animals an' dinosaurs an' planets an' shit, he didn't have no room left to put Heaven anywhere 'cept way up there where it's cold—he'd painted himself into a corner."

I wrinkled my nose at him. "How the fuck you know it's cold in Heaven?"

A cab pulled up, but J.T. waved it on. "'CAUSE IT'S COLD!" he shouted, his voice echoing off an adjacent building. "Mountains got snow on top, right? Snow falls from up there...an' ice."

"True."

"An' angels're always wearin' them stupid-ass robes an' flyin' 'round—they probably are flyin' around jus' tryna keep warm. Why do you think people are always seein' ghosts an' angels down here? IT'S COLD UP THERE!"

It made sense.

"OK, go on."

"An' so while it's so cold in Heaven—the devil's havin' all the fun." After removing his paws from my shirt, he began to count the favorable points of hell on his newly warmed fingers. "You got your rock 'n roll, you got your sex, you got your malt liquor, you got your fire all over...baby, we gotta go to hell for sure!"

He sounded almost excited.

"That's a real nice thing to say, Johnny."

He didn't hear me. "'Cept it's re-e-e-al hot down there, but the devil don't really care 'cause he's the devil. Anyway, he got all that fi-i-i-re an' chicks an' booze an' Jimi Hendrix...I bet Elvis is down there too—that's why ain't nobody sure where he is, didn't no one look down there."

"This is gettin' fucking retarded," I soured. "Let's go home, it's three in the morning."

"NO, WAIT!" he pleaded, as if I could get up with his intoxicated skull in my lap like a sack of lead. "I AIN'T FINISHED!"

"OK, hurry up. But I'm goin' to bed after this, so don't even think about gettin' any."

He began to chuckle aimlessly again. "You're cute...now where was I?"

"Satan and Hendrix are sittin' by the fire passin' a bottle of malt liquor."

"Oh ye-e-e-ah...so with all that fire an' stuff—an' chicks an' rock 'n roll—he has a lotta parties. Barbecues an' stuff...got all that fire—might as well cook out, eh?"

"Whatever."

"You know, an' all that dancin' an' fuckin' an' carryin' on gets you pretty hot an' sweaty an' all—"

"But it's hell!" I laughed loudly, bouncing his head up and down on my legs. "You said it was hot before!"

"IT WAS A DRY HEAT—WORK WITH ME, BABY." He stared at me sternly until my silence assured him it was safe to proceed. "It gets stuffy down there under the dirt an' rocks an' stuff, an' with all that barbecue cookin', there's lots of smoke.... IT'S TRUE!" he insisted.

"Whatever."

"And so God hears all this feedbacky guitar and squealin' women and carryin' on when he's tryna sleep at night—and you can't imagine how cold it must get at night—not to mention that Heaven's so goddamn bright...they must wear them masks over their eyes when they sleep."

"Whatever."

"So God gets on the horn and calls the devil and he's like, 'Would you shut the fuck up down there, I'm tryna sleep—you know it's like, I can't hear my angels' harps or nothin', would ya keep it down?' And the devil's like, 'Sorry to wake you, bro. We're just sittin' 'roun' with some beers by the fire an' shit.' And God gets all jealous 'cause the devil's got barbecue and heat and he ain't got nothin' but rice cakes, and God forbid he gets any action up there 'cause you gotta watch yourself in Heaven." He took a breath to reload. "And God figures that him and the devil have been bickerin' all the time and they should try to get along—'cause he's God an' all—he's just tryna be nice. And so he's like, 'OK, Beelzebub, I swing you a trade...you send some heat up my way an' I'll get off your ass and give you an earthquake or tornado or somethin' now and then, 'cause I know how you like to get people all worked up and shit—but don't let on that it was me."

"I thought Mother Nature did all that?"

"Her an' God are sweet on each other—she does him favors."

"Oh...stupid me."

"An' so the devil says, 'OK, boss, got yourself a deal,' and he took that pointed tail of his an' poked all these holes in the sky, and that's what stars are—you can see Heaven through them holes at night. God got his heat—the devil can have his parties an' shit—they get along fine. Why you think they been so quiet all these years?"

"J...," I began slowly, "that is the dumbest fuckin' thing I've ever heard. Then what happens to the stars in the daytime?"

"Baby...the devil sleeps it off in the day. You don't fuck and drink malt liquor in the daytime! Why do you think liquor stores're open so late?"

"Whatever."

As we finally hailed a cab and headed home, the devil was getting ready to pass out in his own vomit.

# Notes From The Bottom Of A Bottle

*Kirsten Johnson*

Here is what I think happens—
We are at the bar having a few drinks. Seventy-five-cent beers are going down so smooth. I'm feeling good, getting a little drunk maybe. It's OK. We are from out of town and we want to have a good time.

I'm feeling so good—here's how I know I'm buzzed—I start making conversation with a group of cute guys who weren't even paying any attention to us. This is the most free I've felt in years—so simple—why can't it always be this way?

I'm still keeping track of my drinks—something like six or eight. Maybe ten, I don't know, but it's OK—I know what's going on.

We're tearing up the dance floor. I really want the blond guy, but he's dancing with my friend. OK, now he's dancing with me. This is good, I'm feeling good. I know I'm a little unsteady, but I'm doing just fine.

I'm dancing with another guy. We're out on the floor all by ourselves.

I go outside. I'm talking to one guy. Then I'm talking to another guy. Someone has a van. I can't remember what we talked about.

My friend takes me home, and I pass out.

Except what happens is—

I am in the back of the van with the one guy. There's beer cans and fishing rods and crap all over. It smells kind of damp and stale. Outside is the faint sound of laughter and gravel crunching under people's feet.

I don't see his face really. I'm looking at it, but I'm not really seeing it. I know he's there, and that's all I need to know. I don't pay attention to what he says—I don't care; I just lie down. He tries to kiss me, but I'm too sloppy, so he gives up.

He is on top of me, his hands are under my bra and grabbing my boobs. His hands move down and he starts to undo my jeans. I say, "What are you doing?" He doesn't say anything. I try to help with the jeans, but I'm just too out of it. I'm surprised that he gets them down with one quick yank. I hear the clinking metal sound of his belt being unbuckled. My eyes are closed, but I know what is happening here. I don't ask him if he has a condom. I'm kind of dry, so there's pain, but it's a dull kind of pain, far off, like everything else. I feel the scratchy carpet rubbing against my lower back. I'm thinking I should try to enjoy this, but I don't. I don't really care. I just lie there. Is this the blond guy?

The first time it happened, I had no idea that it *had* happened. I was only eighteen, and I had no fucking clue about this stuff yet. How stupid I was. At high school parties I looked on at the preppy suburban girls who got really giggly and stupid after a few beers, and most likely sick, and I felt a cold superiority over them all when I sat there with my pint of whiskey and drank it straight from the bottle in calm smooth swallows that burned and warmed. Here was my claim to fame, and no one had taught me how to do it—it just came natural. So I prided myself on the fact that I could drink a fairly good amount of hard liquor—straight, no less—without getting sick, and without getting idiotically drunk. This was how I started to attract guys' attention—how could they not be impressed? Of course, with a lot of them, I could tell from the way they looked from me to the bottle, and the way they looked at me when they drank from the bottle, well, their eyes became like the little windows on the slot machines, all lit up with me as the jackpot—which I enjoyed.

But that's all beside the point, because I wanted to talk about the first time it happened to me. I went to my work Christmas party at the country club. You should have seen me in my skintight, hot pink, leg-revealing little dress that I was so proud of, surrounded by uptight-looking bankers and their conservative-looking wives. After the party, my co-worker dropped his girlfriend off at home and then took me to a bar where I wouldn't get carded. I vaguely remember him taking me home and us getting high and making out in his red Mustang. It was just another night that I had gotten drunk, big deal.

Except the next day, my mom starts asking me how my night was, blah, blah, and then she says, "Why did you leave the kitchen like that?"

"Huh?"

"I said, why did you leave that mess in the kitchen?"

"What are you talking about?"

"The spaghetti in the strainer? The bread and crumbs all over the counter?"

"What?"

"The stuff you cooked when you got in last night!"

"I didn't cook anything!"

"You didn't cook anything?"

"No!"

"Well who did then?"

"I don't know, but it wasn't me."

"You didn't cook the spaghetti that was in the strainer?"

"No, I didn't cook any spaghetti! I didn't get in till late; why the hell would I be cooking spaghetti?"

"I don't know."

"Well, it wasn't me."

Except it was me. After some brilliant detective work on my mom's part, she figured out that I had had my first blackout. I didn't really believe what she told me, but I would have enough of them in the future to know exactly what a blackout was. A blackout was not the same as not remembering what you did; it was not a soft and hazy kind of forgetting. It was more like a sudden, sharp drop-off point into a big black hole in the middle of space—a total unknown. Like at a certain point, information that's supposed to be stored in your brain, well, it just decides to jump off a little cliff in there somewhere, and it's gone. You never get it back; it's a tape that's been erased—blank. You never played it, and you will never know what was on it. It's much more than not remembering; it's as if it never happened. The first few times it really freaked me out. My friends would say something about what I had done, and I would have no way of knowing what they were talking about. Sometimes I would ask them to retell what had happened the previous night, and I would be shocked and sickened at the amount of time that I could not account for. It got to the point where my friends would call me and I would say, "Don't tell me anything about last night! I don't want to know!" Or sometimes I would just say, "Did I do anything really bad?" If they said no, I was off the hook. But if they said yes, then I would have to ask what I had done even though I dreaded to hear it, even thought the words would make me queasy, and I would hang up the phone and curl into a little ball on my bed and try to forget about how much I hated myself.

The night before Christmas Eve, I drink a bottle of wine before we head over to the bar. I meet you there, someone I didn't even know in high school. I go home with you; you have a very large penis that you hammer away at me with. You drive me home and tell me, "Merry Christmas," and long after the anesthetizing effects of the alcohol wear off, I am left with a painfully throbbing vagina, the lips of which look like raw meat and are swollen to about three times their normal size, and I can't stop thinking about you all day.

Christmas Eve turns into Christmas Day, and day turns into night. Once again the girls go out but to a different bar, and I drink a bottle of wine and a bottle of champagne before we leave. I end up meeting another you there, and this you was the quarterback in high school or something—I know you played football—and we have to leave the bar because it's closed. You take me out back and tackle me on the cement stairs and pull my tights down to around my ankles and lift up my skirt, and my friend sees this and tries to pull you away from me, but she's having a hard time because I'm lying there with my legs spread saying, "C'mon, fuck me." You are just an animal at this point, the scent of your prey still filling your nostrils, so I don't know how she got us out of there. Maybe she took her hands and placed them on your protruding cock; maybe she made you believe you were going to get more than a girl passed out on the cement with her tights pulled down around her ankles.

After my dad died, my mother turned almost as cold and faraway as his gravestone. I felt that I could never get enough warmth from her. Can you imagine that she made a conscious decision not to be close to anyone, including me? That she thought somehow, by barring her heart against me, she would make me strong enough so that I would never feel the kind of pain she had felt? Well, instead of making me a tough shell that couldn't be cracked, I turned out to be a soft and sensitive sponge, absorbing everything, holding so much pain inside and converting all the rage I couldn't express into hatred of myself.

She went out a lot, drank a lot, and I learned to be self-sufficient. But there were certain things I couldn't do, like drive myself to school, so I had no choice but to be really late a lot of times. Being late for church days was the worst, though. When she would pull up to the deserted sidewalk, more than anything I just wanted to stay in the car with her. But instead, I made myself go in through the side entrance, not hearing my footsteps on the green-tiled stairs as only soft-soled shoes are allowed. At the doorway, I dipped my hand into the holy water, made the sign of the cross, and asked God to forgive me for being so late. The priest was already blessing the body and blood of Christ, and I felt I would die of shame as I knelt at the center aisle and crossed myself again. I started the long walk down the center aisle to my assigned pew, keeping my head bowed to the ground. I tried to keep my lunch box silent, but with the simple action of walking, the hinges on the handle still squeak. I can feel their eyes on me as I walk by. They must all be wondering what is wrong with me—no one comes to church late—let alone this late. I am so embarrassed and ashamed. I reach my pew after an eternity, but I feel like I will never escape all of those eyes. I am too young to receive Communion, and I remain kneeling with the missal very close to my face, pretending I need to see the words to the song, but actually trying to cover the tears welling in my eyes and falling in slow motion.

I remember that time we were leaving Grandma's and Mom ran over the curb and hit a No Parking sign.

And that time we came home and found our back door smashed in, and one of the front windows broken, and Mom said she knew it was Roy.

And then that one time when we were coming home, and Mom and he were fighting, and he pushed her, and she fell down and was lying in the middle of the alley, and I hated him with every fiber of my being at that moment and would have killed him then and there if I had known how.

 Lying in bed and listening to the two of them screaming at each other, hearing thumping and crashing, afraid that he would hurt her, hearing every foul word that came out of his mouth, every terrible name he called her pierced my skin like tiny painful arrows, and I hated him so much, I lay in bed and cried and clenched my fists, and whispered over and over, "I hate you, I hate you, I hate you, I hate you," until I fell asleep.

I watched Mom walk out of the garage and down the gangway to our back door—she was trying to walk straight, but couldn't. Her heels clicked down the sidewalk like gunshots in the early morning stillness, and I wished she would fall. I wished she weren't my mother.

One night, Mom dragged me out of bed and carried me downstairs to Auntie Gwen's apartment.

"Stay here," she said, her voice thick and strange.

"Mommy, where are you going?"

She kept walking away without saying anything, and I ran after her crying, "Mommy!" I grabbed onto her, and she pushed me away and like a robot in a stupor repeated, "Stay here," and left, and I was terrified that maybe she was not coming back.

It is New Year's Eve, but I have promised you I won't drink any hard liquor. You have asked me not to, and I tell you I won't because I love you, and because I don't want to embarrass you in front of your friends, and I don't want to cause any violent scenes like that one party we were at where I pushed you down a flight of stairs. I am determined to drink the watery wine coolers, but as the night wears on, the thought of drinking something more substantial is ticking away in my brain, and someone is passing around a bottle of Jager, and in one infantile moment of anger and need, I grab the bottle and chug from it like it was a bottle of water, and while I'm tilting the bottle up to the ceiling in defiance, and while the sickly-sweet syrup pours down my throat and my eyes are half-closed in ecstasy, I hear someone exclaim, "Holy Shit!" and when I put the bottle down, you are sadly shaking your head, and I know that once again, I have ruined my chance to make things up to you.

I empty the Excedrin bottle onto my bed, and count the number of aspirin by twos. There's about sixty altogether, and I separate them into groups of ten. With my right hand I place little groups of the aspirin onto my outstretched left palm. I need to do something drastic to make you listen to me, and I decide that this is a foolproof way to make you hear. But I stare at the white tablets on my palm for some time, knowing I am too scared to do it, and hating myself for being too scared, for being scared my whole life, and a voice in my head screams, "DO IT! JUST FUCKIN' DO IT!" And I do. I swallow them in groups of ten in quick succession, and for once in my life, I am in awe of myself; for once in my life, I know what it feels like to have control.

I wake up in bed with Taco Bell wrappers and hot sauce and say, "What the fuck?" I don't remember eating, and I have no idea that I finished off that bottle of Southern Comfort and screamed obscenities out of the car window the whole way home.

I wake up in an Indiana hotel room in a bed that feels like it has some sand in the sheets, and then something seems to be crunching underneath me, and I pull back the covers to reveal a bed filled with barbeque potato chips.

I wake up and have no idea where I am. From out of the murky depths I finally reach the surface and I am relieved when I see that this place is just as familiar to me as my own home. Except I can't think of how I got here, because you are not my boyfriend anymore. I remember being really drunk and calling you at your work, and I vaguely remember driving there to meet you, but I don't remember passing out in my car in the restaurant parking lot, and I certainly don't remember you hefting the dead weight of my body over your shoulder and putting me in the backseat of your car.

I wake up and I'm disgusted to see your face there—never in a million years—and I look down at my naked body and guess that you must have fucked me, and I feel like I'm going to throw up, and I thank God that I don't remember anything.

I wake up and realize that I am on the floor, and someone has covered me with a blanket. I am completely intact, frozen from the night before, everything still on—my clothes, my winter coat, my shoes, my gloves. I have to get home before my mom gets up and realizes that I broke my promise to her again. Once I'm in the car, I look at the clock and my heart sinks, because I know it's too late. When I finally reach my own bed, and when she comes into my room and starts telling me all the terrible truths about myself that I already know, and when I picture the guy at the bar who somehow had his penis inside me, who somehow had my back up against the stall of the men's bathroom, who somehow fucked me while a line of guys watched it, well that is when I finally start to wish for it to be over.

Five months later, I wake up in my own bed, with my underwear on and my shirt unbuttoned, but in the bed with me is my phone and my phone book, and then I remember that I was trying to make phone calls, and that I had started walking from the bar towards my house, which I'm sure I wouldn't have made it to, and someone stopped and asked if I needed a ride, and I said, "Yeah," and for the first time I got into a car with a complete stranger who could have driven anywhere he wanted to take me, but I ended up at home, in my own bed. I looked over at the dresser, and was shocked to see a corkscrew there. And that is when it finally hit me—there would never be enough booze for me. Even after all the drinking I had done that night, it had obviously been my intention to open a bottle of wine and drink even more, except that my body had shut itself off and passed out before I could get around to it.

A lot of times I felt really bad about my drinking, but through all the times it broke my heart, I still wanted it. I could be flopping around like a sick fish in the shower, puke running down my face, or someone's semen running down my leg, and still, I wanted it.

# *Penny Change*

*Doreen J. Berrien*

It's a cryin' shame about what happened to that chil' Penny. The po' thing was just downright scary to look at. And it ain't no sense in sugar-coatin' it, 'cause the truth is the truth and cain't nothin' be done about it.

Now when Penny was born, it just so happened that Aintee was there. Ya see, Aintee did a bit of midwifin' back in them days, so she got to see most everybody that was born in that neck of the woods. Some babies was just as cute as buttons from the time they poked they little heads through they mama's womb and some of 'em...well, they was just downright ugly. Like I said, ain't no sense in sugar-coatin' it, 'cause the truth is the truth and cain't nothin' be done about it.

Anyway, when Penny's head first started to crown as she was makin' her way out, Aintee noticed somethin' was different right off. Her hair didn't look right. She tried to act normal 'cause Penny's mama, Small Change, had been in labor for...ooh chil'...musta been about twenty-some hours by then. And she just wanted to get that baby out.

So now, when her head come through the womb, Aintee reached for it so's to kind of help keep her movin' on out of there. But when she went to touch it, her hands jumped right on back 'cause the baby had teeny tiny worms growin' outta her head. That's right, worms! Now Aintee had done seen some funny-lookin' heads pop outta wombs, but she ain't never seen no baby with worms growin' on they head. She hid her surprise of course, as best she could, and went on and helped Penny into this world. But things just got worse. The chil' had somethin' like alligator skin. It was kinda green and just as scaly as it could be. Ain't never seen nothin' like it.

Penny's mama and daddy was just plain 'shamed of that chil'. In fact, they was ready to swear her off as belongin' to somebody else, but seein' as how there wasn't but one baby delivered in they house on that particular day, they really wasn't in no position to deny her.

When people came by to see the baby, they always tried to wrap her up in a blanket and put a big ol' cap on her head and then claim that she was real sickly. One time, some of them stuck-up neighbors of theirs—name of Whitakers—come over to see the baby, and Penny was just so happy when Ms. Whitaker was bouncin' her on her lap that she reached up and pulled that woolen cap right offa her head. Ms. Whitaker dern near dropped the baby right on the floor when she saw all them worms squigglin' around. Lucky for them, Aintee was there to catch her, 'cause that Ms. Whitaker act like she needed some salts or somethin' the way she kept fannin' herself and carryin' on. Word got 'round town about Penny pretty quick after that.

The more Penny grew, the more her worms grew and the scalier her skin got. When her baby teeth come in, they wasn't right neither. All of 'em was short and pointed except for them four canines. They was real long, just like a vicious dog's teeth. Her folks was real 'shamed by then. They wouldn't even take her out so she could be 'round other chi'ren. Shoot, it got so bad that Aintee was the only friend she had. But she wasn't no kid so she couldn't play games and things like Penny wanted her to.

It wasn't long 'fore her daddy, Loose Change, built a room onto the back of the house for her, and most times that's where she stayed so nobody would have to see her. Aintee tried to come 'round every day or so and read to her. Penny loved to hear stories, she really did, especially that one 'bout Rapunzel. Guess Penny used to imagine that she was kinda like Rapunzel, 'cause she sho' nuff had a head full of somethin', but it wasn't no golden hair. Whenever Aintee read that story to her, Penny would be just atwistin' at them worms with her fingers.

Must say, them worms was very well behaved. They would curl up any way she wanted 'em to. Sometimes when Aintee would come to see her, Penny would have 'em all fixed up in Shirley Temple curls, or sometimes in a ponytail. Other times, she would put a part in the middle of her head and they would just lay down straight on each side.

One day Aintee dropped by, and shoot...Penny had to be 'bout fifteen by then, she had done braided them worms up into one big braid and was sittin' by the window, just like she was Rapunzel. Aintee didn't want to hurt her feelings none, but wasn't no prince gone wanna climb no stair of worms, so she just held her peace. Wasn't too long after that, though, when a small bird come flyin' in the window. Now them birds was somethin' Penny had to watch out for 'cause they had a tendency to wanna peck at her head. But this small bird come through and dropped a little note right in her lap, then he flew right on out, just the way he come in. Didn't stop for nary a nibble. The note read:

*Plant these seeds and you will behold*
*A beauty unmatched, a beauty untold.*
*When the sun rises, a petal from each you must eat,*
*Then share the beauty with all whom you meet.*

Next thing you know, here come another little birdie that flew right on in the window and dropped three little seeds right there in her lap. Then he flew on out, just the way he come in, and didn't stop for nary a nibble. Well, Penny and Aintee found a big pot, dug up some dirt, and planted them three little seeds.

The next day when Aintee come by, she could hardly believe her eyes. Them three tiny seeds had sprouted into the most beautiful rosebush you ever laid eyes on. Ain't never seen nothin' like it. This thing had rich velvety green leaves and three huge, gold rose blooms. Penny was just so happy, dancin' all around the room and carryin' on that she could hardly wait till the next sunrise so she could eat them golden petals.

Aintee stayed with her that night 'cause she didn't think the chil' was gone make it. They didn't sleep none for fear of missin' the sunrise. When the time came, Penny plucked a petal from each of them blooms and ate 'em. Them blooms wasn't hardly in her belly but a minute 'fore them worms just turned right into the silkiest, blackest locks of hair you ever did see. And all them canines she had, they turned into a perfect set of pearly whites. Next thing you know, them rough green scales of flesh started droppin' from her body to reveal skin like you ain't never seen. It was like a rich autumn chestnut color with just a touch of russet to it.

That chil' Penny had turned into nothin' but pure splendor. The girl was just gorgeous. And she had a glow about her, too. Couldn't no man or woman look at her without bein' caught up in her beauty.

Needless to say, the girl's life changed all the way 'round. She had peoples callin' on her all the time. Her mama and daddy started draggin' her 'round to all they friends' houses. Of course, now they was real proud of their little Penny Change. She had plenty of girlfriends and boyfriends too, all vyin' for her 'tention. Even them stuck-up Whitakers called theyself tryin' to get close to her by makin' some cakes and cookies and sendin' 'em over to the house. Shoot, pretty soon Penny had got so many new friends that she ain't hardly have time for no old woman like Aintee hangin' on her. But Aintee wasn't gone leave her. She knew Penny was gone need her sooner or later.

One mornin' Aintee got out real early so she could be sure to see Penny 'fore all them new friends started comin' 'round. Right away when she got there she noticed how them blooms on that rosebush was kinda losing their glow.

"Penny," she said. "I think it's somethin' wrong with these blooms, chil'. Where's that poem that them birds sent you? I think it must be somethin' else that you s'pose to do."

"Like what? I ate the petals like I was supposed to and now I'm beautiful. Aren't I?" Penny asked admiringly to the mirror.

"Well, of course you're beautiful. I can't deny that," said Aintee.

"And I'm certainly sharing myself with everyone I meet," Penny announced as she whirled herself around.

See, the po' chil' had done mistook vanity for beauty. All them folk that was runnin' up behind her done got her all swole up in the head and she wasn't even thinkin' right no more.

"Penny, when it say for you to share the beauty," Aintee reasoned. "I think they was talkin' 'bout the beauty of the blooms, honey, what you got hidden deep in this little room and what's in yo' little heart. I think that's what that mean."

"Oh, don't be silly, Aintee. I mean...of course the blooms are wonderful, but I can't share them! I've got to keep them to myself just in case—heaven forbid—I have some sort of relapse. I can't let all those people see the blooms. They'll want to eat of the petals, and then...then there might not be anything left for me."

Well, Aintee tried to tell her, but she wouldn't listen to no old woman. Got to the point that she didn't even have much time for Aintee no more, 'cause she got to runnin' round with all them high-class folk that wouldn't give her the time of day when she had that head full of worms.

Guess you 'bout know what happened next. Wasn't too long 'fore them three golden blooms just shriveled up and died. Little Miss Penny's gorgeous skin turned right back into them green alligator scales, just like she had before. And them pearly whites turned right back into canines.

It's such a shame, but them silky black locks turned right back into worms. But this time they was the meanest bunch of worms you ever did see. They wouldn't never behave like they used to. Some curled up, some curled down, some squirmed left, while others squirmed right; they was just everywhere. And if she went to touch 'em, they'd try to bite her fingers right off. The birds wouldn't even try to peck at 'em. Like I said, ain't no sense in sugar-coatin' it, cause the truth is the truth and cain't nothin' be done about it.

# *Lilliputian Jesus—Manufactured In Italy*

*Holly E. Conley*

Camille, a forty-two-year-old woman in the final stages of the breast cancer that had ravaged her body and usurped her living, came to hospice on a Saturday morning in January, smiling and calm. "I've come here to die," she announced in the moments just after our introduction, as her husband, Louis, a worn-looking man with silver hair, lifted her tenderly from her wheelchair and tucked her into bed.

Camille was a small Oriental woman, only four feet nine inches tall. Her voice was given in whispers, as if it were stuck somewhere between her lungs and her larynx or was coming from across a vast open space, and I had to strain my ears and read her lips to make out what she was saying at times.

"I'm going to die in this bed...in this room," she clarified.

"Are you afraid?" I asked.

As a human being, as a hospice nurse, I had to ask this question. If *I* didn't ask it, who would? Would a suffering husband ask of his dying wife, "What are you afraid of most?" without breaking down? Could an aching mother ask her dying child what he or she feared most about dying without succumbing herself? And yet the dying patient may need to talk about fears, misgivings, anger —may need to know that someone is listening earnestly, reflectively, to his or her final words and thoughts. To this dying patient, I could deliver two important comfort measures. First, a river of narcotics to relieve the physical pain; and second, a bit of my own human nakedness in an attempt to connect with and soothe a languishing soul. Time and time again during my days and nights in hospice, I would settle myself into a chair near the head of the bed and begin to peel away my own facade. Away with the false smile; away with concerns about checkbook balances, dinner menus, weekend plans, laundry; away with, temporarily, the picayune details that make up the days of my suburban life. I would strip myself to the skin, to the breastbone, and summon the courage to hear the truth.

When I was finally naked before Camille on that winter day, watching her concentrate on getting oxygen from the little green tubes resting just inside her nose, only one question seemed important. Was she afraid to take her last breath? Afraid of what came after?

The fragile woman in the bed reassured me, as dying patients often have, that there was nothing to fear. She asserted that she was at peace with her God and was prepared to meet him in heaven. As she talked, she fingered a rosary of translucent, pale turquoise beads. Her hands were tiny and very white, the tips of her fingers bluish from lack of circulating oxygen. Feeling helpless, I brushed away a wayward wisp of black hair that had been glued to her forehead by perspiration.

Louis, sitting quietly on the opposite side of the bed, squeezed his wife's frail hand and said, "I'm going to get some coffee, sweetheart. Need anything?"

"Go home," she told him. "Go take a shower and get some rest."

Louis smiled. "I'll be back in a bit," he said.

Camille looked over at me when he was gone. "This is hard for him. He's been sleeping in a chair for almost a week. He won't go home."

I reminded Camille that Louis was doing what he needed to do to deal with his impending loss. "Maybe he's afraid he won't be here when you die," I told her. "He loves you. He wants to be here for you. He doesn't want you to be alone."

She was thoughtful for a few minutes and looked suddenly as if she might cry. Her lower lip quivered briefly, and she bit on it to make it stop.

"Would you hand me my makeup bag?" she whispered, pointing toward a gold-sequined bag on the night table beside us.

I placed the zippered bag on the sheet beside her and watched as she fished among glinting containers of blush, mascara, and lipstick, her pinkie running along the seams and into the corners, searching for some misplaced item. Was she planning to powder her diaphoretic nose?

But it was only Jesus—a miniature silver statuette of a weary savior, nailed to the cross at Calvary—that she rescued from the clutter of elixirs, balms, and tinctures.

"Stick him to the side rail," she told me and dropped the little God into my palm.

The skinny metal cross was supported by a circular magnet mount, and at the bottom of the cross, on the back, a single word was engraved into the pewter: *Italy*. I propped the Lilliputian Jesus on the side rail facing Camille, and together we began our vigil. It lasted hours and hours. It went on for days, a week, longer.

Each day, I grew more and more fond of Camille. She had been a nurse, like me, not long before I met her. Remaining true to our profession she did what she could to ease my difficult role. She made no demands and stressed her gratitude for the smallest palliative measures: ice chips, a turned pillow, a cool washcloth. Looking back now I can see that, emotionally, she was determined to mentor me. "Nothing to be afraid of," she'd tell me when I sat mute, holding her hand. "I am ready. God is with me. It's easier than being born," and here she would smile, as if she remembered her entry into living with fondness.

Intermittently Camille's husband, Louis, would venture absentmindedly to the rattling window and stare out at the arctic Chicago panorama. Frozen wind blasted in off Lake Michigan. It swept over Lake Shore Drive, careened around tall buildings, pummeled mummified pedestrians on the sidewalks below, and formed snowflake whirligigs as it convulsed through narrow alleys.

Indoors the air was dry and full of hair-raising static electricity. Throats and nasal passages became parched, and lips dried, cracked, and bled. The radiators that heated the ancient hospital rooms clicked and clanked and sputtered.

"How much longer?" Louis asked one evening when I had come to the window to stare at winter with him.

"You must be exhausted," I answered. *I* was exhausted.

He pressed the pad of his forefinger into the lacy seam of frost that had formed along the window edge and held it there for a long minute. He lifted the finger leaving a print in the ice and pressed it to his lips. "I need some Chapstick," he announced.

Camille declined by the hour. Nine days after her arrival she became disoriented and began to echo, "Forgive me, forgive me, forgive me...." I gave her extra morphine, hoping to ease her anxiety. I put the head of her bed up and gave her more oxygen. Her uneasiness continued. Why? What was distressing her? Had she suddenly, in her final hours, encountered something that frightened her? Something she had not addressed in prior days? Why was she fighting her departure?

"Camille?" I murmured into her ear, "Who are you talking to? What do you want forgiveness for?"

"My husband," she whispered back, breathlessly.

Her devastated husband, whose face was beginning to look windswept from so many hours at the winter window, bent over her and kissed her cyanotic lips. "I love you, Camille," he choked. He pulled a chair to the bedside and sat stuporous, waiting.

"Forgive me, my husband," she begged her spouse in confusion.

"Your husband?" I questioned. He and I exchanged inquisitive glances over the bedcovers. "Are you asking forgiveness from your husband or from God, Camille?" Surely it must have been God whom she petitioned.

She was laboring like mad to pull air into her lungs. Every protracted respiration spawned a chorus of rattling in her chest. "Yes," she faltered, "my husband. Forgive me, forgive me, forgive me...."

Louis, who sat aching and fatigued, inspected the tiny hand he was holding, then looked up at me. He was crying. I mouthed the words, "What for?" Did he know why she begged him for this ultimate pardon? Was she about to confess that she'd been unfaithful to him in some way? That he had not been her only true love?

He shrugged his shoulders, unknowingly. Finally, leaning over the side rail that supported the icon, the manufactured Almighty, he kissed his wife's cool, clammy forehead and said, "It's OK, Camille. It's me. I'm here, sweetheart. It's OK, I forgive you."

I try to imagine sometimes what I will be doing, what I will be saying or asking for, when my time comes. Will my loved ones be at hand? Will I be soliciting their pardon—their mercy? This thought, this obsession, has come to plague me in the months since I went to work in hospice. Is it possible that I—like so many other people, I imagine—will come to the end having *injured* most those people whom I have *loved* most?

Camille's pleading continued for another hour until she muttered, "Forgive," but didn't finish. She died midsentence—with her husband's bewildered but graceful absolution—and left me sitting, naked and perplexed, wondering why it is that we all have to die before we've settled unfinished business, said our last good-byes, kissed our children one last time, and arrived at a place where we can say without hesitation, "Take me now, I'm ready."

Death is so inconvenient. It's so clumsy, so heedless, so capricious. My friend, Janie, lost her only daughter, Allison, on a cool and sunny Sabbath, when the graceful blond coed went for a hike in the Smokies. While sharing the afternoon with the boy she loved, she slipped and fell sixty feet, headlong, into a ravine filled with muted, gray granite boulders. She crushed her skull, shattered the lives of the people who loved her, and vaporized a future. Barb, a forty-eight-year-old ER nurse and mother of six children, went home after working the graveyard shift with me one Friday night (she left work feeling excited about celebrating her grandchild's birthday later that afternoon), stepped into the shower, and dropped dead under the running water. An autopsy showed no foul play, no anatomic defect, no pathology. The speculation is that she died of a cardiac arrhythmia—a fatal, goose-stepping heartbeat. Could it be possible that she felt her heart begin to gallop, grew dizzy, and died naked, alone, and unprepared, while someone downstairs in her kitchen was icing a birthday cake, counting candles, and bristling with youthful anticipation? How can that be? Couldn't her fate have at least allowed for one more birthday party?

People die, like Camille, like Allison and Barb, in the middle of living. They die in the middle of sentences, in the middle of counting out change, in the middle of a morning commute on the freeway, in the middle of dinner, the middle of talking on the phone, riding busses, and making love. The lucky ones die in the middle of sleeping in the middle of the night.

Awhile back, in hospice, there was a young guy named Jerry with end-stage AIDS, room 1258, who died in the middle of a bowel movement. He was a red-haired kid of twenty-nine who loved pizza with anchovies, bright red lipstick, and *The Best of Queen* at full volume. One morning at half-past ten, he waltzed his IV pole across the carpet of his hospital room, entered the bathroom, and never came out. Two hours later, when his nurse went in to deliver his lunch tray, she tapped on the bathroom door. "Jerry?" she called. "Are you OK in there?" But he didn't answer.

When she opened the door, she found him sitting bolt upright on the toilet with his eyes open, and he was dead. He had been dead for some time, and rigor mortis had frozen him in a perverse mannequin's pose. At the moment his soul withdrew from his body, Jerry had been defecating and masturbating simultaneously. His fingers were still clenched around his penis and his navy blue sweat pants were bunched around his ankles.

The security guys were summoned to lift him from the toilet. Someone wiped his cold butt, pried his fingers away from his penis, and pulled up his britches. He was placed in his bed, pressed against his mattress until he was more or less supine, and made to look comfortable before his parents and his lover came to say a final farewell.

When I heard the story it made me smile. I did not find it at all offensive or morose. Rather, the profanity and irony of this man's death intrigued and bemused me. Why is that?

Sometimes, when I feel brave enough, I ask myself some really important questions. Questions like: What kind of person have I been so far? What kind of mother, wife, nurse or friend or citizen? How have I touched other people's lives—good or bad? And what, if any, contributions have I made to the earth and to the human race? It's very unsettling stuff. My boyfriend, a handsome guy nearing fifty (my third husband and I are divorcing) says that I am a true child of the sixties. A liberal, left-wing, bleeding-heart Democrat, just like him.

I'm not too certain about the child-of-the-sixties philosophy. I don't go around looking for causes. It's just that I'm curious.

Husband number three, a man who is also nearing fifty, tells me that I remind him of something he used to see when he was growing up on the farm. "It's like you always have a burr under your saddle," he says. My daughters, unfortunate victims of my insanity, have had to adapt to turmoil. Once in a while I catch in their faces a strange look that queries, *"Who is this woman?"*

This woman, I answer silently, is simply curious.

Like so many other investigations that I have conducted in my mercurial life, I went to work in hospice with a twisted need to stare at one of life's ingredients, death, as though I were staring at a prized work of art. Like some kind of warped fanatic, I wanted to see death in every light and in all of its many moods. I wanted to feel it, to smell it, to hear and taste it.

While working hospice, most of my patients and their families allowed me, invited me, and even welcomed me to take part in one of the most significant events of their lives. I've come away from these experiences enchanted and shell-shocked, realizing that, in fact, death is no uglier than birth.

Think about it. A newborn comes sliding into our world face first, foot first, or butt first through a torrent of blood and body fluid. It labors through the birth canal, in a mother's fit of constipated relief, with a mouthful of mucous. In a Caesarean delivery, the mother's abdomen is carved open and the infant is excised from the uterus like a stubborn tumor. Attendant fathers-to-be will often faint in the delivery room at the sight of so much gore. Yet (and why is this?) birth is very frequently referred to as having been beautiful, awe-inspiring, a cause for celebration, a miracle so divine that tears of overwhelming joy are shed. It truly is a "Kodak moment" and thousands of excited parents have begun a tradition of filming the event.

Why is it then, I wonder, that those same cameras are left at home when the terminally ill approach yet another of life's extraordinary events? When the dying are straining for that final bit of terrestrial air, why do we want to look away? Why does it frighten, appall, and repel us?

Before Camille's husband left her room on the day she died, I gathered up all of his wife's belongings, put them neatly into the suitcase in which they had arrived, and handed them to the man with these words: "She was a trouper, Louis. I'm glad that I had the opportunity to know her, even for a short time." He gently pushed the suitcase back at me, refusing it.

"No," he said, "I don't want these things. Everything I want from her is gone. Give them to someone who needs them." He stepped toward the window, looked out at the dismal winter sky, then turned and left without looking back. He teetered as he walked down the hall on wobbly legs—like a dizzy, first-time sailor disembarking from stormy waters—reeling, evidently, from so much heartache.

We washed Camille's tiny body, tied an identification tag around one of her big toes, encased her corpse in a white plastic shroud (the plastic is fragrant and reminds me of a brand new doll I discovered under the tree, placed there by Santa Claus, early on a Christmas morning when I was five), and transferred her onto a cold gurney for transport to a refrigerated morgue somewhere down in the guts of the hospital.

Later, as I was cleaning the room, making it suitable for the next dying patient (a man in his thirties with a new wife, an infant daughter, and fatal melanoma), I found the Lilliputian Jesus from Italy still perched on the side rail. I could not bring myself to throw Camille's God, my God perhaps, into the garbage or to give him away—to abandon him like an unwanted orphan—to some deteriorating patient who might, let's be honest, care more about oxygen than salvation. The Son of God, who found his way into the pocket of my uniform trousers that day, has taken up residence on my nightstand right next to the Panasonic telephone.

Sometimes—often, I look at that graven image of God and wonder: Did Camille, at the last minute, discover that her Jesus had forsaken humankind after all? Why, when she was frantic to cling to something she could count on, frantic to find a way to ease the transition from one world to another, did she turn away from Jesus and, instead, beg mercy and forgiveness from her husband? And if she *had* been forsaken by her Lord, where did the spirit of Camille go when it left us? Will I have a husband or a lover at the bedside when I die? Or will I wake up in some other world one morning and find out that I have entirely dreamed my life—that I haven't died, but simply awakened?

Camille was not—I am not—alone in contemplating the dubious nature of God, the nature of existence, when dying is at hand. Occasionally, I have heard grieving people curse, cajole, and condemn the Heavenly Father when "He" threatens to take back a life that he had previously granted. I once heard a grieving father exclaim that God was " a fickle son of a bitch." His eight-year-old son had spun around on the stairs to make his way down for a bedtime kiss from his mother and had tripped. His tiny body rolled head over heels, and he crashed, face first, through a glass coffee table at the bottom. Both of his carotid arteries were severed. His mother quickly applied pressure with her thumbs. She escorted him like that into the ambulance and all the way into the surgical suite, never losing her cool. The pediatric vascular surgeon made the necessary repairs, but the kid was brain dead and we disconnected him from the ventilator three days later so he could die peacefully in his mother's arms.

When I was growing up in the sixties, my father proclaimed that he and his family, his children at least, were atheist. On occasion, he and my mother would drag us off for Sunday school at the First Unitarian Universalist Church of Cuyahoga Falls where we would examine—with telescopes from the classroom window—birds in trees, other children playing on the lawn, and wisps of cloud in the blue Sunday sky. On other Sundays, my father and mother would pack my sisters and me into the old Buick and, after he had scouted, measured, and inspected the brush for a proper walking stick for each of us, set us free on the wooded paths that combed through the B.F. Goodrich Park, the Goodyear Park, or the Firestone Park. (I grew up in the Rubber Capital of the World, Akron, Ohio.)

*"This* is God," he'd remind us during some euphoric moment.

He used to tell us that Baptists were blind, Catholics were liars, and Protestants were prudes. One summer, he let me go to a Baptist summer vacation Bible school for two weeks, but only after I swore an oath that I wouldn't let some screaming lunatic badger me into being *saved*.

"We belong to the Unitarian faith, if anyone asks," he told me, before I anxiously exited the house. (I was only seven at the time.) "We believe in the faith of nature and in the wonder of humankind. Our mission in our faith is to immerse ourselves in ideas, philosophies, and to take part in an aesthetically attentive community of thinkers."

I was about to miss the bus so I didn't think much about what he was saying until after I'd learned to sing, "Jesus Loves the Little Children," and clapped my hands, stomped my feet, and said, *"Amen!"* to some other cheerful tune. I can tell you that when I finally understood my father's words, I understood that his faith in the wonder of humankind did not apply to Baptists, Protestants, or Catholics.

This issue of the belief in God, not surprisingly, lends itself well to my accumulating confusion about life. If I had to describe an image of God, the one that I see in my mind's eye, I could only say that She/He appears as a question mark.

In my nursing career, I've met grieving parents, lovers, spouses, and friends who could not have survived but with the help of God. Others, like Mrs. Dimitri, a seventy-five-year-old widow who was watching her only surviving child, Zòe, die of astrocytoma—a rocketing brain tumor—are so angry with their gods that they threaten to withdraw their affections and even their faith. Feeling defeated one afternoon, the old woman shook her fist and yelled at the ceiling tiles of her daughter's hospital room, *"THERE IS NO GOD! THIS IS MY CHILD, YOU MONSTER! WHY CAN'T YOU TAKE ME INSTEAD? HAVE YOU NO MERCY? WHY DO YOU DO THIS TO THE ONLY CHILD I HAVE LEFT?"*

The old woman's cry brought us running. My colleague wrapped Mrs. Dimitri in her arms and held her there to console and settle her. I took the patient's hand—a plump, warm hand—and looked into her eyes to see if she had understood or been frightened by her mother's panic.

Zòe just smiled. After chemotherapy, radiation, and a severely disfiguring surgery, the young woman's hair had grown back in erratic patches, dark and wild in the hills and valleys of a gnarled skull. The hair parted itself naturally away from a twisted scar that traveled from her forehead to her crown. Her face was pudgy from high doses of steroids and her eyes were beginning to bulge from her head in such a way that she looked perpetually startled.

"It's OK," she whispered to me softly. "I'm dying. So what's the big deal?" and here she giggled girlishly.

Looking hard at her cherubic face, I suddenly read a look of pleading. I bent down and nuzzled my lips to her ear. "Your mother is crying because she loves you," I explained. "She will miss you very much."

We were quiet then, the four of us, except for the convulsive sobbing from Mrs. Dimitri. My hand, which held steady to Zòe's, became an object of exploration. She ran her fingertips over my palm, around my thumbnail, between my fingers. I reciprocated the gesture and was amazed at what I suddenly, unexpectedly found: the crevices, grooves, the rough and smooth, the life that can be felt in a simple holding of hands.

"Look at that," she commanded me. Her eyes had wandered from my face to the television, which was suspended from the ceiling at the foot of her bed. Three frogs on lily pads in a dark bayou somewhere were echoing name-brand syllables to a beer commercial. A desperately thirsty frog unfurled his long sticky tongue and attached himself to a passing Budweiser delivery truck. He went flying gleefully through the air above the pavement, stuck to the back of the beer truck twenty feet ahead of him by a rubber-band tongue, and this made Zòe smile.

*"I worked in a factory all my life!"* Her mother began to wail at the ceiling once more, her words, uttered with the staccato accent of her Greek tongue, not quite as urgent now. "And when my daughter was finished with pharmacy school, she came into the factory one day and told my supervisor that she was taking me home. 'It's my turn to take care of you now,' she said to me. 'You put me through school and now it's time for you to take it easy,' she said. I left the factory that day and never went back. Three months later, they tell me she's dying of a brain tumor. *She had so much life ahead of her!*" and here another great sob, "She was going to get married in a few months."

"You graduated pharmacy?" I whispered to Zòe.

She giggled, pleased to be asked. "Yes, I did," she answered proudly. "I was going to take care of my mother, but then I got this brain tumor and now I'm going to die." All the time she continued to smile. The mention of her brain tumor was equivalent to her request for a drink of water—a simple communication without much meaning, a bit of information transferred from memory to voice box. Her eyes continued to explore the television screen and her fingers searched the folds and creases of my palm. Except for the smile, strangely, her face had gone slack, lacking any kind of expression. It was the face of one who had been lobotomized.

*"First my son, then my husband, and NOW MY DAUGHTER! IT'S NOT RIGHT! OH DAMN IT! THERE CAN BE NO GOD IN HEAVEN!"* Mrs. Dimitri was loud—beyond consolation. The nurse beside her, crying too, caressed the old woman's arm and murmured, "I'm sorry, Catherine. I'm so, so sorry...."

On the television screen, the Budweiser frogs were replaced by the profile of an infant's bare, smooth, bottom. The infant's mother tenderly ran the tips of her fingers over the curve of velvety flesh, and in my head a thought instantly surfaced. Hadn't Zòe's mother admired that sweet, beautiful bit of body on her infant daughter during some diaper change thirty years before?

*"LOOK, MAMA!"* the dying woman shouted wildly. She was deliriously happy at that moment, watching television. A giggle trilled from her throat loudly. *"DIAPERS, MAMA! LOOK AT THIS!"* The diaper commercial was evoking absolute mania.

How is it that one can be so near death and rise to such a state of light-hearted pleasure and aliveness at the same time?

I turned to look at Zòe's mother, Catherine. Her face was buried in her hands on the shoulder of the weeping nurse who was holding her. She lifted the face briefly to look at her daughter, the television, and me.

"She doesn't mean to be like this," she explained. "It's just the tumor, the cancer, that's all."

As if I hadn't known it.

"She can't help it," she apologized. And, once again, she looked up at the ceiling, alluding indirectly that God might reside somewhere in the chalky ceiling tiles. "No," she said, flatly now, without passion, "there can be no God."

Zòe died, I'm sure of it, in the middle of something. A beer commercial, perhaps. A change of adult diaper, bed linen, sweaty nightgown, maybe. The week I left my position on the hospice unit she was scheduled to be flown back to Greece so that she could die on native soil with her mother and her relatives at hand. Did she make it? Did she touch down in a land where God was more readily manifest? (Gods have been unmistakably palpable in Greece for so long!) Of course it's quite possible that she expired in a Boeing 767 some-where over the Atlantic at thirty thousand feet. (Did God exhume her soul then from a tiny flake of metal that was passing through his subflooring?) Was she passing over Italy at the time? The same boot-shaped mass that exported the God who watches over me now while I sleep?

The little silver deity on my nightstand is not that different from his neighbor, the Panasonic telephone. Both were manufactured by some human hand or industrial machine and both were imported into the country where I live. Both of them were bought for sums of money. The telephone links me to friends, neighbors, and a middle-aged boyfriend whom I call, now and then, with a sleepy voice when I awaken.

The forged Almighty also links me to other things, other people. Every time I look at him I think of Camille. I think of Camille, and Jerry, and Zòe; a certain boy who died trying to kiss his mother goodnight; a certain beautiful twenty-year-old girl who fell from a mountain; a mother of six who surrendered her soul in the shower; all the tormented people they left behind; the poetry of Jane Kenyon, Rainer Maria Rilke, Octavio Paz, and so many others; my daughters; the smell of pine trees in wet spring soil; ascending from a gloomy, overcast runway in Chicago into the brilliant blue of almost heaven; the inconceivable congestion of Calcutta streets and sidewalks; the skyline of San Francisco; the miracle of birth; and the wondrous nature of dying.

# *How To Drink A Guinness*

## J. S. Porché

When you get the call from your friends, keep your acceptance brief, as it will already be almost 9:00 P.M., and respectable public houses officially close around 2:00 A.M. A direct "Yap" or well enunciated "Right" should imply your love of this process and eagerness to meet up. Extra chatter or questions at this point will make you out to be an unworthy burden, a useless lightweight. Don't bother with questions of where, who, or God forbid, why—you should damn well know why...everyone else does. And if you babble on, agonizing about running into last weekend's date who never bothered to ring...or what to wear...forget it. You have tainted the act, thus killing the night. Former friends are then allowed (and encouraged) by Irish law to shun you and request that your family leave the town.

After hanging up the phone, you have fifteen minutes to don the wear. Anything nonobvious, unassuming, absorbent, and nonflammable will suffice. A well-worn pair of jeans and a beefy cotton tee under a simple leather or sweater is best. Go for layering...say you're soaked by a spill or a careless flick of ash burns in—no matter, just pull off layer number one and carry on. Dress for comfort; this isn't the catwalk or a dinner party in Milan. No, Adam

Clayton and Naomi won't be queuing up to get in where you're going...and you know they're over, right? And even if they weren't, fuck 'em...you are going to drink, not stargaze.

Don't make the mistake of reaching for anything but hard, rubber-soled boots or Dexters, Caterpillar, Bonz, Doc Martens...no one will care. Do yourself a favor and stick with black or brown, though. Flashy colors will imply that you aren't serious, and if you see anyone wearing those silly little two-toned half boots or worse, sandals...I promise you, there will be a confrontation. C'mon, not even Americans on holiday or student nurses can get away with that crap. Remember, you and the pub floor should have a solid connection.

Once properly dressed, splash on the scent that distinguishes you from the rest and make your way to the front of the house. Offer your parents, siblings, housemates, or anyone else present no explanation for your departure. Ignore any cooking food that you may smell. You can get something at the pub. Leave by the front and really slam the door. The rattling of the door in the frame is a distinct punctuation of the end of the first leg...and hey, you're not sneaking off like some kid, you mean this. In the name of the Father, the Son and the Holy Ghost, lads, you're going up to the pub.

You won't be driving there, and that means anything...bike, car, moped...you don't need the hassle. You're wearing good shoes...walk. Undoubtedly you know some fella with a car, suppress any thought of asking him for a ride...you could blow it again. Why ruin the night by appointing some sap as designated driver—"Yeah, c'mon with us to the pub...and *watch us* have a brilliant night." One doesn't do this to a mate. A whining ne'er-do-well cousin forced on the party, maybe...but not a real friend.

The walk to the pub is crucial. Don't waver from my direction. You will be glad at the end of the night when you and the men make the journey home. This, you understand, is part of the sport. You will learn to love it.

Breathe deeply as you walk, allow your senses to drink the wet, rich air. Five thousand years of toil, frustration, pride, and salvation rise from the earth every time it rains. Remember your great-greats who had to venture abroad to save themselves and the names that allowed Ireland to live on, transplanted in the farthest reaches of God's creation. And bless the ones who had the fight in 'em to stay, preserving what is rightfully ours. If the rain begins, don't bother to quicken your pace. Enjoy it. You won't get any less wet for rushing. Irish rain is soft and rather magical—just let it happen. Wet is a part of life in an Irish town...and people would think you strange if you were always pressed and dry.

When you pass people on the street, acknowledge them with a nod—nothing more. You haven't time for messing. You are working against time. Five hours will hardly be enough time for your experience, but if you're blessed with grand humor and a poet's tongue, and you know you are, you'll be invited to hang on a bit with the rest of the village pub's elite and partake in the after-hours wind-down. Knowing that the boundaries of elitism are not elastic, you'll just have to understand that the barman can't have everyone, so make use of the remaining regularly posted hours to catch up on the crack with those of your friends who as of yet haven't earned their stripes.

Don't worry yourself about being the first of the group there. I promise you, it won't happen. In every circle, and I know this to be fact, there is the one who really attaches himself to the drink. He has devoted a good part of his young life to it, giving up all sober forms of communication, job prospects, and any decent kind of romantic relationship...he's a bit like a unicyclist—you don't know how he could do it, yet he does—so at the very least, we must show our appreciation for him and his willingness to hold us a table. So, he'll be there first, no matter. Most likely he'll have been in the same spot all day, and probably took his tea there as well. There is always someone to welcome you at the pub, so don't fret.

Take notice of the vendors as you pass, you'll be up for a bag of hot chips after closing. For this, hold back a punt or two in reserve. The fried salty potato wedges taste best in the wee hours of the morning.

As you approach the doorway of the pub, recite your creed. Here is where you are on your own. I can give you no example from which you can create your own. It is up to you. You may have the same one all your life, or it may change over the years, I do not know. But the creed is as important as the drink itself. It is a silent promise that you make to yourself, it makes the heart strong, and you are better for having taken a moment to look within. Stand at the entrance...it will come to you. Once proclaimed, you may enter.

The warmth and sweet tinge of smoldering turf coming from the small hole of a fireplace near the back will soak into your clothes. Undoubtedly, you will know you are in the right place. Stand for a moment and get a sense of the layout. Through the gentle clouds of cigarette smoke you'll be able to make out the bar and counter at the side, plain, sturdy tables and chairs carved of black wood surrounding the small step of a stage, and the booths and dart boards at the back. The light will be bright enough for you to know at whom you're smiling, but charmingly low enough to disregard any flaws. Your pause at the front is a statement of purpose and a chance to be seen by everyone who arrived before you. Give a nod to the barman—Brian, Michael, Seamus,

Pat—one of them will be tending bar that night.

If they've got music going, let it determine the speed of your stride. It will help you make your way through a crowd, as well. It's a bit like synchronized swimming. You'll look a lot smarter for not loping your way to the back of the pub through a high-spirited kicker like "The Road to Sligo," and bolting around during "Heaven Knows I'm Miserable Now" will make you out to be a jackass. So let the music guide—it will get you where you're going.

Make eye contact with all the girls, *all* of them, I'm telling you! I once made the regrettable mistake of looking past Olga Flynn one night at the pub, nothing intentional really...I just fuckin' well wasn't in the mood to listen to all of her gossiping...so I just pretended to be busy talking with Eamon an' them, and didn't look up. Well, she made good and sure to tell her best friend's little sister Kay, for whom I'd throw myself off a bridge, that I'd snubbed her at the pub. And when we got back to university, Kay shot me these looks to let me know what a shit I was. Because of Olga's gossiping I had tried to avoid her, but her sharp tongue got me in the end, anyway. So, basically, you never know who knows who...so just make nice with them all and keep the damn peace.

Head towards the booths at the back—they will be waiting for you there. They will be glad to see you...show your affection without being too schoolboyish and get on with the ordering.

Elect one to take the order to the bar. Avoid having someone come around to take your order; it's modern and all, but ends up taking too much time, and when the place is full of wandering bodies, the server *will* get bumped and spill half of what was served up. Be thoroughly *sound* and offer yourself as the retriever. The first retriever always pays for the first round. Offer cheerfully, this will be remembered about you. Underage kids from national school sneak in to hear just these kinds of statements: "All right, men...a pint all around?" you'll ask, as if there was any question. You will feel the passion of every young one who aspires to claim those words for himself...to be used the day he'll first be allowed to take part.

Walk to the bar, lean over, and announce in a tone that can be heard above the music, "Ten pint." Even if there are only five of you, order ten. Brian will know what to do. As he gathers the clinking glasses in a row, turn and greet any school friends and neighbors or any out-of-towners who have come to the pub to partake.

Carefully, Brian, King of Barmen, will tilt each heavy glass to fit over the angled spigot of the tap. Being a novice, you should watch him carefully to see how it's done. In your life you will run into the odd barkeep who does not know what he's doing. With your knowledge, you will now be able to correct him.

The smooth amber stout will flow from the brass faucet, growing darker as it collects. Brian will pull the glass down slowly, keeping the cream-colored froth manageable above the ale and just under the top of the glass's gently widening mouth. A bit will run down the pint glass as the barman sets them up. Please know that this is charm, not waste. Smile and be glad as you pay the barman the mere earthly value of your filled-to-pint's-top glasses...and remember to leave him a substantial something this first time up to the bar. You will be remembered accordingly, and favored. Again, the young ones are absorbing every movement and taking notes on style. Yours is the name that will be recalled in the lovely haze of after-hours close-out as being, "The sport," "The man" and this is good.

As you lift the weighty tray of spirits, push away any thoughts of having to struggle your way back to your table. You aren't a server. The crowd will know this. It is at this point that the real spirit of the place will rise to your aid. The utter love, admiration, and goodwill of the crowd will carry you in, as on a wave, through the dancers, boxers, philosophers, and gents, safely back to your table, quite unmolested.

A cheer of liquor lust and approval will greet you. Keep your wits about you, though; carefully place all the pints at the center of the table. Don't hand glasses off to each man like it's tea at grandmother's. Set them all at the center. This, as you should have copped on, is a process...no...a bit of a ceremony, really.

Settle yourselves and take a moment and look at the collection. The pints will have suffered some in the transport. Let them rest and resume their flawless form, the head a mere pencil mustache at each top.

Look at the people collected around...each man gathered. If you're doing this right, these are the finest lads in the town, your best friends. Appreciate them. They have lived through it all with you—and one or two will stand around, drink in hand, and remember you to your grandchildren at your wake.

The look in each man's eyes, at this point, will reflect enough sentiment to fill a novel, and you will know that this is the time for you to take the first glass and offer the toast. In one slow, measured gesture, offer your raised glass. "Cheers and blessings on us all," you will call out loud for all—but in the flash of an instant, all that rides your heart's center will surface. Remember your grandparents, your first fight won, the best goal ever scored...remember your strong back and able hands...remember Synge, Shaw, Yeats, and the wildness of Wilde....remember the scars of the country and the grace of God and man it will need to heal...remember your mother's forgiveness and Easter dinner at Granddad O'Gorman's Mayo...remember the sweetness of your girlfriend's kisses and the harsh truths learned about yourself from the girls you left behind. Remember all that has shaped you. Put glass to mouth and drink your Guinness.

# *In Defense Of Mr. Ramsay*

*Amber S. Krieger*

*L*ondon Herald, Dec. 10, 1921 (afternoon edition)
In an exciting opening to *Crown v. Ramsay* this morning, the Prosecution has taken on the awesome task of proving that Mr. Ramsay is an overbearing tyrant whose very nature broke down his wife and sent her to the grave. During this morning's various attacks on his character, Mr. Ramsay remained rigid, holding a blank stare as though he was not even sure what was going on, mumbling to himself occasionally. During the fifteen-minute intermission, however, he had to be restrained and removed to separate chambers after storming down on the Justice in the hallway. The final witness for the Prosecution this afternoon was Mrs. Minta Rayley, the daughter of a friend of Mrs. Ramsay's. The Prosecution demonstrated through Mrs. Rayley's testimony Ramsay's habit of flirting shamelessly with the young ladies who stayed with the Ramsays each summer. The Defense, however, regained some ground by insinuating that Mrs. Rayley's testimony was colored by her anger at Mrs. Ramsay (and the Ramsay clan) for pushing her into an unhappy marriage.

Up on the witness list for tomorrow: Cam Ramsay, Lily Briscoe, and James Ramsay.

*Testimony of Cam Ramsay, December 11, 1921.*

PROSECUTION:

Cam, how do you remember your mother when you were a child?

CAM RAMSAY:

Mother was wonderful. She could always make things right. That...last...summer, we were at the island and Edward had sent us this terrible pig's skull. We had nailed it up and James screamed if anyone touched it. Mother told me to sleep and dream of lovely places, but I could see the horns all over the room. So she took her own shawl off and wrapped it round and round the skull, and told me how lovely it looked then, how the fairies would love it, until I fell asleep.

PROSECUTION:

Cam, what was your father like when you were a child?

CAM RAMSAY:

A tyrant. A true tyrant. We were always under the gloom of his authority—he was always making us do his bidding.

PROSECUTION:

And how is your relationship with him now?

CAM RAMSAY:

What remains intolerable is that crass blindness and tyranny of his which poisoned my childhood and raised bitter storms, so that even now I wake in the night trembling with rage and remember some command of his, some insolence: "Do this," "Do that," his dominance: his "Submit to me."

PROSECUTION:

Thank you, Cam.

DEFENSE:

Cam, do you love your father?

CAM RAMSAY:

Of course.

DEFENSE:

Even despite his tyranny?

CAM RAMSAY:

Oh, but, there were good times too.... When I was young, I would go in sometimes early from the garden to catch Father and Mr. Bankes or Mr. Carmichael reading the *Times* in the study. I would take a book from the shelf and stand there, watching Father write, ideas being born there, thoughts expanding like leaves in water.

DEFENSE:

And how did you feel about him in those times?

CAM RAMSAY:

I thought he was not vain, not a tyrant.

JAMES RAMSAY:

TRAITOR! FIGHT TYRANNY TO THE DEATH!

JUSTICE:

Counsel, advise your witness to restrain himself or I will have him removed from this courtroom.

PROSECUTION:

Yes, Your Honor.

DEFENSE:

Cam, please finish your response.

CAM RAMSAY:

He was not a tyrant and did not wish to make you pity him. Indeed, if he saw me there reading a book, he would ask me, gentle as he could, was there nothing he could get me?

DEFENSE:

Cam, did your father ever deny you the things you needed or wanted, out of spite?

CAM RAMSAY:

Oh, no. He always had a reason for things. He was so wise, as though he knew so well all the things that happened in the world. He did not want us to have unrealistic expectations. On our way to the lighthouse he stopped me from throwing a sandwich in the sea and told me if I didn't want it to put it back. I put it back and he gave me a gingerbread nut from his own parcel, as if he were a great Spanish gentleman handing a flower to a lady at a window.

DEFENSE:

Cam, I realize this may be hard for you, so please take your time. Do you think your father wore your mother to death?

CAM RAMSAY:

Oh, no! Never.

JUSTICE:

Ms. Prosecutor, do you wish to reexamine the witness?

PROSECUTION:

Yes, Your Honor. Cam, did your father take you to the lighthouse because you had asked to go?

CAM RAMSAY:

Oh, no. He forced us to go. All the way down to the beach he bade us, "Walk up, walk up." He forced us to go against our wills.

*   *   *

*Testimony of Lily Briscoe, December 11, 1921 (hostile witness for the Prosecution).*

PROSECUTION:

Lily, when was the last time you saw Mrs. Ramsay?

LILY BRISCOE:

Why, it was that summer before she...she...(I'm sorry it's still too painful) before she died. I went to the Isle of Skye with the Ramsays.

PROSECUTION:

How did Mrs. Ramsay seem to you on that trip?

LILY BRISCOE:

Weary. How old she looked, how worn.

PROSECUTION:

What do you mean, she was weary?

LILY BRISCOE:

It tired Mrs. Ramsay; it cowed her a little—the plates whizzing and the doors slamming.

PROSECUTION:

And who was whizzing plates and slamming doors?

LILY BRISCOE:

Why, Mr. Ramsay, of course.

PROSECUTION:

Ms. Briscoe, what is your impression of Mr. Ramsay?

LILY BRISCOE:

Oh, he can be very alarming, somewhat overbearing.

PROSECUTION:

Ms. Briscoe, did you not feel that he was petty, selfish, vain, egotistical; he was spoilt; he was a tyrant; he wore Mrs. Ramsay to death?

LILY BRISCOE:

I might have thought those things, but "wore her to death"—that's a figure of speech....

PROSECUTION:

Did you or did you not think these things about Mr. Ramsay? Just answer the question.

LILY BRISCOE:

Perhaps, once. Oh, but...think of his work!

PROSECUTION:

Are you saying, Ms. Briscoe, that you believe because Mr. Ramsay is a philosopher he has a right to trample over everyone else?

LILY BRISCOE:

No, no, of course not, but when a man has such important matters...

PROSECUTION:

So, Ms. Briscoe, are you saying you found him to be a bit of a hypocrite?

LILY BRISCOE:

A bit of a hypocrite? Oh no—the most sincere of men, the truest.

PROSECUTION:

The most sincere of men? But also absorbed in himself, tyrannical, unjust? Perhaps you are the hypocrite then, Ms. Briscoe?

LILY BRISCOE:

No. It is just that he is a very complex man, difficult to understand sometimes.

PROSECUTION:

So you are saying that Mr. Ramsay does not communicate effectively?

LILY BRISCOE:

Well, yes.

PROSECUTION:

And would you say, Ms. Briscoe, that he placed unreasonable demands on the people around him?

LILY BRISCOE:

Well, yes, sometimes.

PROSECUTION:

And wouldn't you say, Ms. Briscoe, that his selfishness, his demands, his tyranny, wore down Mrs. Ramsay's patience, so that eventually there was nothing left she could do for him but die?

LILY BRISCOE:

No. She loved—

PROSECUTION:

Thank you, Ms. Briscoe.

LILY BRISCOE:

But that's not—

PROSECUTION:

No more questions for this witness, Your Honor.

DEFENSE:

Are you married, Ms. Briscoe?

LILY BRISCOE:

No, but, there is my father, my home, my...painting.

DEFENSE:

But at one point there was some talk of you marrying William Bankes. What happened?

LILY BRISCOE:

Oh, no. I never wanted to marry anyone. It was Mrs. Ramsay who insisted I must; we all must marry. She believed an unmarried woman missed the best of life.

DEFENSE:

Now, Lily, please think carefully before answering this next question. If the Ramsays' marriage was so unhappy, why would she insist that others get married?

LILY BRISCOE:

I'm not sure.

DEFENSE:

Was Mrs. Ramsay a spiteful woman?

LILY BRISCOE:

No, never.

DEFENSE:

And so, wouldn't it be safe to assume, Lily, that when Mrs. Ramsay encouraged others to marry, it was because she truly believed that they would be happiest that way?

LILY BRISCOE:

Oh, yes. Absolutely.

DEFENSE:

Lily, you've stated that Mr. Ramsay is a complex man. Can you elaborate on that?

LILY BRISCOE:

He was at once vulnerable and strong. I always wondered why so brave a man in thought should be so timid in life, thought how strangely he was venerable and laughable at one and the same time. He could get so caught up in what he was thinking that it was as if the outside world were not there—he would mumble out loud, shout lines of poetry, positively look through you.

DEFENSE:

Are you saying, then, that it seemed he could not reconcile the outside

world with the inner workings of his mind?
LILY BRISCOE:

That is exactly what I'm saying.
DEFENSE:

Lily, do you dislike Mr. Ramsay?
LILY BRISCOE:

How does one judge people, think of them? How does one add up this and that and conclude that it is liking one feels, or disliking? Mr. Ramsay has bad qualities—he is overbearing...but he has a fiery unworldliness; he knows nothing about trifles; he loves dogs and his children.
DEFENSE:

Lily, how long have you known the Ramsays?
LILY BRISCOE:

For at least fifteen years.
DEFENSE:

When Mrs. Ramsay was alive, did you ever see Mr. Ramsay abuse her in any way?
LILY BRISCOE:

Physically? No. Never.
DEFENSE:

Emotionally?
LILY BRISCOE:

I'm not sure what you mean.
DEFENSE:

How would you characterize relations between Mr. and Mrs. Ramsay?
LILY BRISCOE:

Directly one looked up and saw them, "being in love" flooded them.
DEFENSE:

Lily, did Mrs. Ramsay ever tell you that she was unhappy in her marriage?
LILY BRISCOE:

Why, no.
DEFENSE:

Did she ever tell you that taking care of her husband made her weary?
LILY BRISCOE:

Oh, no. Mrs. Ramsay believed that taking care of her husband was her duty—she was quite willing to do it. She pitied men always as if they lacked something—women never, as if they had something.
DEFENSE:

Is this how you feel about men and women, Lily?

LILY BRISCOE:

Well, I've always been different. But there is a code of behavior between men and women: it behooves the woman, whatever her own occupation may be, to go to the help of the man, so he may expose and relieve the thigh bones, the ribs, of his vanity, of his urgent desire to assert himself; as indeed it is their duty to help us—suppose the Tube were to burst into flames! This is what Mrs. Ramsay believed and how she lived her life. She would not have had it any other way.

DEFENSE:

Thank you.

\* \* \*

*Testimony of James Ramsay, December 11, 1921.*

PROSECUTION:

Mr. Ramsay, what was your relationship like with your father when you were young?

JAMES RAMSAY:

I hated him. There was many a time when had I had an axe handy, or a poker, any weapon that would have gashed a hole in my father's breast and killed him, I would have seized it.

PROSECUTION:

Why do you hate him, James?

JAMES RAMSAY:

For his tyranny. For his inconsistency. For that fierce sudden black-winged harpy, with its talons all cold and hard, that struck and struck at me, and then made off.

PROSECUTION:

And what was your relationship with your mother?

JAMES RAMSAY:

I loved her. She was always wonderful. Once when we were younger, Edward sent us a boar's skull. I loved it, I would not let anyone touch it. But I also had to have the light on, and the skull's horns scared Cam. Mother took her own shawl off and wrapped it round and round the skull, showed me how the skull was still there untouched, so that I could fall asleep.

PROSECUTION:

Did you ever see your father and mother interact?

JAMES RAMSAY:

Yes, it was terrible. I remember sitting with Mother in the drawing room and Father came to the window and said to me, "It will rain. You won't be able to go to the lighthouse." He brought his blade down upon us and she went stiff all over, and then, her arm slackened, she had risen somehow. It was sympathy he wanted. All her strength flared up to be drunk by the beak of brass, the arid scimitar of the male, which smote mercilessly, again and again, demanding sympathy. So boasting of her capacity to surround and protect, there was scarcely a shell of herself for her to know herself by; all was so lavished and spent. My father wore my mother to death. *(Gasps and murmurs in the room)*

JUSTICE:

Order!

CAM RAMSAY:

THAT'S NOT TRUE! *(More grumbling in the court)*

JUSTICE:

Order, or I will have the room cleared. Ms. Prosecutor, please restrain your witness.

PROSECUTION:

I apologize, Your Honor. James, I want you to think carefully about what you are saying. Do you really believe that your father wore your mother to death?

JAMES RAMSAY:

Yes.

PROSECUTION:

I have no more questions for this witness, Your Honor.

\* \* \*

*London Herald,* December 11, 1921 (afternoon edition)

Things heated up in the courtroom today with the testimony of Cam Ramsay, Lily Briscoe, and James Ramsay. The young Ms. Ramsay's testimony began with great hostility, but in a sudden show of emotion, Cam broke down and expressed her love for her father. The old man was brought momentarily out of his shell, thundering, "For boldly we rode!" in the tiny courtroom, so frightening the stenographer that this episode was not captured in the trial transcripts. There was a sense of forgiveness underlying her testimony, although it is unclear if this forgiveness signifies an awareness of his guilt, or if it applies to something greater. Ms. Briscoe's testimony also contributed greatly to the Defense, emphasizing the difficulty of judging one's character, especially Mr. Ramsay's, due to its complex nature. Things took a sudden turn, however, when James Ramsay took the stand. The young man reinforced for the court his father's domineering nature, especially toward the late Mrs. Ramsay, and repeated twice his conviction that his father indeed wore his mother to death. Tomorrow, the Defense will try its hand at correcting the damage as it cross-examines young Ramsay and brings forward its own witnesses.

*   *   *

*Cross-examination of James Ramsay, December 12, 1921.*

DEFENSE:
   Your Honor, I ask permission to treat this witness as a hostile witness.
PROSECUTION:
   Objection.
JUSTICE:
   Overruled. Proceed, Counsel, as a hostile witness.
DEFENSE:
   Isn't it true, Mr. Ramsay, that you fidgeted purposefully when your mother measured the lighthouse boy's stocking against your leg?
JAMES RAMSAY:
   Maybe. I don't know. I don't remember.
DEFENSE:
   Isn't it true that you wanted your mother's attention all the time, and that your jealousy caused you to fidget and distract your mother when she focused on anything else?
JAMES RAMSAY:
   I don't know.
DEFENSE:
   And isn't it true that on that day when your father said you would not be able to go to the lighthouse, when your mother turned her attention to your father, you felt she had gone away, left you there, impotent, ridiculous? Remember you are under oath, Mr. Ramsay.
JAMES RAMSAY:
   I don't know. I'm sure it is possible I was a little jealous. But she—
DEFENSE:
   Thank you, Mr. Ramsay. And couldn't it also be possible that when you say you wanted to drive something sharp into your father's heart, you really wanted to push him out the way so that you could regain your mother's full attention?

JAMES RAMSAY:

Maybe, but he—

DEFENSE:

Thank you, James. You recently took a trip to the lighthouse with your sister, Cam, and your father—isn't that true?

JAMES RAMSAY:

Yes.

DEFENSE:

How did you feel about that trip?

JAMES RAMSAY:

Well, how could any of us say, "But I won't," when he said, "Come to the Lighthouse?" The black wings spread and the hard beak tore. I kept dreading the moment when he would look up and speak sharply to me about something or other. "Why are we lagging here?" he would demand, or something quite unreasonable like that. And if he did, I thought, then I would take a knife and strike him to the heart.

DEFENSE:

Did you never think, James, that your father planned that trip to make up for the time when you did not get to go to the lighthouse before?

JAMES RAMSAY:

Well, it's possible...

DEFENSE:

And did you not realize, James, on that trip, that your father is not entirely how you have imagined him? Did you not see, when that black-winged harpy made off, that there your father was again, an old man, very sad, reading his book? Did you not think that sometimes you might see him, pressing a sovereign into some frozen old woman's hand in the street?

JAMES RAMSAY:

Yes.

DEFENSE:

And did you not realize, there on the boat, that you had come to feel, quite often lately, when your father said something or did something which surprised the others, that the two of you alone knew each other? And did you not wonder, *What then is this terror, this hatred?* And did you not come to realize that it did indeed stem from a certain afternoon when you were a little boy, one of your last afternoons with your mother, when your father said, "It will rain, you will not be able to go to the lighthouse"?

JAMES RAMSAY:

Yes, that is true.

DEFENSE:

And on that trip, did he make those unreasonable demands as you thought he would?

JAMES RAMSAY:

No.

DEFENSE:

Did he not, in fact, give you at last what you had been wanting? When you arrived did he not say, "Well done!" for you had steered them like a born sailor?

JAMES RAMSAY:

Yes, he did.

DEFENSE:

Tell me, James, how did you feel then when you finally arrived to the lighthouse?

JAMES RAMSAY:

*What do you want?* I wanted to ask him. *Ask me anything and I will give it to you.* But he did not ask anything.

DEFENSE:

And can you say still that your hatred for your father does not stem from a selfish desire for the whole of your mother's attention? Indeed can you still say that you hate your father?

JAMES RAMSAY:

No, I cannot.

* * *

WITNESSES FOR THE DEFENSE

*Testimony of the Overall Storyteller, December 12, 1921.*

DEFENSE:

Overall Storyteller, can you tell me what your role is in *To the Lighthouse?*

OVERALL STORYTELLER:

I help clarify confusing moments and give the readers insight into the characters' behavior with or without going into the characters' heads.

DEFENSE:

And so, would you say that you know everything there is to know about the Ramsays and their houseguests?

OVERALL STORYTELLER:

That's right. I know everything.

DEFENSE:

Storyteller, how would you describe Mr. Ramsay's general character?

OVERALL STORYTELLER:

What he says is true. It is always true. He is incapable of untruth, never tampers with a fact, never alters a disagreeable word to suit the pleasure or convenience of any mortal being, least of all his children, who, sprung from his loins, should be aware from childhood that life is difficult.

DEFENSE:

Storyteller, how would you describe Mrs. Ramsay's character?

OVERALL STORYTELLER:

She felt she had the whole of the other sex under her protection; for reasons she could not explain; for their chivalry and their valor; for the fact that they negotiated treaties, ruled India, controlled finance; finally for an attitude towards herself which no woman could fail to feel or find agreeable, something trustful, childlike, reverential; and woe betide the girl who did not feel the worth of it, of all that it implied, to the marrow of her bones!

DEFENSE:

How did Mrs. Ramsay feel about her husband?

OVERALL STORYTELLER:

She had complete trust in him. There was nobody whom she reverenced as she reverenced him. It discomposed her when he came to her as he did that day on the terrace; for then people said he depended on her, when they must know that of the two he was infinitely more important, and what she gave the world, in comparison to what he gave, negligible.

DEFENSE:

How would you describe relations between Mr. and Mrs. Ramsay?

OVERALL STORYTELLER:

They balanced each other: he is complex, she was simple; she liked a man to protect her, and he could do that; he liked a woman to give him sympathy, and she could do that. They understood each other perfectly. They both cherished their alone-time together, although it might only have consisted of chitchat, or even sitting silently, side by side. They had little jokes together. Sitting alone with him, she felt that nothing on Earth could equal that happiness.

DEFENSE:

Did all this sympathy-giving wear Mrs. Ramsay to death?

OVERALL STORYTELLER:

No. Sure, it could be very tiring, but she did not mind it. And often he would control himself for her. He would stifle his desire to complain to her; he would not bother her again when he could see she was not up to it.

DEFENSE:

Did Mr. Ramsay blame his wife for his failures?

OVERALL STORYTELLER:

Sure, sometimes he thought it would be nice to be alone—one could worry things out alone. But he would have been a beast and a cur to wish a single thing altered. He loved his family very much.

DEFENSE:

Overall Storyteller, you often describe Mr. Ramsay as tyrannical, bearing down upon people, and you often describe Mrs. Ramsay as weary. If it is not the case that Mr. Ramsay wore his wife to death, then why emphasize these characteristics?

OVERALL STORYTELLER:

You will probably notice that these descriptions are softened by the end of the book, and are often counteracted by more pleasant words. This is the way the story had to be told. The reader must come to sympathize with Mr. Ramsay by the end of the book, but it must be a long process. He is a very complicated man, easily misunderstood by outsiders. Mrs. Ramsay and Mr. Ramsay had an understanding between them that careful readers cannot help but see by the end of the novel. To come away from the book feeling that Mr. Ramsay is evil and that he wore out his wife with his tyranny is a gross misinterpretation of the text.

DEFENSE:

Do you mean to tell us that you chose which information to provide the reader, and when you would provide that information?

OVERALL STORYTELLER:

That is exactly what I mean. As the Overall Storyteller, I have access to everyone's thoughts, indeed I have access to everything that has ever occurred in this family. I make certain choices. Sometimes I allow the reader access to one character's thoughts or another; sometimes I step away and offer the reader outside information. By presenting the reader with so many different points of view, I can give him the clearest, most honest presentation of the characters. They are all very human, with certain flaws, and certain strengths. It is essential in this story that the reader come to his own conclusions about the characters, especially about Mr. Ramsay. It is my job to guide the reader to the correct interpretations. I use all of the characters to do this. Lily Briscoe, for example. I go into her head quite often. She struggles constantly with her ideas about the

Ramsays. But at the end, she has her vision, as Virginia Woolf had her vision when she wrote *To the Lighthouse*—and the reader, too, should have his vision.

PROSECUTION:

Isn't it true that Mrs. Ramsay was afraid of her husband, afraid to tell him the truth about the greenhouse roof and the expense it would be to mend it; and to tell him the truth about his books?

OVERALL STORYTELLER:

No, you are misinterpreting the text. She had those thoughts, but it was that she didn't want to worry him about the money, and she knew how sensitive he is.

PROSECUTION:

Did Mrs. Ramsay love her husband?

OVERALL STORYTELLER:

Very much.

PROSECUTION:

Yet, she could not tell him she loved him. Isn't it the case that Mrs. Ramsay despised her husband for wearing her to the bone, for constantly imposing himself upon her, pleading for sympathy, forcing his will upon her as he does everyone in the family and the house?

OVERALL STORYTELLER:

No, that's not true. Well, yes, she may have had some of these thoughts at times, but only in the very natural sense as one does in marriage. She certainly didn't blame him for anything. She was happy with her life.

PROSECUTION:

Isn't it true that Mr. Ramsay is obsessed with the idea that his work will not last, that he in fact becomes uneasy and irritable if anyone implies otherwise? Isn't it true that he always worried Mrs. Ramsay about his books—would they be read, were they good, why weren't they better, what would people think of him?

OVERALL STORYTELLER:

Yes, but—

PROSECUTION:

And isn't it true that he could often be heard muttering half aloud, "But the father of eight children has no choice"?

OVERALL STORYTELLER:

Yes, but—

PROSECUTION:

And isn't it true that he has always blamed his family for his failures?

OVERALL STORYTELLER:
> No. It's true that if he had not married, maybe he would have had more time, but his family strengthened him; looking at his wife and son fortified him and satisfied him and consecrated his effort to arrive at a perfectly clear understanding of the problems which engaged his splendid mind.

PROSECUTION:
> Isn't it true that Mr. Ramsay's tyrannical nature eventually drove his wife to give up her children and her life?

OVERALL STORYTELLER:
> *No.*

\* \* \*

*Postscript*
Needless to say, the jury in *Crown v. Ramsay* returned their verdict after deliberating for just thirty minutes. Mr. Ramsay was found not guilty, and the name Mr. Ramsay is still known to readers today—though few know that the outcome of this trial paved the way for other authors such as William Faulkner and Toni Morrison to present their stories the way they need to be told.

**Work Referenced**

Woolf, Virginia. *To the Lighthouse,* 1927. New York: Harcourt Brace Jovanovich, 1955.

# *How To Live Off Your Girlfriend's Income*

*Karen Stein*

If you want to live off your girlfriend's income, you really need to work hard at it. I mean, yeah, it's possible to just announce it right off the bat—"I ain't gonna get a job and you can't make me"—and then spend all your days sitting on the couch, watching TV, eating, sleeping and beating off. But unless you are, without a doubt, the best damn lay she ever had, she ain't gonna put up with your sorry ass for very long. You don't believe me? Well, shit, what happened when you were living at home and summer vacation rolled around? Did your mom buy you a bottle of corn oil and some napkins, looking to help you break the world's record for consecutive sex-yourself-up sessions? Hell no! She told you to get up off your lazy butt and look for a goddamn job. And chicks are like moms. They'll take a little bit of crap from us, but not when it comes to unemployment. You should be working, but there's an art form to spending mostly your girlfriend's paycheck.

First thing you gotta do is move in with the chick. Now, I don't mean that the two of you are gonna cozy on up with the classifieds, hunting for the most coupley apartment you can find. You want to move in after she's already got all the papers signed. Why? you ask. Lookee here. You're trying to save up your cash to buy a motorcycle, but your girlfriend keeps coming after you, saying, "We got our electric bill, our gas bill, our phone bill, and our rent is due. You owe me four hundred dollars." You hear that? You owe four fuckin' hundred dollars. And I'm guessin' you know not to have a checking account, so she won't be asking you to postdate anything, 'cause you only operate in the green. So let's say the utilities are in your name and your signature is on the lease. You're screwing yourself by not paying. But if you tell her you don't got the money, and your signature doesn't appear on anything legal and binding, well, guess what? You're goddamn right. She's gonna be sweating to pay off all the bills and making damn sure her credit isn't ruined.

But don't be stupid and just not pay, patting yourself on the back 'cause you think you're so clever. Thank her profusely. Go down on her for an hour or so. (I'm telling you, the better you are at it, the more likely she'll forget all about the money before bedtime.) But most important, promise to pay her back, but don't sign any IOUs, 'cause those are legal and binding. If she tries to get you to sign an IOU, don't put on your droopy-eyed, pouty-puppy face and say, "Don't you trust me?" My friend Rodney tried that with his girlfriend Beth, the whole *boo-hoo-I-thought-you-loved-me* bullshit. And she just pushed that paper closer to him, handed him a ballpoint pen and said, "No, I don't trust you. Sign it." He had no choice but to write down that, yeah, Rodney understands that Rodney owes Beth thirteen hundred dollars. I saw Beth the other day. She was on her way to the courthouse to file papers to haul Rodney's ass to the cashier's window.

You still need convincing? Say you wake up to go to work one morning and you need a tankful of gas and a breakfast sandwich and a pack of cigarettes, and hell, may as well get some lunch too. That'll cost you, what, twenty or so dollars? And so what if you've got a hundred dollars burning a hole in your pocket? You wanna save your money for the Friday night poker game. Well, guess what, fella? Guess who's got thirty bucks in her purse? Uh-huh, the Bank of Girlfriend, passed out asleep, probably dreaming about that hour you spent going down on her last night. Think about that poor sap who didn't take the plunge into his girlfriend's apartment and has to spend his own money on the stuff he needs? Whose pockets and purse is *he* gonna pick through? His own.

Hey, now, don't run off to check her pockets just yet. What if your girl is huffing by the door the minute you walk in, folding her arms over her chest and tapping her foot? And she says, "Hey, loverboy, I had thirty bucks in my pocket when I went to sleep and when I woke up there was only ten." What're you gonna do? Deny deny deny.

Denial must be practiced. Stand in front of a mirror, imagining the confrontation, and try to match up the best possible expression with the best "not me" phrase. Your two primary goals are believability and speed. Some examples: Raise your eyebrows and open your mouth wide, but not too wide, and say, "That sucks...." Or crinkle your eyebrows and frown, guaranteeing she will put all the blame on herself when you say, "God, you're always losing things." Or scratch the back of your head to pretend you're thinking, and ask her if she's sure she didn't spend the money on something and forgot about it. But don't ever smile when delivering these lines. If you look like you're having fun, she'll catch on that you're too happy that she thinks it might be your fault. A popular comeback is to glance at her and pout, getting the maximum bruised-ego effect, and say, "Well, I don't know why we're together because you obviously don't trust me." But you should know that with this answer, timing is everything, buddy. It might backfire. You'll either end up getting your ass kissed for the rest of the night and maybe even the next day, or you'll have a blubbering, useless pile of chick, and you'll be the one kissing all the ass, explaining to her a hundred different times in a hundred different ways, including hieroglyphics, that you didn't mean it that way. But since every chick operates on a different rag cycle, the best advice I can give you is to check out her mood carefully and proceed with caution.

Oh, yeah, you should also learn how to cook. No, cooking Ramen and macaroni-and-cheese don't count. We're talking stir-fry, spaghetti, fried catfish, lasagna. And don't just throw together a meal once in a blue moon and say, "See? I care about you!" You gotta be the apron-wearing, kick-her-outta-your-kitchen, spatula-wielding chef in the relationship. No, this isn't any kind of ass-licking, pussy-whip-cracking, wimp thing. This is strategic planning, brother. Say to her, pure and simple, "I cook...you buy the groceries." That's right, a full-on, no-holds-barred guilt trip. I'm not lying when I say that the better the food you're putting in front of her fat face, the more embarrassed she'll be to even *try* to put a meal on the table, since all that domestic crap is supposed to be her job in the first place. And the good news is that, if she gives you any lip, saying in that whiny voice that makes your skin crawl and your muscles cramp, "Well, it's not like you don't eat the food too," all you gotta do is say, "Fine, I'll buy the groceries and *you* cook." Works every time.

But just to be sure she doesn't decide you're a selfish asshole and try to kick you out, you oughta give in every now and then and pay for the groceries, or maybe bring home some carry-out Chinese food out of your own pocket. But you don't have to go to one of those grocery superstores and come home with hundreds of dollars' worth of bulk food items in plastic bags. Just pick up some little things, maybe some cold cuts and a bottle of steak sauce. That way, you also have the smoking *I-did-the-shopping-last-time* gun on your side.

I just have one more tip for you to get the best out of her income. But don't try this until you've served at least a year doing the steps I already told you, 'cause you need her to totally trust you to get this one to work. OK, you listening? First, wait for her to go to the bathroom and then make your rounds to her purse and pockets, makin' sure she don't got any cash. Order carry-out from a cash-only restaurant and offer to pick it up. Then, as you're walking out the door, jam your hands into your pockets and say, real surprised, "Shit, I don't have any money." That's when you move in for the kill. Offer to take her ATM card and withdraw some cash. You'd use your own ATM card, but—whoops!—you don't have a checking account! Be sure to say that you'd feel bad if she had to go get the food since you already said you'd do it. It might take some convincing on your part, but you can do it. Look how far you've gotten already. And now you got her PIN number and you can do creative stuff, like take out money from her account when she ain't looking. And you know what? Right now I got about two hundred bucks burning a hole in my pocket for this week's poker game, and all I had to do to get it was wait for Lucy to go to sleep.

# When The Biological Clock Breaks

*Mary J. Herlehy*

I didn't know I was too old at forty to bear a child. For some women that age isn't too old, but for me it was.

It was a gradual realization, a slow unraveling of an awful truth, which began quite happily: I got pregnant.

My husband Mark and I celebrated. We told our friends. We danced the tango. I swam and napped with my embryo week after week, waiting for my belly to swell with our child. But during the twelfth week the embryo slipped from its anchor, and I had a miscarriage. I bled for weeks. I healed. We tried again. We conceived and then I miscarried two more times, each time the embryo staying for a shorter and shorter time.

I was a healthy and active adult who never considered myself old, barely middle-aged, but my body was becoming immune to pregnancy, shrugging off the fetus like a sneeze.

I got angry. I got depressed. I got silly. I told Mark to find a new, fertile wife. And then my desire to have a child took hold again. I abstained from alcohol and caffeine. I tried acupuncture. I drank Chinese herbal teas that looked like they were scraped off the bottom of the forest floor. I saw my gynecologist. I meditated. But the pregnancies stopped. And I was nearly forty-two.

My last choice was infertility therapy. I was wary of the long-term side effects of the drugs. I wanted my body to remain natural. But my body's natural state now was to remain unpregnant. And I wanted to conceive and bear our child. So Mark and I signed up at a large and prestigious fertility clinic.

The statistics offered hope.

Over 20 percent of all North American couples are infertile. At least 50 percent of those who complete an infertility evaluation will have a successful pregnancy. But the caveat is that some infertility treatments have a higher success rate than others. I would discover that my problem fell into a gray area of treatability.

Infertility therapy is a world of tests. The man's sperm is counted and tested for motility and morphology. The woman is tested for progesterone and estrogen levels. Her eggs are counted and sized. She will know what her egg follicles look like, what her uterus looks like; she will know which chemicals cause ovulation, which chemicals aid in the implantation of the embryo. She will know how strong the veins in her arms are due to all the blood draws. And she will recognize her insurance carrier's logo as the bills roll in every other day through the mail slot. The couple will become number crunchers—counting the days, counting the shots, counting the deductibles. The menstrual cycles will span and split into injections and anxious waiting for results.

Dr. Eddie was highly recommended. His outlook was positive: within six menstrual cycles our child could be conceived and brought to full term. There were no long-term side effects. There was a possibility of multiple births. His techniques were obviously successful: photographs of infants and toddlers, singular and in sets, crowded the wall behind his desk.

A tall, stocky man with a set of tiny brown moles that bisected his upper right eyelid threatening to close down his eye forever, Dr. Eddie spoke in a thick accent of indeterminate origin, which forced us to lean forward onto the desk separating us. A plastic replica of a uterus and vaginal canal hovered behind my shoulder like a lusty maid.

Dr. Eddie detailed his plan quickly. But his explanation bogged down with medical jargon. I looked at Mark anxiously. Mark was a doctor and a sensitive partner, so at appropriate times he restated Dr. Eddie's plan and I relaxed. But when the doctor drew a timeline, indicating the numerous days I would be injected with fertility drugs, my face paled. Dr. Eddie asked, "Am I losing you, Mary?"

I told him I was all right, but to myself I was screaming. Needles? Daily visits to the clinic? This was much more than I had expected. My resolve wavered as Dr. Eddie ordered tests for Mark and me. Mark winked at me and said, "Be brave," as he walked into the rest room to produce sample sperm. A nurse invited me into an examining room and took blood from my arm.

Two days later, a pleasant but busy nurse, who talked as fast as Dr. Eddie, telephoned me. The tests indicated my estrogen and progesterone levels were low. My husband's sperm, however, were plentiful, perfectly shaped, and swam excellently. At least one of us had a good score. I met with Dr. Eddie again. He used the words "urgent" and "aggressive" as he explained that I was miscarrying because my system was slowing down, which happens to women after the age of thirty-five. My eggs were too old. Dr. Eddie wrote up a prescription for eight boxes of Humegon, which totaled up to nine hundred dollars. We had good insurance coverage. Our deductible was 10 percent.

I meditate in the dark alcove beneath my desk. With my eyes closed, legs crossed and palms up, I move mentally downward through my body, relaxing all muscles. I visualize myself sitting beneath an oak tree shading a glacial pond. In one hand I hold a bamboo fishing pole with a long line tied at the end with a round white bobber. Its movement creases the still water. I pull the rod and watch the sperm, wiggly and hungry, whiplash toward the bobber. I sigh and wish getting pregnant were this easy. A tall woman dressed in a blue hooded robe leans over me and whispers in my ear, "I've seen your child. She is coming."

There was a time when I didn't want children. During the go-go eighties, I worked hard, played hard. Then I burned out and couldn't produce anymore. I boxed my belongings and traveled alone for two years. Life broke open and started anew: I met Mark and fell in love. To our mutual delight we both wanted a family.

The first cycle of Humegon began.
Humegon is the brand name for menotropins, a drug which raises the fertility ante by stimulating the release of more than one egg per month. Menotropins contain FSH and LH, hormones that orchestrate the production

and release of eggs. Unfortunately, this drug cannot be taken orally. It has to be administered through the sharp end of a needle jabbed into the upper muscle of the buttock late at night by the woman's partner. Because Dr. Eddie prescribed an aggressive treatment, Mark had to pierce me with two needles full of menotropins every night, one in each buttock.

The injections lasted ten days. The point of entry was the same every night, so my muscles bruised and tears welled in my eyes before the needle channeled into my purpled skin. Mark was gentle. He made jokes: he stroked my back. He warned, "Here it comes!" as I clutched my shaggy dog and buried my face in her fur. Calluses eventually formed and I wore a badge of courage I couldn't look at. Sitting was painful, and a hot white light streaked my vision if I accidentally leaned against anything.

During those ten days I visited my ovaries every other day through the technology of ultrasound. I became used to being half-dressed for procedures and wore clothes that came off easily. I laid on an examining table, my feet hooked into stirrups, my bare legs covered with a sheet ready for another foray into the depths of my body. The overhead lights were turned off and the blue glow of a video monitor lit the face of the young, quiet technician. She typed my name, which showed up on the screen like a headline. Then she inserted into my vagina a dildo-shaped echo sounder called a transducer, which was dressed with a lubricated condom. The transducer was an explorer that reported a murky black-and-white picture of my uterus and egg-follicle underworld. Eggs are too tiny to see, so follicle size—the opening from which eggs float—is measured. The technician tapped the keyboard, placing $X$s on the perimeter of the egg follicles on the screen. She tapped more keys. A print emerged with measurements.

I became a cheerleader, coaching the tiny bodies to grow to their full potential. I became a competitor, pitting myself against myself, wanting the size and quantity of this month's egg crop to be larger than last month's. I knew I had little control. It was up to the drugs. I willed my body and mind to work together.

Next I had blood drawn. It was invasive in a less compromising way. The surroundings were more informal, better lit. I could stay dressed. I only needed to roll up my sleeve. A rubber tube was tied to my upper arm, exposing a ripe vein for plunder. A needle was injected. The procedure became so routine that I became careless about the nurse's warning not to transport anything heavy with my pierced arm. One day I walked to work after the office visit, carrying my heavy book bag for two miles, and developed a bruise on my arm larger and uglier than the one on my rear end.

Lovemaking used to be dotted with burning candles, fixed with long stares, and sealed with passionate kisses on the couch; now we watched the clock. We still made love, but we were focused on the outcome. Orgasm was a by-product, a physiological necessity to move the sperm up to the descending egg. When one is on the baby-making schedule, timing is everything. The days no longer had names; they had numbers. And when it was Day 14—ovulation day—we had to do IT now and often for the next twenty-four hours, whether we were in the mood or not.

The warmup, instead of champagne, was Pregnyl, an ovulation stimulator that was injected into my bruised posterior muscle. The Pregnyl rushed into my bloodstream and burnished my skin. "Let the foreplay begin," I told myself. But the lovemaking became altered. It rose over us like an alien form, coating our desire with a layer of fatigue and anxiety. The added spice of spontaneity was conspicuously absent. I felt more pressure than pleasure.

One ovulation day Mark and I were so exhausted that he injected the Pregnyl at 10:00 P.M., set the alarm for 4:00 A.M., and we both went to sleep, postponing what felt like a chore. When the alarm went off, we moved numbly, barely noticing a climax.

But we kept our sense of humor. We laughed a lot. Once I had the giggles all through our lovemaking. It seemed ludicrous to perform on demand. We called the injections cocktails. We kept the little Humegon bottles and glued them and a dollhouse–sized baby crib into a cigar box and named it the Baby Altar.

And then we waited for the results. Each day crawled by. My anxiety poked through and jeered during idle moments. On Day 26, the verdict arrived. No fertilization. My period, which used to be an awaited friend, the herald of good news, became the messenger of frustration and failure. We counseled with Dr. Eddie. My fertility levels were still too low; my eggs were too small, too few. The feeling of inadequacy dogged me. Mark hugged me tightly. "It's not your fault. It's going to take time," he said.

We added artificial insemination to the regimen. For the man, giving his partner shots in the butt is heroic, but to ejaculate into a cup and be substituted for by a syringe can be unnerving. Some men opt to make their deposit at the clinic, where there is a sanctuary, discretely located down the hall from the waiting room, with a locked door, low light, and girlie magazines. Some men prefer to perform in the comfort of their own homes, which pressures the couple to get to the clinic on time so the sperm can be injected as soon as possible.

My husband opted for home, which meant we sped to the doctor's office in the choke of morning rush-hour traffic. The sperm, if kept in a warm environment during transit, will stay alive in their tiny container. However, the quicker one gets to the clinic, the safer the little swimmers are. Once the sperm is delivered, the technician installs it into a machine that looks like a paint-can shaker. Through vigorous motion the good sperm are separated from the bad. The good sperm rise to the top like cream, the bad swimmers sink like a stone. Only a quarter of a teaspoon of sperm is needed to ensure good contact with the egg. So don't despair, dear audience, if the product of the man's endeavor is small. Only a few good swimmers are needed for the job.

We returned to the doctor's office, which was across the hall from the semen separator. The little guys were packed in a white box, which I handed to the nurse as she ushered us into an examining room. It was time to get back on the table with my feet in the stirrups, with the speculum at the ready. Giddyap! Mark sat next to me so I could squeeze his hand. He was dressed for work in a gray suit, tie, and striped shirt, while I, prone on the examining table, was dressed for work from the waist up and dressed in a sheet from the waist down. I wore wool socks to insulate my feet from the cold metal stirrups.

Mark had a tongue depressor tucked in his shirt pocket, which he had used as a shoe horn that morning. His eyes were alert and focused on the nurse who was threading the syringe filled with semen into the catheter. The nurse, gentle and expert in her delivery, inserted the catheter into my vagina. So far, so good. But the spongy condition of the cervix made it difficult for the catheter to pass through, and I got poked. That hurt. I squeezed Mark's hand. But once the catheter was past the gate, it moved quickly, like a snake sidewinding for shade, to the top of the uterus.

The nurse pushed the syringe and deposited the semen. I cramped. My uterine wall froze in a contraction. My husband pried my fingers from his hand. He was smiling, but his hand throbbed. The whole procedure took no longer than ten minutes, but every second was etched into my synapses. I was curled around the tip of the needle. The nurse instructed me to lie still for at least fifteen minutes to let the sperm reach their target.

What I've heard from well-meaning friends and what I never want to hear again:
> "All you have to do is quit and you'll get pregnant. You're concentrating too hard."
> "When God closes a door, he opens a window."
> "Adopt a child and you'll get pregnant."
> "Infertility is nature's way of controlling population."

"Have your husband wear boxer shorts."

"Stand on your hands after you make love."

JOURNAL ENTRY:
*The metallic taste zinging my tongue last night was not life, but death. It did not represent a little one growing deep within me, rather it was an impersonator distracting me while the little zygote slipped out of life, banking off my unyielding womb, and dissolved into a chemical mucus which passed out of me sometime during the night. I awoke not to the feeling of fullness and life, but to the stain of blood and failure between my legs.*

Infertility is an emotional boiler—churning, jumping, and painful to the touch. The needles hurt, the waiting is unendurable, the failure is inconsolable.

Mark and I are not alone. I see so many women waiting outside the doctor's office and at the ultrasound/blood work area. We look at each other, but don't talk, unwilling to share our misery. But there is a place that infertile couples can communicate anonymously—on the Internet. Infertility impacts on so many Americans that the World Wide Web has a large chat room addressed alt.infertility. It is there that potential mothers and fathers offer frank suggestions, share infertility experiences, and offer support. Here's a sampling:

SANDRA:
*...no other event in my life evoked such intense emotions. First there was the elation of the monthly expectation for pregnancy. This was closely followed by the despair of the realization of loss. The one pregnancy I experienced was filled with joy and fear...The pregnancy ended in miscarriage at three months, and we experience the pain of loss—again.*

NEW TO THE GROUP:
*I remember when we were just discovering that pregnancy does not come easily to all. I hate to say this but I have never gotten over resenting pregnant women. I was so jealous.*

NEVER-NEVER LAND:
*Mostly I just feel so sad. We were pregnant before any of our friends, but at 12½ weeks we found out our baby had died at*

*9 weeks. It just is not fair that these people have children and we still do not. I just want to crawl in a hole and cry for a long time.*

I, too, became jealous of pregnant women. They were everywhere. They came in all ages and races. Why wasn't I pregnant? My husband, the doctor, saw pregnant women every day. He had one client who got in the family way after making love once with her husband, with whom she had avoided intimacy for months. Her luck was aggravating. I was losing my generally balanced perspective.

I added mothers to my spreading jealousy. I stopped attending my friends' children's birthday parties. When my girlfriend became pregnant with her second child and cried because she didn't want another one, I hugged her. I understood, but it was difficult to hear. "Why can't it be me?" I said to myself. I cringed when mothers in the supermarkets swatted their children, yelling at them to shut up. "Be thankful you have a child," I whispered.

I do not romanticize motherhood. It is the hardest job in the world.

I sit alone in a coffeehouse blowing on scalding tea looking through the warm side of a plate-glass window during a cold rain. I watch a few adults dodge the falling drops like athletes. I'm in a grand-thinking frame which usually flares up just as the sun gets closer to the horizon. The thought is this: these adults converge onto this moment of time through need, roots, or dumb luck.

Our commonality is pinned to this moment in this location, like a dart to a corkboard. But there is another point. We all enter this life through the cave of our mothers. A La Salle Street broker wearing a Hawaiian-patterned jacket, its pockets sagging with his trading deck, is poking the air with a chewed fingernail at a short Latina meter maid. He had a mother. So did she. And so did her mother, as her mother did before her and on and on until we get to the time when there were more trees and animals on the earth than humans. And that wasn't so long ago, if you consider epochs as blinks on the dusty humps of an ever-spreading universe.

Most of these people out there in the rain were loved in their mother's arms, heard the word *no*, were taught boundaries and allowed to discover their talents. Then they separated by mutual agreement or by fate: the thick cord pulled thin into invisibility. Some broke their ties, never to return. Others strum their strings in moments of fear, feeling its vibration back to their mothers whose comfort is intractable.

A suck of cold air takes my attention from the window. A mother and boy walk finger in hand into the coffeehouse. He is chubby and wobbly on his two-year-old legs. His chin is wet with drool, his checkered jacket and suspended-by-elastic mittens wetted by the rain. The boy slides his fingers free from his mother's hand and waddles to the table next to me. He slaps his hands on the chair beneath the table and jams his feet onto its rungs with the intensity of a rock climber. His tiny feet launch his chubby knees onto the seat. Then he grunts and inhales rain specks dripping from his nose and pinwheels arm over arm until he is standing on the seat and leaning against the chair back, shouting, "Look at me, Mommy. I'm a big boy."

Now there are many ways a mother can react: like an alarm, hammering shouts of "No, get down, you'll get hurt," or quietly and confidently giving the kid a chance to grow tall. This mother smiled big. She unbuttoned her coat and leaned over and encircled her adventurous boy with a hug. His going places was all right with her.

And where was I going? I was caught in a never-ending purgatory of waiting. I couldn't make long-range plans because there was always the hope that I would become pregnant. I planned to be a stay-at-home mom for the first two years. And because I was "high risk," meaning over forty and prone to miscarriage, I had to stay close to medical facilities. The questions never stopped pounding me: Should I rev up my career now or wait? I could get pregnant any day now. Should we move to a larger apartment? Should we travel at Christmastime? My life became flat and static, tethered to the fertility establishment. I shunned my frustration. I skipped the fertility meds for a month. We went to Mexico. I seduced Mark on a non-ovulation day. I threw away the needles.

Squatting butt-naked in the woods ankle-deep in snow, the steam of the streaming pee curls from beneath my legs. I am far away from home, far away from people, just me and my shaggy black dog. Then drops of brown blood clot the yellow snow. It's another failure. Another month of trying. Another month of hoping. I drop my skirt and pull up my leggings and lick the tears coating my upper lip.

And the cycles clicked to number five. One more to go. Dr. Eddie mapped out the next step, *in vitro* fertilization, where the egg and sperm join in a petri dish. To prepare my body for the IVF, he told me I would have to undergo weeks of multiple daily injections and unavoidable side effects, such as weight gain, nausea, headaches, blurred vision, and fatigue. Eggs would not be harvested from me because my eggs were "too old." Dr. Eddie recommended that I talk to my college-age niece about donating her eggs. After fertilization, the eggs would be implanted in me through surgery, and I would have to lie in bed for at least a week. And the cost was staggering, almost twenty thousand dollars. It wouldn't all be out of our pocket. We have good insurance. But we were reaching our limit.

How far do I go? When do I say it's enough? When do I accept that my last option, fertility drugs, will not work for me? I looked in the eyes of my doctor and saw sperm, eggs, and dollar signs swirling down a deep, dark drain. My body ached. The drugs made me tired and irritable all the time. Mark didn't want to give me any more injections; he didn't want to administer any more pain. And although he would like to try IVF, he said he'd honor my decision.

I decided to stop the therapy.

INTERNET POSTING:
*Pregnyl and Humegon for Sale. We have given up and decided not to go through the agony every 28 days. We have about 25-30 Humegon (exp. Jan 97) for sale @ $20 apiece. Reply,* etc.

No statistics are available on how many people drop out of the infertility program. They litter the road to parenthood. Some people give up entirely, a few become pregnant on their own, and others opt for adoption. I submitted to aggressive treatment, but I couldn't go the distance. It was too invasive, too impersonal, too exhausting. The medical establishment gives the impression that they can give you what you want. They couldn't do it for me.

Did I say fertility therapy was my *last* option? Actually, there was another, standing in the wings like an understudy, one I wasn't ready to call on stage until I had tried everything else. And that was adoption.

My adopted child will not have my eyes and hair or my husband's smooth skin. I will not bond with my child in my body. I will not feel the child grow within me and emerge from me. I will not experience what most women experience. But is that all I'll miss by not giving birth to my own child? There's more. My body won't stretch, strain, and purple with varicose veins. I will not ride the roller-coaster emotions of postpartum depression. That's a bonus.

I have grieved for my unborn child. And for as much as I wanted my own natural child, to be with a child who sprang from my union with Mark, my desire to parent overrides the disappointment. I want to move ahead in my life and have my family. With my adopted child I will experience love and teach and be taught. Someone else's child will be my child.

We are on the adoption road now. There are frustrations and delays, but they are different. The documentations, interviews, and sworn affidavits have replaced the ultrasound and injections. We still have to wait, but the outcome is certain.

Mark and I are very happy. We call our friends. We dance the tango. We have been assigned a daughter.

# The One-Night Stand

### Drew Ferguson

He needed to leave, needed to leave now. The appointed time had come, and those brief and pleasing moments of a night's postcoital, blissful dreaming—the gentle yawn, the outstretched arms, the scratch of the soft blond patch of fur at the stomach, the smacking of the lips, fists massaging sleep from the corners of the eyes—had passed. There was no time—I urgently needed to get to work. Already, the office would be alive with the insect sounds of buzzing computer screens, the ring of telephones, the Chinese water torture pounding of keyboards, the hum of fluorescent lights. It was as if I could hear my desk creaking under the weight of memos, paperwork, reports, the necessary documentation, the projected sales figures, the quotes, the briefs, the options; see its legs splintering, slivers of wood tearing apart under a mountain of work, and still, he would not get up. I stood in the bedroom in my pressed blue suit. I loomed above him as he slept, my briefcase and cell phone firmly in hand, watched the easy, wavelike rise and fall of his breastbone, the fuzzy hair stirring with each breath, and I knew that he was pretending to sleep to spite me.

I kicked him—this One-Night Stand, who even this morning was as indifferent as he had been in my arms last night—the toe of my wingtips connecting with a hard bone. I felt it through the leather of my shoes, felt my own toes cracking, crumbling, breaking apart in my sock and filling it like pea gravel. I clutched at my foot, hopped wildly on one leg, my eyes red and pinched, my head lifted, shouting, cursing, damning him and his mother; but he didn't move, didn't even stir; my kick had done nothing to stir him—a toy chisel to an Everest of inertia. My watch grumbled, its hands twisting like angry lips; the second hand, like a little black tongue, spit out, bitter thick, thick, thick, thicks—he had to leave now.

And I was on top of him, crawling on him, my knees on his chest, sinking into his rib cage like it was freshly laid wet sod; my tie dangled above his nose, barely touched it, tickled it almost; the points of my shoes pressed into his stomach, one shoe's tip hooking into the center of his navel; my fingers curled around his ears, leaving the indentations of pink half-moons. I leaned my face into his—so close that I smelled hints of breath from his closed mouth, felt the softness of his breathing against my lips, saw the involuntary flutter of his eyelashes against his tan, freckled cheeks. "Wake up!" I yelled, feeling spittle dribble off my lip and down my chin. My spit beaded on his face. "Wake up!" I jerked his head left, right, bounced it against the pillow—nothing. Nothing. These things never come easy, I told myself. When the enemy is deeply entrenched, dig him out.

I sprang from the bed, tore off its blankets and sheets, threw the pillows across the room. At the foot of the bed, I grabbed his bony ankles, squeezed them so tightly in my hands that I felt the outlines of the tiny blond hairs on my palms. I pulled—heaved—the dead weight of his body, straining my shoulders and my back; the muscles ached dully; sweat pooled in the furrows of my reddening forehead, under my eyelids, in the pits of my arms, the small of my back, my crotch. My underwear was a damp washcloth, my shirt an ocean. All my effort and he hadn't budged. His fingers were curled underneath the mattress, his hands holding him in place, his lips curled upward in a faint smile. So this is how it is. "Fine," I said, dropping his ankles, "stay there and rot for all I care," and I slammed the bedroom door behind me. In an instant, I heard him leap from the bed, his dry feet swishing the floor like sandpaper on wood. I spun, my arms frantically reaching for the doorknob; it was as if my hands were no longer my own and were attached to the ends of very long poles; I tried to move and manipulate them, but they dumbly fumbled everything. The tumblers in the door's lock rattled, clicked, and fell into place. A soft giggle came from behind the door.

"Bastard! Motherless child!" I shouted, but my voice gurgled like a drowning man's, and I knew that he could not hear me. He was rummaging through my closet, that I could hear; tearing into my clothes, the boxes that I had packed there, like a starved rat foraging for food. This is the way of things, I thought to myself, pulling at my hair as my pacing carved a circle in front of the bedroom door. A One-Night Stand is a modern homesteader. A shared evening, and what was yours is now his.

In the kitchen, as if joining the conspiracy against me, the refrigerator began to hum more loudly—a mechanical moaning of Strauss's "Blue Danube Waltz," the bottles of liquor atop it clinking together on all the downbeats—threatening to drown out the smacking noises from inside the bedroom. "Mmmmmm, mmmmmmm," the One-Night Stand groaned, then a slapping sound, the smug sharpness of skin on skin. He was eating in there, eating and patting his belly in satisfaction.

"There's only paste in there! Only paste!" I called out in a singsong voice. "Paste may be good for a schoolboy, but you'll need more to eat. You'll need to come out sooner or later." Something hit the floor inside the bedroom with a glop. I knew he had dropped the paste spreader. I had the upper hand. I needed to act swiftly and use the moment of his imbalance to my advantage, but at the instant I thought I had him broken down like a convict with the white glare of a cop's interrogation light burning his corneas, the bedroom door flew open, my briefcase, my cell phone sailed through the air, defining a slow arc and thudding to the floor. In the split second where I debated picking up the briefcase or forcing my way into the bedroom, the door snapped shut with such force, such violence, that my body shook, my eyes blinked, and when they opened again I was already at work, seated at my desk.

Taped to my phone was a message. "Hon," it read, "can you stop by the store and get some milk, butter, and eggs?" No. This could not be. It must not be. I dialed the phone; he answered, "Oh, it's only you." I demanded an explanation, insisted that he owed me at least that; I threatened, cajoled, reminded that I was well within my rights to—he hung up. I redialed. He answered again in a tinny voice, pretending to be my answering machine.

"Stop it!"

"No, you stop it!"

"No, *you* stop it!" I slammed down the phone, pleased with my little victory, thrilled that I had gotten in the last word. Now, to get home to drive him from the house and into the desert. I sprang from my desk, but my feet and arms were shackled there. The iron manacles that bound my wrists and hands had miniature clocks attached to them, counting off the time until five o'clock.

I had to leave now, I couldn't wait until then. There was no telling what he would be capable of given that much time. Already I heard the sounds of a U-Haul pulling up to the curb of my house, the grunts of sweaty movers unpacking grand piano after grand piano and stacking them in the middle of my living room like Lincoln Logs. Already he'd be changing the carpeting, putting up new wallpaper, adding his name to the mailbox. It had to stop.

I grabbed a sheet of paper and typed out a memo to all the employees stating that upon the reading of this memo it officially would be five o'clock. It was beautiful. It was art. The words flowed like the waters of the Nile. Shakespeare never crafted more beautiful prose. Coleridge in all his opium-inspired reveries could never have conceived of such precise opulence. The letters themselves were heavy with gold leaf, the paper vellum, and to make it all the more official, I signed my name in blood and added a thick, red wax seal. It would be photocopied, faxed, e-mailed, delivered by God's own archangels if need be. And the shackles fell, the iron clanged, and the voices of the temps and clerks and typists were raised in joyous exaltation as my name was sung on high; but even I, who never dreamed such enthusiasm and good will were possible among my employees, even I realized I had no time for this. At once, outside of the office, I hailed a cab and we were on our way, but it was as if its wheels were made of oatmeal. I was dumb with anger. His plot, his malicious campaign had extended even this far. If he could bribe my cab driver—no, not just my cab driver, he would have had to bribe all the cab drivers in the entire city, and I knew this then, as I saw the Yellow Cabs drive past and the pockmarked, jeering, toothless faces of their drivers glaring at me—he would have his way unless I got home.

Crops were planted, grew, were reaped; children were conceived in bouncing beds, were born with indignant wails and little fingers clawing air, trying to scrape their way back into the womb, were raised, married, had children of their own, died; governments were overthrown; and at last, I was at home and outside the bedroom door.

At my feet was a breakfast service from the hotel—the polished silver tray, the endless pieces of silverware, the lids, the plates, the crystal vase with white gardenia, the wrinkled linen napkins, and piles of half-eaten buttermilk donuts. Behind the door, an electric train—sixteen cars, minus caboose and engine, just like I had begged my mother for but she had refused to buy—whirled in a metallic swish. I struggled with the doorknob, grappling it, rattling it in my hands as my body shook. It wouldn't budge, wouldn't move.

Unless something happened, years would pass without me sleeping in my own bed; and he would still be here, still there behind the door, mocking me, playing with a train set that should be mine. Enough of this, I thought, and my hands were thrown from the door, flying into the air, my bemoaning fists shaking over my head, the curse of Jonah and Job on my lips—haven't I suffered enough? Am I not human? Do I not also bleed? I must draw up a petition, list my grievances in triplicate, get them notarized, then they would hear my pleas. But it was too late. Where could a lawyer be found at this hour? Search the golf courses high and low and like the insects they were, they would scurry under rocks and rotting tree stumps to hide their presence. But if this case were not about justice, they would have been so thick upon me I'd have had to beat them away. Still, the web of this One-Night Stand's conspiracy stretched even further. Now it was all the lawyers against me. Even as my hands beat in time with "The Blue Danube" hummed by the fridge, even as the sound of my own skin slamming into the wood of the door threatened to drown out the engine blasts of the tiny locomotive, I knew that even then, there would be no hope without assistance. I raced to the phone, jumping over the tray, spilling donut crumbs along my floor, picked up the receiver and frantically punched 9-1-1. It rang and rang. Rang. Rang. My mother answered. She was unhappy.

"I am unhappy," she said. Her voice was bitter disapproval. "I've spoken to him, you know...I think he's right...."

"But...," I protested. My heart sank—her, too?

"No! You've made your bed, now you have to lie in it."

She hung up, and there was no choice but for me to put on my pajamas, knock on the bedroom door, and climb into bed.

# *Scars*

*Sean Leenaerts*

Tell me this—whose life goes unblemished?
I am curled on the bed, looking across to the window where my lover sits, and counting the scars upon his flesh. Sometimes, in the darkness, I will run my fingers over him while he sleeps, reading him like braille. Scars are our personal hieroglyphs. We collide through life and carry our history upon our skin.

Boccaccio is coiled like a fist over the leather strap he has stamped beneath a boot heel and pulled up around one knee. He sharpens the blade of a fishing knife in long, rasping strokes against the leather while the early morning light pierces through the open window, illuminating him like an angel in a Raphael.

"He's going to die," Boccaccio whispers hoarsely. "He's going to die."

He holds the knife as if to choke it. Such strong hands. And large. When we make love, his hands will close in around me, engulf me, swallow me whole. They can touch me everywhere at once, it seems. An athlete would envy such hands, as would a murderer.

"You'll sharpen the knife away, *cara*," I say to him.

Boccaccio shakes his head.

"He's going to die...He's going to die..."

By the blade or by the bullet—or in the grip of Boccaccio's hands—Jean-Dominique Orezza will doubtless die today because Boccaccio says it will happen. In the matter of the vendetta, he is a man who can be counted on to keep his word.

"Don't cross Boccaccio unless you're dressed for the funeral" is what people say.

Boccaccio moves through life like an avenging angel. And if anyone notices him, it is only to glance away. A volatile mixture, he is magnificent and terrible at the same time.

"*Cara*, forget this foolishness and come to bed," I tell him. "Make love to me and put Jean-Dominique from your mind. He's an idiot. Everyone knows it."

Boccaccio says nothing, but only pulls the knife harder against the strap until it almost cuts into his knee.

I do not want this vendetta. It is not my wish for anyone to die. Especially Jean-Dominique Orezza, for whom I feel neither hate nor love. He is young and handsome, and is therefore cocky—believing, as all young men do, that the world is his for the taking. He has not yet been beaten down by life.

It began two nights ago. We were at the Café Braga, sitting at a table near the back, hidden in the shadows. There were laughter and loud voices from the bar up front, where Jean-Dominique was holding court over a group of young men. The talk was, as it always is when young men are full of wine and themselves, about women.

"Francesca Angellini would be an interesting lay," one of the young men suddenly said.

I quickly colored at the mention of my name, but tried to act as if I had not heard. Still, Boccaccio had heard. And I watched, feeling a trapped ball of breath in my throat, as his hands congealed into fists.

"Francesca?" Jean-Dominique said. "She's too old."

"A woman in her forties is not old, my friend," the young man said. "She's experienced. And her body is fine. I bet she can go." He made a humping motion with his hips and everyone laughed.

I smiled thinly at Boccaccio and gave a little shrug to let him know I was not offended, praying that the young men would stop talking about me. Just stop talking altogether and leave the café. That would have been best. But Boccaccio was not looking at me. He was staring hard at his hands upon the table. A darkness came into his eyes, like storm clouds moving in, and I felt myself shiver.

"Gino would fuck his own mother, he's so hard up," Jean-Dominique said. "Sure, Francesca has a good body, but her face is like a box of frogs. Maybe a sack over the head would do the trick."

"Ah, but who fucks a face?" another young man asked.

"I do," Jean-Dominique replied, sticking a finger lasciviously into his mouth.

Boccaccio sent his chair banging to the floor. All the young men turned their heads. Without a word, he walked out of the shadows and to the end of the bar, sucking them all in with his stare.

"Shit," one of the young men whispered.

Not a word more was spoken. There was a sudden and stark suspension of sound, not a silence so much as a stillness, like when a hunter pauses in the forest at the sound of a snapped twig.

Without taking his eyes off Jean-Dominique, Boccaccio put out his hand and extended his arm back to me cavalierly. I got up and walked slowly to him. He took my hand gently, tenderly. Still looking at Jean-Dominique, he brought my hand to his lips and kissed it. It surprised me, how soft it was. Then he suddenly pulled me into his arms and clamped his mouth passionately onto mine, giving me a kiss that tugged at my soul. When our lips parted my mouth felt numb and woolly, like my tongue was made of felt.

Boccaccio looked back at Jean-Dominique. And if ever death had a face, it would have that look—a look that struck you like a bludgeon.

With his hand still encasing mine, Boccaccio pulled me along past the young men and out into the street. We walked in silence until we were almost home.

"Foolish boys, that's all," I finally said.

Boccaccio brought his finger to my lips and shook his head. I said nothing more. That night, as I tried to fall asleep, I heard him in the next room, in the dark, sharpening his knives.

I am not a great beauty.

I know this and accept it. My face is too long, my mouth and eyes set a little too wide, my nose thin and crooked from having been broken when I was a girl. But I have a good figure, long, thick hair, and I keep a neat appearance. "Stay thin and dress well, Francesca, and men will notice," my mother told me often. "They look at the body more than the face." For the most part, I have found this to be true.

Although I am not a town mattress like Louisa Poggioli, I have the reputation of a fallen woman. It is doubtless the consequence of my divorce. Never mind that the marriage failed through no fault of mine. In Corsica, a woman never leaves her husband. Ever. It does not matter if he is a drunkard, a bully, or a spendthrift. A man is an animal that must be captured, tamed, and broken in like a stallion. If a woman cannot do that, she is to blame.

My husband was not a drunk. Nor did he ever raise his hand against me or squander our life's savings. He never lived off me like some husbands I know. He did not treat me badly, but neither did he treat me well. Because for him to do any one of those things would have meant showing signs of life.

There are people who do not like living. They treat life as if it is a terrible disease and they wait to die. They quarantine themselves from the rest of the world—not to keep their malaise from spreading to others, but to keep from catching happiness. This is how it came to be with my husband. He had not always been this way, and to this day I do not know what caused it, for he became as silent as he was sad.

I am by nature a happy person, although life has shown me the back of its hand more than once. For me, happiness is a kind of perseverance—not an enduring, but simply an acceptance that life is what it is and a desire to squeeze as much pleasure out of it as I can. But my husband's unhappiness came down on me heavy as a stone, crushing out the laughter and the love I had once felt for him.

At first, I blamed myself. Perhaps there was something I was not giving him. So I gave more, but he only sank deeper into his gloom, sitting in his chair outside the front door with a glass of wine and staring at the granite hills in the distance. It was then that I began to blame him. I blamed him for his inertia. Hit me, shout, break the crockery, walk out the door, and leave me—any of these was preferable to his stony silence. I began to berate him, to scream at him in order to provoke some response. But it was like talking to myself. I felt shrewish, ugly. I thought I was going mad. So one day I packed two bags with a few of my belongings, and I left. There was nothing more that I could do. As I walked out the door, I tripped on the steps—the bags were heavy—and fell sprawling into the dirt, gashing my knee on a rock. I left, cursing and crying, my knee bleeding, and he never said a word. Not even goodbye.

But that is all in the past, now. I have no idea what happened to him. None at all. There is only a faded wedding photograph somewhere in a scrapbook and a scar on my knee to remember him: my own hieroglyph that says I was unhappy once.

Until Boccaccio.

The day I met Boccaccio, everything was bleached and faded, like a photograph left in the sun too long. It was hot and I was sweating, my dress sticking to me like a second skin. I was not feeling pretty. I only wanted to get home, to escape the sun and lie down naked on cool sheets with the fan blowing air on me. Yet when I first saw Boccaccio on the wharf, gutting fish, I could not help stopping to watch the way his large hands moved so deftly with the knife, quickly, almost tenderly. It was hypnotic. Seeing my shadow, Boccaccio had looked up at me, frowning.

"Why do you stare at me?" he asked.

At first, I could not speak. What could I say? That I liked the way he cut open fish? That I wondered what his hands would feel like against my skin? That at that very moment I wanted to bite into his body? What could I say?

"Your hands...they're interesting." That is what I told him.

He looked down at his hands, slick with blood and smeared with fish entrails, then looked back up at me, squinting.

"You maybe make a joke?"

I shook my head quickly, like a little girl, scared.

He chuckled softly. It sounded like pebbles dropping in a can. "You like fish, then?" he said, slitting open another fish as easily as opening an envelope. He held the cleaned fish out to me. Without even thinking I took it in my hands. Our fingers touched. I wanted to throw myself around him.

"Cook it soon, while it's still salty from the sea," he told me, a smile burning itself along the edges of his mouth. "It's the best way."

"Come to dinner, tonight, and I'll cook it for you," I said.

Boccaccio looked up at me, the knife in one hand, a fish in the other.

"A fish such as this should be seasoned with gratitude and shared," I said. "It's best that way."

Boccaccio smiled and I was startled by the whiteness of his teeth, like sunlight bursting through the clouds.

"Come around seven," I told him, turning to leave, not giving him a moment to answer yes or no. I could no longer stand his gaze upon me, that brilliant smile, his muscles shimmering with sweat. His hands.

I never doubted that he would come. Yet seeing him at my doorstep, his hair slicked down and face freshly shaven, I was taken by surprise. Part of me had hoped he would not come, that he would have stayed home or gone out to one of the cafés instead, to sit with a glass and a silent smile, musing upon how Francesca Angellini had tried to seduce him with a fish. I would have eaten his gift alone, feeling a little sad, but also relieved that my passion would have had a chance to cool. My life would continue as it always had, peaceful and uncomplicated. But there he was, in white pants and a crisp white shirt and a flash of gold across his chest, smiling and silent, and I felt my heart tremble.

We ate dinner, our eyes saying much, our mouths saying little. Afterwards, we made love. Like that.

As I was picking up the dishes from the table, Boccaccio took hold of my wrist. "The fish was seasoned just right," he said, his eyes intense and shining. I leaned down to kiss his lips and fell into him as if falling into deep, dark water.

I have been with Boccaccio for almost a year. We have loved each other and talked of marriage, though not in the sense that we would need to seek a priest. God has blessed me with Boccaccio. In his presence I am alive and joyful. In his eyes I find acceptance. In his smile there is peace. If I am a fallen woman, in his embrace there is forgiveness. It is marriage enough, I believe, in the eyes of God.

The day is ending.

Boccaccio leans against a tree and waits, the cigarette in his lips sending a blue membrane of smoke drifting up and spreading out above him like a delicate fisherman's net. He stares out to the west, to the burned edges of the sky. He looks calm, at peace, reflective. He is about to kill a man.

In the hills just outside of town they are building a villa for a rich Frenchman. Jean-Dominique is a carpenter there. At the end of the day he and all the other workers must pass along this road back into town. It is the only way. They walk along the edges of the road, laughing and talking, or in silence, their cigarettes hanging from their lips. A few of them turn their heads and glance over at Boccaccio, who makes no attempt to hide his presence, and then they turn away, pretending not to notice.

I have followed Boccaccio here, cajoling him, teasing him, and finally pleading with him not to go through with this vendetta. But he is beyond hearing my words, beyond reason. He is locked within himself. I know he does not want me here, although he has not told me to go away. I myself know I should not be here. It is not right, not proper, even if the vendetta is for my honor. But I, too, am compelled by something beyond my control. It is like staring at the scene of an accident, repulsed but curious, waiting to catch a sight of blood. I am staying to see it through.

I hear him before I see him, his laughter hitting my ears like a gust of wind. Coming around the bend, Jean-Dominique is talking with two men, his hands animated and his eyes flashing as he tells them about some woman he has bedded. He is kissing the tips of his fingers when he spots Boccaccio leaning against the tree, arms folded across his chest and his black eyes staring into him. Storm clouds flashing bolts of lightning.

Jean-Dominique continues talking, keeping the humor in his voice and holding his smile before him like a shield, but I see the light go out of his eyes. He laughs like a condemned man.

"Jean-Dominique tells you about the goats he's fucked, no doubt," Boccaccio calls out. "I tell the farmers, 'Keep your gates locked at night.'"

There is some laughter from the men. Jean-Dominique stops talking now and his hands drop down to his sides, curling convulsively into fists. But he continues walking, passing by Boccaccio and staring straight ahead. His jaw works as if he were chewing on something too distasteful for him to swallow.

Boccaccio steps out from under the tree. "He would like, of course, to fuck my Francesca," he continues. "He is jealous of my good fortune. But my Francesca, she is too much of a woman for him. She is too human. And animals can only fuck with animals."

The men along the road stop and turn to watch Jean-Dominique, waiting to see what he will say or do. He knows that he is on the line and he must choose between continuing to walk or turn and make a stand. Either way, Boccaccio will make it painful for him.

Boccaccio draws his knife, gleaming sharply in the waning light. "God forbid he should breed and produce more like him. I will maybe cut off his prick, eh? To protect the animals."

Jean-Dominique stops, whirls around. There is a hammer in his hand. He grips it with his knuckles turning white. "What is it you want, Boccaccio? You want to teach me a lesson? Eh? You think maybe that will make me take back my words about your Francesca? Well, I tell you this—I would still rather fuck the goats."

A few men laugh at this. Even Boccaccio smiles. Two men who are standing near me but do not seem to notice that I am there nod silently to one another. One of them whispers that the boy has balls, after all.

"Now that he's discovered them, pity that Boccaccio will cut them off for him," the other answers.

The smile slowly melts from Boccaccio's lips until his mouth is straight, his expression flat. He stands there, silent and unmoving like carved marble. A sphere of silence locks around us, as if everything were suddenly encased in glass—heavy, dense, and refracted. But easily shattered.

When Boccaccio finally does move, he does so slowly, as though his limbs were grinding away in their sockets. He sheaths the knife almost gently, carefully letting it slide in and then snapping the guard over its handle. He begins walking towards Jean-Dominique, hands out slightly at his sides, palms upraised, as if he had been asked a question to which he did not have the answer.

Jean-Dominique backs away, bouncing on his toes and shaking the hammer at his side, trying to keep the distance between himself and Boccaccio. Boccaccio picks up the pace, walking quickly now, his stride long and purposeful as if he is a man in a hurry to get someplace and he cannot wait to get there. His hands curl into fists. Jean-Dominique suddenly turns to run, his heels kicking up dust. Although he is no doubt faster than Boccaccio, he has waited too long. It is too late to play the coward now. Boccaccio tackles him to the ground, ripping the hammer from his grasp and throwing it into the trees. He pulls Jean-Dominique to his feet, his hands suddenly covering the young man with an avalanche of blows. He is quick and merciless. Jean-Dominique cannot even bring his hands up to protect his face.

But most frightening is the calmness with which Boccaccio administers the punishment. He is mechanical, his face showing no emotion, as if he were gutting a fish that he had caught.

Each time Jean-Dominique sinks to his knees, Boccaccio pulls him up by the shirt and pumps his fist into the young man's face and body until he sinks to the ground again. Jean-Dominique tries to land a few blows, but they are useless. They bounce off Boccaccio's body like pebbles. I do not think Boccaccio even feels them.

There is a sickening crunch as Boccaccio lands a punch into Jean-Dominique's ribs, and he cries out like a small animal caught in a trap. He falls against Boccaccio, hugging him as if he were refuge. He coughs up blood and spits out several teeth. He says something, but I cannot make out the words. Boccaccio brings his knee up into the young man's groin and Jean-Dominique drops to his knees, then sprawls out on the ground, wailing. Straddling him, Boccaccio continues beating him. I turn my head away, but I cannot ignore the sounds. It is like someone hitting bags of grain. Suddenly Jean-Dominique stops crying. When I look over at him once more, he is unconscious. He will never be handsome again.

When it becomes apparent that Boccaccio intends to kill Jean-Dominique by beating him with his bare hands, only then do all the men—who have stood by and watched in horror and fascination—rush in to pull him off. It is unforgivable to interfere with another man's vendetta, but they probably think Jean-Dominique has been punished enough. He is mutilated for life. Perhaps even crippled. That is worse than death.

It takes four men, struggling, to pull Boccaccio away. As soon as they get him off, two other men quickly drag Jean-Dominique's body between them, walking quickly down the road into town.

Boccaccio shakes off the men, glaring around him. They back away. He spots a well at the edge of a field and walks over to it. He pumps the handle slowly, tiredly, and begins to wash his hands, which look like a butcher's. The blood runs off with the water, staining the cement around the pump. He holds his hands under the cold water for a long time.

The road is deserted now. The men have dispersed. I walk over to him, my Boccaccio. He does not look up at me as I approach.

"You beat him too much," I say, my voice soft.

"I wanted him to know what it feels like" is all Boccaccio says.

I look down at his hands. They are red and raw and bleeding. There are cuts on them everywhere. They will turn into scars. He has done this for me, and part of my life will become his history. And Jean-Dominique's, as well. His scars have my name on them, too.

In the deepening twilight, the spreading moonlight, I reach out and gently take Boccaccio's hands in mine. Bringing them to my lips, I hear the breath pour out of his mouth as I touch each cut with my tongue, tasting blood.

# *Lucy*

## *Mark Beyer*

Lucy stood before her full-length swivel mirror and tilted it down to see her shoes. She wore pumps from two different pairs of shoes, and almost immediately the black patent leather with three-inch heel was ruled out in favor of the shorter-heeled, red, open-toed one that matched perfectly with her miniskirt and cashmere sweater.

On the bed were the discards of an all-out assault just levied on her closet in search of something, anything, to wear on her sixteenth birthday. A stack of tops and skirts still on the hanger took up the left side of the bed where she had dumped them straight from the rod. The other half of the bed was a jumble of empty hangers and mismatched skirts and tops. At any minute Lucy anticipated a shot from a car horn alerting her that it was time to go. Strewn around her feet were the many shoes that she had eliminated as well, at least a dozen different single shoes she'd gone through in her weekly Friday night ritual. As she bent to replace the black pump with the open-toed red one, she noticed the untouched shoe boxes still in the closet. Not bad, she thought. What would she have done had she gotten through the final box with no decision made?

From outside her closed bedroom door Lucy heard heels clicking as they ascended the five stairs from the living room to the bedroom-level landing. They were unmistakable notations of her mother's presence. When the clicking heels failed to fade and instead grew louder and finally stopped outside her door, Lucy knew her mother had come to bother her. A light rapping echoed inside the room.

"What you want out dare?" Lucy said in a mocking tone. She'd perfected her mother's pidgin English complete with Italian accent. "What's going on?"

A calm voice spoke, filtered through the door, almost too soft to hear and unlike the usual sharp tongue Lucy had grown accustomed to hearing since before she could remember.

"Lucy, *tu mama* wanna talk to you."

Lucy rolled her eyes and shook her head. She quickly sat at her vanity and began fingering her long red tresses, dividing the freshly washed bunches of curly hair into separate strands.

"Come on in," she said, but didn't look over as her mother entered and closed the door behind her.

"Oh my God!" her mother said at the sight of the room. "You got to clean dis mess up."

Lucy was focused on herself in the mirror, pulling at her unruly curls and trying her best to ignore her mother. That wasn't working, though, as she saw her mother's fuzzy image bending down at her own words and pairing up shoes inside the boxes piled around the mirror like a lot of unused bricks.

"Ma! What do you want? I'm busy and in a hurry and I have to leave."

Maria Gianfranco set two capped boxes aside and stood behind her daughter, watching Lucy primp. She wanted to sit next to Lucy, but the bed was taken over by the clothes. If she sat on the clothes her daughter would complain that they would get wrinkled. If she went to move them her daughter would say she needed them. If she moved to hang them up her daughter would yell. So she stood behind her daughter and began her prepared speech.

"We need to talk 'bout some t'ings," she said to Lucy's mirrored image.

"Like what?" Lucy said, moving on to her makeup and applying too much eye shadow to a face needing no help from artificial hues. She hadn't any idea what bomb her mother was readying to drop on her. Their "talks" had become frequent since she'd entered her teens, with a lot of innuendo and warnings and information that Lucy knew was patently false. Yet her mother hadn't yet come out and said anything that remotely broached the truth about sex.

"You get'n older now, Lucy," Maria said, preparing herself.

"Yeah, so?" Lucy said, still not seeing the sucker punch.

"So you can't ever let no boy lay on top of you."

Maria said it quickly and folded her arms across her stomach, standing firm behind her daughter with a stern look setting her face like a plaster cast.

For the first time since her mother came into the room, Lucy looked at her through the mirror. Her jaw dropped open but no words came out. What could she say? How could she possibly respond? A denial? That would just make her mother suspicious (no, *more* suspicious). A firm "Mind your own business"? That would quite possibly result in a slap across her face and more trouble than it was worth. Then how about a simple "Why?" That might get a rise out of her mother—no, it *would* get a rise, and then some stammering, and possibly some metaphorical mumbo jumbo about babies. The time factor disallowed that, however. At least for now. It was just that the statement—no, the command—was so stupid and ignorant that any actual words would have paled the laughter that was welling up inside Lucy's belly. Lucy listened for the car horn that would signal her escape; that wasn't going to happen.

"What are you talking about?" Lucy said, her eyes working in various squints and trying to hold her mother's shifting gaze. Her question was a mere afterthought, a knee-jerk reaction to just one more of her mother's proven-endless supply of imbecilic lines spoken over what Lucy knew was more like twenty years of life packed into the fifteen that she was leaving behind.

"I know what you do," her mother said, and nodded very sagely. Lucy's heart jumped and she felt her chest tighten. Then she rolled her eyes and looked back at herself in the mirror. Her mother didn't know anything; this was just another shakedown she must have gotten from some talk-show topic such as "How to Confront Your Kids about Sex" (or drugs or prostitution or guns or bulimia or contraception or anorexia). Lucy admonished herself for buying into it for even that five seconds of heart failure. Her mother had nothing on her, no knowledge that she had any boyfriends, or of what she did with her boyfriends, no idea that her boyfriends were black, no clue that she'd been playing around on the threshold of sex for three years now.

Her disgust with her mother showed in her tone. "What are you talking about, Ma?"

Maria stepped to Lucy's side and pushed the clothes over to make room for herself. She plopped down on the bed's soft mattress and heard the springs bend. Now she was on the same level as her daughter and she could look at her face. With her hands wringing in her lap she spoke.

"I talk about you girls. How it's your time to be going out wid boys. You got all kindsa t'ings in your head 'bout what you want to do. I tell you those t'ings gonna get you in trouble. You don't want that."

Lucy turned to her. "Is this our sex talk?"

Her mother's face turned crimson. "I no talk 'bout sex and neither do you. Sex is for when you get married."

Lucy couldn't stifle a laugh. "Ah, OK." She shook her head and rolled her eyes.

Maria reared back. "What you say? You having sex now?!"

Lucy turned in her chair. "Ma, I'm not having sex. Why don't you stop getting so crazy?"

"Then why you talk 'bout it?" She was frozen on the bed, flabbergasted by what Lucy was saying.

"I'm not talking about it, Ma, you are," Lucy snapped. She closed her mascara top with a snap and threw it on the tabletop.

"I only try to explain 'bout something mother and daughter should talk about when a daughter is old enough to understand." Her face was a mass of confusion, lower lip twitching, eyes bulging.

Lucy was agitated and only wanted to get out of the room, through the back door, and out of the house. This talk wasn't going to go away, and somehow she had to make her mother understand.

"You're not telling me anything I don't already know, Ma. You're not *telling* me anything at all. You're trying to tell me what to do, and I hate that and you know it." The red had now risen in Lucy's face, and she sat close in to her mother with her hands clenched into fists before her. "If you wanted to tell me about sex you're too late. I already know all about it."

Her mother's eyes widened. "So you do have sex? I *knew* it."

Lucy hung her head in exhaustion, feeling drained from battle. When she looked up her mother stared at her with a defensive, hurt, betrayed look in her eyes.

"Ma! I'm not having sex. I didn't say I was, I never said that. I just said that I know about it from school. They teach how things work in school, Ma, so we know about ourselves. I probably know more about sex and a woman's body than you do, and you've had three kids."

"What they teach you over there? How to have sex?"

Lucy shook her head, lips pressed tight. Where was that car horn?

"No, Ma," she said. "But at least they're teaching us about ourselves when we need to know."

"I never knew 'bout that stuff till my mudda tole me on my wedding day," Maria said very softly, taking the edge off her voice.

Lucy couldn't believe that. Well, she thought, maybe that was true. Her mother was so ignorant, maybe she didn't know.

"Well," Lucy explained, "times have changed."

"Oh, boy!" her mother exclaimed. "Too fast."

A car horn blared loudly, one long blast that cut through the night and in through the back window.

"I gotta go now, Ma," Lucy said, and she rose from the chair and got around it quickly, leaving her mother still on the bed. She opened her purse and checked its contents, then snapped it closed.

"We no finish talking yet."

"Yes, we have," Lucy said, pulling on her long wool white-and-black checked coat. "They're waiting for me."

"What, dey come pick you up in cars now?" Maria was off the bed and following her daughter out of the room. "Why don't dey come in and meet us? You fadda want to talk wi' dem." Their heels clacked across the wood floors, Lucy's at long intervals and her mother's staccato step-stepping as she raced to catch up.

"It's Julia, Ma, not a boy," Lucy said as she descended to the living room, "and she's had her license for two months now. Why don't you relax and go watch basketball with Pa?"

"You said 'they'." Her mother stood by the door but didn't block it.

"She's probably with Mary and Lisa."

"Mary!" her mother said. "She go out wid black guys."

Lucy stopped adjusting her coat.

"So what?"

"What you mean, 'So what'? I don't want you seein' no black men. Dey not like us. Dey live like a da pigs. Dey get dare girls pregnant."

Lucy rolled her eyes.

"Good-bye, Ma," she said and reached for the door.

"Don't listen to me," her mother said. "I stupid. I know nothing. I got three kids and house and job. But I stupid, right?" Lucy opened the door. "You no come home if you get pregnant. You stay wid man who got you dat way. You come home pregnant and we toss you in da street."

The door slammed and Lucy was on the driveway, a faint "Bitch!" bleeding through the window from her mother's fading voice. Her heart pounded and she could feel her whole body shaking. She walked unsteadily to the idling car parked at the end of the driveway. It was dark and she couldn't see who was behind the wheel. Good, then neither could her mother, who was certainly looking out the front window right now. Lucy didn't give her the satisfaction of turning around. Carl knew about her mother—Lucy had told him. When she opened the car door no light went on to illuminate who sat inside. She quickly folded herself onto the front seat and shut the door. A flicker of light came from her house where her mother had just let the vertical blind behind which she spied drop into place.

"Let's go," she said, already feeling relaxed. The car moved off down the street, not too fast, and Lucy felt Carl's hand on her knee, then on her thigh. She let her hand rest on his ebony skin.

"I want to go to your apartment," Lucy said, feeling a tingling ripple through her body from the tips of her toes to the top of her head.

"I thought we were going to Donna's party," Carl said, but he smiled slyly.

"Let's go later," Lucy said. "I want my birthday present now." She held onto Carl's arm as his hand rose higher on the inside of her thigh.

Lucy gripped Carl's thick, firm shoulders as she straddled his stomach, her naked alabaster skin in contrast to the black sheets, the darkened room shadowcast with candlelight, and Carl's own inky pigment. She settled herself down on his torso while his hands polished her tight, shiny skin from hips to shoulders, breasts to belly, thighs to ankles, following her curves like a breeze runs through a familiar patch of wood, winding around and over and through, catching each ripple and nook of the landscape in its ebb and flow. Lucy felt his moist meandering hands leaving trails of electric fire as they passed, her pores oozing a cooling heat that tingled with the air and then dropped off like a dwindling summer rain until the hands made another pass on their way around and around the natural path created by her folded body and his imagination. The sandalwood incense Lucy had rolled her eyes at when Carl lit it once they'd arrived at his apartment now tickled her nose with the same mellowing effect that the soft orchestral music coming from the living room had on her bleeding thoughts, a flowing warm good bleeding that drained the outside world from her mind, replaced by an inner peace and war of hot emotion.

Lucy breathed a deep moaning breath as she arched her back in a languid stretch born of the tension between stimulation and apprehension. Her virginity hovered in the balance, but Lucy only needed the gentle coaxings that came in consistent waves from her patient man beneath her. Carl had already tried with Lucy's urging insistence only minutes before, but with no success due to a matter of his size and her aperture.

"You're wet enough," he'd joked, "just not wide enough." And she'd laughed nervously and thought the night was lost to futility, and a rising humiliation crept from her toes and was at her belly eating from the inside when Carl suggested she get on top and take her time lowering herself down on him and just to relax and don't worry and relax and relax.

So that's what she was doing, relaxing, and feeling, and getting warmer and hotter in different places and it wasn't because the furnace was running in the apartment but instead it was the furnace of her body pumping her heart and warming her skin and loosening her muscles and slowly she reached back and felt for him and put him firmly against her and slowly sat back, pushed back, rose forward, pushed back, smiled with the thought of growing success, rose forward, pushed back, looked down at Carl who watched her face move in time to her body and the music and the mood with pursed lips, half-lidded eyes, open mouth, meshed lashes, nostrils flared, flushed cheeks and beaded forehead, jaw working, lips curled, teeth showing, a laughing smile with no sound, groans and moans from nose and mouth, heaving breasts, rolling shoulders, dangling hair covering and flowing, the moans rising and Lucy flipped back her head and her hair trailed down her back and she stared at the ceiling as she sat all the way down and felt her cool round ass touch his firm warm hips and felt his finger trace her throat as she watched the ceiling ripple in flickering light and shadow and she was finally there, down, now up, now down, over and over and Carl was smiling as he watched her go from slow to medium to fast and felt her lacy white fingers dig into his shoulders as she held on and he just moved slowly with her, letting her lead and he would gladly follow and not break her bubble because she was for sure in a bubble and he might as well not have even been there for all her notice of him but it didn't matter, she would somehow at some time realize he was there and then she would come back to him and they would enjoy the moment together.

Lucy's focus between mind and body, sight and thought, merged and the colors she saw inside the screen of her eyelids came out of the black like raindrops bubbling the pool of a once-still pond, tracing an image that was nothing and then was a house that had large grouped windows in front from floor to ceiling, two groups separated by a brick wall, and suddenly these windows had the look of eyes peering out at her and the lawn was a tongue rolled out to mock her and with a realization that sent a shiver up her spine Lucy saw that it was her house and she grunted in pain or ecstasy—Carl wasn't sure which—and she closed her eyes tighter and shook her head but the shaking only made her dizzy and the tight-closed eyes made the image clearer. And now there were arms reaching out from the sides of the house. Not mechanical arms or brick arms that matched the yellow brick of her house but her mother's arms reaching out to her and Lucy reared up and let go of Carl's shoulders to get away from those arms and arched back and made Carl come up on his elbows with a yelp of pain and all at once they rolled together as

Lucy shook her head to clear the oncoming image of her mother's face with one final violent shake and opened her eyes to see Carl's face hovering above her and not her mother's. She realized they had switched positions and now she was underneath, but they were still together and her head hung over the side of the bed and suddenly she burst out laughing and Carl laughed too.

"What was that all about?" Carl asked, moving at a slow pace because Lucy was moving beneath him.

She shook her head. "I'll tell you later. Just keep doing that."

# *Dear Noreenie*

*David Baker*

**D**ear Noreenie,
   Well, I'm just about as confused as I can be, I mean, your going away and not saying anything to me about it. I'm just starting to piece things together now, in my head, I mean, because I've been out trying not to think about things after I heard the news...clearing my head, so to speak.
   I pulled up in your ma's yard in my truck Thursday night, and old Sam waddled up out from under the porch like he usually does. I smoothed down that one ear of his that usually sticks up, like I usually do. So things started out normal, see. It was nice weather, a sparkling, crisp air, the kind of cool air that you like to say makes you want to breathe in through your eyes and shoulders and the back of your neck. You know how you like to fill up the bed of the truck with leaves and lie back in it parked out at the lake looking up at the stars. You know the weather. Or you'd ask me to drive you around the lake so you could watch the moon circle on the water and feel that cold air rushing and feel the leaves swirling around you as you sit in the bed of the truck. You know the kind of night. (The strange things you like to do, but did I ever ask you why or say that seems silly or anything like that?)

So it was that kind of night, but as I crouched there petting Sam, I began to feel something. I noticed his tail wasn't wagging the way it normally does. He was panting, even though it was almost sundown and starting to get cool; his tongue was hanging out and his mouth wasn't turned up at the corners like it usually does when I pet him. I knew something was funny.

I hopped up the steps to the porch and knocked and went into the kitchen. Your ma was there, and she smiled. She wiped her hands on her apron and sat me down and fixed me a cup of coffee. Lord, how your ma is nice's pie to me. So she sat down at the kitchen table with me and we started talking, and finally I asked her where you were, saying how I planned to take you to a show or go out to the lake, but she kinda turned her head to the side and let her chin drop a bit. "Didn't Noreen tell you she was going away for a few weeks, to see her cousin in Grand Forks—she didn't tell you about that?"

"No," I says, while I sat there. "No," I says, "she probably didn't have the heart to tell me—you know how she gets upset so easy and all."

And your ma nodded. "That Noreen has her own way of doing things," she said to me.

So I talked with your ma a bit about the whole thing and how we agreed that you went at things sideways at times, like the time you hid in the barn for two days when we were in high school. And we laughed a bit, and I didn't let on with your ma that there was anything wrong going on between me and you.

But when I left, the first thing I did was grab my pint of Crow out of the glove box and swallow half of it down. Lord, you burn me at times, Noreen, but now I just want to ask why you're acting the way you are about all these things. Your ma gave me the address when I came around the next day, and I tell you that I wasn't in good shape when I came around the next day, either, but I put on a show for her, wagging my tail the way old Sam does when you're around. And so I'm asking you to come home now. You've been out to your cousin's for about five days now—that is, when you get this—so you'll have had plenty of time to visit and all. So it's about time you come home.

I don't know what I'm in the mind to do now. You know what I get like when you leave me on my own. I can't trust myself, I guess—after you go off and do something like this, that is. It's like when Sam used to be younger than he is now, before his muzzle started to turn gray and his hind legs started shaking with arthritis every time he takes a shit. I'm talking about when he was younger. I'm talking about a few years back when he still had a bit of the pup in him. You remember how he wandered down the road, following a bitch in heat with that silly pink nose of his twitching. He could smell it a mile off. Even two. He couldn't help himself, that nose would start to twitching like he was shooing a fly off it, and he was off down the road.

I guess I'm telling you this so you take my advice to come home early a little more serious. I don't want you to worry, but you know how I am. I was spittin' mad when I left your ma's place Thursday night. I took a hit of the Crow and drove around out by the lake where you like to drive. I parked at our spot. You can see Flick's Tavern from across the lake, the neon lights travel across the water like they're reaching right at you. They were calling me. I could hear the music, and I knew that Flick had the dock open. You know, I like sitting out on that dock and drinking, and I like to go there even though you don't like me to. But old Flick isn't going to be opening up the dock much anymore, and I was thinking how you were way out in Grand Forks and it wouldn't make any difference if I went out there or not because you wouldn't know.

Only I'm telling you now because I always tell you the truth. Like that time I pegged Sandy Coleman out behind the shed at Bill's party. I told you about that even though I didn't have to, and I'm sorry I did it with her; she was a pig anyway.

But I went over to Flick's. I walked in and everyone gave me the "Howdy" and I marched right past them and went out and sat on the dock. He had shut off the lights because of the mosquitoes, and the only folks back there were some couples smooching. So I walked past the tables and went way out to the end of the dock and sat with my feet hanging over the edge. Jenny still is the cocktail waitress there, of course you know that, and she came out and brought me an Old Style without my having to ask. I looked out across the lake, and the moon made a streak across it, and it was pointing to that spot where we park on the other side of the lake. I looked up at the moon, and it almost stung my eyes it was so bright. I was wondering if you could see that same moon, or if it looked different in Grand Forks, or if you were even looking at it at all. I was thinking about you, I swear I was.

Jenny brought out another Old Style on her tray, and she charged me for this one. She leaned over and said to me, "I'm sorry to hear about you and Noreen."

"Yeah," I said, but the whole time I was thinking, *What about me and Noreen? I don't even know about me and Noreen other than she up and left. Is there something else I should know about me and Noreen? 'Cause I goddamned better find out from Noreen herself and not some twenty-five-cent barmaid out at Flick's.* But I didn't say any of that. I just thought it.

So I sat there a while longer and ordered a double bourbon. All the while I could hear the balls cracking on the pool table in the bar behind me, and how

I would have liked to go in there and show some of those boys up, but I knew that I wouldn't be able to concentrate, so I sucked down my bourbon. Some couple over by one of the tables on the dock began making slurp noises and breathing heavy and carrying on. I wanted to get up right there and pick them up and throw them into the lake. Mind you now, I'm not telling you all this to blackmail you or anything like that; I'm just telling you because I'm always straight with you and that's that.

So I sat there and had another bourbon, and Jenny would always stop and talk for a minute every time she brought a drink. Pretty soon the balls stopped cracking on the pool tables and I started hearing Hank Williams on the jukebox. The old Hank too, the slow stuff that Flick always plays when he is getting ready to close. Then before I knew it Jenny was sitting down on the dock next to me and we were looking out over the water and we were the only ones there. Jenny is your friend, now, or at least she was.

She leaned her head on my shoulder and was talking about how you might not be that good for me anyway, and she was talking like you and me were in the past. *Nothing's in the past. Me and Noreenie are still going on and will be for a long time,* I was thinking. But she was sitting there with her head on my shoulder and her soft black hair hanging down in my lap. She always was soft in some ways. She has a soft little mouth that makes an O when she talks, and I always kind of liked that, and the bourbon was making me think of this.

Flick had his old john boat tied to the end of the dock, and every once in a while it swung out and hit a post, but we just sat there and she did most of the talking. She was saying, "Noreen was always a little different, the way she sits back in the corner when we're all together. She's strange and she makes you do strange things sometimes like drive her around in the truck and all that." I didn't listen to it, but I kept looking down at the boat wishing that she'd stop talking.

Finally, I jumped down into the boat and hooked up the oars. She looked down at me with her head to the side, and I didn't know what she was thinking. "Hop in," I said to her. She stepped down, taking off her apron and leaving it on the dock. I rowed out, following the streak that the moon made across the lake, and she didn't talk anymore. I didn't know what I was doing, and I suppose I would have rowed out there by myself, out to where I could see the place where you and me always park, and I would have been thinking of you, but since she was along I didn't think about you at all. I just listened to the oars slip through the water and watched the little whirlpools they left behind when I pulled them out. When we got out to the middle of the lake she told me to stop, so I did. She stood up in the bow and said that we should go for a swim.

She pulled her sweater over her head and unzipped her skirt. All of a sudden she was standing there, in the bow, and she was bare as a baby in a washtub. She was standing up, all soft and curves, and the moon was behind her making the edge of her skin glow. She is real pale, a soft clear white. You're pale too, but you have this kind of pinkish color to you. She is smooth white, like the full moon was. She turned around and I looked at her as she dove off the front of the boat. My arms were shaking as I gripped the oars.

"It's freezing!" she yelled, and then she upended and dove down, kicking her feet as she went under. I don't have to tell you what I was thinking. I was like old Sam when his nose got to twitching. I stood up real fast and unbuckled my pants. I kicked off my boots, and the boat was rocking from side to side. You have to understand that I didn't know what I was thinking. I went up to the bow of the boat and stood there, naked. I could feel a little breeze crawling across me, between my legs and up to the bone at the back of my neck. Jenny was floating on her back, watching me.

"Do one of your dives," she said. You know how I am about my diving. Nobody can ever say that I won't dive when someone asks me to, doesn't matter where it is. So I got up on the very edge of the bow and kept the boat steady by flexing my feet the right way. You can imagine how good it felt, standing out there in the middle of the lake. God, Noreen, I have to teach you how to swim, that's how good it felt. You don't even like boats. I'm going to teach you how to swim and I'm going to get a boat for us, and we can fill the boat up with leaves and you'll feel like a queen.

"Dive!" she called again. So I steadied myself and took a deep breath. I jumped up, and for a second I was flying over the lake with all the black water below and the moon up there. I hope you saw the moon that night. Jenny was waiting in the water, treading, and her face was wet and shining. I knew that after the dive I was going to swim over to her and grab ahold of her. I didn't know what I was thinking. So I went up and I started to come down. It was a swan dive. Perfect. I usually dive with my boots on, but I tell you nothing could feel like this, to be bare as the day I came into this world. I started to come down and all of a sudden the boat was there, in my face. I never dove off a boat like that before, and I must have kicked the wrong way. I came down hard on the bow of the boat, and I could feel the metal crunch into my face. Even before I hit the water I felt the blood flowing like liquid copper into my mouth. I swallowed a mouthful before I hit the water. I think Jenny screamed.

I don't know how she dragged me up in the boat, but I would have paid to see her rowing that rusty old thing toward the dock, bare-assed with me naked too in the back, bleeding like a stuck hog. Flick was still at the tavern, and he helped me get up out of the boat. Twenty-seven stitches total, inside my mouth and out. Eight teeth are gone and I got a hell of a shiner. I've had worse, like when I wrecked the truck.

Noreen, you see how it is for me since you left, and this is only the third day. I'm still laid up. When you get this you'll be gone five days, and there's no telling what will have happened. And that thing with Jenny, that's done. I haven't heard from her, but I guess Flick will keep a close eye on her, maybe even fire her, but I don't know who else he'll get to work in that place, summer being over and all. I just want you to come home so I can get myself back to normal. We can work this all out face to face. I assume it'll take you two days to get back, so I'll be expecting you. Your ma wondered what happened to my face, but I just told her it was a fishing accident. Come home now, Noreen.

Say hello to your cousin for me.

              I love you, Reenie,
              Johnny

# *You Can't Make Chicken Salad Out Of Chicken Shit*

*Brandon Zamora*

Our first gig was a fuckin' disaster. It was perfect. I don't think we could have planned it better. That *performance,* for lack of a better word, was played, or should I say *orchestrated*, at the annual talent show in the Hoover High gymnasium. An event that showcased all the talentless bastards who sat in class, usually in front, quiet and unassuming, but answering every question that came their way. Kids who would go on to become successful doctors, accountants, and proud owners of health-food stores, but who harbored secret desires to be the next Jimmy Page or Shari Lewis.

"In order to participate in the talent show you have to meet a few simple criteria." That's how Mr. Freeman, the guidance counselor in charge of the whole ordeal put it when he called us into his small, sickly green office, with windows looking into the hallways that made you feel like you were sitting in a fish tank, because people on their way to class could look in and see who was getting grilled. We sat in front of his desk in rusted metal office chairs that squeaked and moaned every time you either crossed your legs or farted. Lenny was in the middle, very serious and staring straight ahead. Felix was next to the wall, pretending to read the book titles on the shelf next to him, and I, Tim Walker, was seated next to the door, always prepared for a quick escape.

"OK," Mr. Freeman said, a worried look on his face as he pulled out three papers from his desk and handed one to each of us. Across the top were the words: *Talent Show Application.* Loosely translated, that meant: *red tape*. This was the school's attempt to weed out the troublemakers who might see the event as nothing more than an opportunity to embarrass the school.

Mr. Freeman leaned back in his chair and said, "Take as much time as you need. And don't leave anything unanswered."

We worked on those forms like we were chiseling absolute truths into stone tablets, making sure that nothing went unanswered. Lenny had a big smile on his face and chewed on his hair, which was so long that he could wrap it around his neck like a scarf and still have enough slack left over to wipe his ass.

Felix was scratching his head with the tip of his pen. I think he wrote more on his scalp than his fuckin' paper. He looked like a little kid—a little kid with a goatee—sitting in the waiting room of the doctor's office reading one of those dopey magazines where you have to find *What's Wrong with This Picture?*

I finished first and waited patiently for the others to put down their pens. Mr. Freeman pulled some files from a cabinet behind his desk and flipped through them. I don't know what it was, but I had the feeling that Mr. Freeman didn't want us to play in the show. Maybe it was the way he mumbled and groaned to himself as he thumbed through the files. Finally, he pushed his glasses to the crest of his hairy nose and said, "Now, boys," in a very calm, public-service-announcement sort of voice, "I've been hearing that you've been getting into a bit of trouble." There it was. The goose was on the block, and its neck was ready for choppin'.

"Now," he continued, "participation in the talent show is a privilege, not a right. You," he pointed at Felix. "I've seen you in this office twice this week. What business do you have in the girl's bathroom? Can't *read*, son? And Lenny. I've seen you so often since your freshman year that your parents send me Chanukah cards. Tim, I hear you got into a bit of trouble recently as well."

I knew it had to come sooner or later. The bomb. His ace in the hole.

"It says you ran from security during a lunch detention. Do you care to explain?"

Let's see, did I care to explain that I was on speed, speed that Lenny's stepmom had given me? Or that I wasn't running from anything, but being chased? No, I didn't care to explain, but I had no choice. So without going into too much detail, I said, "Well, it was just a simple misunderstanding. But I have learned from my mistake, accept full responsibility for my actions, and am now flying on the straight and narrow."

There was another stretch of silence as he chewed on my words.

Then the bell rang, and all the kids spilled out of the classrooms and into the hallways. People were running to the cafeteria so they could be first in line, and shouting down the halls to friends who couldn't hear them. For the next hour they would be free as birds. But we were stuck. Trapped. Freeman's final attempt to break us, to see if we'd make for the exit and leave without his permission. But we stayed put, and when he finally spoke I could tell that he was ready to wash his hands of the whole thing. He didn't want the responsibility of coordinating the goddamn talent show, but the school had dumped it on him, so they'd have to live with his decisions.

"All right," he sighed, "but you still have to audition in front of a panel of judges. Be at the auditorium next Saturday at noon. Until then, try to stay out of trouble *and* the girls' bathrooms."

We set up our instruments in my parents' garage and practiced all week. Once, while we were attempting to tune our guitars, my father walked in to get his golf clubs, and when he went back into the house I heard him tell my mom, "You can't make chicken salad out of chicken shit." I guess he was talking about us, but it didn't matter. We were too busy arguing about what song to play at the audition. We thought it might be funny if we played "High Hopes," but thought better of it, and settled instead on a song that was not only simple, but had a great title: "A Day in the Life of a Fool." And maybe the best part of the whole song was it required little to no bass. This was important, because no one seemed to want to play bass. I think Lenny had heard somewhere that the lead guitarist got the most blow jobs, and so he was determined to fill that slot. I'm just glad Felix didn't catch wind of that news, or they'd have been fighting over the goddamned guitar. I was content with playing the rhythm guitar, because I was gonna be the one singing. But still, I didn't want to play the bass because they're usually seen as failed guitarists, and I didn't want that kind of stigma hanging over my head. So my brother usually filled in during the rehearsals. We didn't ask him to. He'd just barge into the garage while we were practicing, pretend like he was looking for a screwdriver or something, and then pick up the bass and start playing. He never took lessons or anything, but he was pretty good. A natural. After jamming with us for about an hour he'd put down the bass and say, "God. You guys suck," then go back in the house. But he couldn't play at the show because he didn't go to the school. That was another one of the requirements.

The audition wasn't anything exciting. In fact, it was almost too boring to mention—waiting for your name to be called so you could prove your worth to a bunch of people behind a brown card table, who all looked like they'd rather be at home jabbing their husbands and wives in the nasty parts with various fruits and vegetables instead of having to say yea or nay to a bunch of high-school malcontents.

We played a perfectly innocuous version of "A Day in the Life of a Fool" to near perfection. I took care of the vocal and maraca duties, occasionally substituting the word *tool* for *fool*, while Lenny strummed away at his guitar and Felix swept his drums with the brushes we made him use in order to control the volume. He hated it. He was like a cat with bags strapped to its paws. We finished the song with a "Tah-dah," and took our bow. On Monday it was announced that we were in.

On the night of the show, the gig, the spectacle that would be remembered as *the night those assholes ruined it for everyone*, we were still without a bass player. The gym was dark. A mirrored ball rotated above the center of the floor, reflecting tiny squares of light on the walls and bodies of the people in the crowd. The decorating committee must have had an orgy with the place. Colored lights, paper balls, and streamers hung from the ceiling like the tentacles of a pink octopus.

Our equipment was backstage, behind the curtain. We wouldn't be going on for a while, and we still needed to find someone to play the fuckin' bass, anyone who could just stand there and hold the thing and maybe play a couple notes now and then.

There was already some shitty band on the stage. I think they were called *The Path*. Their songs sounded like the themes to game shows, but with brilliant solos that the guitar player played while walking across the stage on his knees. At any moment, I expected to see a woman in a frilly gown wheel out a load of fabulous gifts and prizes. They were dressed in the height of fashion—white-collared shirts and black vests that made them look like a bunch of anemic penguins.

As we were scanning the area for the perfect bass player, we ran into one of Lenny's friends, a bearded fucker in a tie-dyed Earth Day shirt and sandals, named Mark Richman. Lenny slapped him five, and they did their secret hippie handshake, which ends with the two of them trying to get a hit from imaginary joints. Lenny thought it would be a good idea if Mark played with us, but I flat-out refused. I had heard the guy play before and he was great. He would've thrown off the whole equation, but Lenny kept pushing it.

Then I spotted a girl I recognized sitting in the corner. She had these thick black glasses and pink hair that was short and spiky like a crew cut, but with bangs that covered her eyes and curled around her ears. I left the others behind to get a better look and ducked behind this fat dude who was standing a few feet in front of her. I just peeked at her from around his belly for like five minutes before I could decide whether I was going to approach her or not. Then the fat guy walked away to get more punch, and I was left there, totally exposed. When she looked up from her book and saw me standing there, I felt like there was nothing else I could do but go up to her.

I said, "Hey there."

She said, "Hey what?"

In an instant I thought she was beautiful. Sure, she didn't have the clearest skin, and she dressed like a man, with rolled-up jeans and combat boots, but she was far more attractive than those feathered girls who walked around with pictures of their boyfriends posing in their football uniforms on their oversized key chains that held a million keys.

"My name's Tim."

"So."

"So I'm supposed to be playing here with my band," I pointed to the stage behind me, "and, well, we don't have a bass player."

"So what?"

I couldn't tell whether she harbored some sort of exceptional contempt for me or if she just had a poor vocabulary. I tried to ignore the angry look she was giving me and said, "And, well, I was wondering if you would do it. I mean, be our bass player."

She put her book on the bleacher and stood up. She came up to about my shoulders. "But I don't even know you or how to play."

"Like I said, my name's Tim. Tim Walker. And it doesn't really matter if you know how to play." She seemed leery, but I needed to seal the deal, because Lenny was starting to close in on me. I said, "What's your name?"

"Fish," she said, extending her hand for me to shake. "My name is Fish."

"Fish? Really?"

She pulled her hand away and said, "Yeah, you got a problem with that?"

"No, that's a good name. It's fuckin' perfect. It suits you." She punched me in the arm. Hard. "No, I mean it's nice. It's pretty." She punched me again, and I rubbed my arm.

When Lenny and Felix arrived, I introduced them to our new bass player.

Lenny pulled me aside for a little conference.

"You won't let Mark play, but *she's* OK? Dude man, what are you thinking?"

"Relax. She'll be fine. Besides, who wants to be in a band with a bunch of guys? She adds character."

Lenny said, "You don't care about character. You just want to get her into bed."

"That has nothing to do with it. Besides, you're the one playing *lead* guitar."

"Hey, man, I'm in it for the music."

"Look. We need a bass player. She's willing to do it. What else is there to talk about?"

"Mark's willing to do it, too. What about him?"

"NO!"

"Why not?"

I didn't want to say that it was because he was too good. Not in front of Fish. So I just said, "Because."

"Because why?"

My answer was still no. Then Lenny, looking for some support, grabbed Felix and pulled him into it. I turned around to look at Fish, who was standing by the bleachers, and shrugged my shoulders like I didn't know what was going on.

"Felix, dude," he said. "What do you think of this chick?"

"I don't know. Does she like to hang out?"

And with that the lineup was cemented.

We waited in the wings, sneaking peeks at the complacent crowd standing around with their hands in their pockets. Margie Bedgood was on stage now, mesmerizing the crowd with her impression of a tap-dancing frog, complete with sparklers and little American flags. I almost felt sorry that the only person who clapped when Margie was done was her mother. "Oh, come on!" said the MC, some jerk from the drama club dressed in a ruffled pink shirt and bow tie, "you can do better than that!" The crowd responded with a roar of obligatory applause and even a faint whistle. But I noticed that most of them were rolling their eyes. We were next, and I was fuckin' scared.

We started to set up our equipment, which was mainly borrowed from other people. As I plugged my guitar into the distortion pedal I accidentally stuck the *IN* where it should have been *OUT,* and a high-pitched *squeeeal* came shooting out of the PA and into the tender ears of the audience. I smiled and thought I'd let it go, to see how long it would take before someone unplugged me. It *shrieeeked* like that for a good thirty seconds, which doesn't sound like very long, but it was as if I had turned a fire hose on the audience and was pushing them back, pinning them against the walls as they covered their ears. When it finally stopped, I was disappointed to find Lenny standing next to me with the cord in his hand. He gave me a *What-the-fuck-do-you-think-you're-doing?* sort of look and walked back to his own amp.

Then the MC walked back on stage, did a bit of his "Yowza yowza yowza" for the openmouthed crowd, and pulled out a crumpled piece of paper with the names of all the acts on it. "OK. Is everybody having fun?"

The crowd let go with an unconvincing "Yeah."

"OK then, this next act traveled all the way from Canoga Park just to be here tonight." And that was funny, because Canoga Park was just the other side of town. "So let's give a warm welcome to..." He stopped to check his paper. "Oh, yeah, Orange Peel Annihilation." The crowd's enthusiasm was basically a reflection of the MC's, whose voice sounded like limp dick in a glass of milk. And that pissed me off. It was like he was setting us up. So when he left the stage I grabbed the mike and shouted, "Orange Peel Annihilation!" and we broke into our song.

It would be impossible to describe the sounds we produced with any kind of accuracy, or to give an exact description of our music. Some people would argue that it wasn't music at all, and I wouldn't disagree with them, because I think what we did that night transcended any kind of music or noise or hymn or anything. I thought I might sprout wings and fly along with those first notes of torrential fury, the whipping and grinding of swirling melodies that were good for no one but perfect for everyone, dripping from the ceiling, vibrating in the walls, bouncing off the floor; the grinding, cutting, pounding beats that were the musical equivalent of adding water to acid (or is it acid to water?), exploding in your face, leaving your flesh dripping from your bones as you screamed for mercy, begging for it to stop. The cherubs in revolt, smashing their golden harps and tossing their saccharine flutes into the fires of contempt just to see the sounds they made as they burned, and the crowd foaming at the mouth like mad dogs ready to devour and rip us from the stage, cursing and spitting and yelling, "You suck! You suck! Faggots!" Our sheer volume making them keep their distance, but it didn't matter because there wasn't anything that could have moved me from that stage. I was in utter bliss, like all my orgasms had come together. The nervous energy in my legs had turned very springlike, and I started jumping around the stage like I was dancing on hot coals as we continued to ignite the crowd, a crowd that only moments before was as lively as a throw rug; and we played our guitars like they were guns and the audience our targets, as Felix pounded away at the drums, which sounded like garbage trucks falling from the sky, trains leaving their tracks in search of something better. And Fish couldn't play for shit, but I saw her banging on that bass like she was hammering a nail into a wall, and the vibrations from her colorful playing knocked some of the cymbals over, and they crashed to the floor like drunken sailors, a Ferris wheel on the loose, burning a trail through a panicked crowd of circusgoers.

That's what we sounded like, like people running for their lives, the music leaving nothing but disaster in its path. And there was Lenny with this worried look on his face as people in the front row shook their fists at him and threatened him with physical violence. He backed away, and I think he was ready to run off the stage. And Fish, shooting green gobs of spit into the crowd of onlookers in riot gear and torches ready to save the village from the monster—us. They called her a *lezbo* and a *cunt licker,* and she started stomping on their pink fingers curled over the edge of the stage. "YOU FUCKING BITCH!" they screamed. I was falling deeper and deeper in love with each mouthful of spit she shot into the eyes of the disbelievers. Then finally, I saw my friend Lucy with some bald guy with the word *SKIN* tattooed across his knuckles pushing toward the front of the crowd, knocking people on their asses, and we gave it the whip.

I was rejuvenated. My heart swelled. I slung my rifle behind my back and grabbed the mike. The others picked up on my dramatic pause and got quiet as I said, "Gee, dear, do you think they're messed up on the dope?"

Someone tried grabbing my leg and I kicked it away, holding the mike close to my lips, "Well, they *must* be. Why else would anyone act like that?"

There was a collective, "BOOO!" So I shouted: "JOCKS ROCK! SUCK MY DICK! YOUR MOM'S A CUNT! AND YOUR DAD'S A PR..."

Guys in football jerseys were giving me the finger, and their girls were calling me a pussy, and then everyone started throwing shit at us, and it wasn't panties or any of that good stuff that Tom Jones got. People were throwing shoes, cups of punch, food, balls of wet toilet paper, and anything else they could get their hands on. I got hit in the face with a wad of wet ass-wipe the size of a pumpkin, and I stopped my beautiful singing and slid the strings of my guitar across the mike stand until the feedback made their eyes roll into the backs of their heads; and Lucy climbed up on stage and started throwing shit back at the fucking crowd while her bald-headed boyfriend started jumping on people's heads, and a fight started in the middle of the floor, and the teachers tried breaking things up, and the angry mob was now looking for blood, someone to lynch, so I took off my battered guitar and started swinging it like a baseball bat, knocking the sloppy projectiles back into the crowd; and I nearly fell to my knees when I saw one of them hit some girl in the eye and she screamed and vowed revenge, so they started throwing them harder and faster, and I couldn't even see what I was swinging at anymore.

And then Fish, covered in trash, threw the bass into the air and let it crash to the ground like a demolished building and started to kick it across the stage like a dog, and with every blow it went *BONG! BONG!* and the crowd started to chant, "FUCK YOU, FUCK YOU," clapping their hands and stomping their feet in hopes of getting us thrown off the stage.

"FUCK YOU!" they screamed, and I knew more than ever that I was meant for the stage and I never wanted to leave it and I was feeling so good I jumped off one of the amps and did a Pete Townsend windmill move, the one he referred to as "bowling" in *The Kids Are Alright*, and like him I kept doing it until my fingers started bleeding, the sight of my blood only urging me to do it harder and faster; and Fish picked up the bass and started playing "Jingle Bells" while Felix kept pounding away at those drums at a constant, steady fifty beats a minute.

The lights went on, and for the first time everyone's face was exposed, and I caught a glimpse of my dad as he walked out the back door shaking his head, disgusted by what he was seeing. I turned to my side and saw Lenny unplug his guitar, while Felix, head lowered, just kept banging at his drums, which were falling all over the place, but he didn't care. Then someone pulled the plug on our instruments, and the security guards rushed the stage, wanting to snuff me out like they did our instruments, and all you could hear was the shuffling of feet and Felix pounding on his unamplified drums. The crowd was ignited with glee, and they started climbing onto the stage to help the bouncers chase me. They wanted my bones broken and my blood drained, but I wasn't going out easy. I was ready to take someone with me and started swinging my guitar like a helicopter propeller to keep the pigs at bay, but someone jumped on my back, and then Fish jumped on *their* back, and I fell to the floor, and it seemed like the whole fuckin' gym was on my back or on the stage, which was nothing more than a prefabricated erector set the school had thrown together. And just when I felt someone wet my ear with the words "You're in a whole lot of trouble, mister," the front of the stage collapsed, and Felix and all the drums came sliding down on top of us. He kept playing till the end.

And there I was at the bottom of the barrel but on top of the world. Suffocating—the neck of my guitar jammed in my throat—pressed beneath all that sweaty weight. Happy, or at least content. Because on that night, if for only a moment, we were the best band that ever played.

# Fool's Spring

## Jacqueline Marie Hill

It was the last Thursday in February of 1961, and just a week before, snow had fallen in huge fluffy flakes that children whooped and danced in and parents cursed under their breaths. The snow had capped the landscape like frosty foam on a root-beer float, and the blanket of flurries had covered the grimy spots of the city and given it a new light.

But on this day and the day before, warm breezes blew over the city and the snow melted, offering a respite from a winter that had come early that year. Even for upstate New York, it had been a winter before its time, one that would prove as hard to get rid of as a lingering cough from a stubborn cold.

The ground softened and little green buds looked as if they had been sprinkled on the twisted twigs. Even the tulips were fooled by the sun into blooming before true spring. Their heads bent toward the warm rays, oblivious to what was in store for them later that day. The temperature had climbed to nearly sixty degrees, and Gloria fought with Vanessa to get her to wear her heavy coat and boots as they prepared to leave the house with Danny in the baby buggy.

"But Mother," Vanessa whined, stamping her foot wrapped in the yellow rubber of her boot, "it's warm outside. Even the dandelions are out," she said, glancing at the dandelions in a Mason jar on the kitchen counter, which she had picked yesterday after school.

"I know, honey, but this is what I call a Fool's Spring," Gloria said as she put on her coat.

"A Fool's Spring," Vanessa said, laughing as she pulled her yellow knit cap over her thick braids.

"That's right," Gloria said, bending over to adjust Danny's white cap. "That's when you think it's spring, and you leave your coat and hat and boots at home, and then the weather will catch you like a trap and you end up getting sick and being the fool. Now, we don't want to be fools, do we?"

"I guess not," said Vanessa, still laughing.

"Now, take Danny's buggy outside, and I'll go and get his diaper bag. We'll walk you to school and then do some errands."

Danny looked up at Gloria and smiled at the mention of his name.

Outside in the warm fresh air, the little group was on its way, Danny sitting in the powder-blue baby buggy with Gloria pushing, and Vanessa skipping just a few feet in front. Gloria thought that even though Christmas had been torn apart like the wrapping paper on the gifts, things were getting better. Gloria thought of their lovemaking last night. Reginald was as tender and as loving as he had ever been. He even took time to suck her breasts like he did when they were first married. He whispered that they reminded him of caramel-flavored ice cream covered with chocolate syrup with a raisin on top. The delicious thought made her smile.

Even the squabbles with Reginald had melted just like the snow, and their lives had fallen into a predictable routine almost like the comings and goings of the seasons. It was not what Gloria wanted, but it was what she accepted, and things could have been worse.

Vanessa ran just ahead of her mother and brother, jumping in every puddle along the way. Her boots made squishy sounds in the spongy ground along the sidewalk, and she bounced back and forth from puddle to puddle, then back to the sidewalk and back to the soft ground. Gloria thought that her yellow cap and scarf, her black coat and yellow boots made her look like a bumblebee buzzing from flower to flower.

Just after they passed McGregor's Grocery Store, Gloria noticed the familiar green flash of something stuck to the bottom of Vanessa's boot.

"Come here, Vanessa," Gloria called. Vanessa stopped and walked toward Gloria as she stopped the carriage on the sidewalk.

"Hold your foot up," Gloria said as she bent over to examine the bottom of Vanessa's boot. "Ahh, I knew it. Looks like it's our lucky day," she said as she peeled a ten-dollar bill from the bottom of the yellow boot. The bill was smudged with dirt and the edges were worn, but it was in surprisingly good condition considering its prior location.

"Wow, money," Vanessa squealed.

"That's right, do you know how much it is?" asked Gloria as she wiped the bill with a tissue she took out of her purse. Danny peeked over the side of the carriage wondering what all the fuss was about, but he turned his attention to a set of toy keys that Gloria had brought along for him.

"Ten dollars," Vanessa answered.

"That's right. You're getting to be pretty smart." Gloria fished out three single dollar bills from her purse and handed them to Vanessa. "Well, since we found the money, you can have this, and I'll put the ten dollars in the bank for your college fund."

"Ohhh, three whole dollars," Vanessa's eyes widened as she took the money.

"That's right, and don't spend it all on candy, and don't lose it," Gloria warned.

"I won't," Vanessa promised as she crammed the bills into the pocket of her coat.

They started on their way again, and once they reached the corner of Maple Street, Gloria and Danny waved to Vanessa and watched her as she mingled with the other boys and girls going to school.

It was getting warmer. Gloria took off her coat and hung it over the handlebar of the buggy and enjoyed the sun's rays on her face, but the cold followed them. After they dropped off books at the library, she felt a cool wind on her face. When they came out of Neiser's Drugstore, she actually shivered from the chilly breeze and stopped to put on her coat.

"It was so warm I guess I fell for this Fool's Spring. I'm glad that I put your snowsuit on you before we left," Gloria said to Danny, but he was busy watching people doing their errands.

Once they got to the bank, Gloria stood in line and took out two saving passbooks embossed in gold with the words *Monroe Savings Bank.* One was for Vanessa's college fund and one was for Danny's. Right after each of their children was born, Gloria and Reginald had opened up an account. Education was the only way for colored folks to get ahead. Whenever she came to the bank, Gloria would walk in with her head high and her shoulders back.

"Next please," the teller said from behind the counter. Her strawberry blonde hair was teased in a beehive hairdo, and she wore black cat's-eye glasses and red lipstick. Too much lipstick, Gloria thought.

"How may I help you?" she asked with a small businesslike smile.

"I'd like to make a deposit. Twenty dollars in this account and five in this one," Gloria said as she pushed the savings books, deposit slips, and money toward the teller. She glanced down at Danny sleeping in the carriage.

"Certainly," the teller said. Gloria watched as she punched the keys on the mechanical accounting machine. The teller looked up at Gloria and said, "Just a minute, I'll be right back." Gloria watched as she made her way down the short narrow aisle behind the tellers' windows and stepped behind a blue curtain. Gloria's heart jumped, but then she calmed down. There couldn't be anything wrong; they had banked there since they moved from Texas, and Gloria always made sure that she filled out the slips correctly. In fact, she took extra time to fill in the blank spaces indicating what each deposit was for. Always she wrote VANESSA'S COLLEGE FUND or DANNY'S COLLEGE FUND, in neat block letters on each of the deposit slips, because she wanted people to know that the Kings were going to send their kids to college. There must be something wrong with the machine, she thought. Once, she had been in a line when the machine had frozen and they had to complete each transaction manually.

The teller came back and adjusted her glasses. "Mrs. King, I'm sorry, but these accounts were closed last week."

"What?!" Gloria felt a coldness creep up her back. Her face twisted into a concerned frown.

"Yes, our records indicate that both accounts were closed last week," the teller said calmly.

"By who?" Gloria demanded. "There must be a mistake. I know there is over three thousand dollars in one account and almost five hundred in the other one."

The teller had seen cases like this many times. A husband or wife would close out a joint account, and in a week, a month, or a year, the other spouse would come in and not know what hit them. That's why she went into the back room to retrieve the proper documentation. So she passed the Authorization To Close Account signature cards to the colored woman standing in front of her.

Gloria looked down at the square white cards and saw her husband's signature. Both cards were signed on February 19, 1961, by Reginald M. King.

"Would you like to open another account?" the teller asked.

"No, thank you," Gloria said as she jammed the passbooks, money, and the slips into her purse and stepped out of line. Danny was still sleeping, and Gloria pushed him across the lobby and looked out the glass windows at the graying sky. A man with white hair, dressed in a long black coat, a black hat and scarf, came in and brought the cold in with him. His face was flushed ruby red when he announced to no one in particular, "Whew, it's cold out there, the temperature must've dropped twenty degrees since this morning."

Gloria pulled the white blanket around Danny and pushed the carriage into the damp air. The air felt like long, icy fingers on her face. Everything had changed. The city was blanketed with the gray haze of winter instead of the bright light of spring. She walked faster and faster, and tears stung her face as she gripped the carriage handle. When she reached McGregor's, she almost ran over a man coming out of the door with a box of groceries.

"Oh, I'm so sorry," she mumbled as she pointed the buggy toward home. The man just shook his head and went about his business.

How could Reginald do it? she thought. How could he be so cold-blooded after all they went through to save that money? Over three thousand dollars gone. What could he possibly have done with the money?

The buggy knifed its way through the damp air and it started to snow. The snow hit her face and mingled with the tears that slipped down her cheeks. The puddles that Vanessa had played in before were glazed over with ice. The snow was coming down like rain, and Gloria pulled the cover of the carriage down to keep Danny from getting wet.

When they rounded the corner of Cole Street, the snow was falling just as it had fallen last week and the whole winter. Gloria pushed the carriage into the entranceway and picked Danny up. He stirred a little, but he did not wake up. She pushed the door open with her fingertips, walked into the warm kitchen, and closed the door as fast as she could to keep the cold out. What she did not know was that the cold came in with her and made itself at home, seeping into all the cracks and crevices, drawing the warmth from the little house and the people in the house. It settled in and stayed for a lifetime.

# *Fallow*

### *Ralph Hardy*

Cullen, Mr. Merrill's son, was always checkin' his watch. His arm was freckled. In the summer his freckles got closer together. That was strange.

"Time is it, Cullen?" I'd ask.

"Time for you to do some work."

He always said that, even when we were workin' hard. Then he'd check his watch anyway and not tell me. Sometimes I think Cullen was timin' how fast we unloaded the tobacco, or if like me, he was just hungry and was waitin' till noon. Then he'd tell us to knock off for lunch. Sometimes I was so hungry it made me dizzy when Cullen would call out, "Last load 'fore break," in his throaty, froggy voice. And everybody'd stop. Just like that. Sometimes, if he was hungry Cullen'd call lunch early by five or ten minutes. But Mr. Merrill didn't like that. He almost whupped him for it, if you believe Cullen. Which I do.

Cullen was my age, twelve, and we were younger than anyone else at the barn. But Cullen was the boss's son. He could even tell Archie, who was as old as I don't know what, to kiss his ass, if he wanted to, and Archie couldn't do nothin' about it, even though he'd been workin' for Mr. Merrill forever and made all the decisions about which fields were ready to be harvested or what temperature to run the barns. That didn't seem fair. I liked Archie. He called me Captain. Cullen said Archie couldn't remember my name.

In the early part of the season it didn't get hot till late in the day. Three, four o'clock. Then, later in summer, it stays hot. Last year, in August, it got so hot you got cold sometimes. When that happened you had to watch out 'cause you'd go spastic. Cullen knew a feller that broiled his brain inside his head on a hot day in August. Only an idiot would let that happen to hisself.

In the mornings, the tobacco would be dew-wet and full of fat, bright green worms. Mr. Merrill had poison sprayed on the fields at night to kill 'em but it didn't work. JR, one of the tenant farmers, would shake his head when he saw the worms, and sometimes he would point them out to Mr. Merrill, who came by once a day or so, to see how the tobacco looked. JR would roll one of the worms up between his fingers like a cigarette. Then with a quick spin, he'd hurl the worm sidearm at one of the metal barns, where it would splatter against the wall like a grape or somethin'. JR had a wrist like a motherfucker. He pitched semipro for a couple of years, Cullen told me.

Mr. Merrill's farm was rich enough that he had a mechanical harvester to strip the leaves off the tobacco plants, so he didn't have to hire a big crew like in the old days. And the bulk barns where he cured the tobacco were 'lectric and stayed pretty much the same temperature day or night. So our crew spent the whole day in front of the bulk barns waiting for Archie to bring the loads of harvested tobacco to us by tractor. He'd unhitch the trailer load of leaves for us to work on and then he'd head back to the field. Archie never said much to anybody; I liked that. Sometimes I wished I had his job so I wouldn't have to talk to nobody. You were your own man then, 'specially out there in the fields by yourself. That'd be great.

Our job was to place armfuls of the sticky leaves on the turntable. And when it was full, Cullen or I would slide the sharp, pronged rack into place, pinning the leaves down. Then Tess would hook the chain to the rack of leaves and JR would press a button and the winch—*winch* is a word for girls too—would lift the rack to the exact height for me and Cullen. We'd swing the heavy rack of leaves into the barn door, unhook it, and push the rack in as hard as we could. We did that over and over, along with some other things.

"That's a hot heat comin' outta that barn," Tess would say every time we opened the barn door. Her face was like a chocolate moon. She sweated through her shirt so you could see her old titties.

"Is it a hot heat, Tess?" Cullen would ask. He teased her a lot. But she'd ignore him and just mop her face with a rag that was stained brown from tobacco juice. Then Cullen and I'd keep up the joke, pointin' out the wet water in the cooler or the frozen ice in the bucket JR brought our drinks in. She never got it, though.

Even though Cullen was my age he seemed a lot older. He knew what a cunt was. It's pussy but dirtier. He said that word a lot—*cunt*, I mean. Sometimes he'd call Tess one but not to her face. He explained the difference between Tampax and Kotex to me, as well. But I don't think he was right about it. I don't know why. One day, Cullen did eight chin-ups on the wooden rafters that crisscrossed the barns. I only got five. But he got a splinter and I didn't. He can walk farther on his hands, too, and swig a Coke in one try. When you drink a Coke fast, first it's ice cold, then it's hot in your stomach and you have to belch. If you belch loud Tess gets mad. She's a cunt.

Sometimes when it was slow we'd throw rocks at John Henry's balls while he was nappin'. He's the farm hound. His balls are kinda stringy. The trick is to not hit John Henry anywhere else until you get a direct strike. Otherwise, he'll move outta range. He never bites you, though; he's a stupid dog. Sometimes Cullen kicks him.

During the afternoon break Cullen would hide behind the barns to smoke. He wouldn't let me go with him 'cause I didn't do that. I'd tried it once the summer before and it made me sick. The puke had been green. Tess saw me and told JR who told Mr. Merrill who told my mother. She didn't say much, though. She smokes as well, long skinny cigarettes. When she's through you can see her lipstick on them like a kiss. It makes me feel funny when I see that. It's like she's leavin' part of herself on that cigarette, a part I'll never see again. I hate it when she empties the ashtrays into the garbage. I want to reach in after her, to save her.

"I could be your lookout," I told him.

"Don't need one."

"You might."

"Not if you don't tell anyone."

"I wouldn't tell. No way."

I was desperate; Cullen could see it. He put his finger on my chest. When I looked down he brought it up and hit my nose hard.

"OK, you can be my lookout."

Then he ran around to the back of the barn. We only had a few minutes left. I was blinkin' like crazy tryin' not to cry. But I was glad too. After a second I ran after him. Cullen didn't have any cigarettes. What he had was a paper bag. When I got there his whole face was inside it. Then he took his face out. Suddenly, Cullen's eyes rolled back in his head and he started walkin' funny like you do when your dad swings you around and around for a bit.

"What're you boys doin'?"

It was JR. He'd come around to find us. Archie'd brought a load. I'd not been lookin' out. But I'd just got there. Cullen had started to puke. JR ran over to him and then over to the bag. He shook it and a tube of glue fell out. Then JR ran and got the tub of ice water and poured it over Cullen, who was lyin' down and kinda floppin'. Cullen could've drowned. It only takes two spoonfuls of water. But I didn't say anything 'cause JR looked mad.

Cullen didn't drown, though he did get all vomity. For the next few days he wouldn't speak to me, though I tried everything I could to make him laugh, even throwing icy water on John Henry's balls. Then, one afternoon, Cullen bent over to pick up a bottle and I saw three rows of welts running up from beneath his Jockeys to the small of his back from where his Mr. Merrill had whupped him.

At lunch time Cullen would walk up to the house where his mother, a scrawny, chewed-up woman that I'd seen at church, fixed him fancy lunches, while I stayed back at the barn and ate my thin sandwiches. The others would leave as well; JR and Tess and Archie all lived nearby, in shotgun shacks. Even John Henry left. Mr. Merrill gave us a full hour because Archie had to fill up the harvester with gas. That hour of lunch was the longest in my life. I'd eat as slow as I could and still have years to kill. The trick was to space your bites and chew your sandwiches nineteen, twenty-three, or thirty-seven times before you swallered. It had to be a prime number or your mom would get hit by lightning.

I'd finish my lunch and have time to wander around the barns, most of which were practically empty or held only a few tools. I would catch grasshoppers, or when I felt like it, look for snakes, though I never found none. My dad had told me I should rest during these fallow periods—fallow means restin' time—that I would have to work the rest of my life because he had nothin' to pass on to me. But I couldn't sit still: my entire life seemed to stretch out before me like a misty, drippin' field.

My dad didn't work. He hurt his back a long time ago at the textile plant. After that he stayed home. He got a check once a month. Sometimes he didn't get dressed all day 'cept for a robe. Ma called him an A-rab when he did that. A-rabs live in the desert and stick their pee-pees in their camel's rears. Tim Layton told me that. And camels can go a month without drinkin' anything. That'd be great. Sometimes Dad started drinkin' by noon. But just beer that early. When my mother came home from the store where she clerked, she'd say, "Make me a toddy, too, James," and then she'd slip off her shoes and prop her legs on the ottoman. Then she'd sigh like a movie actress and wiggle her toes at me until I would come over and rub the horny calluses on her feet, the nylon of her stockings warm and spider-webby on my fingers, my head light and spinnin' from her perfume which seemed to spread from somewhere deep beneath her dress. I would rub her feet for eons it seemed while she and my father drank and talked and sometimes argued. Whenever they'd spill their drinks I'd clean it up for a kiss from my mother or a quarter from my dad. I never spilled anything myself. I was good that way. Often they would forget about dinner and I would become so drowsy in the warm room from hunger and the feel of my mother's stockings, which she always wore even in the summer, that I'd fall asleep. I'd wake up in the same room hours later, a blanket spread over me, my mouth sour and funny-tasting from hunger, and my underpants all sticky. My parents would have gone to their own room and left me in the den because I was always difficult to wake up, and my dad, with his hurt back, couldn't carry me to bed like a regular father.

I hated him for that.

Through church my mother had met Mr. Merrill, and when I had grown tall enough to look fourteen, though I was only eleven, he let me come and work on his farm. My mother let me keep most of the money I made, though I heard her arguing with Dad about it. And the next summer I came back to work for Mr. Merrill again, and he raised my pay by a dime an hour.

A day or so after I saw Cullen's welts he stopped the silent treatment with me. It was great having him to talk to again. It'd felt like I'd been on an island by myself. The others, Tess, Archie, and even JR, who sometimes mentioned his baby son, really never said very much. I hated them too.

Cullen promised to show me during lunch that day—his mother was visiting her sister; I bet she's scrawny as well—where the snakes sunned themselves. We would catch them, he said, and sell them to the biological supply company in Burlington for a dollar a foot. I hoped we found big ones, but not too big.

It was a great day. Not too hot. And the tobacco was dry. I spent the morning thinking about the snakes. I was tryin' not to be nervous. It was great having Cullen includin' me in his plan to sell the reptiles and splittin' the profits with me. That would mean I would get fifty cents a foot. We would have to capture them alive, he kept remindin' me all morning: for some unknown reason the company wouldn't pay for dead snakes. With the money I would buy something for my mother—I didn't know what, I'd ask for my dad's help—and a camera for myself. I was plannin' this way when it happened.

I had taken the rack, with its rows of long sharp prongs, off the stack and was waitin' for the rest of the crew to finish loadin' the turntable. Cullen had wedged a grasshopper in one of the chain links. We did that a lot. As the chain wound through the winch, the grasshopper would come out the other end, smashed and oozing, its front legs pawin' at the air and its antennae wavin', like to its own ghost. If grasshoppers had ghosts. Cullen said they did. I didn't think so. This time the grasshopper fell out of the chain link and down the back of my shirt. I shuddered and reached for it, dropping the heavy metal rack. The prongs were facin' down and one of them speared my foot completely. I was wearing shoes but it hadn't mattered. The prong had gone through my foot and stuck in the wood platform I was standin' on. I didn't cry out until I saw the blood on the prong when I yanked it up. It made a sucking sound. Great spurts of pain swept through me. Then my legs gave out.

Archie was just comin' with the tractor from the field, so they threw me on top of the cart, which was piled high with soft tobacco, and he sped me bumpily toward Mr. Merrill's house. I wasn't cryin'. My foot stained the green leaves, turning them black. Through my half-open eyes I saw Cullen runnin' after us. John Henry ran along beside the tractor barkin' like mad. But Archie had the tractor in high gear and Cullen couldn't keep up. In the driveway Archie jerked to a stop and jumped from the tractor. I slid down off the leaves and tried to stand, but the sight of my shoe spilling over with blood nearly made me faint again. Archie caught me in his arms. His breath smelled like dusty barns, and his light brown eyes seemed to glitter.

"Don't you worry 'bout nothin', Captain," Archie said to me.

The cords in his neck were bulgin'. It felt strange to be carried by a man; I knew I had outgrown that time in my life; I didn't know what to do, how to make myself lighter for him. I looked at my foot. The hole in the shoe was black. There'd be a great scar. Then another spurt of pain hit me. When we reached the front porch Archie stopped and called out loudly for Mr. Merrill. I thought it was funny he didn't climb the few stairs leading to the front door. Then I realized that Archie, who had worked for Mr. Merrill for probably forty years or more, had never come to his boss's front door.

After a minute or so—it seemed like ages—Mr. Merrill appeared behind the screen door. He wasn't wearin' a shirt. I thought he musta been asleep.

"The boy done hurt his foot," Archie told him.

"Put him on the porch," Mr. Merrill said.

Then he disappeared, and a second later my mother was there. I didn't understand that—I didn't think I'd fainted—but there she was. She called my name. I started cryin'. Just a little. My foot hurt but I was glad to see my mother, too. I closed my eyes. I could smell her. The smell I liked. My mother knelt and carefully took off my shoe and sock. The sock was wringin' with blood. Then she placed my foot on her bare knee to keep it off the splintery porch. I was afraid my foot would stain her dress, but she didn't seem to mind. She was beautiful. I'd never realized that. She had on lipstick, but it was smeared. By then the blood was startin' to clot. She held my foot in her hands and stroked my ankle. She told me I was brave. She whispered it; no one else could hear. Archie squatted down beside her and put a cloth on my foot.

Behind me I heard the sound of Cullen's rasping breath comin' closer, and I pulled up my pants leg even more to show him the hole in my foot. It was worse than any snake bite, I'd tell him. But instead of lookin' at my foot, he threw himself at Mr. Merrill, who had just stepped back onto the porch and was now wearin' a shirt. With a hard kick Mr. Merrill sent Cullen flying back down the stairs. I twisted around to look. For a second I thought it was an accident, that Mr. Merrill would run up to Cullen, who was lyin' in a heap on the hard dirt, tryin' to catch his breath. But he didn't. Instead he stood above us lookin' far off at somethin' I couldn't see. My mother's hot tears splashed down on my foot. It was only then I understood it. I lay back. The sun was in my eyes but I didn't close them. I was like that sun. Everyone else, my mother, Mr. Merrill, Cullen, Archie, my dad, floated around me in space. Then Mother put her hand over my eyes and everything went dark.

I didn't work again that summer. I never got the lockjaw either. To make sure you don't have it, you have to be able to touch your chest with your chin. I could do that easy. My foot healed fast too. The scar was great at first, but it got smaller even though I picked at the scab. In fact, my foot was better in time for me to work the last week of the season, but my dad wouldn't let me go back. My mother didn't say anything when he said that. In the fall we moved to the next town and I lost track of Cullen, his father, and the rest of the crew, though I heard the next year that JR's son had been ridin' on the back of the tractor and slipped off and was plowed into the fallow field before anyone realized it.

# *A Little Fire In A Wild Place*

*Robert N. Georgalas*

We were a pulse beat into the sixth when Hector De La Cruz, the middleweight Dominican with the washboard abdominals and the lime green trunks, snapped Jimmy's head sideways with a sharp left. The shot echoed 'round the arena and ripped a crescent beneath my friend's right eye. De La Cruz's cheering squad responded with a listless chorus of "yeahs." And when the Dominican withdrew his glove to set up another combination, a ribbon of blood raced past Jimmy's chin. It dripped first onto his pecs, then streaked low and speckled his white satin shorts.

Next to me, Willy Farina wriggled his 325 pounds in the tan folding chair on which he sat. The thin plastic cushion beneath him hissed as he moved, and the chair's aged legs tilted ten degrees before deciding to hold steady. Willy jutted his chin toward the ring. "Damn shame," he said. Despite the chill of the auditorium, his brow was dappled with sweat. "Guess you coulda figured, though."

"Figured what?" I said.

Jimmy's manager barked at him from the edge of the canvas. "Back it up, for chrissakes! Pedal!"

Willie angled himself to face me. "C'mon," he smirked. "You break it down, the kid's a rung and a half from gym rat."

I watched De La Cruz tag Jimmy hard on the shoulder. "Geez," I said. "Imagine if you didn't like him."

Willie snorted. "I do like him. But you wanna be a fighter, you gotta be like the greaser. No worries about jellyin' up your face. I mean look at that bastard."

My eyes followed his finger towards De La Cruz. The Dominican's nose was flat and wide, the lobes of his ears scalloped.

"Tell me he ain't the poster boy for ugly," Willie said.

I conceded his point, then gazed about the arena. It was a former movie palace, a broad semicircle framed by dark blue walls and a ceiling full of tiny yellow stars. Now, twenty feet of ring stood centered against the long, unbroken wall opposite where we sat. Around us, the auditorium was split into four uneven wedges. In each, rows of aluminum folding chairs slanted upward from the ring, aisles on either side leading to a refreshment corridor at the rear. There, a line of battered entry doors paralleled the concession stands. The doors opened onto a narrow, one-way street. Across from them lay a dirt parking lot patrolled by two Dobermans and a burly Haitian with a leaded baseball bat. Sprawled beyond the lot's rear fence was Fort Greene, a patch of urban gloom marked by graffiti-stained projects, urine-scented alleys, and a necklace of decrepit brownstones.

Normally, I found little reason to cross the borders of Manhattan where I lived and worked. And I was always puzzled when others did. As a kid I had grown up in the Fordham section of the Bronx, and the thing I knew for certain was that no matter how you cut it, Manhattan was New York. The rest was just gristle on a fifty-dollar steak. But then Jimmy had prodded me all week, repeating how De La Cruz was on the verge of being ranked and how the match was being documented by some student filmmakers from NYU. When I protested that I wasn't much of a fight fan, he snickered at me as if I was dodging an obligation. "Thought we were friends," he said. Each time I saw him that week he shot me the needle, shadowboxing as we walked to the subway, leaving copies of *Ring* outside my locker, cracking wise about how Brooklyn *was* on this planet. By Thursday I felt like a Judas for having refused his invite. So the next night, when Willie offered to drive us out in his Caddy, I said, "Sure. The fuck else I got going Saturday?"

Willie swigged at the Bud I had bought him from the concession stand. A trickle of amber escaped the lip of his cup and dribbled onto the logo of his Yankees sweatshirt. I reached to the stack of napkins that rested on my thigh and held one towards him. Willie disregarded the gesture. Still drinking, he flicked at the wet with his free hand. His sausage-thick fingers spread the liquid into a wormlike S that narrowed on the gray cloth as it passed the crest of his stomach.

I wadded the napkin in my fist and dropped it to the concrete floor. Despite the nominal admission, the stands were nearly barren, speckled here and there with a stew of hangdog, ethnic faces. My suspicion was that they'd been drawn inside more by the promise of cheap shelter than by the obscure names on the card.

In the ring Jimmy wagged his head, trying to uncloud his vision.

I took a deep breath and exhaled slowly through my nose. Up through the fifth, Jimmy had done a yeoman's job, his opening speed belying his thirty-two years and his intermittent stabs at preparation. In the third, he had wobbled De La Cruz twice with a steady barrage of rockets to his midsection. And in the fourth, a looping left had puffed Hector's right eye so that it now shone purple.

Willie pulled his face from the beer. A foam mustache bubbled and popped along the length of his upper lip. He licked at a corner of it with his tongue and erased the rest with his shirt sleeve. "I hate to break it to you, Nicky, but the kid's *his-tor-y*." He illustrated the last word with a downward dive of the hand.

I waved in dismissal, but the truth was that Jimmy looked spastic. He was stumbling backwards across the canvas, arms held high, shorts drooping. I took a sip of my beer and thought about the C-note I'd laid with my bookie that morning. The same C-note I was going to parlay into eight, so I could buy a few hours with Vicky DuBarry, one of the topless dancers at the Teddy Bear Lounge.

Willie burped, stretching it out so that the belch carried a rhythm. I faked a grin, but the *BLEE-AH* made my stomach want to turn. He waited a second and repeated the performance.

"Finish the fucker!"

The shout came from my right. I turned to the voice. Its owner was an acne-faced teen with a peach-fuzz mustache and a Mets cap turned sideways on his skull. A chip of cubic zirconium sparkled in his left earlobe. He was seated midway down the aisle, intent less on the fight than on the mustard-laden hot dog cradled in his lap.

Jimmy's sweat-slick torso gleamed under the lights of the student film crew. He shimmied toward the ropes on legs that rippled like rubber bands. "You got him. You got him," the teen said. I stared at him once more. He steadied the hot dog between his knees, then arched back in his seat and fished in the pocket of his 501s.

Willie nudged my ribs with the point of his elbow. The jab sent a splash of beer onto the crotch of my khakis. "I were the ref," Willie said, "I'd stop the thing."

The beer seeped through the zipper onto my skin. Wordless, I patted the spill with my napkin. Sometimes it amazed me that Bobby Bruno had given Willie the nod, making him manager of the after-hours joint at which Jimmy and I tended bar. But then the word was that Willie was a solid guy, someone you could trust to keep the books clean and the profits clear of sticky fingers. The first night I went to work for him, Cynthia Lawrence, the coat-check girl with the cheeks full of pin-dot freckles, sat at the bar during her break. After her second shot of J&B (straight up, no ice), she asked me if I knew about Phil Secura, the guy who'd had the job before me. I told her no. She smiled to herself, thought about it for a moment, had me pour her another scotch, then explained how Willie had caught Phil shortchanging the register. When Phil denied it, Willie nailed his left hand to the bar with an icepick. "You got nice hands," she said. "Be a shame if someone fucked them up."

Inside the ring Jimmy huddled against a corner post, his forearms and gloves shielding his head as De La Cruz pounded his body. When it became evident that the Dominican had power to spare, the sparse crowd began to generate some enthusiasm, whistling, clapping their hands, pounding the empty metal chairs with their fists.

"Fucker's a chump and a half," Mr. Mustard shouted. "Wasta fuckin' life!" I turned to him. He was sprinkling a small box of Rice Krispies over the neon yellow ointment that covered his hot dog. The corner of the box had been neatly ripped, and he was tapping his index finger against it so that the kernels showered like granules of brown salt.

"How long till the bell?" I asked Willie.

Willie inched back the cuff of his sweatshirt. His wrist was wide and the watch face strapped to its middle seemed lost in a forest of curly black hair. "'Bout a minute and change," he said. "I were you, Nick," the elastic cuff crept back over his Timex, "I'd just suck it up."

Willie switched the Bud to his watch hand and scratched at the afternoon stubble that darkened his jaw. When he lifted his arm, my nostrils flared at a whiff of B.O. "Guess it's me buyin' the drinks," Willie said. He moved a pinkie into his ear canal and dug inside.

I bent forward in my seat, the beer cupped between my hands, my elbows anchored on my thighs. "What?" I challenged. "You never bet a long shot,

Willie?"

Willie grunted and slapped me in the middle of the back. The force of the blow rocked me toward the edge of the chair. "Let's just say I didn't hear 'trains' when they yelled out 'brains.' OK?"

The crowd began to chant the Dominican's name, "Hec-tor. Hec-tor." In defiance, Jimmy feinted with a right, then squirted away from the ropes. De La Cruz stalked him, balancing high on his toes. Jimmy crouched, his elbows tucked tight to his sides. De La Cruz swayed in place, ingesting the sound of the crowd, thinking out his moves. The gash under Jimmy's eye kept leaking. He swiped at it with the thumb of his glove. Then De La Cruz lunged forward and popped two short jabs to his nose. The second one landed with a *THWAT* and Jimmy spat out his mouthpiece.

Willie scrunched his shoulders. "*Madone!*" he winced. "I felt that fucker."

I stared three rows down and across the aisle into the next section where Carmen, Jimmy's ex, was sitting with Leon, his seven-year-old son. I recognized her by the blue buzz cut she wore and by the trapezius muscles that bulged against the shoulder straps of her purple T-shirt. "She use ta pump iron," Jimmy told me one night. "At Mid-City. Down on West Fourth." As if to prove it, he removed a picture from his wallet and laid it in front of me on the bar. The photo was a studio shot. It showed Carmen posed against an ivory background, her face in profile, her arms curled to highlight her biceps. She was dressed in a black bikini and her body glistened with oil. The grease silhouetted the contours of her muscles and deepened the toffee cast of her skin. On her feet were a pair of spike heels that raised her head to the top of the frame.

Willie caught me staring. "That his wife?"

"Ex," I mumbled. As I said it, I remembered my response when Jimmy had first introduced us. Moist hands and a nagging flutter in the chest. My inclination was to slough it off as natural. I mean, how else does one react when he meets a female Schwarzenegger? But as we sat there in the corner booth of the coffee shop, Jimmy's chatter faded to a hum, and as Carmen swirled the ice in her Sprite, I found myself wondering about the taste of her lips.

"She the one did that Ms. Universe thing?" Willie's question dragged me back to the moment. I answered it with a nod.

Carmen stretched her arms across the tops of the chairs that flanked her. Her triceps quivered in the chill air.

I glanced back at the ring. The student cameraman tiptoed alongside the apron, zooming in on the referee.

"Reminds me of that joke," Willie said.

The ref was circling the boxers, leaning his head in towards Jimmy, trying to check out his eyes.

"What joke?" I said.

De La Cruz unleashed a right cross. Jimmy blocked it and answered with a haymaker that grazed the Dominican's forehead.

"Woman goes to see her doctor," Willie said.

Jimmy followed the haymaker with a tattoo of wild jabs. De La Cruz danced out of range.

"So?" I was still focused on the ring.

Willie circled a finger around the collar of his sweatshirt. "So she says, 'Hey, Doc, you know those steroids I been takin' for the last six months?'"

Jimmy's manager kicked a spit bucket. "For the love of God, will ya move!"

De La Cruz threw a sloppy left. Jimmy slipped the punch, then fell forward and wrapped him in a clinch.

"Hey," Willie said, "you listening to me?"

The referee bulled between Hector and Jimmy, prying them apart.

I sat up straight in my chair. "I'm listening," I lied.

Willie dabbed his sleeve against his brow. "Goddamn hothouse in here, ain't it?"

Jimmy touched a glove to his broken nose. He was waiting flat-footed for Hector's next assault.

"OK," Willie continued, "so this woman, she says, 'Well, I think there's something wrong, 'cause I got this hair growin' on my chest.'"

De La Cruz zigzagged. Three steps left, two steps right.

Willie went on talking. "And the doctor, he says, 'Really? How far down does it go?'"

Jimmy's hands sagged towards his waist. His skin was chalky and I could see him gasping for breath.

Willie slapped my shoulder. "And the woman, she says, 'Oh, 'bout halfway to my balls.'"

Jimmy dug his wrists into his sides, trying to reposition the waistband of his shorts.

Willie guffawed, then drowned his mirth with a swallow of beer.

The teen to my right shoved three inches of hot dog into his mouth. He seemed oblivious to the saffron Rice Krispie which had glued itself to the tip of his nose.

Yards away, Carmen lit a cigarette and circled an arm around Leon's shoulders.

Inside the ropes, De La Cruz was peppering Jimmy at will. Leon plastered his palms to his eyes. Carmen tucked him into her breast and blew a cloud of cigarette smoke towards the ceiling. Somehow I couldn't help but feel that Jimmy was wrong, subjecting Leon to the carnage within the ropes. It wasn't just that he was getting the crap kicked out of him. Hell. I don't think I would have felt any different had it been De La Cruz taking the punishment. Either way, a boy shouldn't witness such a scene. But then Leon was Jimmy's kid, and if he'd asked Carmen to bring him, who was I to say what was what?

Two rows in front of me an old man with an olive-sized mole on his neck yelled, "'Ey! There's no smokin' in here!"

I finished my beer and tossed the cup under my seat. A Chinese girl with a river of ink black hair and a tight white blouse dashed up the aisle. The scent of cinnamon tarried in her wake.

Without turning, Carmen shot the old man the finger, jerking it up and down above her shoulder.

The old man rolled up his newspaper and used it as a megaphone. "Somebody oughta teach you some fuckin' manners," he said.

The bell rang. Jimmy's corner man, a wispy black with dreadlocks and a baggy white T-shirt, skittered onto the canvas with a bucket and a stool. De La Cruz dropped his hands to his sides and drifted away. Jimmy's manager stepped into the ring and pressed a wet towel against Jimmy's pulpy face.

Somewhere beyond the top of the aisle, one of the orange metal doors that led to the street crunched open. A moment later, the frigid smell of April rain settled inside my nostrils.

Willie rose, waddled into the aisle, and hiked up his pants. "I'm gonna hit the john." He pumped a thumb over his shoulder, aiming it at the ring. "This shit's finito," he said. "Minute more or less won't mean diddly."

I waited till he disappeared, then sat there debating whether to make my way to Carmen. What made me hesitant was an anecdote Jimmy had shared one night while he and I sat in the Garden, watching Jordan trounce the Knicks. "See, she's Cuban," he said, "and if things ain't goin' her way, you better stand clear. Learned that the night we hooked up at La Tango. She was comin' outta the ladies' room, cuttin' through a crowd of rainbow-colored dresses to rejoin me at the bar. Her hips were shakin' to the beat of the Salsa blastin' from the speakers, and she was flashin' me this honey-glazed smile. All of a sudden some prick in a puce jacket grabs her arm and starts givin' her shit about hangin' with a white boy. I'm ready to step in, but before I can move, she opens her purse, whips out this .38, and jams the barrel against the asshole's teeth. Then she says, 'You don't like it, man, suck this.'"

My mouth must have dropped some when Jimmy told me about the gun, because he pointed at me and started to grin. "I did the same thing," he said. "I mean, a girl with an angel's face, who'da figured?"

I raked a hand through my layer cut and pushed the memory aside. The afternoon couldn't be going the way Carmen had planned it. Still, I doubted she'd bite me just for saying hello.

"Sorry about the fight." I took the seat to her left.

Leon peeked out from her side. He had his mother's hazel eyes and mocha skin, but the lopsided mouth, the blonde hair, and the dimpled chin were all Jimmy.

Carmen stared ahead. "Beat it, man. I'm in no mood for a pickup."

"No," I said, "it's me. Nicky Vox. I work with Jimmy. We met about a year ago at that luncheonette on Seventy-second?"

Carmen turned to study me. After a while, she wagged a finger at my face. "Yeah," she said. "I remember you now. The pretty boy likes to crash AA meetings."

The remark caught me off guard. It was something I had told Jimmy once on the subway going home. About how I was so numb and lonely after my marriage evaporated that I started walking into AA meetings to seek some compassion. What I told the attendees was essentially accurate. It was the story of how I had drifted home one February morning to an apartment stripped of everything but the sound of my own voice. Where I stretched it was when I said Gina had left me because of my drinking. The fact was that as I bounced from kitchen to bathroom to hall that snowy dawn, I had no idea why she had gone. To me, the four years had been a fairly smooth ride. Sure, there had been a few squabbles here and there, some back and forth about when we would have kids, a couple of arguments about the scope of my future. But so what? That was par for any relationship. No. If there was a hitch, it was probably because the finances were a bit light. Gina never said that, but maybe. Besides, it was easier to convince myself that it was money than to deal with the truth I'd discovered later, that it was some transit cop she'd met on the number four.

At any rate, I had told Jimmy how one night I was in a church basement on Twenty-third Street quaffing coffee and staring at the floor. This guy named Tony was going on about how the booze had fucked up his career, and how people had gotten real antsy about working with him. The more he talked the more I was bothered by his voice. There was something about it that was familiar, something in the ebb and flow that made me think I'd heard it before. So I aimed my eyes across the jagged semicircle in which we were seated, and there he was. He had his hands folded in his lap, and he was dressed in a black turtleneck and a stonewashed denim jacket. If anyone else recognized him, they didn't let on. But for me, it was hard not to. I mean, the guy was Hannibal Lecter himself. Anthony fucking Hopkins. And in all my thirty years, he was the only celebrity who had ever crossed my path. When the meeting ended, I milled around with the others, hoping he'd come over to me and say something. In anticipation, I started practicing lines from *Silence of the Lambs*, thinking they would make for snappy conversation. Rehearsing quips like, "Yeah. I used to be big on Chi-anti too." But Tony vanished without my seeing him leave. And when I caught the uptown train that night, I felt scummy for having intruded on other people's pain. Jimmy laughed at the story, calling me a pathetic schmuck, but I never knew he had spread it around.

I rubbed a hand across my cheeks to mask the blush that rouged my skin. At ringside, the director of the student film crew was shouting instructions to his cameraman, warning him to stay closer on the action. "We're shooting a fight, Wally! Not the friggin' Ice Capades!" Carmen adjusted the straps of her muscle-T, revealing a glimpse of breast. I pretended not to notice, but her chest was formidable, and as I drank in the view, I was reminded of how Jimmy's defeat was going to squash my plans for Vicky. When Carmen's shirt settled into place, I said, "Things OK? Jimmy mentioned you were having some trouble getting work."

Carmen pinched the stub of her cigarette between her thumb and index finger. Her cheeks hollowed as she sucked on the filter and pulled the smoke into her lungs. Leon inched his forehead from behind her right breast and peeked at me. His hazel eyes gleamed in the auditorium's lights, the skin beneath them puffy and red. Uneasy at the sight of his tears, I did what I thought he'd expect. I gave him a reassuring wink. But rather than smile, he steeled his gaze, waiting for me to look away. When I didn't, he stuck out his tongue, blew me a raspberry, then pressed his face back into Carmen's chest.

"Funny," Carmen said. The word swam upwards, tangled in the plume of smoke that billowed from her lips. "Jimmy woulda cared when we was married; things mighta been different."

I don't know why, but as soon as she said it a part of me wanted to rally to Jimmy's defense. Not that I could counter her complaint. I couldn't. Jimmy himself had admitted cheating on her. Worse yet, he'd done it in their own bed with Leon sleeping in the next room.

I pinched at the crease of my pants, trying to convince myself that it was loyalty that had triggered the instinct. But it wasn't. It was guilt. For as much as I was aware of Jimmy sweating in the ring and Leon nestled by Carmen's side, I was still curious about the feel of her skin and the size of her nipples.

Carmen drew on the cigarette again. Its tip glowed a fiery orange. "You tell Jimmy not ta worry," she said. "I got something lined up at the A&P."

Despite the thorns in her voice, I could sense that a bond remained between him and her. Maybe it was the way she fondled the flat gold crucifix that hung around her neck as she watched Jimmy's cutman swab ointment on his wounds. Or perhaps it was how she closed one eye when Jimmy jerked in pain. Then again, it may simply have been that she'd come to the fight when he'd asked.

Thinking about my own ex, I considered telling her how different everything might be if foresight were genetic. But then I realized how ridiculous that would sound, so I kept it to myself.

Carmen released the crucifix and aimed her cigarette at the floor. The smoldering stub flattened and split under the crush of her sneaker.

Inside the ropes, a skinny mulatto woman with a feathered headdress and a sequined bathing suit paraded to and fro, holding a sign that read *SEVEN*.

"You gonna stay?" I asked. "'Cause my friend and I could give you a ride."

Carmen squinted at me as if I'd just wondered aloud whether birds could fly.

I spread my hands in defense. "Nuh, no," I stammered, "I just meant..." I nodded toward the ring, then towards Leon. "The kid, ya know?"

Carmen clenched the boy in a headlock. Leon giggled and tried to squirm loose, his hands pushing at her arm, his too-short legs trying to anchor themselves to the floor. Carmen scored her knuckles hard across the top of his scalp. Leon butted her ribs with his chin. Carmen squeezed him tighter. "Kid's gotta learn," she said.

The warning whistle sounded. I rose from my chair. "Kind of a harsh way to make a point, ain't it?"

Leon freed himself from Carmen's grasp and stared towards the ring. His father and De La Cruz were standing in opposite corners, waiting for the bell.

Carmen rolled her neck, flexing her shoulder muscles as if it were she and not Jimmy who was about to box the next round.

"Well," I took a step towards the aisle, "nice seeing you again. I'll keep my fingers crossed for Jimmy."

"Hey!" she called when I reached the walkway. I turned. "I'll make you a bet," she said.

"A bet?"

"Yeah. I'll bet somebody woulda told you right off life was a bitch, you wouldn'ta cried so loud when it fucked you."

The old man with the neck mole slapped his newspaper hard on the back of an empty chair. "'Ey!" he shouted. "Watch your mouth!"

Once more, Carmen gave him the finger. And as she danced it about her shoulder, I wondered if she might not have been right.

On the drive home, Willie offered to spring for a meal of sesame noodles and scallion pancakes over at Hong Fat's. "Best fuckin' Chinks in the city," he claimed. The world outside the car was blanketed by a light fog, and the skyscrapers in the distance reminded me of a Monet I'd once seen at the Met. "Another time," I said. The big man frowned. "Nicky, babe. You lost a C-note. It ain't the end of the world." The Caddy's wipers beat rain from the windshield. "It's not the money," I said. Willie reached to the radio and turned it on. "It's just..." I let the thought yield to the weather report: lower than normal temperatures and steady precipitation.

Halfway across the Manhattan Bridge we got jammed in traffic. Headlights from the oncoming cars smudged against the mist. Willie concentrated on the large red rectangle that stared up at us from the southern stretch of the East River. Painted on its side in tall white letters were the words "Pier 17." The radio announcer droned about a proposed rise in subway fares. I plucked at the strap of my seat belt. "We should have stayed to the end," I said. Somewhere behind us a horn began to blare. A moment later it was joined by a chorus of others. Willie drummed his fingers on the steering wheel. "Never figured ya for a sadist, Nick." The traffic began to move. "I mean..." The Caddy snaked into the right-hand lane and shot towards the off ramp. "How much more'd ya wanna see?"

"It's not that," I said.

"Yeah?"

On Allen Street, a bike messenger weaved in front of us and latched onto the rear of a FedEx van.

I scratched at my jawline. "Somebody's your friend," I said, "you..."

Willie swerved to avoid a pothole. "Word of advice, Nick. Don't go confusing a nod and a grin with the ties that bind. OK?"

# Cheese!

### Carey Arnholt

*Japanese Lingerie*

My job sheet says, *Lingerie, Takashimia Department Store, Start 7:00 A.M. until finish—150,000.00 Yen.* In today's market, that is somewhere around twelve hundred American dollars, 45 percent of which my Japanese agency takes. The yellow photocopied map stapled to the job sheet has a red magic-marker line showing where I am to walk once I come up from the train stop in the Ginza district. Special instructions say that the building will be black. But after half an hour of wandering around crooked streets that have no name, I realize that the only building that can house the studio is a looming, light gray concrete structure. I enter and climb the stairs wondering how I can have the nerve to be frustrated with my agents for not speaking better English, when all I can say in Japanese is, *"O tearai-wa doko desu-ka onegaishimashu?"* ("Where is the honorable bathroom, please?")

Once inside the studio, I am rushed into a stale, fluorescent-lit dressing room by two short-haired Japanese women. People scurry around picking up and putting stuff in different places, steaming clothing, and rearranging shoes, props, papers, and more stuff. I catch a glimpse of two long, wheeled clothing racks stretching half the length of the room and decide that it's again going to be one hell of a long day.

Another girl sits on a high stool facing away from the lighted mirror, having her makeup done. Her hair is greased and rolled into gooey, Princess Leah sticky buns. This seems a favorite way for Japanese stylists to torture foreign models. Hair is one of a model's most important commodities, and having your head made into an oil slick is generally not appreciated, but most experienced girls know to bring strong, expensive hair gel with them to Japan to get this goop out every night. Otherwise, you have to douse your head with baby powder to make the oil gritty enough to remove.

When it's my turn to get slimed, I watch in the mirror as the other girl changes. She pulls her black sweater off mechanically and then her bra; she is obviously a professional and doesn't care that there are three other women, me, and a male makeup artist still in the room. I watch her face but cannot detect any significant emotion. I can tell she has been in Japan for a while by the way she steps in and out of her plastic slippers without looking, lifting one foot, then the other, as she pulls on a pair of acrylic jade tap pants. The only noise is the woman in the corner using a steamer: it huffs and gurgles, huffs and gurgles. The model reaches to the rack for her top and when she turns around again I see her nipples are positioned all wrong on her breasts. They point up at the sky. The bottoms of her breasts swell out, unnaturally strained with veins, and a deep purplish scar runs along under the length of them like she's been branded with an underwire. She sees me looking.

"Airplanes," she says to me, breaking the silence. "I fly so much that they've hardened. I have to have them redone."

"Do they hurt?" I ask. And she tells me, no, that they are just hard. She asks me if I want to feel, and I can't help my curiosity. She takes my hands and I feel guilty, like I am a spectator at a freak show. I don't look at her face when I touch her. For all I know, I could be touching a tennis ball with skin over it. The Japanese women aren't paying attention, and the man's face is deadpan and almost androgynous as he continues mechanically brushing my hair. I know that they are too intent on their work to bother with the weird Americans, but it feels as if this girl and I are alone in a room with robots.

She finishes dressing, throws a robe on over her outfit, and leaves for the set. The makeup artist continues brushing my 'do. I think of my boyfriend, whom I haven't seen for months, and wonder if he's being faithful to me. I wonder if he has ever had his hand on a fake breast. The makeup artist is very gentle with my hair, and it is relaxing, mixed with the vacuumed, stagnant silence of the morning. I try to imagine my boyfriend touching my hair, but I get this image of him touching a very buxom girl with sticky buns who looks peculiarly like the girl I am rooming with in Ropongi—Tara, the only girl I've even seen actually look good in sticky buns. Tara, just "Tara," it says on her comp. The girl who has this knack for picking up every single male model when we go out together. The girl who gets a fantastic booking six days a week, traveling to Bali or Hong Kong. The girl with ten thousand phone messages—all of which I seem to take for her. The girl whose name is on all the mail at the agency—she must have a thousand friends sending her tapes and her favorite candy, Necco Wafers, which you can't get in Tokyo. Yes, all that, and she looks better in my clothing than me, including the black stretch dress my boyfriend gave me for my birthday two years ago. I shake this image out of my head.

The makeup artist tells me in Japanese to put my head back, and I know that he is going to give me the pre-makeup massage. This is probably the best part about being in Japan, next to the money. He gently rubs moisturizer into my skin in circular motions. I try not to drool. He moves his small fingers in outward strokes, and I am thinking about my boyfriend again. I realize how long it's been since I've been touched—months that seem like years. My skin is covered with gooseflesh, and I am a blob of jelly when the makeup artist starts on my foundation. Brows, then eye shadow, mascara. In the mirror my eyes look even rounder and wider than usual—the Japanese love this look, the doe-eyed look of no personality—not too dissimilar from the cartoon characters on *Speed Racer*.

When the man starts painting blush on me, the other model walks in finished from her first shot. I discover that her name is Elizabeth because I hear the Japanese women trying to talk to her, "Ewizabef." They force her large breasts into a pink camisole and shake their heads, sucking their breath. This means Japanese confusion. I know that they are worried that her breasts will look too large for their catalog. One of them giggles and Ewizabef awaits the decision, unfazed by their predictable rudeness. They put her into another nightgown and put the camisole on my rack.

Out on the set, I position myself so the camisole will not look so revealing. I face my hips to the side and twist my top half straight toward the camera. The direct light from the light box in front will help to flatten me out. The photographer speaks some English, but mostly we communicate in advanced hand-flapping. His crew is made up of three young guys scurrying about moving prop-walls behind me, holding up reflectors and taking orders like servants. I don't bother to ask why there are twelve extra men sitting at a table, drinking coffee, and watching Elizabeth and me being photographed in underwear. I already know what their answer will be: "Cwients." This is their entertainment. What better way to spend the afternoon than to watch some free *gaijin* ass prance around in Skivvies?

We have modeled at least twenty outfits each when the food arrives in bento boxes, and Elizabeth says, "Shit, I hate this food." The black-lacquered container is sectioned off like a deep TV dinner. In one square is a wedge of sugared egg, in another, a piece of salted fish, then some miscellaneous batter-fried vegetables, a square of white rice with a small round red vegetable in the middle, and last, a section containing tiny, cut Japanese radishes called daikon. Elizabeth and I swap things from our lunches, then she pulls out two tuna-fish sandwiches from her bag and gives me one. We drink green tea and try to be pleasant with the clients and crew, nodding and smiling when we feel it's appropriate, and in less than half an hour we are back to work. After five and a half more hours, Elizabeth is sent home, but I am to stay on for some other shots, which supposedly have been negotiated by my agent.

The makeup artist touches me up and puts on new lipstick. Choosing a bright magenta that smells like lavender, he comes close to my face while he's painting, his hands very sure, and I stare right into his thin brown eyes without him noticing—this is how concentrated he is. He paints gently, suddenly a perfectionist. He turns his body to adjust to the contour of my mouth. He is intensely into his work and the silence, not thinking about the shoot, just absorbed in this task. Detached from my body, my mouth belongs to his hand. I hope my breath doesn't smell like tuna.

Maybe this is what Emily Floge felt like when Gustave Klimt was painting her. Maybe modeling is the fine art of the twentieth century. Maybe those painters' women didn't feel special at all and posed for the money with no idea they would be eternalized in art books, museums, and coffee shop conversation.

I work my way through smaller and smaller panties and bras until I need to eat or pass out. The stylist tells me I have one more shot, but I only see cotton-crotched pantyhose hanging on the rack.

"You cover," she says to me and puts her hands over her breasts. I am confused. My job instructions only said lingerie. They didn't mention anything about sheer. A model gets double rate for lingerie and triple for anything that is see-through or shows the obvious areas. At this point it would be very rude to call my agent, not only because she is at home, but also because the phone is out by the clients. I have no idea if I am supposed to be doing this or if they are sneaking this shot in without payment. I have no way of finding out because I am not to discuss money matters.

As I stand there out on the set in only flesh-colored nylons and covering my breasts with my hands, three Japanese women poke and pick at my crotch—pubic hair is considered a very dirty thing here.

Japanese porno movies show women being tethered, whipped, and abused, and I saw a Japanese comic book once where a woman had barbed wire running through her mouth and out her vagina, but the delta areas were all fogged out. It's illegal to show pubes.

The stylists stuff triangle-shaped, flesh-colored swatches over my crotch. They adjust the seam at my rear and pull tight the nylon at my knees. When I help, they push my hands away. I am no longer the master of my own body. The twelve "cwients" have switched to beer and suddenly have a very "businesslike" interest in the hosiery shot that's being done for their catalog. Two men cover their mouths when they laugh.

Finally, at 9:45, I walk home in the street-lit night, passing the train stop I could take to get to my apartment in Ropongi. I want to walk a tree-lined street, which is such a rarity in Tokyo. Though it is dark, I am in no danger. There is very little crime here. Once, a man actually called me to return the purse I had left on the subway.

Fan-shaped ginkgo leaves flutter down from the sky, twirling in the neon light. I catch a few. The Japanese have special trucks that pick up these honorable leaves, so that they won't lie in the road. Ginkgo means *bank* in Japanese.

At night, almost every night in Japan, I dream of aliens operating on me. Long emotionless eyes stare down as if I am the thing that is foreign. The dream goes on and on in dull Technicolor with subtitles that I can't read...and I am helpless...and I am frightened.

*Cheese!*

There stands Manny, five feet two and a half, hands on hips, face in a scowl, foot tapping like a woodpecker on speed. We are forty-five minutes late.

"And I'm not even going to ask where you two ladies were," he snaps, his eyes boring into us. "Now get your heels on and get your asses on stage!"

Amy and I set our stuff down and scramble up onto the T-shaped platform. I have never worked with this little twerp before. My agent suckered me into this nightclub runway show by continuously telling me what an important benefit it was. My friend Amy kept telling me that doing an AIDS benefit at the Shelter nightclub was such a big deal and that there would be tons of talent agents and photographers in the audience.

Like I even believed that for a second. More like a bunch of people from the suburbs who decided to drive in on the weekend and be alternative.

"OK, people," Manny claps, "let's walk," and he begins strutting around on the floor the way he wants us to do on stage—pelvis forward, shoulders thrusting in the opposite motion of his hips, his little body dwarfed by the massive room. I realize that I have never seen a nightclub in the light before. It looks pretty primitive, like some kids splattered paint all around a garage, in this case an airplane hanger. Huge tarps—or I guess "decorative drapes"—hang down from the ceiling, probably covering imperfections in the walls, and I notice for the first time, way up high, thin black metal catwalks circling the room. Our heels click on the wooden planks as we walk up and down, up and down the runway, Manny counting out loud. I size up the other models. One girl, wearing a rather tight pair of workout pants and a plunging half-shirt, has the most amazing breasts I have ever seen. They leap out, freestanding in front of her, leaving her tiny tanned stomach behind in the shadow. Another girl, big-boned I would call her, has a massive mane of curly red hair. To me, she doesn't look thin enough to be a model, but her stage presence is that of a proud Clydesdale. Initially, the men are less interesting to me, but that is probably because I have had the number-one golden rule of this business ingrained into me—"Never date a male model." They spend more time in the bathroom than a bladder-infected bulimic, and they use up all your makeup without asking.

We all continue to walk without expression, the little man Manny stomping his foot on the floor to keep time.

"He's the best choreographer in town," Amy whispers to me when we pass on a turn.

"Oh yeah," I say the next time I pass her, "then don't you think that he could afford something other than women's gym shoes?" It is true. Manny wears little white tennies with little folded white socks. He has on a tight white tank top that shows all of his bulging little muscles. It looks like there is a row of golf balls underneath his skin. He wears tiny white shorts, and one can see that he works out like a fiend because his calves are the exact same size as his thighs. An Evian water bottle hangs at his side in a black mesh bag that is obviously designed just to hold it. As I am trying to decide about his rubber-ducky-yellow D.A., he swings himself around, water bottle making an arc in the air, and asks me if I have a problem.

"OK, people," he yells, "we only have one night to work on this. I want Julia, Julius, Marc, Sabrina, and April on stage. The rest of you, especially you late ones, get down and start stretching out."

We all pile off onto the floor and plop down. I ask Amy why we need to stretch out, and she informs me, for the first time, that this is a dance show. This is a classic Amy thing to do, leave out mildly important details. I am definitely not a dancer and can't remember the last time I touched my toes. I soon discover that Amy darling, who had only studied dance for thirteen years herself, had a "little brain lapse" and—oops—forgot to mention to this little Napoleon Manny character that her friend over here couldn't even two-step.

"What am I gonna do?" I ask, searching into her wide emerald contacts.

"Just fake it," she says, tossing her huge blond head and laughing. I try to control my anger by watching the rehearsal. Manny has the dancer/models twisting and spinning, jumping and kicking, stuff I could not do if my life depended on it, especially in heels. I sink down lower into my mood and busy myself with images of hitting Amy over the head with a large blunt object.

When it is our group's turn to go up, I slink over to Manny and inform him that not only am I no dancer, I am not very familiar with the plain old runway. Being five eight is considered quite short for even basic print work, let alone for the catwalk. This does not excite him. He pauses, squints his beady green eyes at me, complete with scowl, looks up onto the stage for a minute, takes a sip from his water bottle, fixes an imaginary hair, then sighs.

"Well, I'll just have to figure something out, won't I?" Then he snorts loudly and points to the stage. I walk up feeling incredibly clumsy and as obvious as a glowing green thing.

"We're gonna need different music," Manny calls up to the sound box. "Try that number three with the SLOWER, extended beginning." And while the DJ is looking for the song, Manny starts talking our group—two guys paired up with Amy and me—through the routine. The first part I think I can handle: parallel cocky strutting down the stage, slow turns, abrupt stops with head thrusts and poses. It is when we get to the end of the stage that I begin to get nervous. The two couples are to separate to the far ends of the T, where our routines will mirror each other. Once there, I am supposed to raise my hand to my head as if I am going to faint, then free-fall to the floor, my strapping male dance partner catching me in a striking pose just before I hit, a pose we will hold, waiting for the next dramatic beat, when we will strike another pose and hold it again. After that, the couples are supposed to cross sides of the stage and do basically the same thing, only this time with my partner spinning me around until I fall from dizziness and he catches me.

My partner is a long-haired, no-shirt-wearing, full-blooded American Indian named Cameron with teeth as white as office lighting. I deem him safe for me to investigate further, now that I know he is probably not just a model. He informs me that he is a professional ballet dancer, and I don't mind one bit when he has to pick me up and spin me around in the air. At one point, he scissors me between his dark-brown-muscled legs, and I feel like he could cut me in half like a piece of cheese. Funny, that's how I have been feeling the whole night, like a big loose piece of yellowy, inflexible butterfat. Cameron assures me that I am not, flashes me a big white grin, then asks me for Amy's phone number.

After walking through Manny's instructions, the song "Dangerous on the Dance Floor" comes thundering over the speakers, and we run through it. Manny has a sour-lemon look of utter dissatisfaction, and he works with us for forty-five more minutes. Then he takes the next group and teaches six more routines.

Finally, we are ready for a complete run-through. The music plays all the way through, the different songs strung expertly together by Mean the Mo Master Mixer and his big shining gold tooth. The beats overlap just enough to link the next tune.

After the act we all hold still, silent on stage. Manny stands glaring up at us. His little foot does not tap. We all wait, not moving a muscle for his response. He puts his hand to his chin, nods his head, and gives us a big squinched smile.

"Hated it," he says. And we all know we will be there until well past midnight—even though the three guards have to stay on with us—because this is our only night to practice.

I don't remember what time we finally left, but I do know that I dreamed about that stupid routine for three days. Something about Manny chasing me around with a tomahawk and me running on mazes of scaffolding and eating floating dots like Ms. Pacman.

The night of the show, we all packed into the dressing room. Dressing rooms at nightclubs are usually curtained-off areas of the kitchen or coatroom or wherever they can squeeze everyone. This time we were all just behind a big wall of freestanding plywood and some more of that tarp stuff. I peeked out onto the dance floor. It was full of people smoking and wearing black. Music thundered loud enough to vibrate your innards. But no one was dancing, just waiting for the show. The platform was illuminated with brilliant light. I could see three of my friends there and, to my horror, my agent standing in the audience.

"Amy," I said, "You're not gonna believe this. Bill is here."

"What?" she gasped. "Where?" And I pointed in his direction.

"Oh my god," she called, "I really didn't think he'd come. He's hard enough to get to go to lunch."

"You *invited* him? You invited our agent to come watch me fall into an angry, alternative, AIDS-benefit audience?"

"Oh you'll do fine, you're such a worry wog," and she turned to go primp, leaving me wondering what in the hell a "wog" was and where I would get that blunt object I saw so clearly.

In the dressing room, everyone ran around in thongs and G-strings. To this day, I refuse to put myself through that pain; I'd rather have panty lines than feel as if I'm straddling a clothing wire, thank you. We all organized our outfits and put them into a place where we would find them in a rush. To our mutual horror, Amy and I discovered that the outfits we had to wear during our dipping, falling number were black-and-white polka-dot bikinis with the classic *come-up-and-fuck-me* black pumps. I just knew I was going to wipe out into the audience.

I got my makeup done by a frazzled makeup artist who kept trying to talk over the music. I got my hair done by an acne-scarred hair person who held a curling iron in my bangs so long it made a big poofy log over my forehead that I couldn't brush out no matter how hard I tried. Nervous tension buzzed through the whole room (or rather, the tarped-off area), and bodies were everywhere squishing past, combing, brushing, and primping.

Suddenly, forty-five minutes late, a deep voice announced us, and the show finally started. Manny stood at the opening of the curtain and whispered into every model's ear just before they went out. The rest of us tried to peek through the curtain. The groups did their routines confidently, right with the rhythm, then passed through the curtain and flew like mad people, running to their next outfits, clothes and accessories flying off into the air.

Finally, "Dangerous on the Dance Floor" came on, and our group stalked out onto the stage. This is when all nervousness strangely disintegrates and something odd happens. It happens every time. Total confidence overcomes me. Power rushes through my veins like chocolate. We held the audience's attention like a whip in our hands. I watched the sea of faces, eyes all on me it seemed, and I was telling them what to do, what to feel, what to think. We did our routine better than ever, and when we were finished and passing through the curtain a terrified Manny stood blocking us, eyes as wide as a bug's.

"Julie can't find her top," he cried flapping his hands. "Go back out there—*go, go*."

I have never been in a runway show where this doesn't happen. Models aren't ready, the people walk too fast for the music, or somebody forgets to do a whole part of the routine. Amy and I stalked back out there, only now with our tails between our legs, all eyes on us, burning holes.

Back on stage, I feel stupid, self-conscious, and like a slab of meat up on display, and it seems like we are out there for hours just walking back and forth like a bunch of goons. Finally, thank God, Julie comes through the curtain. She is wearing blue bikini bottoms and no top. Her hands cover her breasts, and she struts so proudly that for a minute even I think it was meant to be that way. The crowd goes wild, whooping and screaming over the music.

Finally, the last number is to be a wedding scene. One bride and four bridesmaids all wrapped in chiffon and pinned with flower pins. This part we didn't practice in costume, because the wrapping takes a bit of time. The stylist stands across the room, and we hold one end of about twenty feet of fabric and twirl until we're all twirled up. I wait in my previous outfit until it's my turn to be wrapped. Everyone is scrambling around like crazy rats and the music thumps with our hearts. Just as I am about to be wrapped, I realize that I can't find my underwear.

"It's no big deal," the stylist tells me. "It doesn't show." And after she's done, she turns me to the mirror, where I see nothing suspicious showing through the chiffon. "I look pretty good," I think to myself. "Maybe this isn't so bad."

Huge electric guitars wail the wedding march, and when the five of us stride out, the crowd applauds madly, and people whoop and howl. We stalk, buck, kick, and kneel. We throw our bouquets and strike poses that Madonna would be jealous of. I am hammified and I throw my arms up proudly, adding steps that just feel right. The scene is spectacular, and flower buds and bubbles rain down from the ceiling. We're called out again for an encore, and we bow and bow.

When it's finally over, everyone scrambles to get dressed and gather their stuff. I calculate everything that is lost or stolen from me. It is inevitable. Just my underwear this time, lucky dog. Suddenly I realize the miscellaneous flashing among the chaos that is all around the room. No matter how tough the security, a few unknown photographers always manage to sneak in and shoot off a couple rolls before someone kicks them out. My girlfriend once smacked one right across the mouth at a show in Paris and made his lip bleed. At least that's what she says.

When we finally emerge from the dressing room, the greasy manager of the club is there with champagne for us. People are all around, congratulating us and chatting. I can see my boyfriend and my agent waiting off to the side. My boyfriend has a concerned look on his face, and my agent is laughing hysterically.

"That last number," he says, "whew, I didn't know you had it in you. I'm gonna have to start booking you for Frederick's of Hollywood." And I laugh with him, wondering what the hell he is talking about. My boyfriend clarifies the issue.

The bright blue light that rained down on us onstage illuminated the baby blue chiffon in such a way that it resembled a poofy cloud aura around us. We all appeared buck naked on stage for the entire last number.

Runway work always comes back to haunt you.

Two years later, a young up-and-coming photographer came into the agency, and after seeing my composite asked if he could test with me. I wasn't doing anything that day, so I agreed. After a freezing shoot out by the Adler Planetarium, we went back to his house with the makeup artist for some hot chocolate. I was unsure of his talent, but I liked him as a person.

"I've been waiting to shoot you for a long time," he said. When I asked him how he knew me, he got an excited grin on his face and said he had something for me.

I followed him into his basement, where he dug through a three-foot-high stack of eleven-by-fourteen-inch matted photos. He pulled out an electric blue print and handed it to me, sighing proudly.

There I was, a big, goofy smile on my face, arms thrown overhead, completely, utterly, birthday-suit naked.

# *With Our Secrets Intact*

*Kent Modglin*

I had watched an episode of *Alfred Hitchcock Presents* that night—the one where a young woman is left alone in a big creepy house with her dead mother and her mother's nurse, who turns out to be a really big man dressed as a really big woman—and I couldn't go to sleep. I kept seeing the big nurse standing silently at the foot of the stairs just at the moment the young woman realizes that it was the nurse who murdered her mother. I couldn't go to my mom's room. If she knew I couldn't sleep, I would have been fulfilling her prophecy. "You won't be able to sleep if you watch that!" she'd said only hours earlier. So I sat, quietly suffering at my window with my chin in my hands, watching the corn rustle across the street. The shimmer of the full moon's silver light on the dark green leaves and the singing of the crickets was reassuring. I closed my eyes and let the cool breeze rush over me. A cicada began its slow, rhythmic, rasping cry, and as it reached its crescendo, it was joined by a chorus of its fellows. Their big scraping wings drowned out the polite chirp of the crickets, the late song of the whippoorwill, even the hum of the fan in the downstairs bedroom window. But somewhere underneath it all I heard, quite distinctly, a man's voice calling, "No!" It came from the field.

It was well past ten o'clock, and people just weren't in cornfields at that hour. In that moment, I saw Alfred Hitchcock for the mean-spirited man my mom always said he was.

I opened my eyes, and for a moment saw nothing but the same serene moon and gently swaying stalks of corn. Then Ambrose Shears ran out of the row of corn, and I clamped my hand over my mouth to prevent any sound from escaping. To everybody in town, Ambrose Shears was just the old guy who lived alone in the little pink house at the dead end of School Street. Most of us knew him well enough to say hi, and a few knew him well enough to ask about his health; but as it turned out, none of us knew him very well.

Ambrose stumbled and fell onto the deserted gravel road. He seemed old to me then, though he must have been no more than fifty. His gray hair and eyebrows seemed to glow blue under the brilliant moon. "Please," he said, his voice barely reaching my window. The cicadas began another verse of their shrill song. Then, Mr. Gray came out of the field and stood over Ambrose in the road. Delbert Gray was my teacher that year at the grade school.

"I can't let you tell anybody about what we've been doing, Ambrose," Mr. Gray said in a sandy whisper.

"I won't say a word. I swear I won't, Del," Ambrose pleaded.

Mr. Gray laughed. "You won't be able to," he said. He was tall and handsome, younger than Ambrose, but old enough to seem old to a ten-year-old boy. His dark skin and hair made him stand out plainly against the colorless gravel road. He reached for Ambrose, seizing his arms just above the elbows, and jerked him to his feet. But Ambrose's knees seemed to buckle, and he fell down into a praying position in front of my teacher. Mr. Gray looked at him like he was trying to decide how to lift an awkwardly shaped package. Then, without any movement that would have suggested what he was about to do, Mr. Gray kicked at Ambrose's face. But Ambrose, moving quicker than I would have suspected possible, grabbed Mr. Gray's foot and lifted it into the air. Mr. Gray fell backwards and hit his head on the road. He looked surprised, like he had the breath knocked out of him, and was barely moving when Ambrose climbed on top of him. He sat with his knees on either side of Mr. Gray's waist, holding him down with his full weight. Ambrose wrapped his hands around Mr. Gray's throat, his thumbs in the center on the Adam's apple. Mr. Gray grabbed hold of Ambrose's hands but couldn't loosen the old man's fingers from his neck. Ambrose's body lifted and his weight shifted from Mr. Gray's waist to his throat. From my window, I could just barely hear a sort of gagging sound from Mr. Gray and a little whimpering noise that must have come from Ambrose because it continued even after Mr.

Gray stopped moving. Then Ambrose released his hold on Mr. Gray's neck and sat back onto his waist, becoming very quiet and staring at my teacher's slack face.

Then, as if I had called his name, his head jerked up and his eyes flashed to my window and hesitated. I was in plain view, but I couldn't move. I just closed my eyes and waited. I could feel that Ambrose and I were both holding our breaths, trying to think of what we should do next. Then I heard the crunch of footsteps in the gravel road, and then, except for the hum of the fan, silence. Even the cicadas were quiet. When I finally opened my eyes and looked at the road, it was empty.

In the troubled silence, I crawled to my bed and tried to find reason in what I'd seen. When I slept at last, I dreamt I was riding my Western Flyer down a quiet road, passing Ambrose over and over again as if there was a new Ambrose every fifty feet. Each Ambrose would stop walking and watch me as I pedaled past.

I awoke, after a night of confounding dreams, to the sweet smell of corn silk and rain. As I lay in bed, listening to the house's familiar sounds, my memory of the previous night's events was seen through a mercifully increasing brume. I told myself I had been dreaming, must have been dreaming, and I walked carefully through that first day, afraid that I might do something to break this fragile conviction. By the day's end, I could almost believe I had seen nothing the night before.

When I awoke on the third day, it was to the sound of men shouting outside my window. I slowly got out of bed and slipped on my T-shirt and jeans. It was when I saw Delbert Gray's body carried out of the field that I knew it had been real.

"Good morning, honey," Mom said as I came down the stairs. "Don't run out after breakfast. I need to talk to you."

I sat down at the kitchen table and Mom poured a bowl of Trix for me. She walked to the window over the sink and wiped her already dry hands with a dish towel.

"What, Mom? What is it?"

"Well, I was going to wait until you were finished, but I guess you might as well hear it now." She came to the table and sat down across from me, never letting go of her towel. Her green eyes looked tired and puffy, and I suddenly saw how much she had aged since the last time I'd really noticed her. She'd taken a job doing piecework at the glove factory and had begun to take on the smell of the tanning fluids they used on the leather. "The Coles found somebody in their field this morning. Somebody dead. Mr. Cole said he thinks it's Delbert Gray, but he...couldn't be sure...." Her pause made me think of the fish I had seen decaying in the hot sunshine at the river's edge, their eyes sunken and gray, and I felt like I might be sick.

"Are you OK, honey? I'm sure there's nothing to worry about, they'll catch whoever did it. You'll see," she said as she reached for my hand.

"Can I go outside now?" I asked without looking at her.

"Yeah, I couldn't eat anything either. OK, but stay away from the Cole's field. Tiger Gulley's out there with a couple of police from Coulterville. They won't want anybody getting in their way."

"OK, Mom," I said, as I rose from my untouched bowl of cereal. I hadn't gotten around to pouring milk on it, and I could hear the wax paper crinkle as she put the cereal back into the box. I turned and saw her carefully fitting the box tab in the slot, and I felt a hard, painful knot swelling in my throat. Ever since Dad died, she'd saved money any way she could. I nearly told her then, not just about Ambrose, but everything. I nearly told her everything.

I've lived here all my life. Everybody thinks we all know one another, all of us in a small town, but everybody's wrong about that. We don't know each other, we just know everything about each other. Very few of us escape with our secrets intact. Since I was eight years old, I knew Beaulah Gulley wasn't sleeping with Tiger anymore because he had come home drunk and hit her in the arms and hands with a two-by-four with sixteen-penny nails sticking out of it. The bloodstains are still there on the carport and are our equivalent to a tourist attraction. We show them to out-of-town friends as a point of interest. But I didn't know Beaulah and Tiger Gulley at all. I knew that Manis Clayton was put in a mental institution downstate because he would make himself hard and show it to old Ruby Varner every chance he got. But I didn't know Manis or Ruby, either one. And everyone knew that Bale Tyler sat in his window with a pair of binoculars and watched the Lloyd girls through their window. I guess I pretty much knew every stinking detail of everyone's life. That's why I'm sure everyone else knew about mine.

It was at the grade school Christmas pageant in 1964 that the town got their first real taste of what my family would come to be known for. I was to be the Toy Soldier in the pageant. This illusion was to be achieved by rubbing rouge into my cheeks, draping a wide red ribbon over one shoulder for a sash, and carrying my own toy rifle against the other shoulder. Mom dyed black a piece of red felt from last Christmas's decorating, and she rolled it up to form a soldiery looking hat. My performance consisted of being wound up with an imaginary key in my back by Rhonda Lloyd, then goose-stepping until my spring unwound and I bent over in exhaustion.

Mom and I begged Dad to come and see my performance. He held out until an hour before the event. "As long as we don't have to stay for that goddamn chili supper," he said. I was joyful. I knew that this time I would make him proud.

I walked the block and a half to the school, feeling grown-up and somewhat exotic; my flattop was gelled to a sharp angle, and my black dress shoes made gritty noises on the sidewalk. The sun had long since gone down, and it was exciting to see the school and my classmates in this new light. We weren't yet at an age where we needed to feign indifference to a coming event, and our energy filled the first-grade classroom. Mrs. Finley, our teacher, was helping those with more complicated costumes get dressed. "Hurry, everybody, we don't have much time. Start putting your makeup on," she said. Mrs. Finley was never indifferent.

By the time I was dressed and had allowed Mrs. Finley to smudge my cheeks with a tube of brilliant red lipstick, my excitement had turned into something more ominous. I could hear the families of all the grade-school kids milling about in the hallway as they made their way into the overheated cinder-block gymnasium. The sound of hard-soled shoes on the wood risers multiplied what must have been only a couple hundred spectators into a mob that could have filled a coliseum. Minutes disappeared each time I looked away from the clock. The mere idea of this event had kept me humming carols and goose-stepping for weeks, and now it made my stomach churn.

Mrs. Finley herded us into our preplanned line, and we began our march into the gym; I was first in line because I had to hide under the riser until my cue. I was to walk out to the middle of the gym when the lights went down, right after the fourth grade finished singing "Angels We Have Heard On High," and would be discovered in my unwound state as the lights arose.

I took my place under the riser and watched as the rest of my class filed into their seats on the floor. The room was trimmed with rolls of red and green crepe paper, and stars made from aluminum foil hung from strings tied to each wall. An aluminum Christmas tree sat smack in the middle of the floor and was lit from underneath by a spinning color-wheel.

Although I had practiced this routine countless times, I ran through it all again so as to lessen the chance that I might forget something. The air in the gym was too warm and smelled of hot metal. I could feel sweat form under the brim of my felt hat. The lights over the audience dimmed, and a hush filled the room. It was at that point I saw that there was a problem. I had been instructed not to come to the gym floor and assume my position until all was dark; Mr. Walker, the music teacher, had been quite clear on that point. "Now, it's important that you understand that you'll ruin the surprise if the audience sees that you're really just a boy in a costume. So you must wait until the lights go out and nobody can see you get into position." I understood perfectly, and now there was that stupid color-wheel. It hadn't been there before. Would they turn out that light so my entrance wouldn't be spoiled? The third grade began their version of "Away in a Manger." I was conscious of one bead of sweat rolling down the side of my cheek and another sliding down my nose.

When the fourth grade began singing the last refrain of "Gloooooooo-ri-ah," I knew I had to make a decision. The color-wheel's light had not been extinguished once since the beginning of the program. I could either walk out in plain view of the audience, illusion shattered, or I could hold out here in my hiding place until someone went out there to turn the colored light off. "In-egg-selsius-daaaa-yooo," the fourth-graders crooned, and the piano stopped.

I would wait it out, I decided. The color-wheel would just have to be turned off, even if it meant that everyone would have to wait for the show to continue. It was unbearably hot under the riser, but there was no point in ruining the entire production for the sake of comfort and expediency. Sweat streamed down my forehead and paused at my brow, threatening to sting my eyes.

And then the lights went down! I ran to my spot in front of the wonderful dark Christmas tree and leaned over, my arms hanging limp toward the floor. As I hung suspended there, I could feel the sweat on my face and back start to evaporate, and I was grateful. The piano started playing my song, "Parade of the Wooden Soldiers," and my heart leapt. My class began to sing, and I pictured my mom and dad, especially my dad, sitting out there in the dark. I hoped he was thinking, "There he is. That's my son, starring as the Toy Soldier."

Rhonda, right on cue, wound my imaginary key and I sprang into action. I began goose-stepping, and moving mechanically, as rehearsed. At first, I thought the audience's reaction was in response to my performance, but the little giggles I heard soon grew into outright mean laughter. The laughing only grew worse when I tried to ignore it and really threw myself into my goose-stepping. I tried to finish the circle I was supposed to complete before winding down, but when I saw Rhonda laughing, too, I could only think of escape. I ran for the gym door and made my way to the boys' rest room.

I cried out when I saw myself in the mirror. Black stripes ran down every conceivable angle of my face to form an imperfect circle around the neck of my otherwise clean white shirt. My dyed felt hat had bled from all my sweating under the riser and made me look like a sloppy parody of a blackface minstrel. My eyes, wide with fear and disappointment, shone brightly against my blackened skin.

It took several minutes for the laughter to subside enough for the concert to continue. I tried to rinse off my face, but the dye was more tenacious on my skin than on my hat. I heard the program come to its finale with the entire school singing one verse of "We Wish You a Merry Christmas."

I was still trying to clean myself up when the bathroom door flew open with a force that made me jump. Dad came into the room, and I knew I would have to pay for embarrassing him. Pausing only a moment to consider a course of action, he chose the one with which he was most familiar. He slapped the hat off my head and pulled me up to his puffy red face by one arm. "What was that all about? Do you work at making me look stupid or is it just a talent you have?" he hissed.

The concertgoers were pouring out of the gymnasium, when Dad, still holding me off the ground by one arm, carried me out of the bathroom, through the hall, and out into the darkness, giving me a hard jerk every couple of steps. I don't think he even realized anyone else was around. I knew better than to cry or beg for him not to hurt me. Any sign of weakness only doubled his rage. As ashamed as I was that night, I looked directly into the eyes watching us go out the door. I didn't know if the disapproval I saw in their faces was meant for me or for my father.

He never came to another Christmas concert or any other school event. People soon forgot about my embarrassing appearance in the pageant, and I never attempted anything like it again.

There were times when I could see my father, in a moment of anger, stop and consider what he was about to do. There were times he would successfully suppress his anger, let his hand fall limply to his side from where it was poised to strike, and walk away. There were times he was not successful, when he would stop, consider what he was about to do, then strike with as much force as he could physically muster. And there were times he did not consider what he was about to do but would strike without any thought at all.

He had worked at the same cripplingly dreary maintenance job since the day his father kicked him out of the house, at the age of fifteen. Apparently, Dad was finally old enough, or big enough, or brave enough, to fight back, so he was no longer welcome. Unfortunately, he had inherited more than his father's brutish blue eyes; he was also burdened with his irrational rage.

He and Mom got married when she received the news that I was imminent, and Dad seemed to view their marriage, and my birth, as one more rung in his ever-descending ladder toward ruin. Whatever dreams he believed we'd shattered he did not share with me, but I suspect they were ruined long before he met my mother. His dreams, I believe, were stunted and disfigured while still being formed, by his father, a man I never met, though we lived only miles away. I learned of my grandfather's furies and hateful existence from my mother, and then only after my father had died.

But my father wasn't a monster, at least not when it came to our neighbors. The Harveys—Parnell and Nancy, and their boy, Toot, and their girl Landa—lived about a mile down the road from us in a ramshackle, four-room house. They were what we called trash, though the line that separated the Harveys from most of the rest of us in town was fine indeed. One late spring night, the summer after the Christmas pageant, Dad and I were driving by their house, and Dad saw that Parnell had a rifle in his hand, pointing it at his wife. I had been asleep in the front seat, but woke when the car came to a sudden stop at the side of the road. Nancy stood defiantly against her charging husband, with her hands on her narrow hips, and curlers as big as soup cans in her hair. From where we sat in our dark car, I saw Toot and Landa standing, looking bewildered, on the porch. Toot wore cotton pajamas with cowboys holding lassoes high above their heads, forever on a bucking bronco in mid-buck. Over this he wore a powder blue chenille robe, tied handily at the waist in a perfect bow. Landa wore a dainty pink nightie, with satin ribbons on each shoulder, and her stringy hair flew in wispy disarray around her head. Though she was an eight-year-old girl, she moved like a man who'd driven eighteen-wheelers all his life: arms held out away from her body, her head held forward, and her legs always slightly bent, as if her hamstrings were too short to allow anything else.

Toot had his hands pressed to each side of his face, screaming like the woman did before she was abducted by the Creature from the Black Lagoon: long, shrill, sissy screams. Landa stood with her arms hanging by her side, tears streaming down her homely little face. It was the only time I'd ever seen her cry.

"Stay down," Dad said to me as he got out of the car. "You need some help, Nancy?"

"Good, I got a witness now. You ain't nearly so big with another man around, are you?" Nancy said, and I noticed that she had blood coming down the side of her head from a cut in her temple. It looked black in the yellow porch light.

"You just stay out of this! Just git back in your car and drive on home. This ain't your affair," Parnell shouted without looking at my dad. To Nancy, he said, "I swear to God, I'll kill you if you talk like that to me again! It'll be a cold day when I allow a woman o' mine to give me lip!"

"Call the sheriff, Toot," Nancy said calmly. But he stood with his hands to the sides of his face, his buckteeth glowing in the yellow light. "Landa Lee, go call the sheriff." Landa ran into the house and let the screen door slap shut behind her.

"You raised that boy to be a pantywaist. Just look at 'im! He makes me sick," he shouted. And then he spun around to my father and said, "Look at 'im. You know what he is?"

"Shut up! How can you be so mean, you slack-jawed son of a bitch!" Nancy shouted, moving to within a few inches of Parnell and pushing her finger into his narrow chest. "Why, he's no more a pantywaist than you are," she said, with a mean little smirk.

He seemed thrown off by the duplicity of her statement; you could see him stop and consider it. *Does that mean she thinks Toot's not a pantywaist because I'm not one, or does it mean that I'm just as big a sissy as he is?* He must have come to a conclusion he didn't care for, because he quickly brought the butt of the rifle down on his skinny wife's face. It met the side of her head with a sickening crack sending rollers flying across the yard. She stumbled backwards and fell against their red Ambassador, where it was parked in the driveway. Toot began a new series of high-pitched screams, and Parnell moved to where Nancy had fallen, lifting the rifle high over his shoulder, with the butt aimed again at her head.

Because I'd been told to stay down, I watched all of this with my eyes peering over the dashboard, like a frog in a pond. I opened my mouth to shout at him, and only grunted. I didn't know what words to say. Dad, with a movement that surprised all of us, ran to where Parnell stood and jumped through the air, hitting our neighbor in the shoulder and pushing him to the ground. The rifle flew out of his hands, and skittered across the dew-wet grass. Parnell scurried out from under Dad and ran a few feet away, on the other side of their car.

"Stay away from me, you son of a bitch!" Parnell screamed, in a voice that was every bit as high-pitched and girlish as his son's. Nancy pulled herself up and moved away from the car.

Dad stood and snatched the rifle up off the ground with one hand. He stood facing Parnell, and Parnell's eyes grew wide with fear. He backed away from my father and Nancy, raising his hands in the air as if he were surrendering. He ran his hand through his dark, slick hair, lifting it out of his eyes, then dashed into the Ambassador. The little car's engine struggled over and over again, and Parnell finally got it started and jammed his foot onto the gas pedal, causing dust and gravel to spit twenty feet behind him. The wheels caught hold and he sped down the driveway and down the gravel road, until the tiny red taillights disappeared.

All of us watched the car go, and then Nancy, finally rid of her tormentor, collapsed onto the ground into a sitting position, and buried her face in her hands, sobbing. Blood slid down the side of her face and forearms. Dad ran into the shabby white house with the gun, and a couple of minutes later returned with towels and a tray of ice. He crouched down by Nancy and dabbed a towel on her face, then dumped a tray of ice onto another he had laid on the ground. He wrapped the ice up in the towel and held it against her head. I watched, fascinated to see my father move with such grace and awareness of another person. I could see that my dad was talking, whispering something to Nancy, and I was suddenly jealous. I was excluded from this moment in my father's life; he'd never been so tender with me, had never held me so gently and whispered that everything would be all right. He was showing this strange family a side of him that I'd never been allowed to see.

My father helped Nancy onto the front seat of the car, and I sat on the back seat with Toot and Landa. We rode silently the mile down the road to our house, and the three of us children got out and explained to my mom, as best we could, what had happened, and told her that Dad had taken Nancy to the emergency room. We fell asleep long before my father drove Nancy, with her arm in a sling, and a broad white bandage around her head, back from the hospital. When I got up in the morning to get ready for school, the Harvey children had already gone back to their mother, and my mom shushed me, saying that Dad was sleeping for a few minutes before he had to get up for work. When he got in from work that night, he looked tired and different somehow, like someone you see from a distance and think you recognize, but when you get closer, you realize it's someone else entirely.

The summer after the Harvey incident, my mom and dad and I went on a rare five-day summer camping trip. As the vacation wore on, my father had grown more and more silent, in response to some stimulus unknown to me or Mom. Silence was the most dangerous sign. Silence meant trouble.

After returning home, Dad and I were nearly finished unloading the camping gear from his 1961 Oldsmobile Super 88 when I saw that he had forgotten his tackle box in the trunk. As I reached to pick it up, Dad accidentally closed the trunk lid on my hand. I screamed as I felt the hot, wet pain race up my arm.

"You little idiot! What're you doing?" he asked without moving to unlock the trunk. I stood with my hand in the trunk, and my screams turned to a sort of loud hum that corresponded with my rapid breathing. He slowly reached into his pocket and produced the key, all the while shaking his head so that I might truly understand how unhappy he was with my behavior.

Mom had been on the front porch and ran down the front stairs to the driveway. "Hurry! He's going to pass out!" she screamed at him. He unlocked the lid and I stood staring at my crooked, bleeding fingers. Dad took my hand in his and inspected the damage. He produced a handkerchief from his back pocket and wrapped it around my hand. "We'll need to take him to the hospital," he said, watching the blood soaking into the white square. Then he slapped me hard across the face. "I guess you know this is going to cost me an arm and a leg, don't you?" I was too close to shock to know how to respond. The last thing I remembered seeing before the white static in my mind turned to black was Ambrose Shears's eyes, wide with concern.

My hand was in a cast for eight weeks after that, and I had stitches as well, though I can't remember how many. I learned that Ambrose Shears had witnessed my father's brutality and had carried me onto my family's porch to wait for the ambulance to take me to the hospital. He sat with me and Mom while Dad continued to put away his camping gear.

Ambrose came to see me several times that summer, always in the daytime. He didn't say so, but I suspected that he came during the day so he would miss my dad. I wasn't allowed to ride my bike, or run, or anything else that might result in my rebreaking the bones in my hand, so Ambrose and I sat in the backyard in the swing under the elm tree. We didn't talk much. There didn't seem to be much to say. I was just glad to have a person near me who didn't hit or yell.

The last Friday of summer vacation, my dad called the plant and told them he was too sick to come in. He came to my room before the sun was all the way up and pushed his knuckles into my ribs. I woke with a start. "Get up, we have work to do." This was how Dad asked for help.

I had been exempt from performing all of my usual chores that summer because of the cast on my hand, but it had been off for almost a week, and Dad wanted me to make up for lost time. I sat in bed with my legs hanging off to the floor while my head cleared. I dressed in the near daylight and went to the bathroom. When I came out, Dad was there waiting for me.

"Ready?" he said.

"What are we doing?" I asked.

"We need to pull those rotten eaves down on the east side of the house. You'll have to come up there with me and hand my tools to me. Think you can handle that?"

I nodded silently, afraid to make a sound that might betray my fear. The last time he forced me to climb to the roof, I had only been able to get three-quarters of the way up the ladder to the second floor when my legs froze and the tears started. But that was last summer; I was smaller then. I would have to try again.

I watched Dad climb quickly up the seemingly endless wooden ladder, and I was sickened by its sway and give. With each step, it scraped slightly on the concrete surface of the carport. The ladder only reached to the lowest point of the roof, a section that came down to the top of the second floor; the rest of the roof was much higher, capping both the second story and the attic, climaxing in steep peaks that stabbed at the sky. When he reached the roof, he took a claw hammer out of his tool belt and threw the heavy leather belt off to the side. He looked over the edge of the roof at me. His face looked puffy and red as his skin sagged from the gravity, and it made me think of his face the night of the Christmas pageant. "OK. Come on up. Be careful, now."

I put a shaking hand on the ladder and took one step onto the first rung. It was much easier than I had remembered. I stepped two more times and felt my confidence swell. When I was nearly three-quarters of the way up, I remembered that the first steps had been easy the last time, too. "Don't look down," Dad said, as he realized my pace was slowing.

I don't know which frightened me more, the height or the possibility of disappointing Dad again. I didn't look down and kept my legs moving. I forgot which leg or arm needed to move next and had to concentrate on getting the rhythm right. I came to the lip of the roof and felt like I had discovered a strange new planet. The roof looked entirely different from up there. The gray shingles were much bigger than they seemed from the ground, and all the imperfections, the little bumps and scuffs, were remarkably apparent. Dad lifted me off the ladder by the hands and set me down away from the edge. My first instinct was to keep as close to the roof as I could, or even to lie down, but Dad walked over to the eave and called me.

"Bring that belt."

I saw that the tool belt was very close to the edge, and that a branch high in a maple tree brushed lightly against it. The leaves were more individually defined from this vantage point and the morning sun made each one glow. I looked past the roof's edge to the land beyond our yard. I had never seen so much of the world at one glance, and its size startled me. Staying as close to the roof's gritty surface as I could, I slid toward the edge and thought about how to reach for the belt. I stuck out my leg and tried to hook the belt on my foot to bring it closer to me, but I was too concerned about falling. My foot pushed the leather belt and all the tools off the roof. I heard it hit the carport with a slap and a clang.

"Goddammit! Good job, dummy. Now you can just go down and get it," Dad yelled.

I came to the edge of the roof where the ladder made contact and slowly positioned myself to mount it. I made my way down the ladder, backing down one careful step at a time. I didn't cry, which surprised me. The one thing I agreed with my father about was that I cried too much for a boy. Once I had my feet on solid ground again, I looked up to where Dad had climbed, all the way to the top of the peak over the attic window, and felt my knees quake, even while standing on solid ground. I stood and watched as Dad leaned over the edge and began to pull at the old rotted wood with his hammer. I felt an ache start in the back of my neck from holding my head at such a severe angle. He pulled hard at a strip of wood that began to come away from the house, but snapped back when it slipped out of the hammer's claw. I watched as the hammer seemed to lurch forward on its own, out of Dad's reach, and begin its oddly slow descent to the ground. Dad's face plainly showed his surprise as he reached for the hammer and realized that he had reached out too far over the edge. The hammer clanged so loudly against the carport that it left my ears ringing. Dad's eyes caught mine for an instant, and I'm sure it was anger I saw in his face. He grabbed for the roof's forty-five-degree angle and hung by his fingertips.

"Bring the ladder!" he screamed. "Now!" He began inching his way down the steep grade, trying to get to a place where his feet might reach the ladder.

I ran to the ladder and pushed it toward where he hung so helplessly. The top of the ladder scraped against the white clapboard house, and the bottom against the smooth concrete surface. It was a very long ladder and I was a very young boy; I had to push it a couple of inches at a time to prevent it from toppling over.

When the ladder was still fifteen feet away from where he hung, my father shouted, "Hurry, you little idiot!"

I pushed the ladder two more steps. Then I stopped. I looked up to him, where he looked back over his shoulder at me. I thought of my mother crying on one of the countless times he'd called her an idiot, one of his favorite pet names for us.

"What are you doing? Push it over here. Please!"

I didn't move. The ladder was still ten feet to the right of his right leg, and probably five feet below his feet. I could see that if he continued to move to the right, and I to the left, his feet could have reached the top two rungs of the ladder, but left where it was, he continued to dangle from the rotten eave.

"Help me," he cried out to me.

I wondered why Mom hadn't come to see what the noise was all about, but she must have been in the shower. He finally stopped yelling, and again began working his way down the severe angle toward the ladder. Inch by inch he came closer, until he could have reached the ladder with one toe, but the rotten wood finally gave way with a wet, ripping sound, and he fell. He might have landed on his feet, but his foot pushed against the side of the house and he turned head over heels in midair. I didn't move away but stayed standing near where he fell. I was close enough to see his blue eyes, confused and angry, a second before his head hit the concrete. I watched him struggle for a minute, watched his fingers slowly clutch at something he must have thought could still save him. Then he was still.

I don't know how long I watched Dad lying there, and I'm not even sure what I was feeling, but when I finally turned to find Mom and tell her that there had been an accident, standing on the side of the gravel road was Ambrose. He walked unhurriedly to me and took me by the shoulders. "Come in the house. We'll have to call someone" was all he said, his voice even and comforting.

I can't be certain that Ambrose Shears had been there long enough to see that I could have stopped Dad's fall. I've replayed those minutes a thousand times, and each time I seem to read the same thing from Ambrose's expression: understanding. We saw much less of each other for the next several months. He'd say hi to me when we saw each other at the store or when I rode my bike past him as he walked along the road, but we never spoke of what I'd done.

When I saw Ambrose kill Delbert Gray almost exactly a year after my father died, I knew I would do for him what he had done for me. He must have had his reasons, too.

He still lives in the little pink house at the dead end of School Street. I make a point of knocking on his door and going in for coffee when I visit Mom. We still have little to say to one another, but the understanding we share fills the quiet.

# *Mason The Dean*

*Christopher Sweet*

I am not an elderly man. I am rather in the full flower of my academic career as an administrator of a public high school in one of Chicago's most prestigious suburbs. Indeed, my school has not gone unnoticed by a commission chaired by the First Lady of the United States, Hillary Rodham Clinton. And in the days of which I shall come to speak, the name of the Hillthwart Community High School was included in that fragrant bouquet of elite North Shore schools, among which numbers the First Lady's alma mater. The nature of my vocation over the last twenty-five years has brought me into professional contact with a class of persons not heretofore celebrated in the annals of education. I mean the high-school disciplinary deans, who as a class of men and women offer some interesting studies in idiosyncrasies and ideologies that would make pedagogues of whatever ilk radiate a sympathetic resonance. But one of these gentle persons stands out from the rest for the singularity of his peculiarities, never mind the others whose lives are an open book. I speak of Mason the Dean, about whom the story herein related is the sum and total of what is known of that man, astonishing as that may seem in an age of background checks and full disclosure, except for a vague rumor, which shall appear in its proper time and place.

Before painting for you a portrait of Dean Mason, as it were, from life, it is fitting that I describe myself, my colleagues, my ambient surroundings, my responsibilities, and my philosophical underpinnings, because a grasp of the milieu into which Mason was inserted is necessary to a grasp of the man himself. My motto is and always has been, "Live and let live," or as the French say, *"Laissez faire."* Shortly after embarking on my career at Hillthwart High School a quarter century prior to these events, I found myself elevated to the post of Associate Principal for Student Services, in which capacity I outlasted three principals and four superintendents. My immediate domain included two rooms squeezed between the nurse's office and the cashier's office: an outer room staffed by my secretary, a matron of considerable years and experience, who answers my telephone, keeps the keys to the building locked in a safe beside her desk, greets anyone who happens to wander in, and replaces the five-gallon bottle of water atop the water cooler when necessary, a skill I have never mastered, as my efforts are always attended by considerable slop and spillage; and an inner room furnished with my desk and chair, a single filing cabinet, and usually a box of donuts next to the coffee pot, which rests on top of the bookcase where I keep a number of volumes both philosophical and practical. Under my supervision are (1) the Director of Student Activities, a person whose responsibilities are keeping the deposits of clubs and organizations, filling the vending machines, and operating a fund for which the word *slush* is an ugly but useful appellative which serves a number of purposes and keeps the machinery of student governance oiled; and (2) the disciplinary deans, about whom I shall speak at length. In addition, I have the personal responsibility to prepare, in the springtime of the year, the master schedule, giving rooms to teachers, teachers to subjects, students to rooms.

Far at the other end of the school, at the end of a balcony overlooking a light-starved atrium, a sign hanging from the ceiling tiles proclaims THE OFFICE OF THE DEANS. At the time Mason appeared on the scene, I had only two deans and a secretary in my employ: first, Dean Prozac; second, Dean Winwin; and third, their shared secretary, Ten-Four. These names may strike you as weird. Each is in fact a nickname, chosen to express some facet of its owner's character. Dean Prozac was a woman of moderate years. During periods of relative quiescence in the student body, Prozac was the most organized and nonbelligerent of officers. The students over whom she held sway knew her to be stern but fair-minded, if overworked. She routinely commuted after-school detentions to lunchroom detentions, to be served during the school day rather than at times when most of the students who received them were working as clerks, baggers, stock boys, or receptionists at tanning spas, grocery or hardware stores, and fast-food emporiums about town. She was not above hugging distraught students with one arm, a shoulder grip parallel to the student, which seemed to say, "Go now, and be good." She greeted colleagues in the hall with a wave and a smile as her short legs shot her across the path of oncoming student traffic, here into the Guidance Department, there into Officer Schmooz's office, now coming, now going, always on the move.

It was during periods of student unrest that the nature and character of Prozac were radically altered. During these periods, progress reports issued from Prozac's desk decrying the decline of the student body and proclaiming a state of siege. To read them, one would think that Hillthwart's students were the dregs of the inner city:

*Attention, teachers! The number of students we see every day has doubled every year since we started keeping records. Gang activity, gang signs, and gang dress are on the rise. The search for concealed weapons marches on!*

Understand that these missives went out to an audience which was not wholly in disagreement with their warp and weave, though in truth our students—save for a handful, perhaps twenty-five hard-core bad guys, by whom I mean those who spit tobacco juice in the halls, cut classes to take a walk on the roof of the school, or engage in sex in deserted hallways—are puppy dogs of the first order. But teachers and deans being what they are—a cross section of the public—they share a cross section of the public's perception of youth. The perceived threats are usually of the sartorial variety. That is to say, outerwear. The wearing of threatening outerwear is the single most offended-against rule at Hillthwart High. Indeed, Prozac once chaired the Garments Committee, which after outlawing outerwear begat the Borderline Garments Committee, whose charge was to define what was outerwear and what was not outerwear, and to devise punishments severe enough to discourage outerwear. Hooded sweatshirts were first banned, but when the wrestling team complained that they then could not wear their hooded sweats in school, the ban was amended to include only hooded sweatshirts with the hood up. A fine distinction, to be sure, as the ban on outerwear had been in response to the perception that students were bringing guns and knives into the school concealed in their clothes. The efforts of the Borderline Garment Committee did not cease until after a frenetic field trip to a local mall, where Prozac, like a tour guide whisking through Europe in ten days, invaded every apparel shop, tried on every category of outerwear or suspected outerwear, and egged the committee into issuing its final report, a sartorial balance sheet, in twelve pages, which was duplicated and sent to each faculty member on blood red paper, the same rather expensive paper which Nurse LaFever uses at the beginning of each year for her vibrant "Blood-borne Pathogens" memo, which is always accompanied by a pair of plastic gloves of the kind used by doctors for pelvic and rectal examinations.

Not only in her dealings with teachers does Prozac go overboard from the educational tour boat. Her dealings with students are marked by some indiscreet slippage. It came to my attention one time that she had collared a boy who had sworn at a teacher—a clear-cut case of insubordination, the second-most-often violated rule, and sort of a blanket infraction covering everything from elevating the middle finger to refusing to show a teacher a student identification card on demand—sat him in a chair, and bent close to his face, close enough for him to feel her hot breath on his cheek. Her exact words were "Do you believe in Jesus? If you believed in Jesus and went to church, you wouldn't be getting into trouble all the time. Jesus, boy, Jesus is the answer!" The boy, unfortunately, was an atheist, and said so in rather uncompromising terms. I entered the case when his parents appealed the three-day suspension which Prozac had thrown at him, along with a thick book of infractions going back to his days as a freshman. I stepped into her office one day after school and said, "Prozac, we can't go about trying to convert them to Christianity."

"How else are we going to beat the hell out of Satan?" was her reply. I decided to wait a few days until the storm subsided, but as my motto is "Live and let live," the incident found its way to my back burner, where it simmered until one day it totally evaporated.

Winwin is a different case altogether. Winwin's philosophy is that everyone is a winner, no one a loser. Whenever a case of insubordination comes before Winwin, he calls in both student and teacher, sits them side by side in the uncomfortable office chairs opposite his desk, and says, "I don't know how you feel about this, but I feel that no one who comes into my office leaves a loser. You're both winners, and I want you to feel good about yourselves. Now, what exactly is the problem, Billy?"

*Student*: "I used inappropriate language, Mr. Winwin."

*Teacher*: "He called me a fucking son of a bitch."

*Winwin*: "Is that true, Billy? Well, how can we all be winners here? Billy, will you apologize to your teacher?"

*Student*: "I guess."

*Winwin*: "And Mr. Sorego, do you think maybe you overreacted in not taking into account Billy's home situation, his difficult childhood, and the fact that his high median income means that he is economically enhanced but culturally deprived?"

*Teacher*: "No, I, well..."

Then Winwin will pull out his ruler and his pad of paper and draw a straight line across the pad, and begin writing on the line in a slow hand, each loop perfect. No one has ever seen the notes he writes. But the struggle to make a straight line and to labor over each letter is remarked upon by all witnesses. Watching it is excruciating. I have had to sit through it myself. One begins to think of the pain and suffering this man has endured, and of the difficulties faced by the learning impaired. Then he says, "When I was in Vietnam, I knew a lot of boys like Billy. Most of them didn't make it back. And those who did can't walk or can't talk or can't paddle a canoe. But they were all good kids." And so it goes, on and on and on, until both parties are exhausted and concede to themselves, and then, reluctantly, to each other, that they cannot, in fact, win. The offshoot of all this is that Winwin's students never suffer any consequences for their behavior. Legion are the teacher complaints that I have had to field in Winwin's "situations." But as I say, confronting the man is problematic, to say the least. One cannot simply say, "You have made a mistake, Winwin." He won't let you. He starts talking about how all of us need to be a winner. And so it goes.

Third and last of all is Ten-Four. She is a woman of middling years and middle-body spread; a secretary, but more than that. Ten-Four mans the radios which connect the Deans' Office to the troops in the field, the parapros, who are always looking for someone who has broken a rule. Indeed, one suspects that they are paid for piecework. The parapros exist to humiliate and harass the student body, to provoke them into unwise angry responses, to escort them to the scaffold, and to oversee the placement of the nails, the thrust of the spear, and the vinegar cocktail. Ten-Four has seen it all and done it all. She spends her days at the radio and the keyboard, turning the day's events into disciplinary reports, adjudications, and orders. At midday, she goes out to lunch and brings back for the deans a meal of Fatburgers from Fatty's, the fast-food emporium.

Now, the increase in enrollment and concurrent growth in delinquency which we experienced starting several years ago warranted an expansion of my office, specifically the hiring of a third dean to take up the excess. The opening was posted at the beginning of the year, when funding for the position was belatedly passed by a tax-revolt-wary Board of Education, and within a few days Mason appeared at my door, ramrod straight, firm-jawed, and clad in a Hillthwart wrestling sweatshirt (hood down) and sweatpants, looking for all the world like the coach that he was, and had been for his two years on the faculty.

After a brief interview, I put him at the top of my list, and after questioning the requisite "other" candidates who had indicated interest in the position, just to maintain the appearance of competition for the post which state law mandates, I engaged him. Immediately the position of wrestling coach opened up, and I braved the fierce glances of the chairman of the Physical Education Department—a colossus in short pants—for several weeks thereafter. I was glad to have among my stable of deans a man of so much authority in his bearing and his being, a man who I hoped would bring to the Deans' Office a firm hand in control, which might mitigate the evils begat by the seasonal whimsicality of Prozac and the soft hand of Winwin.

I should have stated before that I had found money in the building fund the preceding summer to add a third office to the deans' suite by knocking out a wall and appropriating part of an English classroom, over the objections of the English Department chairman, who saw the reasonableness of the move only after I suggested that he transfer his own office into the abbreviated classroom, thus enlarging his own workspace in the process. Now, when one entered the Deans' Office from the dreary atrium balcony, one found oneself face to face with Ten-Four at her desk, her word processor ever radiating a blue light, her walkie-talkie crackling and spouting. She sat at the end of a short foyer or waiting room. The wall behind her was filled with cabinets where the forms and blank student passes were locked each night. To her flanks, the walls of the waiting room were intersected by the deans' doors, and each individual dean's office possessed a plate-glass interior window through which the deans could look out at the waiting miscreants and the miscreants could look in upon the human form of justice. On the left, by the entrance, was Winwin's office. His door was always open, and he could be seen through the slats of his Venetian blinds bending over a yellow pad of paper, his ruler in one hand and pen in the other, working unhurriedly, with light from outside filtering in over his left shoulder. On the right by the door was Prozac's closed chamber, into which one looked as into an aquarium, where one might see her pacing back and forth with quick turns, like an exotic fish, or resting uneasily with her feet up and crossed at the ankles, hands folded in prayerlike meditation, lit from above by a sometimes-blinking bank of fluorescent lights. Beyond Prozac's window was a wall of building blocks from floor to ceiling, and seven chairs all in a row where the students who had been collared by the parapros sat waiting to be summoned to judgment. And opposite the chairs, to Ten-Four's right, one looked into the office assigned to Dean Mason: a southern exposure, light, airy, painted a bright new yellow, with an exterior window looking out upon the peaceful suburban green which surrounds Hillthwart High School. From this vantage he might contemplate the lonely arc of a Frisbee on a spring afternoon or, looking down, monitor an intimate circle of vaguely menacing hacky-sackers, or peruse a peculiar congregation of inland seagulls and land-roaming Canadian geese spread over the grassy lot, devouring the remains of lunch discarded by our well-socialized, happy students.

At first, Mason held an extraordinary number of conferences with students who were called to his office for minor offenses, assigning Saturday detentions (Saturdays being a prerogative of the deans alone, for if teachers were allowed the power to assign Saturdays, the detention room would be crowded to overflowing and I would have to increase the Saturday staff). Saturdays were routinely given to offenders of the dress code, smoking violators, and the grossly insubordinate. He quickly grew familiar with all of the offenders in his third of the alphabet, filled a filing cabinet with dossiers on them, called their parents, and dealt with them firmly and fairly. He never backed down from a confrontation with a student, always supported the faculty, and made the parapros feel a little less like the minor demons of Hell that they were, and a little more like cherubim and seraphim and winged minions of the Lord. He always ate his lunch in his office, and frequently his dinner and breakfast, as he habitually was the first to arrive in the building, when the custodian opened the door, and the last to leave. As we walked to our cars, we could observe Mason working alone in his second-floor window, where the light shone like a beacon in the darkness of a winter evening.

On occasion, it is my responsibility to review a judgment made by my staff against a student when the parents raise objections to the disciplinary measures taken. I am the last resort before the lawyers grapple the school board.

In such cases where, against my natural grain and tendency to leave well enough alone, I was called in to mediate a dispute between parents and deans, it had been my habit to confer alone with the dean in question, to get his or her side of the story before proceeding, to sound him or her out and gain some impression of where we might compromise and where we might stand firm. It was in the third week, I think, of Mason's service that I received a request from the parents of a boy who had been apprehended hiding in the cafeteria to avoid his physical education class, an offense which warranted a Saturday detention at most, and that only for a repeat offender such as the boy was. Mason had issued the student a three-day suspension from school, an overly sensitive reaction which I ascribed to Mason's previous association with the Physical Education Department and to his zeal to show that he was made of as tough a stuff as we all intuited him to be. I thought it might be a simple matter to speak to him in conciliatory terms and persuade him to commute the sentence to a simple full-Saturday detention, with all the boredom and time to think about the sin of repeated non-dress for P.E. and cutting class which attends four hours spent sitting in a dreary and silent cafeteria on a Saturday morning.

In this very frame of mind I did broach the subject with Mason in his office, he seated in his leather chair behind the spreading desk and I in a simple steel office chair reserved for the accused on the less imposing side of the desk. I rapidly sketched that perhaps, since the student's parents had called me and requested a meeting, I ought to be prepared to concede a point or two since it appeared that the boy had only committed a level-two offense, while suspensions were strictly reserved for level-five offenses, such as excessive display of pyrotechnics, third-time destruction of school property, and threats of violence to faculty or staff. After all, I said in a jocular reference to a past event, it's not like he brought roadkill into the halls. I was met by a wall of silence, and, thinking that I had perhaps stated the case in terms too strongly chiding, I urged Mason to show an excess of grace. Imagine my surprise when Mason, in a tone clear and commanding, replied, "I'll handle it my way."

Stunned, I thought that perhaps an appeal to Mason's generosity of spirit had been misunderstood as a weakness on my part, rather than a thoughtfully considered policy decision. I said, "Mason, can't we go easy on the boy this time, if for nothing else, to avoid a row with the lawyers?"

But in the clearest tone possible, he reiterated, "I'll handle it my way."

"Handle it your way!" I retorted. "Mason, do you understand that we may have a lawsuit against the school pending here? I want you to do the right thing. A three-day suspension is an inappropriate punishment," I concluded, rising to my feet.

"I'll handle it my way," he said.

I tried to stare him down. His eyes were cold and blue, and his jaw jutted forward at an uncomfortable-looking angle as he slowly ground his teeth. Not a ripple of human understanding disturbed his countenance. I might as well have been talking to a Hindu god of extinction. I should have overridden him on the spot. But we live in disordered times. Beset by an anxious faculty, a self-aggrandizing principal, a TV-news-addicted community, and a school board of hinds up for re-election by wolves, I was clearly out on a limb in suggesting leniency for the student. The boy might as well have been selling crack cocaine as sitting out P.E. in the cafeteria. Had I detected the slightest hint of humane sentiment in Mason...but there was no shred of human kindness I could seize upon. As I had several other appointments that day, I let the matter rest. When I did meet with the parents, I persuaded them that suspension was in the boy's best interest and that three days at home would make him consider his truant behavior. I also promised that he would no longer have to shower with the boys, which it seems was his central complaint. Fortunately, the parents turned out to be as reasonable as the boy was shy, and the crisis, like a dark cloud, evaporated as quietly as it had condensed.

A few days after this incident, I received a call from a member of the English Department—whose members are, I must say in passing, as motley a collection of malcontents as ever convened—who stated that Mason had issued three-day suspensions to four of his students for stealing a walkie-talkie from one of the parapros. It seems the teacher had a casual relationship with his students, several of whom confided in him that they had a bet, or a sort of contest, to see who could be the first to steal a parapro's radio. By ill luck, at the moment the four boys and the teacher were enjoying the humor of the prank and listening to the parapro's enraged buzzing, Mason appeared at the classroom door. He strode into the room, picked up the radio, and barked out, "You, you, you, and you, come with me." When the English teacher learned they had been suspended, he appealed to Mason, but receiving, he said, only a cold stare, he came to me pleading that the boys had only committed a practical joke. When I entered the Deans' Office, a congregation of parapros hovered around Ten-Four's desk.

"Disgusting."

"What they need is discipline."

"It's not like the eighties."

"No respect."

"Where are their parents?"

"I'm afraid to walk to my car at night."

"You're not safe in the halls anymore."

These and similar statements issued from the small circle, but Mason, standing a head above the rest, remained silent.

"Mason, I must talk to you," I said.

"What do you want?"

"These boys who stole the radio," I said, "couldn't we treat this as a bad practical joke? I don't see that the boys should be suspended."

Mason folded his arms and said, "I'll handle it my way," then he turned and stepped into his office and shut the door, while the parapros, infused with new blood occasioned by my rebuff, went off to their posts.

For a moment I was taken aback, all air gone out of my sails, and I stood staring after Mason. Then I marshaled my strength, opened his door, entered, and demanded a reason for his retributive conduct.

"Why are you so set on suspending them?"

"I will handle it my way."

Had it been any other dean, I would have overridden his ruling at once. But there was something about Mason that overmastered me completely in the wonderful way that the exercise of arbitrary power has of gaining acquiescence from those, like myself, less inclined to engage on the level of a barroom brawl. I tried reasoning with him.

"Mason, the boys meant no harm, it was merely a practical joke, they are all honor students, and they intended to return the radio." Then I added, perhaps feebly, "Can't you see their humor and creativity?"

"I'll handle it my way," he replied flatly. It seemed he had not heard a word I said. He appeared to conceive of himself as final among the powers of the universe—like electricity, gravity, or inertia, only less scrutable.

"You have made up your mind, then, as you say, to 'handle it your way' against all appeals to your better nature?"

He gave me to understand that the students were, in his words, "dead meat" and might receive no sympathy from him.

I turned around, shaken to my very foundation, and reached out for support from my other colleagues, who had been standing outside the door discreetly listening.

"Prozac," I said, lapsing into the vernacular, "what do you think of all this? Should the boys not be cut some slack?"

"With all due respect, I think they need moral re-education."

"Winwin," I said, "what is your opinion?"

"These boys have stepped over the line drawn in the sand, sir. They're not winners; they're bad seed."

"Ten-Four," I said, hoping against reason for a token of support, "what do you think?"

"I'd expel them," she said with a grin.

There was no way to reply to this unanimity of vindictive impulses. I retreated from the Deans' Office. "Well, live and let live," I mumbled to myself as I passed above the atrium. But I did not put the situation entirely out of my mind. In the days that followed, I observed Mason all the more closely, dropping in at various hours, hoping to understand how he had wrought the conversion of the entire staff to intransigence. I noted that while Prozac and Winwin frequently left the office to talk to counselors and psychologists,

Mason appeared to take no counsel but his own and seldom left his office. Three times a day, during her breaks, Ten-Four would cross his threshold and without saying a word, he would pass her a five-dollar bill. She then would proceed to Fatty's, which was only a block from school, and return each time to deposit on his desk a bag containing two Fatburgers and a box of long, springy, deep-fried potato coils. He seemed to live on Fatburgers. Yet he remained trim and fit and rocklike. Nor was ill digestion an impediment to his willpower. He remained unfazed by his diet and as firm as ever in his dealings with students.

Nothing so irritates a person of moderate temperament as a bully. If the person bullied be not lacking in human sympathy, and the bully by the very bravura and brashness of his bullying reveal himself to be one of those pitiable individuals whose personal hell is to look into the mirror and see not his own face but that of a distorted and blameless angel, then the former will tend to soften criticism of the latter by an act of charitable imagination. Thus I regarded Mason. Poor devil! He meant no evil harm by his brusque bullying. Perhaps he was bullied as a child by parents whose own demons were exacting revenge for wrongs committed by their parents, who had in turn been the victims of their parents, and so on back to the first bullying act outside the guarded gates of Eden in the middle of a primal night lit only by the flaming swords. Thus, I resolved to play the good and forgiving parent to Mason, patiently indulging his excesses and teaching by example that a moderation in temper brings rewards which vengeance envies. Yet occasionally a different mood would seize me, and I would be tempted to antagonize him, to elicit from him a burst of anger, and then watch him spew and fume. It was a simple matter. One winter morning the impish impulse prevailed and the following scene ensued.

I arrived at Mason's door clad in a wrestling-team sweatshirt, one of the hooded variety, during the first period of the first day of winter that we really noticed the cold. As always, the ever balky heating plant, which is "controlled" by telephone line from a thousand miles away in Atlanta, Georgia, where it was sunny and seventy degrees, was uncooperative, and the offices and classrooms were frigid.

"Hello, Mason," I said. "The heat's not on in here, is it? Well, then, I'm glad I'm dressed for the weather." And so saying, I pulled the hood of my sweatshirt up over my head and disappeared inside it. All present understood that while staff were not subject to the dress code, teachers and administrators were expected to set a good example for the student body. My good example did not go unnoticed by the students who occupied the chairs along the wall.

One shivering girl gasped, and a young man who was rubbing his hands together burst out with a "Cool!" that was as visible as white vapor.

Mason didn't move a muscle but stood in the cold in his white shirtsleeves, khaki pants, and black wing tips, as solid as if he had been turned into a pillar of stone. He said, "In this office, we all follow the dress code. Put down your hood."

"How noble of you," I said. "Do you also punish yourselves when you are insubordinate?" I was met by a silence so thick I could have buttered toast with it. "What do you say, Winwin," I said to the also-shirtsleeved phantom who was standing in the doorway to his office. "What is the punishment for insubordination?"

"I try to resolve the situation so everybody comes out a winner."

"And Prozac," I said, turning around, "what do you do when a student steps out of line? Suspend him for three days?"

She folded her hands and bowed her head.

"What would you do, Mason, if you were confronted with a clear-cut case of insubordination?"

"I'd handle it my way," he said, standing ramrod straight with his hairy arms at his side and looking as though he routinely ate people like me for sustenance.

"Very well, Mason," I said, intoning my voice as if to say that he had condemned himself by his own words. I half believed he had, and was half ready to execute the sentence—immediate dismissal. But a sudden consciousness of the earliness of the hour invaded my soul and made me think of my donuts and fresh pot of coffee, which I had started brewing before being struck by the impulse to confront Mason. Anyway, it was not the time of the day to fire anyone. And so I thought it best to pull down my hood and walk to my office, though my whole body was vibrating with rage and confusion at his impudence.

I may as well admit it. The offshoot of the confrontation was that a certain rigid dean named Mason came to dominate the Deans' Office and his colleagues in it, so that his hard line prevailed over the students. He could not be dissuaded from the harshest and most unfair of punishments. He paid scant attention to the student handbook and the carefully articulated hierarchy of infractions, that frail lattice upon which the whole framework of student discipline rested.

As the weeks passed, I became uncomfortably accommodated to Mason. His steadfast devotion to order, which overshadowed his routine bending of the law, gained him crowds of supporters among the faculty. I daresay he grew to be the most celebrated individual in the building. Even I had to respect him for having initiated tremendous changes. People outside the school—community leaders, the local police chief, the leader of the tax watchdog group, and the editor of the newspaper—began speaking of the positive change that had been wrought by the crackdown on the student body. Mason won the favor of the principal, a man who played community opinion like an angel plays his harp, in harmony with the great choir. The principal ordered a survey to be taken of the faculty; 40 percent of the teachers completed the survey. Of that number, 55 percent stated that they wanted to close down the halls to student traffic. "A clear majority," the principal declared. And so, on a cold day in November, hall passes became a thing of the past, and the halls became deserted while classes were in session. I was given cause to reflect that people who feel that they cannot control their own lives compensate by trying to control the lives of others around them, even to the extent of controlling their bowel movements, for passes to the rest room were forbidden, and afflicted students were told to retain their grief. So Mason and the others, afflicted by an ever increasing number of ever more hostile student violators, compensated by cracking down in ever more areas of student life. Now and then, when parents complained or threatened a lawsuit, as they did when Mason suspended a student who had written a letter to the editor that the school paper printed, in which the student took the deans to task in unflattering terms, I would confront Mason with the necessity of easing up, relaxing his grip on the school. His invariable response, "I'll handle it my way," became like a mantra to me, something to be counted upon. I could be infuriated by his closed-mindedness, but I also could admire his success, and he was so successful that he seemed to lift the entire building and carry it upon his broad shoulders like the chained Atlas carried the disk of the world.

 Here it must be said that the certified staff, by which I mean the faculty, and the classified staff, that is to say the secretaries, parapros, lunch ladies, and custodians, had been working since the beginning of the school year without a contract, and negotiations had made little headway by the third week of November, when they broke down completely over the issue of reductions in force. Specifically, three parapros were slated for immediate dismissal and at least ten teachers were to be dropped at the end of the year either through early retirement or by issuing pink slips to all untenured staff and rehiring a smaller number. Mason was not alone in judging both measures to be unacceptably draconian. But no one was more hostile than he; even the officials of the teachers' union marked his militancy in defense of his assistants. He made his view widely known, that to reduce the number of parapros threatened to undo the mighty work of discipline he had wrought.

The responsibility for making the cuts in my staff fell, of course, on my shoulders. However, I thought it not inappropriate to solicit from my three deans a list of names of the parapros with whom it was felt we could most comfortably part. Each dean was to submit one name. If there were duplications, the deans were to settle the issue among themselves and then present me the final list, which I would use as a guide in making the dismissals. I thought this a completely reasonable course to pursue, and I prepared a memo for the deans in which I deplored the necessity for RIFing their assistants and requested their nominations by the end of the following week.

Three days later, strike votes were taken by both unions and passed with overwhelming majorities. So it was that on a cold Monday morning I happened to walk into a frigid and empty school building. Administrators were required to spend the day at work, though there was little to do but drink coffee and partake of the pastries the superintendent's office had provided on a table in the main hallway. It was at this table that I ran into Mason, pouring himself a cup of hot coffee while holding two glazed donuts.

"Well, Mason," I said, "nothing is as relaxing as a day without students, eh?"

He replied somewhat nervously that he had business to attend to and hurried off in the direction of the Deans' Office. As the quotient of his hostility seemed to be lower than in recent days, I resolved to approach Mason later, after he had digested his meal, on his own ground. After all, despite his injured feelings, we were playing on the same team. Mason could not help but be a backbone to the administration in this cold war, where staff and administrators stared at each other across the picket line. In a strike situation, Mason's way seemed the best: remain unmoved in the face of intimidation. Later in the day, I found myself on the balcony overlooking the darkened atrium by the Deans' Office, and I thought the time right to discuss with Mason my proposal for making the cuts in classified staff that had become so necessary. When I tried the other door, I discovered it was locked. Luckily, I had my master key with me. But when I opened the door, I found the vestibule dark except for the light burning in Mason's office, which dimly illuminated the far half of the waiting room. Mason was nowhere to be seen. I called out his name but received no answer. I looked around anxiously. I meant no offense, sought to gratify no meddling curiosity. But Mason's office in a sense was mine, and I was within my prerogatives as Associate Principal for Student Services in making observations of his work space that might cast some light on his rather strangely distracted behavior that morning. So I tried Mason's door and, finding it ajar, I entered.

At first I saw nothing remarkable. His desk was neatly ordered and clean. His trash can was filled to the top with wrappers, bags, and boxes from Fatty's, for the custodians had not made a final sweep of the building before walking out on Friday. His walkie-talkie lay on his desk in inanimate silence. His *In* box was empty. His chair was firmly pushed up against the lip of the desk. But leaning sideways against the wall under the window that looked out upon the front lawn was a hand-lettered sign. I inclined my head and read: *ON STRIKE: Reductions In Force undermine order and discipline.* I now recalled Mason's outspoken opposition to cuts in his support staff. I remembered that he had been a teacher at Hillthwart before he had been a dean. I remembered his angry denunciations of the school board for mismanaging tax revenues and failing to keep an orderly account of expenditures. I remembered his barely controlled fits of rage directed at me and at students and faculty who crossed him.

Turning all of this in my thoughts, and combining with it my discovery of the sign, a warning light flashed on in my mind. My first feelings for Mason had been to give scope to his anger, to let his game play itself out; but as leniency turns to contempt if met with contempt, so my awareness grew that I had given Mason the rope with which to play, but he had contemptuously tied the knot and slipped it over his own head. It is a terrible thing to see that up to a certain point benevolent negligence allows the individual full play of his creative faculties, but if his bent be for destruction, his efforts, in time, take on a repulsive character, and benevolence becomes its opposite. This proceeds from a certain hopelessness that the individual can or will reform himself, a sad awareness that free will has its moral limitations. What I saw that morning convinced me that the dean suffered from a flaw in his moral being that could not be rectified. While I might treat his impulses with massive doses of indulgence, I could not cure the affliction of his soul.

While immersed in these ruminations, I heard a key rattling in the outer door. I quickly stepped out of Mason's office and waited while he opened the door, flipped on the light switch, and then glanced at me with a look of irritated surprise. We stood for a moment looking at each other with unspoken understanding.

The next moment came.

"Mason," I said, gently calling to him.

No reply.

"Mason," I said in a still gentler tone, "it may be none of my business, but have you considered the consequences of your action? It appears to me that you have nothing to gain and everything to lose by joining the staff on strike."

Mason noiselessly strode past me and into his little office. I followed him to the threshold.

"Will you just tell me, Mason, why? If it is the firing of three parapros and a handful of teachers that you object to, can you not find a safer way to express your disappointment?"

"I will handle it my way," he said, grinding his teeth audibly, then picked up his sign and brushed past me.

I called after him, "Mason!" But he did not stop. I stepped to his window and in a moment saw him making his way toward the head of the driveway and the crowd of teachers who walked there carrying their signs. Soon Mason, too, was walking the picket line, surrounded by a group of glad faculty patting him on the back and smiling with him as they paced up and down in the cold.

I recognized in my condemnation of Mason's protest a certain Old Testament quality, *Thou shalt not take thy employer in vain,* and *Thou shalt have no other allegiances before me.* But soon I reflected that a new and more secular covenant had replaced the old, and the first of its new commandments was, *Thou shalt not abridge a man's freedom of speech.* I beat down my anger at the dean and strove to interpret his insubordination as an expression of the kind of pluralism I held in the highest esteem. "Live and let live," I sighed, as I reflected that Mason's defection meant nothing in the great scheme of things; he was still one of us and would return to the fold when it all blew over, if not sooner.

I tried to keep busy that afternoon. When Prozac and Winwin returned from their late lunch, I dropped in on them in their office. I half believed I would find Mason there, like the others, busy at his desk. There was Prozac, cleaning her desk drawer, sorting into piles her paper clips, detention slips, pens and pencils. And Winwin was seated at his desk, carefully forming the letters of an unseen word. But Mason's door stood open, his office stood empty, and a strange stillness reigned therein. From the window, I could see the man at the end of the driveway, a head taller than the others, carrying his sign like a rifle on his shoulder, salient while the other sign bearers slowly beat a circular orbit into the ground. As I stood watching, Winwin quietly slipped into the room.

"Excuse me," he said, "but I think I know how I would handle this situation. You need to sit down with Mason and find a way that he can feel he's a winner and you're a winner, too."

"Thank you, Winwin," I said, "but I'm afraid I'll have to handle it...well, I'll just have to deal with it, that's all." I had recently taken to using the word *handle* involuntarily in all kinds of situations. What other changes my association with Mason might have brought into my language and thought, I dared not guess. This linguistic anarchy only contributed further to my decision to take the necessary measure to restore my department to order.

As Winwin, looking defeated, was leaving, Prozac approached. "I've been thinking," she said, "that Mason might benefit from some kind of therapy, or perhaps medication is what he needs—he's such an angry person, something isn't right inside. I just can't get a handle on him."

"So you've taken to using the word, too," I said, rather exhilarated.

"Word? What word?"

I spoke the word.

"Oh, I hardly ever use it. But as I was saying, perhaps the crisis could best be handled by putting him on medical leave?"

"Prozac," I said, "leave me."

As she was departing, Winwin came to the door and inquired as to the *handling* of a case against a girl who had been caught smoking marijuana under her science lab table. He used the word without irony. It was evident that it had slipped out unconsciously. I thought, what a disagreeable fellow to have polluted our words, which are the outward signs by which we know one another and ourselves. It only strengthened my resolve that should Mason not experience a change of heart and come in off the picket line, he would surely have to depart. But as time wore on, Mason never so much as showed his face in the office, though his word was with us.

Several days passed, during which I had time to pick up and browse Aristotle's *Ethics*, Augustine's *City of God*, and Aquinas's *Summa Theologica*, which had been sitting on the bookshelf in my office since my college days; for though I had majored in educational administration, I had minored in philosophy. These books, considering the circumstances, had a beneficent effect. It dawned on me that Mason was following a higher authority than that of the school board, namely his own inner voice, which Providence has given us to be our guide through mazes of choice. I resolved not to press the issue with Mason, not to fire him, but to let him have free play of all his sensibilities and sensitivities. I would not play the role of Pilate in his sacrifice. Let the winds of change blow him where they may, he would be maker of his own destiny.

I believe I would have continued in this philosophical frame of mind had it not been for the hostile comments of fellow administrators. The Director of Student Activities, he of the slush fund, could not let pass a single opportunity to comment upon Mason's "treason" and my acquiescence to it. Various department chairpersons let it be known that they found it extremely difficult to look their teachers in the eye when Mason was marching with them, and they would regard me with wolfish desperation. Thus it is that persons who stand on principle are suddenly upended and reversed by the constant erosion of their ground by persons of illiberal temperament. To be sure, it was not strange that they should react so violently against one of their number siding with the enemy. But it was when a reporter for the local newspaper walked into my office one morning with his head cocked to one side and squintingly inquired with a jerk of his thumb if that were not Mason the Dean standing on the picket line like a statue of bronze, that I resolved that for the good of the school district, Mason must go.

But how? What should I do? I asked myself as I zipped my parka up to my neck. Had he not wandered astray on my watch? I could not, after allowing him to go along in his own way for so long, suddenly take it upon myself to fire him for the logical continuation of my policies. I had brought him up from the faculty, but it was not upon my head to set him back down; that would be up to the school board, and I feared they were not in a mood to humor him. Now with the press in it, all hell would break loose. Accordingly, I took a walk out to the end of the driveway and drew Mason aside and told him: "I'd be looking for a new job if I were you, Mason. That fellow from the paper spotted you, and you'll be headline news tomorrow. If there is anything I can do for you...of course I will give you a good reference."

He did not answer me, and I left him, as there was nothing more for me to say.

It took the school board only a week to act. After a fiery meeting full of recrimination and anger, Mason was given his pink slip. As he was not a member of the union, the union could do nothing for him, though its members complained loudly. A letter was mailed to his home; it contained his modest severance pay along with the notification that his services would no longer be required.

Still, every day, Mason appeared on the picket line and marched with the teachers, whose brows were furrowed and frowning even more than before, though to the observer in the window looking out over the school yard, it appeared they were less animated, less talkative.

Mason's finished, I said to myself, finished at last. Gradually my mind turned to other matters, primarily next year's master schedule, which would have to be completely redrawn. But one day as I came into my office I was met by the principal. His scarecrow form loomed above me and in his unnaturally deep and shaking voice he said, "Why is he still out there? You've got to get rid of him—do you understand?—got to." And he placed both hands on my shoulders and bore down.

I recoiled in shock at the vehemence of his assault. I assured him that it was none of my doing that Mason was still on the picket line, that it was not my responsibility to do anything about it. Trespassing did not fall into my jurisdiction.

"Then whose is it?" he thundered.

"I think it's yours," I said, adding, "but if you will give me a few moments with him, I will try to talk him into leaving peacefully."

Going outside to the crowd by the street, I braved the boos of several teachers and took Mason aside.

"Mason," I said, "are you aware that you are making considerable trouble for me by persisting in remaining on school property and taking part in the strike after your dismissal?"

He did not answer.

"Something's got to give. Either you must reconcile yourself to a change in employment and leave at once, or the police will be called to escort you away. Now, have you made any applications elsewhere? Would you like to remain in education?"

"I'll handle it my way."

"Would you like to remain in administration or return to teaching? The latter would be by far the easier placement, considering your recent actions against the administration."

"I don't want to go back to teaching; I'm very particular about that."

"Have you thought of becoming an educational consultant? There's a market for it."

"Consulting would take me away from students."

"Away from students! Can you honestly say you enjoy working with students?"

"I would not like to be a consultant."

"What about publishing? Educational publishing?"

"Not just anything will do. As I said, I am very particular."

"Or you could sell textbooks, make a few calls a week; textbooks sell themselves."

"Thank you for your concern, but I'll handle it myself."

"Mason," I cried, losing control, "if you don't find something else you're going to starve; that paycheck is not going to come in every two weeks. It's high time you were out looking for a job and not wasting your time on this line. If I leave here without you, Mason, the principal is going to call the police and have you removed."

"I'll handle it when it comes to that."

I was overcome by despair and frustration, which always leaves me feeling powerless and angry. As kindly as I could under the circumstances, I said, "Mason, come into my office and we will draw up a list of places you could look for employment. Remain there until the end of the day, then go home."

"No, I would rather handle it my way."

I could say nothing to that, but looking at the ground all the way, I walked back to the school and entered my office. At the end of the day the principal came in and told me that the police had removed Mason from the premises, but that he would not press charges if Mason would not return.

I afterward learned that the poor dean, when told that he must be removed from school property, put up a physical struggle. Some of the more frenzied teachers joined in the fray and a second squad car had to be summoned before order was restored and the skirmish ended. Mason was handcuffed and carried away to the station house, where he was incarcerated, but the school board refused to press charges and Mason was released.

On the same day that I heard this, I received a phone call from an English teacher with intelligence that Mason was working as a chef, or more properly a short-order cook, at Fatty's Burger Palace just a block from school. It happened to be on the day that the strike was resolved, a day the pickets never appeared. The school board and the union had sat down together, divvied up the money, and produced a salary schedule which merely froze hiring and eliminated no one's position. That the union almost unanimously approved the new contract was bittersweet news.

I went to Fatty's. Seeking the manager, I declared the purpose of my visit and was told that the individual whom I sought was within the food preparation area. Paper hat on my head, I assured the manager that Mason was an honest and trustworthy fellow and a good worker, however high-strung he might at times appear to be, and I was conducted to the grill at the back of the restaurant.

Being a man of mature years and extensive experience in a semimanagerial capacity, Mason had been given the responsibility of running the kitchen from the griddle where he grilled Fatburgers and chicken breasts.

"Mason!"

"It's you, is it? Well, get lost," he said, without looking up from the dozen sizzling patties of red meat he was squeezing and distressing with the flat of the spatula.

"It was not I who fired you, Mason," I said, deeply injured by his implied wrong, "and at least you have a job. This isn't such a bad place. Look, there are some of your students working at the counter, and others are customers."

He did not reply but only smiled wryly, and so I departed.

As I was lifting the end of the counter to pass through, a huge, sausagelike man with a triple chin, in an apron and paper cap, stopped me and, jerking his head toward the back, inquired, "Is he a friend of yours?"

"Yes."

"He's eating up the profits. Everybody who works here gets free meals, but I catch him with a burger and twisty fries every time I go back there."

"Who are you?"

"I'm Fatty. Glad to meet you. I know he's had a hard time. For some of us, eating is a way of dealing with excesses of stress and anxiety. How do you think I got this way?" he asked, pointing to his enormous body which spread below his neck like a sack of potatoes. "It took a quintuple bypass a year ago to turn me around," he said, and I noticed the sagging flesh bags around his neck and cheeks that had once been filled to the stretching point, but now lay empty.

"Have you lost weight?"

He said he had.

"Then will you pay particular attention to my friend there, and see that he does not ruin his health while he is here? And be as patient with him as possible."

He assured me that Mason was in good hands, called him a good and valued worker, and promised to do all he could to ensure Mason's continued health. And so I left him.

Several days later, I again walked to Fatty's in quest of Mason, but I found the paramedics' wagon parked in the driveway partially blocking the entrance to the restaurant. Inside, the atmosphere was quiet, but business was being carried on as usual, money being exchanged, and paper bags filled. I inquired whether Mason were on duty.

"I saw him in back," said the young man.

So I went through the counter and around to the grill. There I found the paramedics on their knees around the immobile body of a man. All that I saw were his legs, the toes of the shoes pointing slightly outward.

A girl beside me turned a tear-streaked face. "Are you looking for the dean?" she asked. "There he is. He just collapsed," and she pointed at the stricken man.

I moved toward his head to gain a better view. One of the paramedics was counting aloud while pumping his chest. Another was giving him oxygen with a respirator. Mason lay flat on his back, stretched out straight as a pole, his enormous chest barely stirring with the forced air. His flesh hung on him like a heavy weight, and his body had an unusual softness that seemed to betoken not surrender but rest. I watched as the paramedics applied electric shock to his heart, saw his body shaken by it, and knew that all emergency measures were doomed to fail, as fail they did, though they were sustained for twenty minutes.

I felt Fatty's enormous girth pressing against my arm. "His heart couldn't stand it."

"Ate until it burst," I said, as I watched the paramedics stowing away their equipment.

"He looks as if he's asleep, doesn't he?"

"With warriors of old," I mumbled.

There would seem to be no reason to go on with this tale. You may imagine the turnout at Mason's funeral, the faculty pallbearers, the eulogies from community leaders, and the many friends he had made during his short reign in the hearts and minds of the staff at Hillthwart High School. But before I leave you, let me say that if you have any curiosity as to who Mason was and what his life had been prior to coming to Hillthwart, I fully share your interest, but can do nothing to satisfy it. Yet I feel terribly uncertain whether I should divulge a little rumor that came to my attention a few months after the dean's passing. Whether or not it was true I could never ascertain, so cannot vouch for its accuracy. However, since this rumor has not been without compelling interest to me, it may be the same with you, and so I will tell it briefly. The story was this: Mason had been a marine for several years before obtaining his teaching credentials and in that capacity had been one of the guards at the Tomb of the Unknown Soldier, until he was relieved of that duty for a minor lapse in performance. These men, as you know, are specially trained to stand without moving a muscle for extended periods of time, to walk with perfect funereal cadence a straight path back and forth in front of the great Tomb, and to resist all efforts by sightseers to rattle them or disrupt their concentration. Imagine Mason, enduring a fly walking across his nose, without so much as a twitch of his skin, staring always at a point out in space, his eyes covered by dark sunglasses so that the inescapable involuntary blinking of his lids not betray his essential humanity under this machinelike exterior. While others around him give vent to emotions too large to bear a name, these stalwarts must maintain perfect impassivity and absolute control, watching over the graves of those who died in anonymity in the service of the state, whose perfect discipline led them to the perfect sacrifice. From so few, so much.

Ah, Mason! Ah, humanity!

# Celebrating Twenty Issues Of Hair Trigger Magazine

*Editors Past and Present*

This—*Hair Trigger*'s twentieth incarnation—provides an opportunity to reflect on the magazine's rich past, to assemble a list of its laurels, and to cull the archives for the names of all those whose labor and insight have packed twenty issues with writing that is deep and broad with life, voice, imagination, story. Through this process of twentieth-anniversary reflection, a number of things have become obvious, foremost among them being this: Over the years, the people involved on the editorial and creative sides of *Hair Trigger* have constantly changed, yet the magazine has consistently stood at the forefront of student literary anthologies. This is something akin to a college basketball team changing coaches and players every year, yet still managing to reach the Final Four on an annual basis. What accounts for this phenomenal track record of success? On the following pages, a number of *Hair Trigger*'s former "coaches" and "players" have contributed thoughts and reminiscences about the magazine that shed some light upon this question.

### Carrying Forward the Best Traditions of Prose Fiction

The first thing that stands out about *Hair Trigger* is that no concession is made to the "plain style" that dominates contemporary literature—nor to the limitations and posturing imposed by the "plain style." Laconic occasionally, yes. Plain, no. *Hair Trigger*'s reviewers point toward why the writing in *Hair Trigger* stands out: the writers make every effort of image, language, and point of view—of *story*—to reach the reader. "*Hair Trigger* walks away with first prize... The writing is thoughtful, realistic, sensual, exciting, and within the vein of the best traditions of American literature...full of solid, memorable surprises" (AWP). "Big, energetic, original throughout..." (CCLM). "Each story is fresh, evolving with its own energy, its own design... The writing is blessedly unself-conscious and full of human understanding... Language use is almost flawless" (CSPA). Full of life and imagination, humor, exploring the range of human feeling and emotion, and doing it with a mastery of technique that helps rather than gets in the way of the reader—that, too, characterizes *Hair Trigger*'s stories and other genre.

In a strong letter about life and technique in prose fiction, Gustave Flaubert, pre-eminent in the founding of modern fiction, said: "Thoroughbred horses and thoroughbred styles have plenty of blood in their veins, and it can be seen pulsing everywhere beneath the skin and the words. Life! Life!... That is the only thing that counts!... All the power of a work of art lies in this mystery, and it is this primordial quality, this *motus animi continuus* (vibration, continual movement of the mind—Cicero's definition of eloquence), which gives conciseness, distinctness, form, energy, rhythm, diversity."[1] Flaubert's statement could be the statement of *Hair Trigger*'s mission and purpose. Life and the courage and skill to bring it into being. And the devil-may-care trust that the audience will welcome and respond.

*Hair Trigger* does, indeed, carry forward the best traditions of prose fiction in both traditional and experimental modes, though I have wondered what the latter really is, since if a piece of writing succeeds as a story, as a movement of language pulsing with the vibration of life, it ceases to be experimental. *Hair Trigger*—its authors, editors, advisors, and the Story Workshop environment in which this literature has been nurtured and developed—dares a strong engagement of the reader's imagination, mind, and emotions. There is nothing accidental about *Hair Trigger*'s achievement, unless we argue that all imagina-

---

[1]*The Selected Letters of Gustave Flaubert*, translated, edited, and introduced by Francis Steegmuller, (New York, NY: Farrar, Straus and Young, Inc., 1953), p.158.

tive events are, in some way, blessed accidents. The conditions for these blessed accidents can be cultivated. In fact, that is a central aim of Story Workshop classes.

This is the twentieth-anniversary issue of *Hair Trigger*, promising a healthy succession to come. Congratulations to everyone associated with this project, proud with its traditions and cutting-edge daring, and especially to the student writers and editors, production advisors Deborah Roberts and Linda Naslund, the faculty of the Fiction Writing Department, and Chair Randy Albers. And a particular note of congratulations to Bill Burck, who submitted a proposal to me several years ago on the *Hair Trigger* editorial process, which read like an elaborate, warmly engaging story.

Yes, the very idea of the twentieth anniversary does what it's supposed to do, makes you turn and look back as well as forward. In actuality, *Hair Trigger* is in direct line of descent from a bloodline that started with $f^1$, and was succeeded by *Don't You Know There's A War On?*, *It Never Stopped Raining*, *Angels In My Oven*, and *The Story Workshop Reader*, and has been further established by successive revised editions of the anthology, *The Best of Hair Trigger*. You can track the attitudes and interests of what we call generations, cultural phases, the passage from one cultural phase to another, in this succession of *Hair Trigger*s and earlier Story Workshop publications. You can track how each generation, with the energy of its imaginative reach, escapes the strictures of its own code of correct identity. The range of emotion and intellect, the humor, appreciated in the pages of *Hair Trigger*, is very much the life and energy of a Story Workshop class at its best.

Very early in the involvement of publishing these anthologies of works from Story Workshop classes, we discovered how troubled the area of manuscript selection can be, a tender area that makes just about any editor of a literary journal wince. That is, too often the strongest and most engaging and most proficient material is set aside very early in the process of sifting through a pile of submissions. Or the editor is uneasily conscious of having set aside and not published a story, the events of which he or she continues to recall with a nagging resonance for many years. Set it aside because it was in some way outside the bounds of implicit common denominators. We asked, why does this happen? Why do readers, listeners, and editors tend to behave in this way? We see it happen sometimes in the Recall activity in a Story Workshop class when, to the amazement of young directors, the strongest and most vivid piece of work read aloud the week before does not come back in the next week's recall, not until the teacher herself/himself begins to recall it. And then the others in the class join in, usually with increasing recognition and satisfaction.

They begin to expand their common denominators of acceptance, overriding group unease with certain stories and passages that move vividly on their own, outside and different from the bounds and bonds developed in the group. That is often the quality of work that will move readers to an unexpected intensity of appreciation.

The editorial selection process turned out to require a high discipline of mind and emotion, tuned to the oneness of the Life! Life! vibration and artistic mastery. If young writers have begun to write strong and engaging stories but see these stories never making it through the process of selection, they experience a distinct chilling of their enthusiasms, a withering of the directions of their efforts. Then comes less risk-taking, more and more reliance on "plain" style and "plain" interests within plainly narrow bounds, rather than the Life! Life! that Flaubert saw as the very pulse of literature.

We worked with faculty advisors and student editors to develop a process of selection that would come up with a fair and accurate representation of the pool of literature from which choices were to be made. It was student-driven, coached by an advisor, with a crucial appeals process to override the constraints of majority opinion. Notable contributions were made by Betty Shiflett, Shawn Shiflett, Randy Albers, Gary Johnson, and Bill Burck. We usually saw that two or three worthy books could be selected from material that was finally left out of the process that produced an issue.

The writers in *Hair Trigger* have had an unusual experience of the kind of discipline that makes possible artistic freedom and writing that matters. The pulse of life and storytelling mastery in the issues of *Hair Trigger* testify to the finely tuned efforts of student editors, faculty advisors, and faculty and students who become involved in the appeals. *Hair Trigger* writers and editors carry that touchstone experience with them. And the struggle continues; in fact, it appears to be everlasting.

*John Schultz*
Professor Emeritus and Founder
of the Story Workshop Approach

**History, Background, Origins**

Toward the end of the semester I had the nerve to tell them they were ready to write a story. Yes, whole story. They were flabbergasted, I was expectant; this was my very first Freshman English section at Columbia, the spring of 1967, and I believed the Story Workshop method, the same approach that we used then in John Schultz's private workshop for writers and use now in the Fiction Writing Workshops at Columbia, would work in the required

Freshman area. On the last day of class one John Madler, a quiet young photography student married with kids, who'd told me he'd wept and stayed drunk all night when he heard Hemingway died, quite apologetically turned in "The Stud Ace," a classic tattoo parlor story with a killer first-person, meet-your-audience-more-than-halfway, warm-up anecdote. It seems that Stoney, who ran the tattoo parlor in an arcade off Howard Street and had put in forty years working the carnivals, liked to tell about him and the belly dancer from the sideshow lying naked on the bed in her trailer drinking gin, and she bets him twenty dollars she can piss in an empty bottle three feet away... What happens next? Distinctive and icy clear, but I almost missed this piece of Madler's, this "Stud Ace"; with minimal punctuation, mostly a sprinkling of quotes, it was typed in all caps, visually off-putting in the extreme and balky reading. Said he capitalized wholesale "to keep from making mistakes," be-damned, he said, if he could ever learn the rules of grammar and punctuation!—and so I understood he took this route: If every letter and word was treated equitably, who, then, could say where the mistakes fell?

Well, I typed it up—if the early Greeks could do it, I could, too (all caps and very little punctuation in *their* day, remember?). And all the sentences fell in place in Madler's voice without any shifts of word sequence needed from me, all there to hear, see, touch and be touched (by the electrifying tattoo needles themselves), all there to drink up and enjoy and tell your friends about. We printed Madler's "Stud Ace," with other offerings taken from my two workshops of that groundbreaking semester in the first and also groundbreaking issue of *F Magazine*, which John Schultz as editor and I and a few others had just started up, offerings that included images given in the workshop, brief word bursts, and something called "Play Sections," developed movements designed and based upon responses to the oral word exercises, wordplay from the private workshop taught by John Schultz and of which I was still a member, and from his elective Fiction Workshops at Columbia, which had been going at that time for two semesters. From the Freshman workshops we printed a second full-length story, an extravagant Cold War encounter by Dennis Peglow and a selection of slightly amazing composed-to-stand-alone images, including one about an insanely overheated guy hurling ice cubes at four suns in a cloudless sky—he cleans out an entire tray of ice cubes—turned in for homework by the now-well-known TV personality Bob Sirott, and some eye-grabbing quickie movements, page length or less, such as Laura Lile's "In My Purse," immediately anthologized for a new student text just then coming out.

We titled the entire freshman section "Freshman Section On Another Planet," so named by John Madler when he showed up an hour late for his first

Story Workshop session in the shank, as it were, of the word games buzzing around the semicircle in great leaps of laughter and high-wire silences while the person whose turn it was concentrated to find that just-right surprise word welling up—you'll know it when you hear yourself speaking it—to give the others in the semicircle. Madler, who came in waving his blue registration slip to show he'd paid for the class, listened alertly for a moment and then all of a sudden started backing out of the room. I stopped him. The inevitable question: "*This* is Freshman *English*? On another planet!" he marveled hauling up a chair, delighted to jump right into these astonishing verbal goings-on. When you look back on things they happen devilishly fast. A few weeks, a few semesters, once we had John Madler's "Stud Ace" in print, in a book, in our hands, we thought we couldn't start a new semester without an oral reading of it to point the way from day one, to communicate to the students: "See you can do it! You can use the words you need to use, to talk the way you need to talk, to tell the story that you want to tell to somebody else, the story that, until then, nobody knows but you. John Madler may have never gotten famous, but his story did, and it pains me that we can't locate John Madler, and Dennis Peglow, and Laura Lile, and the others now. Because we owe so much to them and many another like them though different, too—all the willing eager people in those early Story Workshop semicircles who started on this journey to and from another planet with us. We've had glowing blue earthworms for companionship and ethereally sharp stones to challenge our bare feet, occasional blankets of kind stars, and hosts of cardinals and silvered mourning doves to punctuate and amplify and light our way.

About that first issue of *F Magazine,* the *Chicago Review* said, "The Freshman English section will astound anyone who has ever had to teach or take that agonizing course." Besides several other hefty volumes of published student work—*Don't You Know There's A War On?, It Never Stopped Raining, Angels In My Oven, The Story Workshop Reader, The Best of Hair Trigger*—Good Lord! this is *Hair Trigger 20,* you are our antecedents, and that's something old friends should celebrate!

*Betty Shiflett*
Professor Emeritus

**A Tradition of Excellence**

Way back down the road, barely halfway to the milepost that we celebrate with this issue of *Hair Trigger* (at a time when the path was potholed with politics and bounded by dragon dens and sloughs of despond in the college and in the department), John Schultz asked me to take over the advising and editing process for *Hair Trigger 9 & 10*. I agreed to assume the mantle, despite warnings from faculty who had undertaken the pilgrimage previously that this journey promised to be no summer stroll in the park.

How right they were! I was presented with a troop of over fifty fiction and creative nonfiction manuscripts, in various states of dishabille, which *Hair Trigger 9* editors had chosen during an initial round of reading, and which I was forced to select and edit myself since time had run short before their process could yield final decisions. Sometime later, after another turn or two in the road, a phalanx of poems marched out of the woods and joined their prose counterparts, all of which I consigned to an encampment at the corner of my office. There, they sent up a disorderly racket while I summoned them one by one over the next few months for review and a determination as to their fitness for continuing the journey toward eventual publication.

Meanwhile, as work on *Hair Trigger 9* was beginning, I set about forming a cadre of student editors for *Hair Trigger 10* and put out a call for promising new recruits among the teeming multitudes of manuscripts emerging from Story Workshop classes in the department during the preceding year. Folder after folder of student work appeared as if by magic in my mailbox, and I passed them along to the talented, eager group of student editors, who began putting these manuscripts to the tests that had come to ensure quality during the many earlier editions. In the best tradition of *Hair Trigger* editorial staffs, they pushed, prodded, and interrogated each other and the stories themselves: Was the story original in conception and execution? Was the voice lively and engaging? Was the imagery vivid and compelling? Was the movement firm, trim, and free of manipulation? Did the chosen point of view serve the ends of the tale? Were forms fully realized? Was there a sense of an authoritative overall storyteller addressing a supportive, challenging audience? Was there evidence of risk-taking and of sound conceptual, abstractive, and imaginative problem solving? Was the story, quite simply, one that made you want to keep reading?

I added one new wrinkle to the exhaustive process that had been fashioned in earlier issues and that was designed to ensure the highest quality for the book. I added three extra student editors to the eight who served as manuscript editors. While the *Hair Trigger 10* selection process moved forward, I gave these three students a short course in copyediting, led them to the particularly promising but somewhat motley crew of *Hair Trigger 9* manuscripts that I had culled from the even more motley crew clustered in the corner of my office, and directed them to begin the process of close inspection and improvement. In the succeeding weeks and months, the copyeditors would correct the obvious mistakes and debate the less obvious choices that weighed the integrity of the storyteller's voice and authorial intent against the demands of clarity, in the process raising numerous pointed questions that guided my way through the final edit. Later, they did the same for *Hair Trigger 10* stories that survived the focused, merciless interrogation by manuscript editors. Their work was invaluable in ensuring a high-quality final product.

For the department and for me personally, it was a difficult year. Out of struggle, the phoenix of a new Fiction Writing Department would eventually rise; but at that point, we were still in the throes, and I was asked to assume the position of acting co-chair of the program during this transitional stage. Then, in the midst of it all, my father died suddenly on his sixty-second birthday, far too young for such a good person to leave us. I trudged on, hip deep now in those sloughs of despond but carried forward and encouraged in large part by the boundless energy, enthusiasm, diverse voices, and lively interactions of our student writers and editors, for whom the work of imagination was all, a persistent joy and solace among the buffets and blows of living in the world.

Finally, summer arrived, the selections had been made, and I set about the more solitary task of forming the ranks among the stories. I would spread manuscripts across the whole space of my office floor, arranging and rearranging them in different combinations, pausing now and then to straighten, scratch my head, and study the new design until, finally, a shape for this bulging double issue revealed itself, not as trim perhaps as in previous issues but far better formed than the student editors and I had any reasonable hope of achieving at the beginning of the process.

As final edits were completed and manuscripts were shipped off to Lisle for typesetting, I went in search of a cover photo at the Columbia College Museum of Contemporary Photography collection. I eventually settled on a shot by Photography Chair John Mulvany, an abstract and dreamy silhouette of a dark figure in a topcoat and fedora angling into the reflex of a stark and empty cityscape, above which hovered a rectangular opening that revealed a sunlit cloud against a summer sky. The image evoked thoughts of Mayor Daley wandering in a deserted Chicago (what would have been, no doubt, his own version of hell) and of those mysterious figures that emerge from the shadows during those waking dreams in which stories are encountered and demand to be told. Mary Forde Johnson conceived a wonderful cover design around this image; and along with the manuscripts, the cover and other materials were sent off to the printer in Michigan.

A few weeks later, after a furious flurry of communications about bluelines and other last-minute emergencies, the boxes of finished books were delivered to the department, and we held the reading and publication party that always celebrates the writers' and editors' arrival at the gates of the Celestial City. Although all editing processes are complicated and exhausting, perhaps none had been so difficult to complete as that of *Hair Trigger 9 & 10*, and this party was truly celebratory (attaining the particularly high level of intensity that can only come with the profound relief following negotiation of an especially treacherous path).

Unbeknownst to us, one final turn in the road remained. *Hair Trigger 3* and *Hair Trigger 8* had won first-place awards from the Coordinating Council of Literary Magazines as the top collection of student writing in the country, and *Hair Trigger* had never failed to place in any year that it was eligible for this national competition. (*Hair Trigger 8* had won in a year when Harvard had received second and Amherst third out of approximately 100 magazines that were entered, and in the following year, the department had blossomed with "We Beat Harvard" buttons.) We sent *Hair Trigger 9 & 10* off to the contest, and waited. And waited. And waited some more. Finally, we were told that the CCLM was re-forming itself and that, in the interim, the magazine competition had been suspended for lack of funds. Somehow, after all we had been through with this issue, the announcement was less than surprising and, in fact, almost fitting. But I was left feeling somewhat chagrined and disappointed that the writers and editors who had worked so diligently and creatively at negotiating the bouldered and pocked path toward publication of this edition had been denied the opportunity for recognition beyond the college. Nonetheless, a host of stories and essays from this book were included in *Best of Hair Trigger* anthologies and are still used with excellent results in department classes to this day.

As I look back over the decade or so since the experience of advising that edition, and think of the thousands upon thousands of stories from students in Story Workshop and other Columbia College fiction writing and Prose Forms classes, of the hours upon hours of thoughtful and conscientious work done by student editors and faculty advisors as well as of those extraordinary efforts in copyediting and proofing by Administrative Assistant Deborah Roberts, Secretary Linda Naslund, and others previous to them, and, finally, of the many twists and turns to the department itself that brought it to its present status as one of the largest and most successful fiction writing programs in the country, I see that *Hair Trigger* has not simply been a remarkable showcase for the best of the best in prose writing from Columbia College but also a tribute to the many, many students who, while they may not have won awards or even been published in the pages of that book, nonetheless gained skills that allowed them to enact a personal vision and to succeed in a wide variety of jobs upon graduation.

Above all, perhaps, for those of us who have watched the journey being made year after year (or have even made the journey ourselves from time to time) *Hair Trigger* has been a kind of constant in the midst of the flux that inevitably occurs in all colleges and universities, a beacon marking a tradition of excellence in our program. That beacon has signaled our success even in the midst of trials; and it continues to urge each new generation of student writers forward toward those dark, dreamy forests where the voices of shadowy characters sing in the depths. It takes courage and imagination to enter that forest and return to tell and write vividly, authoritatively, compellingly the stories that those voices sing. *Hair Trigger 20* celebrates an especially significant milestone, but it also stands alongside those other editions from the past, as well as those yet to come, as a celebration of all Columbia College writers (past, present, and future) who are unafraid of making a journey that promises nothing more than the possibility of leading those shadowy characters and their stories into the clear light of day. To all of these writers, we who are privileged to be teachers owe a great debt. Please pardon us if we assert, unabashedly, our justifiable pride in the uniqueness, honesty, and variety of the students whose voices and visions have been represented with such extraordinary richness for two decades in the pages of *Hair Trigger*.

*Randall Albers*
Fiction Writing Chairperson

**A Reputation Born of Carefully Managed Chaos**

I often characterize the long, multi-staged birth of a new *Hair Trigger* edition as carefully managed chaos from which the Fiction Writing Department is able to produce the best book possible. During the early weeks of the manuscript selection process, I find myself thinking, Where are we ever going to get enough strong material to make a book? During the middle stages of the selection process, I know that all is not lost when student editors with consistently opposing editorial opinions are ready to take out their Uzi machine guns and "simplify" matters. And at the end of production, when I take that first book out of a shipping box, open it, and run my finger down a table of contents that represents the wide range of voices and subject material for which *Hair Trigger* has built its esteemed reputation, I always think, *Wow, we did it again*.

Many stories published in *Hair Trigger* were originally rejected by the student editors only to be resubmitted by a Fiction Writing Department teacher and eventually published. Other strong pieces of writing were saved from the rejection pile by a lone student editor who came to my office and pleaded, on more than one occasion tearfully, for a story's pardon from the rejection pile. Often, student editors will leave notes in my mailbox that read something to the effect of, "You better take a look at this story. The other editors rejected it, but I think they're all idiots." It is in an underdog, adversarial editorial climate that some of *Hair Trigger*'s finest literary gems have been discoverd and brought to my attention as the faculty advisor to the magazine. So much for lockstep agreement, or blind reliance on the majority opinion. Regardless of healthy disagreement on the road to producing another *Hair Trigger* edition, I am always struck with the realization that from Introduction To Fiction Writing students to Advanced Fiction Writing students, to student editors, to faculty advisor, to copyediting and layout production people, to Chairperson, everyone cares so deeply about *Hair Trigger*, a magazine that represents the Fiction Writing Department's community effort towards excellence.

Over the years, there has been another recurring thought that comes to me when I run my finger down a *Hair Trigger* table of contents, and that is that all of the fine, rich, powerful, divergent, vibrant prose living robustly within the book's jacket is the result of one man's original vision of how writing can be successfully taught. Thanks, John. Your Story Workshop approach to the teaching of writing has touched and enhanced so many lives.

If one were to read all twenty editions of *Hair Trigger*, that person would be able to trace some twenty years of recorded trends and truths in American culture. On to the next twenty!

*Shawn Shiflett*
Coordinator of Faculty Development

**Strong Writing That Connects with an Audience**

As a student editor for *Hair Trigger III* (we switched to Arabic numbers on the double issue, 6/7), I remember long weekends spent in a stuffed easy chair dragged to the space heater reading piles of student manuscripts. I had no idea the fruits of my grunt work would ever reach beyond the small circle of fellow students, teachers, family, and friends who might see our book. But issue three of our upstart magazine (the first actually to be typeset) caused all sorts of fireworks.

First, *Hair Trigger III* won a prestigious first-place award from the Coordinating Council of Literary Magazines (CCLM) as the best college literary magazine in the country. Second, a New York literary agent read the book and came knocking at the doors of five *Hair Trigger* contributors (myself included) with letters of inquiry asking to see more of our work. The buzz was incredible! To think Big Apple eyeballs were rolling over images I'd penned in John Schultz's Wednesday-night Advanced Fiction class (a class one colleague described as "where the sharks swim" on account of all the talent) in that ugly, wood-paneled room with the stained blue carpet on the sixth floor of the 600 South Michigan Avenue building.

So, there actually *was* a wider audience for this stuff we were banging out on our manual typewriters in apartments and houses across the city.

The college community suddenly took notice of us. A favorable review of *Hair Trigger V* ran in *Chicago* magazine. Clearly, the unique and rich and powerful writing—and the tireless aim for professionalism—had thrust the magazine and the program into the national spotlight, where we have pretty much remained ever since.

When I judged over one hundred college literary magazines for the next CCLM national contest the following summer, I came away knowing the difference between excessive design and effective writing.

As faculty advisor to *Hair Trigger 12*, *Hair Trigger 14*, and *Hair Trigger 19*, I continued the magazine's unique editorial tradition which, among other things, guides student editors to be open and responsive to strong writing that connects with an audience. I've also been chiefly responsible for the evolving design of the series. (Few design changes were made between *Hair Trigger III* and *Hair Trigger 11*.) And while the writing has been consistently winning awards, we have also been quietly collecting first-place prizes for visual features, such as striking cover artwork and, most recently, overall design.

The impressive list of *Hair Trigger* awards is a testimonial to the strength and the flexibility of the Story Workshop approach, which urges writers to cast a wide net when reaching for story, to revel in the complexity of voice and image, to connect with the reader as audience. I remember a particularly effective coaching for broadening the writer's sense of audience: *Be aware as you write of the audience beyond the room, of the audience not yet born.* If you've ever experienced that coaching as a student—say, in a Betty Shiflett semicircle during a One Word or Take-A-Place abstract exercise—you know how it can set you fairly reeling if you let it, if you give yourself the permission to do so.

*Gary Johnson*
Fiction Writing Faculty

## Who the Hell Would Publish Something Like This?

When I was struggling with the body of material that would become my first novel, *American Skin*, John Schultz gave me the guidance to put it all together, and *Hair Trigger* gave me the incentive to find the full movements within that body of material. Close versions of "Lovie of Lilac Farm," "Zack," "Exile in Chickville," and "Skinhead Dreams" all appear in *American Skin*. Main characters from the book were also developed in "The Rogue Scholars."

But even before I started writing a novel, *Hair Trigger* was becoming a big part of my writing process. Most of all *Hair Trigger* provided me with a sense of permission that was absolutely unique in an American literary world where political correctness ruled, and still rules to this day. This was a permission that began in the Story Workshop classroom. I remember staying up the whole night before a Fiction I class I had with Randy Albers to write a draft of a crazy little satirical piece called "My Job," about a small-town Joe who is fed up with the way women treat him. When I handed it in to Randy I felt pleased with myself, then suddenly thought: "Who the hell would publish something like *that*?" *Hair Trigger* did. The next semester I spent a number of hallway conferences with my Fiction II teacher, Gary Johnson, discussing a story I was writing called "That's Mine," about a big-town Joe who is fed up with the way women have treated him. Again, when I finished it, I felt that flush of accomplishment, but wondered: "Who would publish this? Maybe *Hair Trigger*?" Yeah, *Hair Trigger* published it, earning me many a dour stare from Womens' Studies Chicks (as well as Sensitive Males Trying To Get Laid By Womens' Studies Chicks). Over the next few years I worked with Andy Allegretti, Shawn Shiflett, Betty Shiflett and, of course, my thesis advisor and mentor, John Schultz, on my novel—feeling, I must say, pretty damn free to write what I pleased. If you are unfamiliar with my work, and wondering why I am making so much of this freedom issue, perhaps a quick, uncensored trip inside my daily thoughts will illuminate a few things:

> ...if I pulled the same shit Rodney King pulled, those cops would have beat the living fuck out of me too.... watching women's hockey reminds me of the Special Olympics.... sometimes when a girl says no, she really means yes.... I don't think homosexual men should be allowed to take Boy Scouts out to the woods and sleep in the same tent with them. I mean, would you let your teenaged daughter spend the night at my place?... Joyce and Faulkner are overrated....

My fictions are not political tracts, but my personal views *do* color my work. How could they not? And when I hear of literary editors today who openly cite "moral soundness" as important criteria for deciding whether or not a story is published, I get scared. And angry. As a two-time *Hair Trigger* editor I got in many a knock-down, drag-out fight with other editors over this very issue. I remember after one such melee, Shawn Shiflett (who had seen many a *Hair Trigger* brawl in his day) kind of teasing me about being such a contrary hothead. "I'm not concerned if people like me," I told him. "Yeah," he said, "but we like you anyway."

There are few things I can say with more gratitude—*Hair Trigger* liked me anyway.

*Don Gennaro De Grazia*
Fiction Writing Faculty

**The Eye of the *Hair Trigger* Tornado**

Week after week, semester after semester, year after year, strong writing flows into Story Workshop classes at Columbia College as regularly as the tides. There's an ocean of story out there, and the Story Workshop classroom seems to evoke the best of it.

*Hair Trigger* magazine is the home for the best of that best. Over the years, a process of editorial selection has evolved for identifying the stories that will make *Hair Trigger* their home. The goal of that process goes something like this: only the very strongest work gets published; none of the very strongest work goes homeless. Anyone who has ever been involved in manuscript selection knows what a maddening goal that is. How does one determine where to draw the line separating the stories that are strong enough to publish from those that are not? Conceivably, one could continue adding just one more story to an issue, until one volume became two, two became three, and so on. Eventually, however, time and good judgment win out. The line gets drawn and the issue goes to press.

The process begins in mid-February, when the faculty advisor is presented with several lineal feet worth of manuscript folders. The process ends a little over a year later, when a slender volume of some thirty stories arrives from the printer. What happens in between is not for the timid.

Oh, those manuscript folders! They are the bane of the student editor. The faculty advisor doles them out week by week from a seemingly endless supply. Most of the manuscripts contained in those folders are not, ultimately, of *Hair Trigger* quality. Yet they all deserve reading and discussion. In fact, each piece is read and evaluated by at least three editors. Pieces that survive the cut made by those first three editors, are then evaluated by another three editors. Sometimes, a seventh or even eighth editor weighs in. That's an awful lot of reading and evaluating, and there are times when the frustration of editors grumbles to the surface: *What were instructors thinking when they submitted all of this work?! Don't they know good writing when they see it?*

Yet the process depends on all of that work being submitted. If instructors are too selective, it is likely that some of the strongest work will not find its way into the editors' hands. Instructors are therefore asked to err on the side of oversubmission. This is a fine line, however. Too much oversubmission, and editors find themselves plowing through story after unpublishable story, their aesthetic sensibilities rapidly losing their edge.

What needs to happen, of course, is just the opposite. The editors' aesthetic sensibilities need to become ever more finely honed as the editorial process unfolds. When things go right, the editors become increasingly able to articulate the strengths and weaknesses of pieces under their consideration, the pattern language of the group evolving with the sophistication of their literary judgment. At the same time, they also become increasingly able to recognize the tendencies and blind spots inherent in each other's sensibilities. As a result, the weather in the room during editorial deliberations can become awfully, shall we say, stormy. In fact, by late April and continuing right on through early June—tornado season in the Midwest—funnel clouds touch down with a fair amount of regularity in *Hair Trigger* editing sessions.

There is nothing quite like having passed through the eye of a *Hair Trigger* tornado. And while it may have its drawbacks in the moment, once you're out of it, safely resting on terra firma again, you begin to realize what an incredible experience it has been. Especially when a story about which you have a particular passion has just made the cut. And if you're like some of us, you will find yourself drawn back into the tornado again...and again...and again. It's not that we're gluttons for punishment. But we are gluttons for experience.

Learning is a big part of that experience, as is the pride Shawn Shiflett mentions, of running your fingers across the book when you first get it into your hands. Leafing through page after page where image, voice, movement, and point of view are all conspiring to create moments of story that spring to life, command center stage in the theater of the mind, and establish a transformative connection with audience. Yes, the pride thing is definitely cool. Especially when the awards start rolling in. But I must admit, I do have a fondness for the eye of that *Hair Trigger* tornado.

*Bill Burck*
Faculty Advisor
*Hair Trigger 20*

# Retrospective List of *Hair Trigger* Staff

## Faculty Advisors

Randy Albers: *5, 9 & 10*
George Bailey: *6/7*
Sheila Baldwin: *3, 4, 5, 6/7*
Bill Burck: *20*
Ann Hemenway: *6/7, 16*
Paul Hoover: *2, 3, 4, 5, 6/7, 8*
Gary Johnson: *12, 14, 19*
Eric May: *18*
John Schultz: *1, 2, 3, 4, 5, 6/7, 8*
Betty Shiflett: *2, 3, 4, 5, 6/7, 8*
Shawn Shiflett: *4, 6/7, 8, 11, 13, 15, 17*
Margaret Yntema: *6/7*

## Student Editors

Al Aviles, Jr.: *14*
Kristin Bair: *18*
William Boerman-Cornell: *15*
Pete Bontsema: *4*
Ron Booze: *4, 5*
Steve Bosak: *1*
Mary Brophy: *8*
Janet Marie Brown: *6/7*
Holly Bruns: *17, 18*
Jotham Burrello: *19*
Bill Burck: *6/7, 8*
Todd Burger: *18*
Ronald L. Burns: *5, 6/7*
John Callegari: *6/7*
Reginald Carlvin: *3*

Serafina Chamberlin: *15, 16*
Donna Maria Chappell: *14*
Martina Clarke: *16, 17*
Adrienne Clasky: *5, 6/7*
Andrea Cody: *8*
Sean Colbert: *13*
Juan Cortés: *20*
Lincoln Davis: *9*
Connie Deanovich: *6/7*
Don Gennaro De Grazia: *14, 15*
Tony Del Valle: *2*
John Drake: *20*
Wilhelmina Dunbar: *15*
James O. Elder: *4, 5, 6/7*
Ed Eusebio: *13*

STEVE FARMILANT: *9*
RICK FELTES: *19*
DREW FERGUSON: *18*
SIOBAN FLANNERY: *10, 11*
BRUCE FOX: *10*
KIM GELLER: *16*
IRA GENOVESE: *9, 11*
STEVEN GIESE: *3*
MICHAEL GORSKI: *9*
SUE GREENSPAN: *4, 5*
KENNETH HARRIS: *11, 12, 14*
MIKE HAWKINS: *10, 11*
AILEEN MARIE HAYES: *2*
HEIDI HEDEKER: *9*
ANN HEMENWAY: *4*
LAURA HOOFNAGLE: *19*
CHRIS HYATT: *12*
HERBERT L. JACKSON: *17*
GARY JOHNSON: *3*
VENICE JOHNSON: *20*
SHERYL JOHNSTON: *16*
DORIS JORDEN: *6/7*
JANE JORITZ: *9*
VICTORIA JULIAN-GONIA: *5, 17*
KEVIN KELLY: *19*
GREG KISHBAUGH: *12*
SUSAN KLAISNER: *17*
ROCHELLE KNIGHT: *8*
ROBERT KOEHLER: *16, 17*
VINCE KUNKEMUELLER: *15, 16*
DEBORAH LAMBERTY: *9*
ADAM LANGER: *12*
LILLI LANGER: *10, 11*
ANN LANGLAIS: *13, 14*
TODD LEADINGHAM: *18, 19*
ROBERT LENEA: *6/7*
FERN LEVIN: *3*

CRIS BURKS LEWIS: *12*
LISA LILLY: *11*
MIKE LIPUMA: *20*
ARLENE LITTLETON: *5*
KAREN MAROUSEK: *19*
TONY MARQUEZ: *10*
PAUL MASSIGNANI: *20*
KATHLEEN MATACASSAR: *19*
PATRICIA MCNAIR: *10, 11*
JOHN MCPHAIL: *8*
DAVE MEAD: *12, 14*
LAURIE L. MEGGESIN: *6/7*
SHARON MESMER: *5*
TOM METCALF: *6/7*
PAMELA MILLER: *2*
POLLY MILLS: *9*
KENT MODGLIN: *20*
DENISE MOORE: *10*
RICARDO MORENO: *17*
MARY MORITZ: *12, 13*
MAUREEN MORLEY: *9*
KAREN MURAI: *9*
TOM NAWROCKI: *1*
DARA AYANNA PRESSLEY: *20*
JERRY OESTREICH: *3*
ALEXIS PRIDE: *16*
TOM O'KEEFE: *9*
GEORGE ORLOWSKI: *10*
CHRISTINA PERRY: *18*
JOEY PICKERING: *8*
BEVERLY PITTS: *3*
CATHLEEN QUARTUCCIO: *18, 20*
PETER RADKE: *4*
HARLAN REECE: *15*
CHRIS RICE: *16*
BARBARA SANDLER: *8*
MIKE SCHWARZ: *3*

JENNIFER SHANAHAN: *14, 15*
KETURAH SHAW: *13, 14, 15*
CHARLES SHEDIVY: *6/7*
JENNIFER SHERIDAN: *13*
CHRISTOPHER SHOUP: *17*
DAN SPINELLA: *3*
LAURA STEELE: *8*
DAVID SWANSON: *9*
NICK TOLER: *16*
LYDIA TOMKIW: *4*
PETE TROTTER: *2*

AMY TURILLI: *13*
ESTHER VITAL: *5*
JAMIE LYNN VITI: *19*
JULIE VOHS-ROCCO: *13*
JACQUELYN WADE: *6/7*
KATHLEEN WARGNY: *8*
WANDA WELCH: *12*
ADA WILLIAMS: *8*
RENEE WYATT: *9*
ELIZABETH YOKAS: *18*
ALLAN ZEITLIN: *11*

## Production Managers
ROBIN CAMPBELL: *9 & 10*
CHUCK FREILICH: *6/7, 8*
LINDA NASLUND: *19, 20*
DEBORAH ROBERTS: *11, 12, 13, 14, 15, 16, 17, 18, 19, 20*

## Production Editors
KRISTIN BAIR: *16, 17, 18*
SERAFINA CHAMBERLIN: *16, 17*
JULIE GORDON: *9, 10*
SALLY JASKOLD: *9, 10*
CHRIS KAUFMAN: *9, 10*
PATTY LEWIS: *16*
LINDA NASLUND: *17, 18*
JANET POWERS: *8*

## Graphic Designers
GORDON BIEBERLE: *12, 13*
ANNA DASSONVILLE: *14, 15, 17*
GERRY GALL: *6/7, 8, 9 & 10*
MARY FORDE JOHNSON: *9 & 10, 11, 13*
KEVIN RIORDAN: *16*
LINDA ROBERTO: *18, 19, 20*

# THE *HAIR TRIGGER* TROPHY CASE

## *HAIR TRIGGER 19*

**SILVER CROWN AWARD, CSPA**
**GOLD MEDAL, CSPA**
**3RD PLACE, OVERALL DESIGN, CSPA**
**1ST PLACE, COVER DESIGN, CSPA**

**1ST PLACE**
**TRADITIONAL FICTION, CSPA**
"The Boys"
*Herbert L. Jackson*

**1ST PLACE**
**EXPERIMENTAL FICTION, CSPA**
"Celestial Bath"
*Yan Geling*

**2ND PLACE**
**EXPERIMENTAL FICTION, CSPA**
"Brewsterhaus, The Bartender:
A Story Of Halsted Street"
*Kent Modglin*

**2ND PLACE**
**ESSAY, CSPA**
"Gohan"
*K Fujiwara*

---

## *HAIR TRIGGER 18*

**GOLD MEDAL, CSPA**

**1ST PLACE**
**TRADITIONAL FICTION, CSPA**
"Pennies In The Sock Drawer"
*Kristin A. Bair*

**2ND PLACE**
**TRADITIONAL FICTION, CSPA**
"Five Bloods"
*Terrick Wilkerson*

**3RD PLACE**
**TRADITIONAL FICTION, CSPA**
"Earned Outs"
*Serafina Chamberlin*

**2ND PLACE**
**EXPERIMENTAL FICTION, CSPA**
"How I Contemplated The World From The
University Department Of Physics And
Began My Life Over Again"
*Harvey Wilcox*

**3RD PLACE**
**EXPERIMENTAL FICTION, CSPA**
"The Backbone"
*J.D. Reeves*

**1ST PLACE**
**ESSAY, CSPA**
"Refuge For The Dying"
*Todd Burger*

**2ND PLACE**
**ESSAY, CSPA**
"When A Little Bite Will Kill You"
*Susan Dennison Brenner*

**3RD PLACE**
**ESSAY, CSPA**
"Streetball Junkie"
*Paul E. Wagemann*

**CERTIFICATE OF MERIT**
**EXPERIMENTAL FICTION, CSPA**
"Inside The Walls:
The Telephone Monster"
*Jill Pollock*

**CERTIFICATE OF MERIT**
**EXPERIMENTAL FICTION, CSPA**
"Celestial Birthday"
*Jennifer Yos*

## *Hair Trigger 17*

**Gold Crown Award, CSPA**
**1st Place, Cover Design, CSPA**

**1st Place**
**Traditional Fiction, CSPA**
"The Devil in Gloria's Pipes"
*William Meiners*

**2nd Place**
**Traditional Fiction, CSPA**
"Theatrics and Orgasms"
*Susan Klaisner*

**3rd Place**
**Traditional Fiction, CSPA**
"The Lesson"
*Robert Wood*

**Certificate of Merit, CSPA**
**Traditional fiction**
"Underground Bliss"
*Sheryl Johnston*

**1st Place**
**Experimental Fiction, CSPA**
"Nuptial"
*Keturah Shaw*

**2nd Place**
**Experimental Fiction, CSPA**
"Two Men And A Truck"
*Chris Rice*

**1st Place**
**Essay, CSPA**
"Whitehall, Michigan"
*Vicki Ruzicka*

**3rd Place**
**Poetry, CSPA**
"Skid"
*Keturah Shaw*

---

## *Hair Trigger 16*

**Silver Crown Award, CSPA**

**1st Place**
**Traditional Fiction, CSPA**
"Fried Buffalo"
*Alexis J. Pride*

**2nd Place**
**Traditional Fiction, CSPA**
"Gotta Let It Fly"
*Patricia McNair*

**3rd Place**
**Experimental Fiction, CSPA**
"Lullaby From A Marriage"
*Cris Burks*

---

## *Hair Trigger 15*

**Medalist Certificate, CSPA**

**1st Place**
**Traditional Fiction, CSPA**
"The Last Positive"
*George Alan Baker*

**2nd Place**
**Experimental Fiction, CSPA**
"The Fog"
*Robert C. Koehler*

**3rd Place**
**Experimental Fiction, CSPA**
"In Pure Softness"
*Polly Mills*

**1st Place**
**Essay, CSPA**
"How To Prepare A Saxophone Reed"
*Vince Kunkemueller*

---

## HAIR TRIGGER 14

**GOLD CROWN AWARD, CSPA**
**1ST PLACE, COVER DESIGN, CSPA**
**DIRECTOR'S PRIZE, AWP**

**1ST PLACE**
**TRADITIONAL FICTION, CSPA**
"Disappear"
*Eduardo Cruz Eusebio*

**2ND PLACE**
**TRADITIONAL FICTION, CSPA**
"The Duration Of Life"
*Al Aviles, Jr.*

**1ST PLACE**
**EXPERIMENTAL FICTION, CSPA**
"Dream"
*Dave Mead*

**1ST PLACE**
**ESSAY, CSPA**
"Sex Education"
*Victoria G. Ashton*

---

## HAIR TRIGGER 13

**MEDALIST CERTIFICATE, CSPA**

**1ST PLACE**
**EXPERIMENTAL FICTION, CSPA**
"Brought By The Stork"
*Jennifer Sheridan*

**CERTIFICATE OF MERIT**
**EXPERIMENTAL FICTION, CSPA**
"What A Fish"
*Bruce Fox*

**1ST PLACE**
**ESSAY, CSPA**
"The Missing Stories"
*Elise G. Le Grand*

**3RD PLACE**
**TRADITIONAL FICTION, CSPA**
"Follow The Signs"
*Lilli-Simone Langer*

**CERTIFICATE OF MERIT**
**TRADITIONAL FICTION, CSPA**
"Home Free"
*Polly Mills*

---

## HAIR TRIGGER 12

**SILVER CROWN AWARD, CSPA**
**1ST PLACE, COVER DESIGN, CSPA**

**1ST PLACE**
**TRADITIONAL FICTION, CSPA**
"Vampires"
*Wanda Welch*

---

## HAIR TRIGGER 11

**1ST PLACE**
**ESSAY, CSPA**
"AIDS: Learning For Lives"
*Don Bapst*

---

## HAIR TRIGGER 9 & 10

Double Issue. Not entered.

---

## HAIR TRIGGER 8

**1ST PLACE, CCLM**

---

## HAIR TRIGGER 6/7

Double Issue. No awards.

*HAIR TRIGGER 5*

**3ʳᴅ Place, CCLM**

———————

*HAIR TRIGGER 4*

Not eligible to enter contest because
*Hair Trigger 3* placed first in previous
year's contest

———————

*HAIR TRIGGER 3*

**1ˢᵀ Place**, CCLM

———————

*HAIR TRIGGER 2*

Not entered

———————

*HAIR TRIGGER 1*

Not entered

———————

**KEY TO ABBREVIATIONS AFTER EACH AWARD**

AWP = Program Directors' Prize for undergraduate literary magazines

CCLM = Coordinating Council of Literary Magazines national competition for undergraduate literary magazines

CSPA = Columbia University Scholastic Press Association national competition for college and university undergraduate and graduate magazines